Into the East

The Returning

J. A. Davis

BLACK ROSE
writing™

ISBN: 978-1-61296-471-3

PUBLISHED BY BLACK ROSE WRITING

www.blackrosewriting.com

Printed in the United States of America

Suggested retail price $17.95

Into the East is printed in Plantagent Cherokee

Editor: Amanda Sievertson

Acknowledgments

Thank you to all the fans of the first installment of the *Into The East* series. We appreciate all the kind and encouraging words and reviews. You have blessed us greatly.

I want to thank my lovely wife of nineteen years and my children who encouraged me to pursue a goal that I didn't believe was possible.

But above all, I give thanks to the One who sees all things.

"Professor Seegertun! Professor Seegertun! Are you ok!? What happened to your office?" the strapping young student asked while trying to awaken his battered and bruised professor as he lay unconscious.

Sluggishly, the aging professor stirred, "Aaron? Is that you?"

"Yes professor."

"Are…are they gone?"

"Who Professor? I don't see anyone. I came by because you never showed up for class. Dr. Seegertun, we need to call for an ambulance or something. That eye of yours looks awful."

As Geoff shifted from his left side, a large knife could be seen protruding from just below his rib cage.

"Oh my God, Professor, you're bleeding! We need to call 911!" He quickly threw down his backpack while searching for his phone. As the phone was ringing, he tried to find anything to stop the bleeding.

"Aaron wait; I need to tell you something."

After frantically speaking to the 911 operator, Aaron said, "Hang on Professor, I've got 911 on the line. They'll be here soon."

"There isn't enough time son. I need you to listen to me."

Panicking, Aaron said, "What do you mean?! No, no, no, no… Professor, you can't die on me! What am I going to do?"

In a calm clear voice, his beloved mentor and friend said, "Aaron, look at me. Please…look at me."

As his hands continued to shake while holding the bloody rags against the open wound, the trembling grad student attempted to compose himself.

"Remember the ancient metal relic I showed you?"

"Yes."

"The ones who did this; they want it. You cannot let it fall into their hands."

"Prof…Geoff, I don't even know where it is."

"Yes you do. It's where I put all my important finds."

Tears flowing down his face, one hand on the phone, the

other drenched in blood, he asked, "Why? What is it? Uh…why me?"

Reaching up to touch his cheek, with a fading voice, he said, "You were always like a son to me."

As he breathed his final words, he lost consciousness and slipped away. As the sound of the sirens grew louder, drowning out his cry, Aaron just sat there, holding the one man who treated him more like a son than a student.

Looking around at the piles of paper strewn all over the floor, he found the following email.

From: Rabbi Yaakov Moshe
Date: Friday, April 22, 2016 - 11:57am
To: Dr. Geoff Seegertun
Subject: ancient relic

Please do not contact me anymore about your finding. I've already been visited by several of these so-called men asking me far too many questions about your relic. I suggest you destroy it immediately. If I'm right, the ambitions of that masochist party which tried to kill my ancestors, has never died. Their lust for ancient knowledge will never be satiated. I repeat, do NOT contact me again.

Aaron quickly grabbed hold of the paper and pushed it into his coat pocket just before the paramedics, and the police came rushing through the door.

Into the East

The Returning

Chapter 1

"How long My Lord, until we remove this vile, wretched filth!?"

"Patience. We are not obligated to remove these *precious* souls. Our adversary will do so in good time. All we must do is bring their separation to completion."

"But haven't we done that? There are only a few left. Can we not deal with them directly?"

"A few is all that is needed to thwart our plans and to keep the line from being broken. Direct intervention among them is far too risky. Or have you forgotten what happened to the others and their mingled offspring?"

"But My Lord, if we don't stop this so-called *giver of rest*, he will inevitably bring about our demise."

"You fool! If you intervene, your end will be most assured!"

"Forgive me My Lord. I just…I only long for vengeance."

"Don't you think that I long for that as well? Subtlety, however, is the game we must play."

"Yes My Lord. If I might say however, I am surprised they are so easily led away from…"

Slamming his fist down onto the cold black stones that encircled his throne he thundered, "Do NOT speak their name!"

The servant cowered as he always did before his master, and started to speak once more. "Forgive me My Lord. As I was saying, they are so easily misled from…him."

The menacing ruler of the darkness eased back into his blackened throne and uttered in a soft, sinister tone, "Everyone needs a master." From his distant fortress, set on one of the heavenly bodies that circled Shemesh, he motioned towards Araz as he continued, "They are incapable of leading themselves. They have no original thoughts of their own. They must be given to them. The truth resides within them, as it was from the beginning, and yet they refuse to heed its call. Therefore, I give them the desires of their flesh, and a master they can lust after. Even if it leads them to their demise. Foolish mortals."

"But My Lord, why are they so incapable of seeing the truth that is both within and without?"

"Because they don't want it, you simpleton! They want lies! Deception is far more appealing than the truth, and I'm the one to give it to them! Deception always brings comfort in the night, but pain in the morning. The dawn is breaking, and they still want nothing less than a heap of lies."

"Soon, however, these clever fabrications will no longer be able to overcome the obvious My Lord."

"Yes, yes indeed. The razing will soon be upon them, but it will be too late; for their minds and hearts are long gone. They wouldn't know the truth if it stood before them."

Looking upwards toward the heavens, he continued, "The stars have already begun to shift, and the hosts are beginning to move out of their course. Their destruction is a foregone conclusion."

"What of Aaranon My Lord?"

"What about him?" he answered dismissively, hiding his deeply rooted concerns.

"Will he be turned before it's too late?"

"I easily kept Zeul from the truth, didn't I? The son is no different than the father. He seeks revenge, yet lies to himself and others about his true intentions. Vengeance. A subtle, yet ever growing iniquity that consumes its victim until there is nothing left. Nothing left but a rotten shell of a being. Besides, Aaranon is the least of our problems. That so-called *comforter* and his aging grandfather have begun to prepare for the razing. If they complete it, they will destroy everything for which we have worked. We must do all we can to stop them."

"But I thought you said we could not intervene?"

"Again! You fool! Have you not learned anything? Leave it to me. When the time is right, Zeul will lay before me, begging to remove that promised one and his family."

"Very good My Lord, very good."

"Yes...it is all...very good!" Halail said as he and his servant laughed; their voices echoing throughout the dark abode from which he commanded his sinister legions.

Chapter 2

He slowly pushed open the creaking door to the dark and dreary pub located on the outskirts of another small village. It was no different than any other pub among the lower-class. Just a place for udamé to drown away their sorrows and complain amongst themselves of the incessant oppression they experienced from the UAK. However, with all the new laws being enacted, along with MSS troops and spies running throughout the villages, it became increasingly difficult, if not impossible, to express one's self openly.

He scanned the room, a habit he'd developed in the past year, looking for anyone who could potentially recognize him or cause him any unnecessary strife. It was rare for him to venture out into the public. It was necessary, however, to pick up a few supplies as he made his way east to find and rescue the ones he loved.

He did his best to disguise his appearance by removing his golden locks and allowing his beard to grow much longer than he'd done before. He dressed his head in a number of tattoos reminiscent of the foresters of old who once moved about the woods with ease.

He dwelt among the tall kyder trees to avoid detection while he slept. For protection, he made his clothing from the hides of gloths and ohemas. A hood provided a covering for most of his face, allowing his once gentle, yet now rough exterior, to slip into its shadow when necessary.

He carried everything he needed with him, with the exception of a few items he kept hidden, in the event of theft. As the UAK continued to introduce new laws, taxes, and regulations onto the lower-class, robbery, kidnapping and the selling of souls began to increase.

As he moved across the floor, no one looked up from their table except for one udam sitting in the darkened corner of the pub. Aaranon noticed him but thought nothing of his presence. He made his way to the bar to order an ale and pick a few supplies from the store that was located in the back.

Aaranon tossed down an old coin and just said, "Ale."

The barkeep looked at the coin and then glanced in the direction of the dark figure resting in the corner.

Slowly, the shadowy presence broke through the darkness and into the light that drenched the entryway. As he moved towards Aaranon, the barkeep scurried out from behind the rickety old bar and into the back. Several others quickly hurried out the door, leaving just the two of them to decide the fate of the other.

The udam leaned against the bar, attempting to catch a glimpse of Aaranon, who was wearing his hood. "From your appearance I would say it's been awhile since you've come down from the trees."

Turning his head slightly to avoid being seen, Aaranon said nothing.

"Apparently you haven't heard. All citizens of Araz must have an identification card to make a purchase. It's against the law to use the old coinage."

Aaranon gently grabbed hold of his knife, which he kept tucked up under his left sleeve, preparing himself to make a quick getaway.

Taking notice of the movement the udam said, "I wouldn't do that if I were you."

Aaranon could now feel and hear the breathing of something enormous that was just a few *ama* behind him. As he turned and looked down at the floor, he could see the massive claws of an MSS trooper. He slowly turned back towards the bar and gently reached for a small device in his right sleeve.

With a slight grimace on his face, the upper-class law

enforcement agent said to Aaranon, "I don't think you have anything up there that will get you out of this."

"I disagree," Aaranon said as he pushed a button on the device. Immediately, the MSS trooper fell back and hit the floor, leaving a large indentation in the stone covered ground. Aaranon then quickly pulled the knife from his left sleeve and slit the throat of the bewildered agent who immediately fell to the floor; writhing in a pool of blood.

The barkeep quietly looked around the corner to see only Aaranon sitting; waiting for his order.

"Can I get that ale now?" he asked.

In a trembling whisper the udam replied, "Yes sir."

As the barkeep was sloshing the refreshing brew into a mug, Aaranon moved over to the MSS trooper. He leaned over and, being careful to keep it contained within the surrounding flesh, he removed the implanted farspeak device. He then stored it away in a container he kept in his satchel. Next, he removed several tracking devices from both the MSS trooper and the dead agent. He then smashed them against the hard floor, destroying them completely.

Sitting back at the bar, Aaranon quickly drank the ale and then gave a list of items for the barkeep to retrieve from the store. "I need these," he said with a calm demeanor.

"Yes sir, right away," came the barkeep as he quickly headed back into the store room to fill Aaranon's order.

While the barkeep focused on his duties, a few of the patrons cautiously entered the pub, gazing at the once feared yet now silent corpses.

One concerned soul said to Aaranon, "Sir. You need to get out of here before they come."

With an inward, resigned sigh he replied, "It will be awhile before they arrive."

"How did you do that?" asked another patron.

"What god do you serve?" inquired another.

As the barkeep came back with the supplies, Aaranon laid

down several old coins on the well-worn counter.

"Sir, these are free. You don't need to pay me."

Aaranon just left the coins and grabbed the sack of supplies and headed for the door.

"Sir, who are you?"

With the light streaming down upon him in the open doorway, Aaranon paused, without turning around, and answered hesitantly, "Loha."

Soon after, he moved down the road and off into the forest, leaving the patrons to stand among themselves and watch. The barkeep said to the others as he continued to gaze at Aaranon, "Can the old myth of his returning be true?"

Chapter 3

The past year did nothing to abate the emotional scars that continued to plague Dihana. She grieved day and night for the loss of her precious Aaranon. She longed to sit by his side as she moved her hands through his beard while he talked about his many adventures.

Since their separation, she did nothing but continually hide herself away in his quarters. She laid out his uniforms and covered herself with them. As night turned into day and back again, she cried out rivers of tears and anger onto his bed.

She grieved for the loss of Rohu and her mother, Sari, as well. She uttered very little to anyone except to occasionally spew out her venom towards the mingled servants, or use them as whipping posts to release her pent up rage and aggression.

To seek shelter from her despair, she climbed down to the bottom of every bottle she could find. Unable to obtain solace however, she destroyed priceless furnishings, pottery, and tapestries throughout the castle. Darham attempted to comfort her, but her fury for his lack of concern would not be appeased by his measly platitudes. He appeared indifferent and emotionless for the supposed passing of her dearly departed brother.

Her father, as well, did very little to comfort her; leaving her to her own devices. However, unbeknownst to them, Zeul had other plans for their lives.

One night, as she walked about the castle drinking her way to another evening of inebriation, she came to her mother's quarters. The doors had been locked a few odes after her death. While gripping the handles, she thrashed against them, attempting to gain entrance, but to no avail.

Ever since Aaranon's funeral, Zeul had numerous UAK soldiers positioned throughout Quayanin castle. As Dihana kicked and pulled at the doors, one of the UAK soldiers came to assist.

"Your Highness, may I help you with something?"

"Dack yeah! You can open these dack'n doors," she said, slurring every word.

"Your Highness, I'm under strict orders to leave these doors locked."

"Really? Strict orders huh? Is that from my so-called ruler of a father?" she asked as she poked him in the chest several times with her finger.

"Yes Your Highness, King Zeul said..."

Dihana waved her hands as she interrupted, "Oooo...King Zeul said; King Zeul said. Well...*Princess* Dihana says you better open this door, or I'll rip your sack off and use it for a purse!"

As the young cadet nervously covered his privies, he said, "Your Highness please, I mean no disrespect. I have my orders to leave this room locked. If I break those orders, I will face..."

Dihana took the bottle she was holding, threw it at the wall behind his head and screamed, "I don't care what you will face! I don't care if you die! I don't care if they throw you on the fire as a sacrifice! I don't even care if they take everything away from you because he took everything from me!"

Dihana slumped to the floor and wept uncontrollably as the guard looked around to see if anyone was watching. "Just open the door. Please open the door. I just want to see my mother's things."

He quietly disengaged the lock and helped Dihana to her feet.

"Your Highness, please don't tell anyone."

She held onto the guard as best she could and said in a desolate tone, "Who would I tell?"

Removing the key from around his neck, the handsome young cadet said, "Just please lock the door when you leave."

"I will," she said as she fumbled for several moments trying to place the key around her neck.

As she started to close the door behind her, the guard softly said to Dihana, "I'm so sorry for your loss, Your Highness. I lost my mother three years ago."

"What is your name?" she asked.

"Micah, Your Highness."

Through the door, she reached out and gently touched the guard's hand and said, "I'm sorry Micah. Please forgive me."

Confusion swept across his face as he wondered why the Princess of the Alemeleg would ever apologize to someone like him.

Closing the door, Dihana's eyes took some time to adjust to the darkness. She didn't want to open the curtains or turn on any lighting out of fear of being discovered. She finally made her way to her mother's bed.

She flopped down on top of the comforters and a mountain of dust flew into the air. She didn't notice however; with the room spinning from her drunken stupor, she finally passed out and fell into a deep sleep.

***

As the wind blew through her golden locks, she found herself walking through a beautiful wheat field that was ready for harvest. In every direction, she could see nothing but wheat. There were no buildings or structures. There were no clouds in the sky, and the light of Shemesh continued to shine for what seemed like days on end.

Dihana didn't know where she was, but continued to walk through the tall wheat without getting tired or exhausted. As she caressed the stalks, she could see that none of them had any kernels left on them. They were empty.

She looked off towards the horizon to see three blurry figures in the distance. As she drew near she could tell that it was two udamé and one wudam. It didn't take long, but as she moved closer she could see that the wudam was her mother.

Joy filled her heart as she raced towards her mother, calling out her name. Within a few moments, she could see that the other two were Rohu and Yohan. Dihana soon threw herself into her mother's arms while Rohu and Yohan joined in the embrace. All four of them wept tears of rapture, unwilling to be the first to let go.

Sari pulled back slightly to gaze at her beloved daughter. She said as she dabbed away her tears, "We don't have long dear, and I need to tell you something."

"Oh Mother, I don't understand. Have I died? Where is Aaranon? Where are we?"

"My little princess. There is so much I wish I could say, but we only have a moment."

Dihana looked confused as she continued to embrace all three of them, "I don't understand. What do you mean?"

"I need for you to listen to me carefully. Can you do that?"

"Yes Mother."

"In my room, behind my bed, you will find a secret compartment. You can open it by pushing the olive branch on my bedpost."

"What's in there?"

"You will find a set of scrolls. I want you to read them, but don't let anyone else see them, and don't let anyone else know you have them."

"Mother I don't understand, if I'm dead then where is Aaranon?"

Sari looked up towards Rohu and Yohan, who were quietly watching Dihana. Their countenance was like that of a divine being. Rohu had a full head of hair and not a scar to speak of anywhere on him. Yohan radiated a peace about him that was beyond her comprehension.

Sari continued, "You will soon take a journey. But first, you must read the scrolls. They hold the truth. They reveal why the razing must come."

Dihana looked around at the scenery and then back at her beloved family members. She soon realized that she was not on the surface of Araz, but somewhere else.

Sari continued, "You understand now?"

"I think so," She paused for several moments as she tried to take in everything. A smile worked its way across her face as she said, "Aaranon isn't dead, is he?"

All three of them smiled at Dihana as the burden of her loss began to lift. In its place came joy and happiness. As they held one another, the ground began to quake and dark clouds moved in from every direction. The wheat started to fall to the ground, and the light of Shemesh diminished. Dihana grew fearful, but the others displayed nothing but peace and tranquility.

Sari gently caressed Dihana's cheeks and looked deep into her eyes as she said, "The time is short. The hour is close at hand. Read the words written in the scrolls and obey them, for they are life."

As Sari continued to look into Dihana's eyes, a large cracking sound jolted her beloved daughter. She looked down and could see the ground ripping apart beneath her feet.

"Mother!?"

***

A deafening boom knocked Dihana out of her mother's bed and onto the floor.

"What the dack?" she screamed as the room continued to move ever so slightly. From the ceiling, pieces of stone and dust collapsed to the floor. The shaking continued for several moments until it finally ceased, leaving her dazed and befuddled.

Gingerly she walked to the door avoiding the rubble scattered about the room. Being careful not to draw attention to herself, she slightly opened to door to glimpse out into the hallway. She could see several mingled servants and UAK forces running about the castle. Micah rushed to the entryway to confirm her safety.

"Are you alright Princess?"

"Yes, yes I am. What happened?"

"It appears we've experienced another ground quake. This one was much worse than the previous. Several require medical attention. Do you need anything?"

"No. I'm fine. I'll stay here until things calm down."

"I believe that would be a good idea, Your Highness," Micah said as his eyes never left hers.

Dihana closed the door and went back to the bed to wait until all the commotion had subsided. As she laid there listening to the ruckus just outside, she looked up and saw the olive branch on the bed post.

She thought to herself, *Did that truly happen? Did I see my mother, Rohu, and Yohan? Oh, if it were only true! What did she tell me to do? Read...read...what did she say to read? Scrolls?! Yes...scrolls. But what scrolls?*

As she continued to ponder the dream, she slowly moved her hand over the engraved olive branch. As she scrutinized it, she stated out loud, "Can it be true?" Once depressed, she heard a small compartment open behind the bed.

In the dark, she could see what looked like ancient scrolls tucked inside the small opening. Quickly she moved back to the doors to ensure they were secure. Then to the windows she scurried to confirm that no one was near.

Tiptoeing her way to the secret compartment, she carefully removed the scrolls. As she unrolled them, a small unassuming piece of parchment drifted to the floor. Because she couldn't see the writing, she picked it up and carried it near to the window to let in a small amount of light. After reading it, tears filled her eyes and poured down onto her soiled dress. She gleefully whispered to herself, "It's true; Aaranon is alive!"

Chapter 4

With the incident at the pub far behind him, Aaranon journeyed back into the forest to continue his preparations for rescuing Dihana and Darham. After numerous attempts over the past year at getting close to Quayanin castle, he soon realized that it was going to be far more taxing than he anticipated. Zeul had thoroughly fortified the surrounding forests of Hoshier with UAK forces as well as placing additional MSS troops to provide greater security.

The UAC, under Zeul's control, continued to pass laws that made it nearly impossible for anyone to move about. In time's past, the UAC only positioned upper-class agents in the small towns and villages scattered throughout Araz for the purpose of collecting taxes and enforcing the laws. Now, however, they embedded an MSS trooper with each agent to carry out any punishment they so desired.

Most, if not all, of these agents, ruled with impunity. They took whatever they wanted - food, equipment, wives, husbands, children - nothing was kept from them as long as they meet their quota to the UAK. A few villages tried to protest formally to the UAC, but they experienced even harsher punishments. A handful even attempted to rebel openly, but soon discovered the full power of the UAC. All of the villagers who rebelled, along with their families, were hauled off to become sacrifices or prisoners. Their towns were destroyed with multiple thermal-collapsers as a witness to anyone else who might wish to defy the kingdom.

Due to the MSS troopers' genetically designed capacity for violence, agents were given the ability to control them through an implanted device. After numerous attempts, Aaranon was able to isolate the frequency and the code on the devices. This gave him the ability to kill with just the push of a button. This method was a more primitive way of communicating with the embedded implant, and he had to be near the MSS trooper for it to work. Due to these factors, Aaranon preferred to abstain from using this advantage unless it was necessary.

Another problem he discovered, was that the frequencies and codes changed from time to time, hence the need for him to remove the device from the MSS trooper once it was dead. The removed device would have a set of updated codes from which he could then use to reprogram his improvised trigger.

Killing an agent and his MSS trooper, however, can draw too much attention, something he hoped to avoid when he left the safety of the forest to pick up a few supplies. Since he was caught using the old coinage, however, he knew there was only one way out of that pub. It was either kill or be killed. Fortunately, no one recognized him, but word would soon spread that an udam named Loha had the ability to kill an agent and his MSS trooper. Regardless of the repercussions, he needed to focus his attention on getting his beloved family members back before something dreadful happened to them.

***

As he came near to his temporary dwelling, which was high up in the trees, he could see an udam hanging upside down from a limb. It appeared he was in a trap and, possibly, still alive. He didn't want to get involved out of fear that he might be recognized by someone, so he attempted to move around without being seen. As he stepped across a limb however, he broke it, stirring the udam awake.

"Hey! Hey you! Can you help me? Can you cut me down before they come back?"

Aaranon glanced out the side of his hood and continued to walk on, ignoring the udam's pleas for help.

"Oh, for the love of all that is good! They're going to sell me as an Apostate and sacrifice me in one of those wretched temples or sporting arenas!"

Against his better judgment, Aaranon replied, "Well then, I guess you deserve whatever you get for being an Apostate."

"Oh come on! Do I look like a dacking Apostate to you?"

"I don't know. I haven't seen one in a while."

"Of course not, no one has seen one in a while because they are all dead."

"Then why would they want to sell you as one?" asked Aaranon.

"Really? Apparently you've been spending too much time in these trees. The altitude must be eating away at your brain."

"Do you always insult the person you want help from?"

"Look, I humbly beg for your forgiveness. But if you haven't recognized, times are tough. People'll do anything now to earn a day's wage."

"So what is the going rate for an Apostate these days?" asked Aaranon.

"How should I know? Maybe you should wait around and ask the mooks who set up this trap."

"Maybe I'll cut you down and turn you in myself."

"Look, if you cut me down, I can give you some of my provisions. I can get you whatever you need. I live in a small village not too far from here. Just please, cut me down before they come to take me away."

"No, I don't want to get involved. I have problems of my own to deal with; I don't need yours," Aaranon said. He turned away from the udam and walked off into the forest, leaving the udam to dangle from the rope.

Desperate, the udam shouted, "They took my wife and sister!"

Aaranon stopped his forward progress and just stood there, thinking about Dihana.

"Look," The udam pulled up his sleeve and revealed a tattoo

of his wife and kids on his arm. "My children need me, and I need them. Haven't you lost someone you love? Wouldn't you do anything to get them back? Please, get me back to my children, and I'll do anything for you."

Not wanting to expose himself to others, but feeling the pain of his own personal loss; he walked over to where the rope was tied off. He cut it and gently lowered the udam to the ground.

"I will never forget this. My name is Pernel. What's your name?"

"Go home Pernel," said Aaranon as he walked away.

Before they could get too far, however, Aaranon and Pernel soon found themselves surrounded by several udamé who returned to retrieve their catch.

"Well! Would you lookie here! We gots two birds with one stone. They's gonna make for a fine prize don't you think Jezatha?"

"I sure does, Sargon. They make for a fitten' pair to sell. But they don't compare to that one thing of a beaut' that we took over a year ago."

"Ah yes. She was a beauty wasn't she? We had funnin' with her, didn't we Larzo?"

"Oh what fun she was. You could tell someone took care of her. Like a temple maiden for them uppity uppers," said Larzo.

"Oh yea. I don't think we've found such a beaut' in a long time. Remember how long it took to get her to break? She wasn't going down without a fight that one," said Sargon.

"She screamed for some mook, remember? What was that name she yelled out Jezatha?" asked Larzo.

"Who cares? I just know these two ain't much for lovin', but they will bring a fittin' price at the stadium."

"Aaron I think it was. No, no. Aaranon! Yeah...that's it. Aaranon. Like he was some kind-of-a saver that would come to her rescue," Larzo replied.

Before he knew it, a rage within Aaranon built until it soon consumed every fiber of his being. Pernel was shaking uncontrollably and tried to appease them. "Look here gents. I have plenty of provisions back at my house, and you're welcome to all of them. I have a pack animal that you can take as well. Just please, let us go."

"Well, that's right kindly of you there dear sir. Along with selling you, I think we'll take up your offer," said Jezatha.

Sargon grabbed hold of Pernel's arm and lifted up his sleeve to reveal the tattoo underneath. "Lookie here Larzo. Looks like we have a few more offerings to sell. This just keeps gettin' better an' better."

"No! Please, they're only children. Please don't touch them, just take me!"

"Only children!? Well, they's the best kind of lovin' in the temples," said Thaddius as he grabbed hold of Pernel and threw him into a small cage.

"And what about you forester? Do you have any children you be wantn' to save?"

Aaranon slowly pulled out the two massive blades he had strapped to his back that once belonged to Rohu. He then turned to face the bandits while pulling back his hood, revealing the fury he was about to unleash.

"Oh righty then. Looks like we've gots a fighter on our hands."

Each of the bandits began pulling out their weapon of choice, leaving Pernel to sit inside the cage and watch the whole spectacle unravel.

Sargon turned to Jezatha, "Why don't you let me give this one a go? He looks to be a bit feisty."

"As you wish kind sir. Just remember he's no use to us dead."

Sargon pulled out a blade from his side and began moving slowly towards Aaranon. They both began to circle one another, looking for an opportunity to strike. Jezatha was becoming impatient and yelled out, "Just take him down, Sargon!"

Sargon lunged towards Aaranon but with a quick sidestep and a swift slice from Aaranon's blade, Sargon's head fell off his shoulders in one quick motion. As the others stood there, they watched Sargon's headless body fall to the ground.

Aaranon turned and calmly asked, "Whose next?"

Each of the bandits screamed in anger and proceeded to throw every weapon at Aaranon; but to no avail. With rapid motion, Aaranon killed each of the bandits except for Larzo, who was waiting off to the side. He was biding his time while the others wore him down.

Pernel, however, was attempting to reach a crossbow that had fallen off the back of one of the dead bandits. He was having trouble reaching it through the small openings in the cage but continued to do all he could to obtain it.

As Aaranon was wiping the blood from his blades, Larzo took off his cloak, revealing a plethora of tattoos, scars, and an assortment of piercings. He then began methodically swinging his blades, showing his talent in sending many unfortunate souls to the great beyond. When he finished his display of combative skill, he positioned himself for the attack and said to Aaranon, "These dead mooks wanted you for money. I want you for a trophy."

Aaranon began swinging his blades, revealing his level of skill and ability. Planting his feet in a fighting stance, he answered Larzo, "I just want you dead."

Larzo gave a sinister grin, "So, what should I call you before I cut your head off and mount it on my wall?"

Just as they started to lunge at one another, Pernel was able, finally, to pull the crossbow up and fire its one and only arrow into Larzo's chest, dropping him to the ground. Stunned, Aaranon stood up and looked over at Pernel as if to say, *I had this!*

He then leaned over Larzo as he was gasping for his last breath and whispered into his ear, "I'm Aaranon you dacking piece of dung!" He then stood over Larzo's body and with one slice, removed his head and kicked it into the woods.

After Aaranon had freed Pernel from the cage, he proceeded

to pilfer through the dead bodies, looking for old coinage and provisions he could use. Pernel couldn't contain his gratitude and begged Aaranon to come with him to his village.

"Please, let me give you my provisions. I owe you my life."

As he continued to search through the bandits' supplies for anything useful, Aaranon replied, "You owe me nothing."

"My daughter makes the best stew you will ever have. It's her mother's recipe. You look like you haven't had a home-cooked meal in a long time. Please, let me do this small thing. I won't ask anything else of you."

After setting the pack animals free and hiding the bodies and the cage in the woods; he looked up at Pernel and thought about how grateful he would be if someone returned Dihana and Darham to him. He also realized that he would not be able to free his loved ones by himself. He would need an ally. But could this stranger be trusted?

He said to Pernel, "Alright, but just for tonight. I'll leave before daybreak."

Chapter 5

It had been almost a year since Ravizu's initiation into the organization that ruled the UAC from behind the scenes. Several hundred *ama* below the surface of Heock, Ravizu and Zeul made their way through the massive hewn stone tunnels to meet with their fellow members of the Kahe'Akaba; also known as the Dark Brotherhood.

With Zeul's ascension to the throne of thrones and sole power given to him by the council, he could now move forward unimpeded with all his plans to prepare for the razing. In spite of Ravizu's initiation as a member of the secret organization, Zeul continued to keep his son in the dark about the looming cataclysm until he deemed him worthy enough to know. Ravizu was led to believe that the underground cities were safe havens in the event of an uprising from the populace.

The complex was created many years ago by Zeul's mining company without Ravizu's knowledge. The cave system had multiple levels reaching deep into the ground. It was easily ten times the size of the city above it. A multitude of mingled servants provided all the manual labor necessary to build and maintain such a colossal infrastructure.

Virtually every amenity was made available to those privileged enough for admittance. Underground aquifers provided plenty of water, while large domed caverns provided room for growing crops and livestock. An iridescent glow, primarily greenish in color, covered many of the walls, providing the necessary light throughout the tunnels.

This, of course, wasn't the only underground complex. Numerous other cities were built and linked together through a vast tunnel system that stretched across all of Araz; all of which were accomplished by Zeul and his company.

The two of them, along with the other members of the Dark Brotherhood, entered into their most sacred of chambers. A mammoth set of granite stone doors, which sealed the only entrance into the room, were closed behind them; leaving them to wait in the dark for their master to arrive.

A low hum came from the members as they started to chant the ancient name of the one that promised them ascension to godhood. As the chanting continued, it soon reached a feverish pitch, echoing against the stone walls which were polished to a glass-like appearance.

In the middle of the chamber, a small glimmer of light could be seen piercing the darkness. Radiating outward, one could now see the members in their long black hooded robes standing in a circle looking toward the growing illumination. As the light increased in intensity, the chanting grew to an extraordinary level. Instantly, the light consumed the entire room, prompting everyone to become silent and fall prostrate.

The light not only pierced the darkness, but it also pierced their souls. It spoke of knowledge and wisdom that no udam could attain in their present state. Virtually every soul that stood in its presence could not resist its overpowering call to obey its every command. No one that is, except for a few. However, the few who could resist its power were nowhere near this hallowed dwelling.

Soon after, a thunderous voice spoke from the light and declared, "Rejoice brothers! For the time of reckoning is close at hand!"

Every member of the Kahe'Akaba uttered in unison and without moving a muscle, "Praise almighty Halail!"

Chapter 6

Walking together through the forest, back to Pernel's village, Aaranon barely said a word, leaving his new companion to fill the air with his nervous bantering.

"I truly do appreciate you helping me out of that predicament back there. My children will be grateful as well. They will be so excited to see a real forester. No one of my age has seen one in such a long time. My forefathers told me stories of how your kind walked among the trees. He said you were named wind-walkers because you seemed to glide through the air as you moved about the forest.

"If you don't mind me asking, how long have you lived out here by yourself? You don't appear to be that old. But, as you know, it's difficult to accurately tell someone's age until they are more than four or five hundred years old.

"Have you always been a forester, or did you have to move out here because of the kingdom's constant oppression? Which, if I might add, is getting worse and worse every day.

"I'm sure I'm among good company when I say this; I sincerely don't like this new Alemeleg. I mean, so what if he lost some of his family? That doesn't mean we have to suffer for his loss, do we? I've lost my wife, both parents, a sister and three brothers to those temples and arenas. And we are most certainly not Apostates I can assure you of that!

"Who, in their right mind, can follow a deity that allows all of this evil to run amuck in the world? If he's so merciful and gracious like the Apostates say, then why hasn't he thrown off this disaster of a government and installed a benevolent ruler? In fact, why do we need any ruler? Can't we rule ourselves?"

Aaranon walked a few paces in front of Pernel, hoping to

make it clear he didn't want to talk, but his chatty and annoying companion continued to drone on.

"I like those leathers you are wearing, did you make those yourself, or did someone else do that for you? They look like ohema and gloth hides, which if they are, I can only imagine what it took to hunt them down. Is the skin of the gloth really that hard to cut? I heard that the hide is almost impenetrable.

"My father wasn't much of a hunter. He was primarily a farmer like myself. In fact, the reason I'm away from my village is because I was venturing out to look for a particular herb we use for stomach aches. My son, he's been having trouble keeping his food down. I think he ate one of those new plants that are popping up all over the place. They're like nothing I've seen before. If I'm correct, I think they're something the UAK is creating in one of their disturbing labs; like those MSS troops they've been putting all over the place.

"I'm not sure if you've seen one of them up close, but they are *not* natural I can tell you that! And those dacking agents! They do whatever they want since they get an MSS trooper assigned to them. They take food, property, our wives and children. In time's past, we would just wait for the right time and kill them. They learned very quickly not to mess with us. But now? They do whatever they want. It would be wonderful if there were a way to kill those monsters without being discovered."

Thoroughly annoyed Aaranon finally said, "Has anyone ever told you, you talk too much?"

"Ooohhh yeess! My mother used to say, 'That mouth is going to get you killed one day, Pernel.' She was an excellent lady. Knew her stuff she did."

"Maybe you should have listened to her," Aaranon said as he continued to walk faster.

"I agree with that. Saying too much can get you into a big

mess; like back there. I should have shut up about my family. Imagine if we didn't kill them. They would have come back here and taken them."

"We?"

"Well, mostly you, but I did manage to kill that one mook. But, I must confess...it was a lucky shot. I didn't know how to work that silly thing. I just got lucky. Just like with you coming along at the time you did. If you didn't come by, I would be sold by now."

Exasperated, Aaranon asked, "How much further?"

"It isn't much further. Up that hill," Pernel said, pointing toward a path that veered off to the right and up a mildly steep slope. Pernel continued, "So, why are you out here? I haven't seen you in these parts before today. Are you passing through, or looking for a place to stay?"

Aaranon, wanting the incessant chatter to stop, tersely stated, "I'm just passing through."

"Ah, I see. So where might you be headed? I heard the forests of Tarshish are a great place to hide away. It's mostly untouched woodlands. No energy taps. No UAK patrols. I've heard it's great if you want to disappear. I've also heard it isn't so great if you want to live but, after watching you, I don't think you would have a problem taking care of yourself. So, are you headed to Tarshish or somewhere else?"

Aaranon stopped dead in his tracks and said to Pernel, without looking at him, "If you don't mind, I prefer to keep silent so I can hear if anyone or anything is approaching."

"Oh right! Most magnificent! Keep your ears open and your mouth shut. I agree. How can you know if something is coming unless you keep a lookout for them, right? My father taught me that when I was..."

Aaranon gave Pernel a look that said, *SHUT UP!*

"OH! Right! Got it."

***

As they began the climb down the hill that lead into Pernel's village, Aaranon could see several quaint little homes, both on the ground and in the trees. From a distance, he could see small gardens planted throughout the village with only a few pack animals available for tilling the ground.

The streets between the homes were, primarily, covered in dirt with only the town square, located near its center, covered in cobblestone. There was a small temple to the Ayim made of brick that appeared to be there only out of a requirement from the UAK and not out of their desire to worship.

In the trees, he could see winding staircases that circled the tree on its way up toward the main dwellings. Between the trees, rope bridges connecting the various homes could be seen. Some of the trees were also hollowed out in places, allowing them to find shelter inside their massive trunks. Some of these trunks were up to two hundred *ama* in width, which could easily fit several udamé laying down end to end.

Once Aaranon and Pernel reached the outskirts of the village, several children came running toward them yelling, "Uba! Uba!" Pernel took off running to greet his children, leaving Aaranon to continue at his preferred pace.

As Aaranon watched them embrace each other, he couldn't help but think about Dihana. He longed for the day when he could once again hold his precious flower. He even thought about Amana and wondered if he could find her once again.

From time to time, he entertained the thought of making her his bride. Maybe they could have children. Maybe they could make a life out in the forest near Emet with Nahim and his family. But for now, these were only far off dreams.

Knowing what his father and the UAC were capable of, he didn't have any ambitions whatsoever to reclaim the throne. All he wanted to do was get back his family and go as far away as he could.

For now, however, he needed to focus on his plan of rescue. He knew he needed help, but he didn't trust anyone. After his father had stared back at him through the visual when he sat helpless in that dark and dreary cave, he believed that Zeul would do everything in his power to find him. Therefore, anyone could be a possible spy sent out by his father.

Once Aaranon was close to Pernel, the children pulled back and hid behind their father, fearing the worst.

"Oh, no, no, no. Children, I want you to meet the udam who rescued me. If it weren't for him, I would not have returned."

Aaranon continued to wear his hood pulled across his face, hiding himself. The children slowly moved out from behind their father and circled around, looking him up and down. One of the toddlers started poking on Aaranon's leg checking him out. The others looked at the two blades tucked away securely on his back while another tried to pull at his satchel. Aaranon quickly pulled it away from the little one, prompting the others to run with haste behind their father once more.

"I'm sorry about that. They are very curious. We don't get many visitors here you see."

Aaranon gently replaced the satchel to his side.

"Why don't I introduce you to some of the elders in our village? I know they will be happy to see you," said Pernel as he motioned for Aaranon to follow him.

***

While walking past the small cottages toward the village square, several people stepped out of their humble abodes to gaze at Aaranon and whisper among themselves.

"You must forgive them," said Pernel. "Like I said, we don't get many visitors. We can meet with the elders in the council hall. They should be there at this hour of the day."

Almost every small town had a body of elders that acted as a ruling council for that particular community. These councils were not officially sanctioned by the UAC but were relics of a time long gone. Hundreds of years ago they governed every aspect of their village, from the passing of ordinances to the punishment of criminals. Now they only rule in small matters of dispute. Every other matter gets handled by the upper-class law enforcement agent for that region.

"Elder Dalltun and Elder Stol, I would like for you to meet my new friend. As I was out in the woods gathering herbs, I was captured by the bandits."

Elder Dalltun's eyes became red while a small tear could be seen moving down his cheek.

"Were they the ones who took our people?" asked Elder Stol.

"I believe so. But they won't be stealing them anymore. My friend here rescued me and killed all of them."

Both of the elders took a moment to look at Aaranon with immense gratitude. Aaranon could see a heavy burden being released from all the years of being terrorized by a force they could not overcome. He could also see a deep sadness across their faces for all the loved ones they had lost to those heartless criminals.

"Then he deserves our everlasting friendship and gratitude," said Elder Dalltun as he turned to Elder Stol and then back to Pernel.

"Yes, I believe so. I would like to invite you to stay with us as long as you like. Anything you want is at your disposal. Please, don't hesitate to ask," Elder Stol thankfully offered.

"I thank you for your offer, but I'm needed elsewhere. I promised Pernel that I would have a meal with him and then be on my way."

"I would beg you to stay, but you seem to be an udam on a mission. However, until you leave, please know that we are here to serve you. Ask, and it shall be given to you," said Elder Dalltun as he extended his hand to shake Aaranon's. As Aaranon slowly extended his arm to reveal a deeply scarred and weathered hand, both of the elders recognized an ancient symbol on the two blades protruding from behind Aaranon's back.

"May I have the honor of knowing your name?" Elder Stol asked as excitement grew in his eyes.

"Loha."

Elder Dalltun's hand began to tremble as he held onto Aaranon's. He asked Aaranon once more, with hope shining in his eyes, "What did you say your name was?"

Aaranon slowly pulled back his hood revealing his bald head and rough countenance and then looked into the eyes of each of the elders and said, "Loha."

Both of them kneeled before Aaranon while Elder Stol spoke just above a whisper and said, "He carries the blades. It's true. Loha has returned to us."

Chapter 7

As Aaranon looked down on the two elders bowed before him, he couldn't help but wonder if this had anything to do with the stories of Rohu.

He looked at them in mild bewilderment. "Why are you bowing before me? Get up!"

"We're sorry Lord Loha, but we've been waiting for your return for so long," said Elder Dalltun with tears streaming down his face.

"What are you talking about?" Aaranon said.

"Centuries ago you saved this village from the giant heboram that plagued these hills. They took our crops, our animals, and even our families from us. If it weren't for you, this town would have been swept away for good," said Elder Stol as he continued to look in sheer amazement at Aaranon.

Elder Dalltun continued, "Legend says that the ancient gods took you to their abode and made you commander over their armies and that one day you would return to set us free."

"Why do you think I'm *that* Loha?"

"Because the symbol on your blades bear witness to the first Loha. These were the markings of his family. All of his children and his wife were killed, leaving no heir. But there they are, on your blades. If you are not him, then who are you and how did you come into possession of his markings?"

Aaranon's mind started to race as he thought about the situation he found himself. He needed help, but he had no one to trust. If these elders believed him to be connected to the first Loha, then they might be willing to influence some of the stronger udamé to go with him. They might even fight for him, but he needed to be cautious. Once again, he struggled with the temporary comfort of a lie over the steep path of telling the truth. Convenience, however, was what he needed at the moment. The truth would just have to wait once again.

After carefully considering what to say, Aaranon finally answered, "They were given to me by him. He trained me in all the ways of war. He then returned to the gods. His mantle now rests upon me."

At that moment, another villager came running into the council chambers with a great deal of enthusiasm. "Elders! Wonderful news! A forester came through and killed the local agent and his MSS trooper at the pub. It was truly..." The villager's words trailed off, and his face became white as a sheet as he looked at Aaranon. He then said, "IT'S YOU! You killed that MSS trooper without even touching it!! How did you do that?"

Both of the elders turned back to look at Aaranon. Once again, they found themselves speechless.

Chapter 8

As Aaranon ate his soup, he could see out of the corner of his eye all of Pernel's children staring at him. Through the window, he could also see the villagers walking slowly past, attempting to catch a glimpse of the one they anticipated returning, but never fully believed that it would come to pass.

Pernel, noticing that Aaranon was getting a bit agitated by the attention, motioned for his children to stop staring and eat their soup before it grew cold. Soon, a knock came at the door, prompting Pernel to excuse himself and see who it was.

After several moments of a mildly heated discussion, Pernel returned to Aaranon and asked if some guests could visit with him. Aaranon hesitantly said yes and soon the entire house was filled with villagers shuffling into the cramped quarters, hoping to speak with the apprentice of the legendary Loha.

"I apologize for the crowd, but some of the villagers wanted to speak with you before you go," said Pernel.

Aaranon beheld their faces and saw within them something he had not seen in a very long time; hope. "That's fine."

The first to step forward was an elderly udam who could barely stand upright. The room immediately grew silent as he stepped out of the shadows. The only sound was the whistling of the wind through the numerous cracks in the walls.

He was assisted by a few family members. As he moved past Pernel, he gave him a look of disappointment, causing Pernel to look away.

Even though Aaranon was sitting down, the elderly udam had to look up to see him. As he drew near, he looked deep into Aaranon's gorgeous blue eyes. He stared at him for several moments without saying a word. Soon after, a smile could be seen forming in the corner of his deeply wrinkled and aged mouth. He said in a quiet yet gentle voice, "This one has walked with Loha."

With those words, tears of joy began to fall down the faces of all who gathered there. Others started to speak in whispered tones to one another, and a sense of euphoria proceeded to sweep throughout the room. The elderly udam then pulled on Aaranon's sleeve prompting him to come closer as he whispered. "Do not forget what he told you."

Aaranon immediately recalled Rohu's warning of seeking revenge. Wondering how this old udam knew, he simply nodded his head.

The old udam then turned, with the help of his family, to slowly walk out of the cottage and back into the night.

Turning to Pernel, Aaranon asked, "Who was that?"

"His name is Isma. He is our oldest elder."

"What's so special about his presence?"

"That is the first time he has spoken in over a year," Pernel replied as he stared out the door in awe.

Finally, the silence was broken when a female voice from the back of the room said, "May I speak with Loha?" As she made her way to the front, you could see deep anguish across her face. "My name is Ita and my husband's name is Oseph. The bandits took him and sold him. I have not seen him for two seasons. I miss him so much. Can you get him back for me?"

Almost immediately, a barrage of requests came streaming out, one running over the top of the other.

"They took my children and sold them to the temples."

"They took my wife; I don't know if she's alive."

"I lost all hope until you came."

"Please help us. You're our only hope."

"Someone needs to stop this reign of terror. We can't live like this."

"Can you help us?"

"We want to fight back, but we don't know how. Can you teach us?"

Pernel shouted to the sea of people that now engulfed the tiny rickety shack he called his home. "Everyone please; he has somewhere else he needs to be. He's only here for tonight, and then he will be on his way."

As everyone continued to pour out their requests, Aaranon couldn't help but feel the same longing they all craved; to once again be reunited. How could he ask them for their help if he wasn't going to reciprocate?

Aaranon slowly stood up and raised his hand to quiet the crowd. It didn't take long before the room once again grew silent. All waited to listen to every word that would pour from his lips.

"Not long ago, I too had my family taken from me."

Throughout the room, whispered gasps punctured the silence.

He continued, "Over the past year, I've learned that I am unable to rescue them on my own. To fight an heboram is one thing. At least with them, you know who the enemy is. But when you fight the kingdom, you don't always see them coming. They could be anyone in this room."

Each of the frightened villagers looked at one another with an uneasy suspicion.

He continued, "They are elusive and subtle, and they are everywhere. I realize now that I cannot fight them on my own. I need help, and I need help that I can trust. But in order for me to trust you, you must also trust me. It would be indecent of me to ask for your assistance if I did not first offer mine in return.

"But please hear me when I say this; what you are asking for, will more than likely lead to your death. If you were to liberate your loved ones, the UAK would see it as opposing their rule. They do not see your family as people, but as property of the kingdom. If you take your loved ones back, then you are stealing from the kingdom and swift punishment will follow.

"I think most of you know what happened to the towns and villages that rebelled against the UAK. Not only did they deal harshly with those who fought against the kingdom, but they were heartless in their treatment of their families and their villages.

"What you are asking of me is to put everyone's life in this village in jeopardy. That includes not only yourselves, but your wives, your husbands, and even your children.

"If you want to know how to fight. I can train you. I cannot, however, prepare you to live with the aftermath of what would come if you choose to go down this path. I'm afraid that it will only lead to your destruction. I can carry the burden of my personal fate, but I cannot carry it for others. That will be your choice to make."

Once Aaranon finished speaking, Elder Dalltun stepped forward, prompting the others to remain silent. "My father told me of a time when we were free. There were no kingdoms. There were no Alemelegs to rule with an iron fist. Everyone lived as they pleased, and did as they so desired.

"Our children know nothing of that time. If we continue to allow bandits, agents, and nobles to have their way with us, no one will be left to tell the stories of old. Loha, we know all about the risks. We live under them every day. If you are committed to helping us, then we are committed to helping you. Our word is our bond."

Aaranon glanced around the room and saw everyone nodding in agreement. As he looked around that insignificant, crowded shack of a home, he could see a glimmer of hope making its way across their faces. Something he had not experienced for himself in a very long time. With an ever so subtle smile, he uttered, "Well then, tomorrow, we begin."

Chapter 9

Zeul and Ravizu made their way down the hall at the UAC headquarters to speak with Dihana and Darham in Zeul's office. Because of Dihana's anger over the loss of Aaranon, Zeul felt it would be best to wait before making his announcement to both of them.

"Father, I understand you believe it is necessary to retain pertinent details close to your vest. However, if you wouldn't mind, I would like to know who we are going to speak with before we arrive."

"I suppose I can tell you now since you will know soon enough. I'm going to have Darham take Dihana as his Betwudam."

"Father, I mentioned before that I would gladly take Dihana as my bride."

"Ravizu, do you take me for a fool? Once she is in your hands, she would most assuredly find an untimely demise."

A sinister grin crossed Ravizu's handsome face. "It wouldn't be untimely…it would be right after I had my way with her."

"I told you; I have a need for her. That's why I've kept you from her this past year."

"Alright, but would you mind telling me your plan? If you include me, I could…help you."

"Ravizu I told you before, when you're ready to know I will enlighten you. However, you are not ready just yet; you still have much to learn when it comes to the art of subtlety."

**

Dihana and Darham sat quietly in Zeul's office as a few mingled servants stood in the shadows, waiting for orders. The tension between the two was high as this had been the first time they had been near one another in over six odes.

Dihana tapped her foot as she waited impatiently for her father to come meet with them. From time to time, she would stop her foot to look back at the door to see if she could hear him coming near. When the doors didn't open she would let out a gruff sound, cross her arms, and continue to tap.

"Dihana, if you wouldn't mind. Please stop tapping…"

Dihana started to tap both feet in rapid succession and then said, "Oh, I'm sorry. Did you say something Dung-ham? I couldn't hear you through the tears over the loss of our brother."

"Dihana I need to tell you something, but…"

"You need to tell me something?" she said as she looked up towards the ceiling and continued. "Did you hear that? He needs to tell me something. Now what can *Dung*-ham tell me that would be so important that he couldn't tell me less than a year ago? Hmmmm! Let me see. What could it be? *I'm sorry I wasn't there for you Dihana while you were grieving over the loss of our brother.*"

"Dihana…"

"Or is it, *I'm sorry I've been such an ASS for not caring at all about Aaranon even though he loved me dearly.*"

"Dihana please, let me…"

"Or maybe it's, *I'm sorry Dihana for not looking out for you. Leaving you open to the possibility that Ravizu might come at any moment and 'take care of you' like he took care of Aar…*"

Dihana's words trailed off as she fought back the tears. "No! I'm not crying anymore. I don't think there is anything you can say to me that would make a difference. You mean nothing to me, Darham. I don't know why Father has called both of us here, but after tonight I don't want to see you again."

Before Darham could say another word the doors opened, revealing Zeul and Ravizu walking together into the room.

Dihana and Darham turned around in their chairs to see both of them. Immediately Dihana turned back to one of the servants and yelled, "I need a drink, NOW!"

***

It didn't take long for Zeul to make his announcement while showing little to no concern for Dihana's repeated requests to be left alone.

Once she and Darham were allowed to leave, Dihana immediately walked briskly out of the room, leaving Darham to catch up as they both made their way down the long UAC hall. Darham tried to get her to slow down, but she wouldn't listen. She continued out into the plaza and made her way to one of the local cafes to further drown her sorrows.

While closing the massive doors, Zeul took a moment to watch his two children run away from him. He then spoke briefly to Ravizu about Dihana. "Ravizu, did you notice something different about Dihana?"

"Let me see...angry, drunk, sarcastic, hates me, doesn't suspect you; and yet still as beautiful as ever. Nope...nothing different."

"I sense she is suffering from the same illness as her mother."

"Father, if you're insinuating I poisoned her, I assure you..."

"I want you to search Sari's old room. Look for anything out of the ordinary."

"Like what?"

"Secret compartments maybe? Ancient papers or scrolls."

"What are you getting at?"

"All in due time Ravizu, all in due time. Take a few of your guards and have them search the room. If you find anything out of place, bring it to me."

"Certainly Father. I'll let you know what I find."

***

Darham was finally able to catch up and sit next to Dihana just as she was downing her first ale.

"Didn't you hear me back there *Dacking*-ham!? I said I wanted nothing to do with you. You are a dacking piece of dung!"

"May I please say…?"

"NO! You don't get to say anything. You knew I needed you, and you let me down."

"Dihana, there is a reason as to why I couldn't come to you."

"Oh, were you too busy having sex with your maidens in the temple."

"It isn't like that."

"Or maybe you were just too drunk to come see me."

"You mean drunk like you."

"SHUTUP! Dack you Darham! Dack you! I drink because of the pain. You drink because you don't want to listen to people."

"That's why I couldn't see you," said Darham trying to explain himself.

"OH! You didn't want to experience my thoughts, see my grief did you? That's just like you Darham, or *DUNG*-ham. You don't want to feel or care about anyone do you."

"That isn't the reason!"

As Dihana continued to berate Darham in public, he slowly pulled out a thick metal collar from his coat that he quickly put around Dihana's neck when she wasn't looking.

"WHAT THE DACK IS THIS!?"

Darham stood up and grabbed hold of Dihana's arm, pulling

her out of her chair. "Forgive us folks, my Betwudam is having a bad day so we will be going now."

"No, we are NOT leaving, I haven't finished my drink you sack-licker. Get your hands off me or I'll…"

Darham spoke loud enough so everyone could hear. "Or you'll do what!? You're my Betwudam now, and I can do whatever I want! So shut the tarsis up you wench and do as I say or you'll find yourself as a sacrifice in the temple!"

Several of the udamé sitting in the cafe applauded and shouted in agreement. As Darham dragged her away by her arm he whispered into her ear, "We need to get out of here. I have something to tell you, and you're not going to believe it."

Chapter 10

Darham was finally able to pull Dihana into his sky runner and begin heading back to Quayanin Castle. He put the ship on autopilot and made his way to speak with Dihana in the forward cabin.

The assault on his ears began as soon as he passed through the cabin doors.

Tugging on the thick piece of metal around her neck, she bellowed, "Where in TARSIS are you taking me and what is this thing you put on me you idiot?!"

"Let me explain..." was all that Darham could get out before Dihana began punching and kicking him with all her might.

"I'll let you explain you son of a wench! I'm going to kill you where you stand!"

"AARANON IS ALIVE!" screamed Darham, while he continued to cover himself as she threw a fury of punches into his head and side.

"What?! What did you just say?" Stunned, she backed away and looked at Darham in complete bewilderment.

"I said Aaranon is alive!" he said as he slowly picked himself up off the floor and rubbed his wounds.

Dihana stood there, just looking at him for several moments. She then flung her arms around him, squeezed him tight, and kissed him several times on the forehead. Through her tears she whispered, "I knew it had to be true. Oh, thank the ancient one!"

Dihana continued to hold onto him while he slowly put his arms around her.

"How long have you known?" she asked as she gently pulled back and wiped the blood from the corner of his mouth.

In a soft, squeaky voice he answered, "If you don't mind, I

need to sit down for a moment. Your foot found my privies one too many times."

"Darham, I'm so sorry, it's just that I was so angry with you."

Dihana then punched him in the arm, causing him to give her a confused look.

"What was that for you crazy w…"

"Aah! I'm not a wench."

"So why did you hit me again?"

"That's for not telling me you knew. How long have you known?" she asked.

Darham curled up in the seat to protect himself once again in anticipation of the flurry of fists that was sure to follow. He then whispered, "Six odes."

"SIX!!" she yelled as she doubled up her fist to strike, but then pulled back.

"I'm so sorry Dihana. I wanted to tell you, but…wait a moment. You just said that you knew it had to be true. What do you know?"

While Darham sat curled up on the soft, white sofa that stretched the length of the cabin, Dihana slowly backed up and then plopped herself down on the floor.

As she tried to catch her breath she said, "It's somewhat difficult to explain."

"We have a long trip back. You can take your time. Especially if it doesn't involve hitting me," Darham replied, with a slight grin as he nursed his wounds.

"Well…I had a dream of my mother, Rohu, and Yohan. I don't know if I crossed over to the great beyond, or if they came to me, but I know it was them."

Intrigued, he leaned forward and asked, "Really? What were they like?"

Dihana glanced out the window as the light of Shemesh shined through, reminding her of their countenance. She said, "You should have seen them Darham. There was a peace in their eyes I had never seen before."

"What do you mean?"

"It's hard to explain. It's as if they had no worries anymore. No fear. No sadness. No pain. I could feel that flowing from them. They were at rest."

"What else?" He stared at Dihana, hanging on her every word.

Grinning, she said, "You should have seen Rohu. He had hair!"

"Hair!? Seriously?" he laughed at the thought.

"Yeah, and he had no scars to speak of, anywhere. Mother looked younger than me. She moved without the help from any servants. The dream was just like the ones Aaranon had, but I could speak with them." Dihana's eyes grew red as she recalled the scene so vividly.

"What did they say? Did they talk about Aaranon?" he asked as he used a cloth to clean up some of the drying blood from his lip.

"They didn't say anything directly, but I could sense from them that Aaranon was still alive," she said. She thought about mentioning the scrolls and the letter she found in Sari's old room, but decided to keep that to herself for now. She still didn't know what Darham was up to and wanted to find out more.

"Was there anything else?" he asked.

"No, that was it. So how did you know he was alive?" she asked.

"I'm sure you're wondering why that collar is around your neck."

"Oh this! Noooo... I just thought it was your atrocious taste in jewelry. Besides it doesn't go with my dress or my shoes and the color is soooo last season."

"I'm glad to see you still have your sense of humor," he said.

"Yeah. So go on, tell me why I have this exquisite celab collar clamped around my neck," she said sarcastically.

"You have a device implanted in the base of your neck that allows our wonderful father to see your thoughts. And that exquisite *piece of jewelry* creates a false thought-signal while blocking the real one from the implant."

"What!? I had my suspicions we were being watched, but this?" she yelled while tugging on her collar.

"Bear with me as I tell you a long tale."

"Like you said, we've got plenty of time," she replied while lying down on the floor.

"As you know I could read other people's thoughts. What I didn't know is that it was not a natural ability. There was an implant in my head like the one you have. I learned however that it had a malfunction that allowed me to read other people's thoughts. Even those who don't have an implant."

"So the one I have goes only one way. Father can read mine, but I can't read his."

"Correct."

"But why did Father want to know our thoughts?"

"Our father isn't who he claims to be. One night, about seven odes ago, I was at the villa sleeping off one of my many long evenings. As I was laying there, I could see Father's thoughts vividly. Even better than my own."

"What did you see?"

"Normally for him it would be boring and mundane things. How to pass laws, how to advance the family, and so forth. But on this night I saw more than I wanted to see. I saw him talking to a bright light."

A look of confusion crossed her lovely face. "A bright light?"

"I can't quite explain it, but there was a tremendous voice that spoke through this light. They were talking about Aaranon as if he was alive," he said.

"How do you know it was Father's thoughts and not just a dream?"

"I could see Father talking about his plans of giving every upper-class law enforcement agent an MSS trooper. Two odes later he made the announcement on the visuals. There were other things as well that confirmed to me I wasn't dreaming.

What I saw was real."

"Give me a moment while I try to fathom the craziness I just heard. Father can read my thoughts, but I cannot read his, he can also read your thoughts but you can read his and the thoughts of everybody else as well?"

"Well...not exactly. The part about you is correct. The part about me, however, has changed. The technology in that collar is the same kind that is now in me. I can no longer read other peoples thoughts. However, when Father tries to read mine..."

"He gets a false reading," she said as she completed his thought. Dihana continued, "So why did you stay away for six odes?"

"For one, I knew Ravizu would not come after you. Zeul explicitly forbid him from touching you anymore."

"Anymore? You mean he knew what Ravizu did to me? And he did nothing!?"

"Like I said Dihana, our father isn't who you think he is."

"Darham! If you can read his mind, then why didn't you see all this before? You could have warned all of us a long time ago."

"The only thing I can think of is that he must have been sending out false signals. But then apparently something went wrong, and I was able to see who he truly was."

"So what were the other reasons you didn't come around?" she asked.

"The other reason is that I've been busy putting together our escape plan."

"Huh? What do you mean?"

"Zeul has something planned for you and me. I'm not able to see what it is exactly, but whatever it is, it isn't good. Since he made you my Betwudam, even though it isn't a typical rescript, I think he will make a public announcement on the visuals in the near future. I'm guessing he wants Aaranon to see that you and I are still alive."

"If Aaranon sees that broadcast, he may try to come back,"

she said enthusiastically.

"I'm guessing he's already tried but has been unable to do so. Father has stationed UAK and MSS troops all over Araz. It's becoming difficult for anyone, other than the nobles, to move throughout the world."

"Do you know what this *light* is that Father speaks to? Is it one of the Ayim?" she asked.

"Last year, when I spoke with Aaranon about first born sacrifices, I told him I read the thoughts of someone who knew of an ancient evil that is worshipped by a group within the UAC. I never thought our father could take part in such a thing, but I think that light, or entity, is that evil force."

"Where does it come from?" she asked.

"I have no idea. It might be the Ayim, or like the Ayim, but more powerful. I'm not quite sure."

"Is that why our charming father wants Aaranon back? He wants to offer up Aaranon as a first born sacrifice to this thing? You know, finish what he started?"

"I think so."

"Well great, so what do we do Darham? Where can we go to get away from all this evil?"

"I think we need to find Nahim."

"Nahim? Who's that?"

"I don't know. But as powerful as this entity is that Father bows to, it still cannot get near to this Nahim. It seems to be in fear of him," he said.

"Well...let's go find this...Nahim...or whoever he is. Maybe he can help us."

"That's what I was thinking. He's somewhere in the forests of Tarshish in a town called Emet."

With shock and bewilderment in her voice, Dihana asked, "Tarshish!? Isn't that the location of the Apostates?"

"Again...everything is not as it seems," said Darham with a slight chuckle.

"I'm shocked. No, I'm numb. I can't fathom what you're

telling me. It all sounds so surreal...and...and...well, crazy!" she said.

"Tell me about it."

"I tell you what, just to help me, let's start from the beginning and fill me in on everything you know so far. Then fill me in on how we're going to get out of here, find Aaranon, and make our way to Emet to see this...Nahim."

For the rest of the ride home, Darham revealed everything he knew about Zeul, Ravizu, and Aaranon. Darham laid it all out before her, from the meeting between Ravizu and Zeul that Aaranon could see from the cave, to their worship of Halail deep in the underground tunnels.

Chapter 11

Unbeknownst to Dihana and Darham, there were other passengers onboard the sky runner that evening. Servants of Halail moved through the walls of the ship without resistance. They made their way to the forward cabin to watch and listen to the two of them as they tried to catch up after not speaking with one another for so long. The only sign of their presence was a slight chill in the air; quickly dismissed by Dihana and Darham as the cool of the night.

***

"Look at the two of them. Do they even suspect what Halail has in store for them?"

"Do any of these wretched souls know what awaits them in their near future?"

"The girl knows. But we can still use both of them for our purposes. We just need to move cautiously."

"Why did Halail allow this disgusting piece of meat to see his father's thoughts and the conversations he had with our Lord? I thought Zeul wanted to use these two as bait to pull in Aaranon?"

"You fool! You're just as inept as these worthless beings. It matters not what Zeul wants. All that matters is that we break the ancient line."

"What then are they for?"

"Once Zeul knows of their escape to Emet, which we will make sure they achieve, he will have no choice but to go after them."

"Ahhh!! I see now. But what are we to do with Aaranon?"

"Halail has other plans for him if this does not work. But this will work. Because if it does not, you and I will not like the consequences."

"We must go. Our Lord awaits to hear of our progress."

***

As the servants of Halail moved out into the night, Darham and Dihana noticed it warmed up slightly once again, yet suspected nothing.

Chapter 12

Four odes had passed since Aaranon agreed to train the udamé in Pernel's village. The focus of their training was to function solely as a rescue squad to redeem their family and friends from captivity, and to defend themselves if they came under attack. He had no intention of becoming an offensive force against the UAK. The villagers were outnumbered, outgunned, and under skilled. Their best hope was to accomplish their mission, retreat to a safe location, and leave no evidence behind.

As the udamé trained night and day, along with continuing their routine duties of farming and hunting; the wudamé helped by manufacturing weapons with Aaranon's guidance. Some of the younger wives took on the roles of spies and lookouts for any possible incursions from an MSS trooper or an upper-class law enforcement agent.

Even the older children participated by acting as runners between the different camps, carrying messages that they would memorize. Aaranon established, early on, multiple camps in various locations far outside the village in order to protect their numbers. Once they determined no one was watching; they began combat training. When a stranger from another village or an agent were approaching, a signal was given. The signal gave them enough time to hide their weapons and pick up their rakes and sickles to appear as if they were just merely going about their daily routine.

Other operations, however, needed to be concealed far away from prying eyes. Carved into the massive trunks of the trees that surrounded the village were a few secret chambers. Within these hidden rooms, Aaranon and others worked on the remote trigger devices used to disable the MSS troops.

Once again Aaranon felt like an Armada commander, putting into practice all that he learned from the Academy. He also incorporated all that Rohu taught him, even though he knew these skills were meant to teach him how to survive and not for war. To achieve the best possible outcome, Aaranon knew they'd have to utilize primitive weaponry, indigenous docile animals, and native skills. He also realized he no longer had the luxury of relying on the advanced technology he had grown accustomed to while serving in the military.

As Aaranon and Pernel were walking through the village to go and check on one of the camps, Elder Isma motioned for Aaranon to come speak with him. Turning to Pernel, Aaranon said, "Why don't you go ahead and check on the udamé. I'll see what Isma wants, and I'll catch up with you later."

Pernel replied, "If I were you, the less you speak with him, the better. He's not like the other elders. He tends to be…uh… stuck in his old ways if you know what I mean. He also doesn't make a lot of sense. I think he's losing his mind."

"I'll be fine. I'll find out what he wants, and then we'll head out to the fields for more training," Aaranon said as he smacked Pernel on the back.

"Hopefully, my shoulder has healed after the last time we sparred," Pernel said as he rubbed his arm.

"You'll be fine. You're a natural fighter."

From his broken-down porch, Isma continued to stare at Pernel with a disappointed look; causing him to turn away and lower his head as he walked away.

"Good evening Elder Isma," said Aaranon.

"Good evening. Please, have a seat next to me," he said, gently patting the old wooden chair that was adjacent to him.

"What can I do for you Elder?"

"What can you do for me? I think a better question is, what can I do for you?" said Isma with a slight grin.

"Well, uh, I hadn't actually thought about asking you to participate, but if you would like to you can help out in the…"

"That's not what I meant young Loha."

"Oh…so what did you mean?"

"I want to tell you a story."

"A story? Alright," said Aaranon as he thought about Pernel's warning.

Isma gently put his hand to his chin and looked up slightly as he searched his memory. "Long ago, possibly over six hundred years now, I once knew an udam who lived a simple life. He was a farmer like me. He had a wife, a few sons and daughters. He was happy. He was peace-loving. He was always willing to help out his neighbor. He even helped me and my family on numerous occasions. Then one day, trouble came in the form of rain; a lot of it. This udam lived in a valley area. It was great for farming, but not so good when the rains came."

Aaranon immediately thought about the story his mother told him of his father.

Isma continued, "It was terrible. I had never seen such a rain before. It was as if the heavens opened up and poured down all they could. He was away that day in another village visiting friends as I recall. By the time he returned, all had been lost.

"I tried to do what I could, along with my children helping, but it was too late. He lost everything and everyone. Have you ever seen what that can do to someone?"

Aaranon's eyes began to grow slightly red as he said, "Yes, I'm very familiar with that."

Isma continued, "I tried as best as I could to console him, but his grief turned into anger, his anger to rage, and his rage into vengeance."

"Vengeance?" Aaranon asked. "Vengeance against whom?"

Isma slowly looked up and then pointed to the sky.

"The sky?" he asked, hoping for further explanation.

Isma continued without revealing any further the target of the udam's anger. "This udam once believed as I still believe. Let me ask you. Do you know why I do not speak except to you?"

Aaranon took a moment to ponder his question; searching

his mind for a reason as to why. Aaranon said, "Pernel mentioned you did not speak for over a year until you spoke to me that day at his house. I must say I am a bit curious. In fact, I'm curious about a lot of things when it comes to you," Aaranon said as he wondered if Isma had a similar intuition like that of Rohu.

"Have you ever tried to get an ohema to do what you want?"

"Huh?"

"It's a simple question."

"I don't mean to be rude, but what does this have to do with the udam who lost everything?"

Isma just sat there waiting for Aaranon to answer his out of place question.

Aaranon, with a look of confusion, decided to appease him and said. "Well...I have tried. You certainly cannot make them do something if they do not want to do it."

"Exactly, young Loha. It's very much like pushing a rope. You have to lead them; you can't drive them. Very different from say, an ananin. They can be blindly driven into the side of a cliff or into the ground without even thinking about it. But an ohema, they must be led."

"What does that have to do with you not speaking and the udam you mentioned?"

A smile came across Isma's face, and he chuckled a bit. "I learned that udamé are like ohemas in some aspects; you can't drive them; you must lead them, and they're both extremely stubborn."

"That is true," Aaranon replied with a mild grin.

"They both have something else in common," said Isma as he leaned closer to Aaranon.

"And what's that?"

"They are both dumb."

"How do you mean?"

"The ananin can be driven to its death, but the ohema can be led to it. They both go blindly, but the ohema thinks he knows better."

Aaranon looked at Isma with bewilderment; wondering where he was going with all of this. Aaranon asked, "So... again...what does this have to do with your silence and the udam?"

"As Elder of this village, it was my duty to lead these people. For years, I tried to drive them to do what was right, but they would not listen, and then I tried to lead by example."

"So what happened?"

"Someone, or should I say, something else has taken up residence in their hearts."

"Isma, I don't think I understand what you're getting at," said Aaranon trying to anticipate Isma's leading.

"I'm grateful that you are here...young Aaranon," said Isma as he sat back in his chair.

In a panic, Aaranon stood up quickly and looked around to see if anyone was going to come for him. He wondered how in the world Isma knew his real name.

Aaranon reached for his blade. "Who are you, and how do you know my name?"

"Have a seat. Your secret is safe with me. The udam I told you about; the one who lost his family. He is your father, Zeul. He was an udam like you."

Aaranon cautiously sat back down and removed his hand from his blade, but still kept an ever vigilant watch on his surroundings.

Isma continued, "I see a peace in you Aaranon, like I saw in your father before he lost everything. But I also see suppressed rage and anger. Odd how one can have both attributes, isn't it?"

Aaranon had a slightly harsher tone in his voice. "Obviously, I now have many more questions, but you still haven't answered my other one. Why did you stop speaking?"

"Because, I only speak when someone is willing to learn. And you, young Aaranon, are still willing. But, you also have your father's stubbornness. Rohu was keenly aware of that."

Aaranon once again looked around to see if anyone else was listening. He leaned closer into Isma and asked, "How do you know Rohu?"

"Rohu and I, or Loha as I called him, were quite good friends. He told me much about you."

Aaranon slumped back in his chair looking confused and bewildered. He gave up trying to anticipate where Isma was leading.

Isma continued, "I'm sure you have many questions to ask, but, suffice it to say; I know how to keep my lips shut. Your secret is safe with me."

Aaranon tried to slow his thoughts down. He didn't know where to begin in his questions.

Isma once again continued, "Let me say this for now. Rohu knew you might not listen to his request. He knew you would try to rescue your family. He even knew our paths would cross. Let me ask you a question. Why did Rohu go to so much trouble to save you? Even willing to die to accomplish that mission?"

Aaranon sat there thinking the obvious. That being, that Rohu knew his life was in danger and wanted to keep Aaranon alive. But why did he need to stay alive? For what purpose? He never fully considered the question before.

Isma said, "Rohu never told you why you needed to be safe because he knew you would not understand nor accept it."

Aaranon asked with growing frustration, "What? What would I not accept or understand?"

"Come closer," said Isma as he motioned at Aaranon. As they looked into each other's eyes for several moments, Isma finally said, "You are not yet ready to know. You must first pass through much tribulation. You must face a similar journey that your father took. Guard your heart Aaranon; for evil seeks to consume you like it did your father."

Pausing for several moments, Aaranon just looked around in confusion. Thoughts were racing through his mind. He tried to discern if Pernel was right about Isma, or if he had a profound wisdom like that of Rohu. He finally said, "I don't understand. Are you saying I'm going to lose my family like my father did? My sister and brother? What do you mean?"

"You are willing to learn Aaranon, but not right now. You being here is proof of that," said Isma as he once again leaned back in his chair.

Aaranon sat there just staring at Isma. He thought to himself, *What in the world is he talking about? He acts like I have a greater purpose, but he won't tell me what that is. Apparently Rohu knew what that was and was willing to die for it, but even he didn't tell me what it was. He only told me to read the Apostate's scrolls and go see some old udam in a village. What am I willing to learn that all of these villagers are no longer willing to learn? But then again, he says I'm not willing to learn it now. He talks in circles. I don't understand what he's saying. It doesn't make any sense. He reminds me of... MOTHER!*

Isma interrupted his thoughts by saying, "Well, you won't learn anything here by staring at me."

"Uhh, right! I have much to do. We'll speak...uh...goodbye," said Aaranon as he quickly headed out to meet Pernel; trying to quiet his mind so he could focus on the mission at hand.

Chapter 13

"I would ask, where are we descending to and why, but past occurrences tells me that would be pointless," said Ravizu as he stood next to his father.

As the walls of the cave continued to rush past, Zeul enquired, "What did you find in Sari's room?"

"We found nothing except for a small hidden compartment behind her bed. It was empty," said Ravizu as he looked slightly perplexed over the fact that the elevator was still descending. He continued, "Father, I don't recall any of our mines going down to such a depth. How far down does this go?"

Zeul, unfazed by the question asked, "So you found nothing?"

"No, I found nothing. You must know I'm telling you the truth," Ravizu said while pointing to the back of his head.

"Although I doubt you would remember, your implant was removed during your initiation."

"Uh...no I don't remember that. Why was it removed? I thought you were the mind, and I was your hand, or something like that," said Ravizu as he mockingly waved his hands in the air.

"Now that you belong to Halail, he is your master; he doesn't need our devices to keep track of you."

Ravizu took a moment to compose himself as he thought about the implications of what his father just told him. His initiation into the Dark Brotherhood was a blur. He recalled a blinding white light as he stood naked in front of an altar. Out of the light came a thunderous voice that was completely imperceptible. Soon after he experienced a searing white hot pain in the middle of his forehead. The pain felt like hot lava being poured into his mind. After that, he remembered nothing.

"May I ask, what were you hoping to find in Sari's room?"

Zeul slowly walked over to the control panel and pushed the stop button; bringing the elevator to a complete halt. Without turning towards Ravizu, he asked, "What do you know about the Apostates?"

Ravizu stood there for a moment wondering what his father was up to. He began to grow nervous as he realized he was a few thousand *ama* below the surface with an udam who believed the highest quality anyone could possess was betrayal. He then said, "If you don't mind Father, I would like to continue to our destination."

Zeul methodically made his way toward his new apprentice and gently brushed Ravizu's long black hair out of his eyes. "It's a simple question son. The Apostates, what do you know about them?"

Ravizu gently backed away from his father while tilting his head to get away from Zeul's hands moving through his hair. "Well uh, not much except they are an excellent source of blame for all the things we want to accomplish."

"That's right! They are an excellent source to blame for all our problems. We can create change through conflict while pointing to them as the cause of the commotion."

Zeul continued to stare directly at Ravizu as he spoke. "Sari, my dearly departed wife, was an Apostate. I gave you the idea, or should I say, *thought*, to poison her. You thought it would somehow destroy Aaranon. But the real reason she needed to die is because she took up their doctrine."

"Not that I care for what they believed, but what did their doctrine entail?" asked Ravizu.

Again, ignoring his question, Zeul continued, "The secret chamber behind her bed. I believe Sari had hidden away the ancient scrolls. If I'm correct, Dihana is now in possession of those scrolls."

Already knowing the answer to his question, Ravizu asked it

regardless, "So, these scrolls. They contain the Apostate's doctrine?"

"Yes."

"That's why you asked if Dihana seemed different. You believe she is now, like her mother was," said Ravizu as he tried to understand where all this was going.

"What do you know about the razing?" asked Zeul.

Again, he tried to comprehend Zeul's line of questioning, but he had great difficulty understanding his leading. "Uh...well... nothing?" he said.

Zeul paused for a long time. It appeared as if he was carefully choosing his next words. He said, "An ancient foreseer, one of the Apostates, proclaimed that one day we would see a great cataclysm."

"But Father, the Apostates, what do they know about anything? They are unsophisticated, uneducated bottom-feeders. This so-called *razing* could only be a myth if it came from them, correct?"

Zeul turned around and pressed the start button on the elevator, causing it to return to its rapid descent.

"Father. That can't be true. Can it?"

Zeul looked over his shoulder at his confused and bewildered son and replied in a matter of fact tone, "It isn't true for everyone."

Chapter 14

As Aaranon headed toward Pernel after speaking with Isma, he could feel a great heaviness overcoming him like a dark storm rolling over the land. Rather than immediately going to train with Pernel, he quickly headed deeper into the woods in order to get away from everyone.

Listening to Isma speak of his father and Rohu, along with the thought of losing Dihana and Darham, was more than he could bear. He didn't want anyone to see him as he wept profusely.

Finding shelter in the hollow of a tree, he finally let out the pain and anguish he had suppressed for over a year. His mind once again began to race with thoughts that tumbled down like the tears from his cheeks.

What if I become like my father? How could he have ever been like Isma? Is this what happens to an udam who loses everything? Am I going down the same path as him? I cannot allow myself to become like him!

Oh, how I wish Rohu were here. I need his guidance. I need his friendship. I need his help! I don't know if I'll be able to rescue Dihana and Darham. What if they're dead, then what?

And what of these villagers? Even their oldest elder will not speak to them because he believes something else has taken up residence in their hearts. Is it the same evil that's in my father's heart? Can I even trust one of them?

What have I done? I should have kept walking that day I saw Pernel. Better yet, I should have listened to Rohu.

But what about Dihana and Darham? Wouldn't Rohu understand? Wouldn't he know that I needed to rescue them?

And now I'm supposed to have some greater purpose, but neither Isma nor Rohu would tell me what that is. Isma said I'm willing to learn, but not right now. What does that mean!? Oh, if I had wings I would just fly away and leave this place!

As Aaranon continued to hide in the tree; attempting to compose himself before meeting up with Pernel, the servants of Halail observed him without his knowledge.

"Did you hear what Isma said to him?"

"Yes you fool, I was there as well."

"What is this greater purpose that Aaranon serves? I know of no foreseer that spoke of him."

"Why do you ask me? I have no knowledge of it either."

"Can this be a threat to our plans!?"

"Isma's time is drawing to a close. He will soon suffer the same fate as the others. We must try and learn what Aaranon's purpose is to be sure he isn't a threat."

"We have tried so many times before to break the line, but nothing has succeeded."

"Shut up you fool! If Halail heard you speak like that your fate would be worse than the Ayim."

"I'm only stating the obvious. You know, just as well as I do, the number of times we have tried and failed to stop the inevitable. Do you really think we can go against *him*, and survive?"

"If you express doubt in Halail one more time..."

"Please! I will speak of it no more. This plan of ours, it must...it will work."

"Good, make sure you continue to believe."

Aaranon finally composed himself enough to exit the tree and head back toward Pernel. As he stepped out he felt an extremely cold breeze pass around him. Pulling his blades, thinking a portal had opened, he quietly investigated his surroundings. After confirming he was alone, he assumed it was just a cool midday breeze and proceeded on toward Pernel.

Chapter 15

Shemesh was beginning to set behind the hills, indicating the end of another day. Pernel, along with a few of the other udamé from the village, were going about their business of farming the land as they waited for Aaranon to return and begin their training. As Aaranon was approaching, he could see a law enforcement agent and his MSS trooper off in the distance, riding in a mobile cart and coming towards the group.

Fearing the worst, he pulled his blades from their sheath and moved cautiously through the trees while looking for an opportunity to strike. Soon, Aaranon was close enough to activate the device to kill the MSS trooper, but it wasn't working. He attempted to change to another frequency, but none of them worked. Apparently the UAK caught on and changed the codes.

Aaranon signaled to Pernel that danger was approaching. He intended to get over top of the agent and his trooper to strike from above, but Pernel signaled back to stay out of sight.

Aaranon thought to himself; *it might be best if I do stay back. If I'm not successful in disabling that beast, then he and the agent will destroy the whole village. Plus, if they cannot handle a small incursion, then how will they be able to deal with hundreds or even thousands of MSS troops coming after them? I'll wait to see what he plans on doing before I do anything.*

The agent demanded, "Which one of you is in charge?"

Pernel responded, "I am, kind sir. This field is mine and these are my workers. How may I be of assistance?"

The agent methodically walked around the group while his trooper stood like a statue at the perimeter of the field; waiting for his master's bidding.

"I am agent Sayir. My companion over there; well...he needs no introduction. It appears that a rogue forester is wandering through these woods. The previous agent for this district did not have, shall we say, an opportunity to complete his conversation with him. However, the barkeep, after a bit of persuasion, mentioned his name was Loha. Does that name sound familiar to any of you?"

"If I may speak, kind sir. We do not receive too many visitors in this part of the forest," said Pernel, trying to keep calm.

"Too many? Well then, does that mean you may have a few pass through these parts from time to time?"

To show deference, Pernel bowed his head. "I apologize for my incorrect statement agent Sayir. We haven't had anyone pass through here in a very long time,"

"Why do I find that hard to believe? There is a main road that passes through this area just a few thousand *ama* from here, and yet, somehow, nobody has passed through this district?"

One of the other villagers, Yaren, started to grow enraged over the agent's presence and decided to answer for himself; something he would soon regret. "You heard what he said. Nobody has come through here. So why don't you take your pet and leave?"

Without even glancing to look back at the trooper, Sayir signaled for the MSS trooper to come and eliminate the unfortunate villager who chose to show defiance. It didn't take long for the beast to move across the field, leap into the air, and swiftly remove Yaren's head with its razor sharp claws.

Aaranon sat helplessly in the tree. He tried desperately to dial in the correct code and frequency on the remote device, hoping to kill the beast, but nothing was working. He was able to get Pernel's attention, indicating he wanted to do something, but Pernel made it clear that Aaranon needed to stay hidden, even if it meant the death of his friends.

"Now, let's try that one more time, shall we? The forester,

have you seen him in these parts? Because if you have, you need to tell me right now. If I find out you know of his whereabouts, I will not only kill the rest of you, but your wives and children as well."

Pernel attempted to appease the agent, "I swear to you kind sir, we know nothing of this forester. If we hear of something, we will most assuredly contact you. I just ask that you please…"

Sayir motioned for the beast to grab hold of Pernel around the neck and lift him into the air as he moved closer to speak with Pernel.

"Listen to me you miserable piece of flesh. You don't ask anything of me, do you understand? I give the orders in this district. I don't *ask* anything of you. I *command* you! Do you understand?"

Pernel was only able to whisper *yes* before he passed out. Sayir motioned towards the trooper; indicating he wanted him to drop Pernel.

"The rest of you, let this be a warning. If you hear anything, you will notify me. Understand?"

The other villagers responded in muffled unison, "Yes sir!"

"Good! I will return from time to time to make sure this village is functioning properly and in accordance with UAK law. Your last agent did not serve his position well. I will not make the same mistake."

Agent Sayir and the beast returned to their mobile cart, leaving the others to try and revive Pernel as well as grieve for the loss of their friend.

***

As soon as it was safe, Aaranon climbed down from the tree to check on his friend. When he did so, he noticed Pernel had a scratch across his neck; courtesy of the trooper.

One of the villagers asked, "What's wrong with him? Will he be alright?"

"Quickly! I need some water!" commanded Aaranon.

"Is he breathing? Is he going to live?"

"MSS troopers can excrete venom from their claws and it can either paralyze or kill their victims. The wound doesn't look to be that deep, so he should recover."

Benohi, Yaren's brother, weeping and clearly enraged, demanded, "Why didn't you stop that dacking beast like you did before!? That thing killed my brother! You could have saved him!"

"I'm truly sorry about your brother. I tried to stop him, but they must have changed something," said Aaranon. He continued to work on Pernel, using some herbs he carried in his satchel and the water that was given to him.

"Well, you didn't try hard enough! Look at my brother. Look at him! That thing took his head off. How are we supposed to go up against these beasts? Even you can't stop them. Some savior you are!"

Aaranon looked up at Benohi and replied in a stern voice. "I told you this wasn't going to be easy. That was only one MSS trooper. Imagine hundreds, even thousands coming after you. And not only you, but your wives, your children, your mothers and fathers; everyone you love and care about. They will not stop until everyone who is connected to you is dead! I'm sorry about your brother but if I showed myself, he wouldn't stop with your brother or me. He would have killed everyone in the village."

Pernel whispered, "He's right."

Aaranon tried to help him sit up. "Pernel, are you alright? Can you move?"

"I can't feel my legs."

Aaranon reassured him, "The poison should wear off in a few days."

Pernel turned towards the others as best he could and said, "If you want to blame anyone, blame me. I brought Loha to our village because he saved my life. The elders agreed to this path that we had chosen. Loha is correct. If he came down, that thing would have killed us all."

With tears making tracks down his dirt-stained face, Benohi pleaded with Pernel, "I understand that, but after this one incident, how can we ever hope of getting back our families? If the high and mighty Loha can't save us against one beast then what dacking hope do we have?"

Pernel asked Aaranon to hold him up while he spoke to his friends. "Listen to me! The first Loha was an udam like all of us. He had a family like us. He lost loved ones...just...like...us. But he didn't run away and hide. He stood his ground and fought.

"He fought so that others would not lose the ones they loved. If you want to give up and run, I will not fault you. Every day I want to run and hide. I want to take what's left of my family and go where they cannot find us.

"But somebody has to say, Enough! Somebody has to fight against this tyranny. Loha has come, but not to save us. He came to guide us.

"If any of you want to leave, you're free to go. But as for me, if Loha will continue to train us, then I'm staying. I want my wife and family back, just like you. But what I want even more is for our children and our children's children to live in a world without fear. If we run and hide now, the day will come when a place of safety will no longer exist."

Pernel then turned to Aaranon, looked deep into his eyes, and said softly, "Promise me you will remember what I said today. My words are true."

Aaranon looked at Pernel in confusion; wondering why he made him promise to remember. "I promise."

One by one, each of the udamé stepped forward and pledged their commitment to carry on the fight for their freedom.

Pernel continued, "Good. But for now, let us mourn our brother."

While Aaranon carried Pernel on his back, the others brought their dead home to bury him in his family's tomb.

As they were walking back, Pernel said to Aaranon, "I don't blame you Loha. You've given us hope. Even in spite of this incident."

"I think the UAK discovered that I cracked their code to the MSS troops. I'll need to figure out how we can incapacitate them. If we can't do that, then we have very little hope of rescuing your family. I'll need to look at the device from the one MSS trooper I killed to see what went wrong," said Aaranon.

"I believe in you Loha. I know you have been sent for a greater purpose."

Aaranon didn't reply but thought to himself; *You're not the only one who thinks I have a greater purpose.*

Chapter 16

The mine shaft elevator doors finally opened to a cavernous room that stretched for several thousand *de-ama* in every direction. As Zeul and his son stepped out, Ravizu couldn't believe what he was seeing.

Before them was an army of mingled servants building massive ships. He'd never seen these ships before and then to be so far below the surface of Araz, deeper than he knew to be possible, Ravizu was stunned. "What is this?"

"We believe it's time you learned our destiny," replied Zeul.

"We? Our? What destiny?" asked his bemused apprentice.

Zeul commenced walking through the vast shipyard, prompting Ravizu to follow. "We used the Apostates, like I said earlier, and will continue to use them to further our agenda. We needed to consolidate power, but the people needed a reason for going along with it. Even after we consolidated the kingdoms, we still knew that it would take *persuasion* for the useless masses to accept a supreme leader. Before we could rule the world unchallenged, we needed for them to give us their consent. The truth would not suffice, of course. So fear was our best ally."

"Fear?"

"Yes, fear. Fear of what the Apostates would do if allowed to continue their *so-called* reign of terror."

"When you say, 'we believe it's time…,' are you referring to the Brotherhood?"

"Yes, as well as our master."

"If you don't mind me asking, I understand that Halail is now my master, but, who is he, or it? I assumed he was one of the Ayim, but after asking many questions without answers, I thought that eventually you would get around to telling me."

Zeul turned towards Ravizu and gave a slight grin, "All in due time, son; all in due time. For now, however, you've been permitted to see this place and understand its purpose."

"So what is the need for all of this? These ships don't look like anything we currently have," replied Ravizu as he noticed that all of the ships had sealed cabins and no outside decks for people to walk about.

"The Apostates serve many purposes for us. One I've already mentioned. The other is their ability to see into the future."

"They can see the future. How?"

"The *how*, isn't important. The fact that they can *is*. The Apostates spoke of the razing for hundreds of years. Many, including myself, ignored their drivel. But when we made this discovery, we learned that their warnings were not mere fear mongering."

Zeul walked over to a visual to access the star charts and other information. Motioning for Ravizu to come near, he said, "Let me show you something." As he waved his hand across the console, an image of a small red star appeared on the visual.

"Because of their warnings, is this why we have been working to eliminate them, to silence them and turn the populace against them? So the people cannot prepare for what is to come?" asked Ravizu.

"That is one of the reasons."

Ravizu tried to push aside the thoughts of the Apostates ability to see into the future. He wondered, how could they have such prowess if they were inferior to the nobles? Rather than asking about their abilities, Ravizu came near to the visual to see the image Zeul was pulling up.

"Father, this looks like an actual picture; like it was taken high above Araz. In fact…," Ravizu paused as he drew nearer to the screen, "…it looks like this image was, somehow, captured while standing on Evla. But how is that possible?"

Zeul pointed over towards one of the ships, indicating how

they were able to leave the surface and travel to the small planet, Evla, which moves around Araz.

"How's that possible? I thought that our ships could only move by way of the stationary energy taps. Have you been able to extend the range?"

"I'll get to that in a moment. But look again at the screen. Notice that small red star?"

"Yes, but what is it?"

Zeul waved his hand across the screen once again to show the same red star, only slightly smaller. He continued, "This is what it looked like from Evla over three years ago." He moved his hand again to reveal an even smaller image. "And this is what it looked like over ten years ago."

As Ravizu continued to think through the implications, he said, "It's moving toward us. And if I'm not mistaken, it's coming up from the south."

"That's correct. It's getting closer. And every day that it draws nearer, it has an influence on Araz."

"The ground tremors," said Ravizu as he now realized the source.

"Exactly. As this star makes its unwavering trek towards us, it will soon have a profound impact on our world," he said as he watched his son begin to fill in the missing pieces.

"The underground vaults, the cities, the tunnels. You're not worried about the people fighting against the government. You're concerned about that star."

"I knew you would catch on."

"And the ships?"

"As the star draws nearer, we will need to retreat to a safe location until the calamity passes."

"A safe location? You mean Evla?"

Zeul shook his head.

"Where then?"

"Mu'udim," replied Zeul.

"Mu'udim?! But…it's…how?!"

"You already know of the new metal we found almost one hundred years ago. It's gray in color and is primarily in a liquid state. We learned that once it's heated to an extremely high temperature, it displays some incredible properties. The resonator cores on all ships contain this metal, giving us the ability to fly. However, it wasn't until a few decades ago that we discovered a fuel source that was capable of generating enough power to be independent of the energy taps. It's difficult to harvest from the rock, but it holds tremendous power in quite a minuscule package."

Zeul paused for a moment to watch his son think through what he'd just heard. Mu'udim is the planet next to Araz that encircles Shemesh. It only appears as a small point of light in the night sky. To travel there would take several odes.

"How do you travel to Mu'udim? Do you open a portal for the ship to pass?"

"At present, we can only open portals for small items at short distances, and for a short amount of time. The power required is far too great. We are, however, working on a solution for that," replied Zeul.

"You're working on a portal between here and Mu'udim?"

"Yes, but the Brotherhood has something much further in mind."

Ravizu was confused. "Further than Mu'udim? Where could that be?"

"All in due time son. All in due time."

"Of course. How silly of me," Ravizu replied, dripping with sarcasm. He continued, "So, rather than a portal to Mu'udim, we travel there by these ships?"

"Yes," replied Zeul.

"How long will it take?"

"At present it takes almost seven odes."

"At present? You mean we've already been there!?"

"We've been traveling there for the past few years. We already have a small colony established," answered Zeul.

"A colony! I see that I have much more to learn," replied Ravizu looking confused and overwhelmed.

Zeul once again began walking through the vast shipyard, speaking as he went. "Notice something different about this ship?" He asked, pointing to a smaller craft that appeared to be unable to hold any occupants.

"It's smaller than the others, but still quite large. It looks like there is no room for passengers. Wait?!" Ravizu drew closer to look inside one of the open doors. "That's one of the largest MCR's I've seen. Other than the one at the UAC."

"This ship will be set in orbit around Araz traveling from north to south. In order to save our accumulated knowledge, we needed to replicate the information to several safe locations during the calamity. This is just one of them."

The gravity of the circumstances and the depth of the crisis began to sink in. "How bad will the calamity be if we need to leave the surface and head for Mu'udim along with saving our knowledge in something that will circle Araz like a tiny planet?"

"We don't know exactly how bad it will be. Our experts have been attempting to calculate the trajectory of the red star. At this point, it isn't clear how close it will come to us. But we're taking multiple precautions just in case."

"What will the underground cities and vaults hold if we plan to leave the surface and head for Mu'udim?" Ravizu asked.

"Supplies, seeds, animals, mingled servants - everything we need to rebuild the world in our image. Out of the ashes will come a new Araz," replied Zeul.

"What about the rest of the people? What will be their fate?"

With a dismissive air Zeul answered, "I believe the one thing this world has taught us is that only the strong and wise will survive."

Ravizu laughed without a shred of concern. "Well then, I guess we will need to take plenty of mingled servants with us to do our bidding since the bottom-feeders will no longer be available to do the work."

"Yes. Exactly."

Chapter 17

"Master!"

"What is it?" Halail asked; every word dripping with condescension.

"We overheard Isma talking with Aaranon.

"And?"

"He said that Aaranon has a greater purpose."

"I'm waiting!" he growled, knowing Aaranon's real purpose, yet unwilling to reveal any concern.

"He did not explain, My Lord. He even said Rohu knew of it, but never spoke of it to Aaranon. We fear that somehow Aaranon will interfere with our plans if we don't eliminate him."

"Are you losing faith?" asked Halail in an accusatory manner.

"Not at all My Lord. I only wish to keep you informed," the servant stammered.

"Well then, fear not! For I have it all under my control."

"Of course My Lord. I would never doubt you."

"What was Aaranon's response to such drivel?" asked Halail.

"He hid himself away and cried like an infant. Very pathetic! But he said nothing."

"He is weak. He cannot harm us," replied Halail confidently as he masked his growing trepidation.

"Yes My Lord, he is fragile. However, should I remove him?"

"If you wish to suffer the same fate as the Ayim, then go right ahead," he said, waving his hand.

"Forgive me My Lord. I only wish to serve you and do what is best for our kind."

"The Ayim!" Halail said with a maniacal laugh. "They wanted something that they could never possess. Their attempt to stop our destruction was admirable, but they did not understand the Ancient Law when they made their pact with one another. Interference isn't possible without these pathetic life forms' consent. Even then, it must be done *subtlety* and not *directly*. And to think they pleaded their cause through one of these vile pieces of dust to try and save themselves."

"Yes My Lord, what fools they were."

"You have zeal like the Ayim, but you must temper it with wisdom," replied Halail.

"Yes My Lord. To learn from you is pure wisdom."

"Now, what do you know of our true enemy?" asked Halail

"He has completed a large portion of the structure."

Halail slammed his fist down on the massive throne he rested upon, causing the sound to reverberate throughout his dark and ancient palace. He yelled, "If he completes the work, then he will survive the razing, and the line will go unbroken! That ancient prophecy cannot come to pass! Do you understand!?"

The servant cowered before Halail, "Yes My Lord."

Chapter 18

A brisk wind was blowing gently through Aaranon's long golden locks as the light of Shemesh shined down upon him. He scanned the horizon to see that he was no longer in the forest, but once again standing in the midst of the same vast wheat field he had seen in previous visions. It began as it did before, but it wasn't long before the scenery changed. A tall figure in white appeared on a hill a few *ama* in front of him.

The beautiful figure was brandishing a blade in one hand and a shield in the other. To behold him was like looking into Shemesh. His clothing was without stain or blemish. His presence aroused a great deal of fear and dread, but at the same time he emanated a peace that was beyond understanding.

Aaranon felt within himself the need to run and hide from his brilliance, but was frozen in place, unable to move a single muscle. As he continued to look at him, the tall figure said, "Fear not, for I have heard the cry of my people, and my line will not break."

As Aaranon was about to ask what he meant, the tall figure spoke again.

"Watch and observe! For herein lies your purpose."

Immediately, Aaranon found himself flying upward into space at a great speed. He was soon far beyond the surface of Araz and found himself floating in outer space. As he looked down at his home planet and Evla, he heard the voice of the tall figure say, "Turn around! Watch and observe!"

As he turned, he could see a large red beast with two horns and four legs off in the distance running towards him. As the creature was getting closer, he could see two large heavenly bodies moving near to one another. As the beast came near, it caused the smaller planet to break apart into millions of pieces. One of the larger pieces flew off and collided with the second planet. Rather than destroying it, it was absorbed like a sponge pulling in water. The red beast then continued its journey towards him unabated.

He was then immediately dropped back down on the surface of Araz. He once again found himself standing in the middle of a wheat field. Dark clouds were forming on every horizon, and the light of Shemesh began to diminish. Soon after, a small white creature appeared on a hill in front of him. The petite creature emanated a brilliance like that of the tall figure. As Aaranon was watching, the voice once again said, "Turn around! Watch and observe!"

As Aaranon turned, he could see the horned red beast running towards the small creature. Aaranon felt within himself an overwhelming desire to stand between the beast and the white animal on the hill in order to save it. As he was moving to shield the creature, the ground beneath his feet began to shake violently and break apart. He could hear the hooves of the beast behind him beat against the ground with every step. Before he could reach the small creature, he felt the sharp horn dig into his back.

***

Aaranon leaped out of bed holding his back and crying out in pain. He quickly pulled off his coat and shirt to examine himself. As he continued to confirm that he had no injuries, the tall figure appeared behind him and said, "Remember what you have seen."

Aaranon, startled and afraid, turned around and fell back against the wall of his room; a room carved into the side of one of the prodigious trees.

The tall figure said again, "Remember what you have seen, for the time is short."

Pernel immediately came running into the room to find Aaranon holding his arm across his face as he sat against the wall, shaking terribly.

"Aaranon! Are you alright! What happened?"

"Look out Pernel! He has a weapon!" screamed Aaranon.

Pernel looked around the room and said, "Who has a weapon?"

"He does, over there...," said Aaranon as he pointed over towards an empty wall. "He was just there," he said looking perplexed and still shaking from the experience.

"Who was? I don't see anyone." Pernel continued to look around the room as if someone might be hiding.

Aaranon stood up hesitantly. He slowly and cautiously walked over to the space where the tall figure was standing.

"Aaranon?"

"I swear someone was standing here," he said with a great deal of frustration in his voice.

Pernel continued to look at Aaranon as he walked around the room, dazed and confused.

Pernel was perplexed. "Aaranon, are you sure you weren't dreaming?"

"Uh...I...I could have sworn...," he replied as he reached down to put on his shirt and coat.

"I've noticed lately that you've been having trouble sleeping. It looks as if you're having terrible dreams," said Pernel as he helped to straighten up the room.

"I...I...think that's what it was," said Aaranon as he was scratching his head trying to figure out what just happened.

"Do you need anything? Can I get you something to eat or drink?"

"No. No, I'm fine."

Both Pernel and Aaranon stood there for several moments; each trying to figure out what just happened.

"So...do you remember what it was you were dreaming?"

Aaranon vividly recalled everything he saw, but didn't want

to speak of it until he had time to think it through. He said to Pernel, "No, I don't remember it. It must have been nothing."

"It sure didn't look or sound like nothing. You were screaming. As if you were being...killed."

Aaranon sat back down on his bed. He ran his hands over his bald head thinking about the vision he just experienced. He couldn't help but want to believe it was only that; a dream. But it was far more than that.

As he continued to ponder the meaning, Pernel interrupted his thoughts. "I actually came up here to talk to you about something if you have some time. If not, I can come back later."

"No. I mean...yes. I have some time. What did you want to talk about?" Aaranon asked as he looked up at Pernel.

"Well...you know me. I tend to talk...a lot. I say many things. Sometimes I speak because...well...I'm nervous, as you know. I need to say that... Well, what I want to say is...,"

"Wait, you're up and walking now. I see the poison has worn off."

"Oh...oh yes. I guess that is one thing I wanted to show you."

"Do you have any residual pain or numbness?" asked Aaranon.

"I still don't have complete feeling in my toes, but I'm sure that will come back soon. The herbs you recommended have been working."

"Good! We are almost ready for our first raid, and we need you at full capacity before we go."

"Right! In fact, that's why I wanted to talk to you for a moment. What I want is...uh...what I mean is that I wanted to say is...,"

Aaranon continued to stare at Pernel with a confused look; wondering why he was now having trouble speaking.

"...that day in the woods. When the agent came; I asked you to promise me that you would remember what I said."

"I remember," said Aaranon.

"If something happens. If something were to happen to me,

or to you. I just wanted you to know that…I just wanted you to know that I'm thankful that our paths crossed."

"As am I. Is there something particular on your mind Pernel?"

Pernel was about to speak once more, but quickly grabbed his forehead with his hand.

"Are you alright Pernel?"

"Yes, I'm…quite…alright," replied Pernel as he rubbed his head.

"You don't look fine. Is there something wrong with your head?"

"It's just some head pain. That's all. Probably left over from the poison." He sputtered, trying to hide the magnitude of the pain.

"So…what did you want to tell me?"

Pernel continued to rub his head and neck. He finally said, "It's nothing really. I was just nervous about our first rescue attempt. I wanted you to know that if something were to happen, you have my deepest gratitude."

"You have mine as well, Pernel,"

"Good then. I will see you later, yes?"

"Yeah. Give me a moment, and I'll go down with you."

"Please, take all the time you need," said Pernel as he hastily walked out of the room. He walked down the flight of stairs that wound around the circumference of the tree. He paused for several moments to grab hold of his head and try to ease the pain that felt like a tremendous weight crushing his skull. He whispered, "Alright…alright."

Chapter 19

"Lord Ravizu! It is a pleasure to see you again. I hope your trip was enjoyable?" Inquired the lead scientist of the Grenaldi clan.

"Hello, Healer Greyson. It is a pleasure to see you as well. I gather that my new companion is ready?" asked Ravizu as he embraced the one who was the gifted mind behind the creation of the mingled servants and MSS troops.

"You can skip the title if you like. I don't do much *healing* around here," he said with a chuckle.

"Well, you certainly have healed my spirits. I am so looking forward to this," said Ravizu as they both walked side by side down the vast laboratory that housed multiple birthing chambers for many of the newly created mingled creatures.

"I'm so sorry to hear about Ballar. I did not realize how desirous he was of you. Sometimes loyalty and devotion can turn into obsession. I believe we can avoid that with your new companion."

"Yes...he was very devoted to me," said Ravizu, hiding the truth of his death.

"I must say, it is very exciting to see how many of the new MSS troops your father has requested; I don't think we've ever been so busy. They've been working out much better than I planned."

"Yes, Father has been quite busy with all the changes taking place," he replied while hiding the fact that this was the first time he was hearing about the new MSS troops.

"It is of no concern to me, but his request for several more mingled servants is a bit interesting. Do you know what their purpose shall be?" he asked cautiously.

"Only the Ayim would know that. I'm not privileged to see,

and I have no desire to know, the inner workings of the UAK. I have enough to tend to when it comes to the family business," Ravizu said, hiding the coming destruction that would soon consume all of Araz.

Pausing for a moment at one of the chambers, Ravizu looked in through a small window to see how the mingled creatures were grown. Looking inside he could see a wudam stretched out on a table with multiple tubes and wires connected to her.

"Greyson, are these mingled creatures?" asked Ravizu, looking perplexed.

"Oh yes, I forgot. You've never been here to see how we create our...*children*," he said with a smile. He continued, "To answer your question, no, these are not mingled, they are unmodified hosts. We are however refining the process so we can use either a mingled creature or an artificial womb. But so far, to obtain the best results, we use a non-mingled host."

"How many births can you get from just one wudam?" asked Ravizu.

"If it's a mingled servant, upwards of three or four before we discard the host. For an MSS trooper, however, we can only achieve one birth. The host is incapable of living beyond the delivery. It's quite a sight to see one being born. There's not much left of the host after the infant finishes eating," replied Greyson.

"So...from where do the wudamé, or hosts as you call them, come?"

"Mostly lower-class villages. We take some from the temples, but only those who are not fully spent. However, we have been birthing our own hosts for some time now to make up for the shortfall."

"Your own hosts?"

"Oh yes. We keep the girls for hosts, and the boys are used for either labor, target practice for the MSS troops or as fresh meat. All of the girls however are kept underground in the labs. They will never see the light of Shemesh. Imagine if the populace found out about our baby mill. There certainly would be a riot among the populace then," said Greyson as he laughed maniacally and smacked Ravizu's shoulder.

"Yes, I'm sure they would be quite disturbed to learn of your procedures," said Ravizu without showing a shred of remorse for the unfortunate souls who found themselves in such a place.

"Let's make our way to the living quarters where you can meet your new companion," said Greyson pointing towards a long hallway. He continued, "After you meet your partner, we will begin the implantation procedure. I will have my best surgeon, Mishna, take care of you."

"You don't perform the surgery?" asked Ravizu with some concern.

"Not anymore. For as much as I can enhance my own flesh, it seems that age has finally caught up with me. It has become difficult for me to perform such delicate work. But I can assure you, that Mishna will take good care of you."

"And the implant, you can guarantee that this will link me to this new mingled servant?" asked Ravizu.

"Oh yes! You will have complete control and ability to see and hear everything. It will be an extension of you. We will just need to insert the device at the base of your neck. Right here to be exact," said Greyson as he reached up underneath Ravizu's black hair to point to the spot on his neck where the farspeak device will go.

Greyson continued, "Hmm? I believe you have an implant already."

Ravizu, not wanting to reveal his previous implantation by Zeul said, "Oh that. That was from an accident when I was a child. It's been there for quite some time."

"Oh. Well then…we will be careful to work around it. We need a good connection to your spinal cord in order for it to work," replied Greyson. He continued, "Ah, here we are. I will leave the two of you alone to get acquainted. When you're finished, you can find me in my office. We will begin the implantation procedure then."

"Thank you. I won't be long," said Ravizu as he stood outside the room of his new companion while Greyson walked away.

Taking his time, he slowly opened the door and stepped inside. Across from him was a figure sitting in a dimly lit room, waiting for its new master to arrive. Ravizu waved his hand across the console, turning on all the lights. With its back to Ravizu, he gently walked up behind his new companion that was waiting patiently for its first order.

"Stand up," he said. "Now look at me and remove that robe."

Slowly the new mingled servant stood up and removed its robe revealing a beautiful black haired, dark complected figure of a wudam. She slowly turned around to look at her new master. She asked in a soft, yet firm voice, "Am I pleasing to you, my master?"

Ravizu took several moments looking her up and down, admiring the female version of himself. "Oh yes, you are very pleasing to me."

"May I ask, what shall my name be?"

"Let me see. Since you are a part of me what name would be worthy of you? I believe I will call you…Lilith."

"Thank you Master. Lilith is a beautiful name," she said as she stood there without a stitch of clothing, hanging on his every word as if everything that poured from his lips were divine.

"You may address me as your Lord. I like it better than master," he said as he embraced her beautiful form. He continued, "Soon, you and I will have an unbreakable bond. Everything you see, I will see. And whatever I think, you will do."

"I wouldn't want it any other way My Lord," she said as she started to caress her new master.

***

While lying face down on the operating table, Ravizu could hear the group of surgeons gathering around to begin the procedure.

"Lord Ravizu, my name is Mishna and I will be taking care of you today. Do you have any questions before we begin?"

"How long will this take? I have things to attend to."

"You will be able to leave before Shemesh sets over the mountains. If I may, we will begin administering the sleeping potion," said Mishna.

"That's fine. Greyson said that you're the best."

"Oh yes, My Lord, I am...cut from the same cloth as he," replied Mishna, referring to himself being a copy of Greyson.

"Oh! I wasn't aware of that. Well then, proceed," said Ravizu, with some relief in his voice.

"As you wish," said Mishna as he pointed to one of the other surgeons to administer the potion that would put Ravizu to sleep.

Within a few moments, Ravizu was fast asleep, allowing the surgeons to begin the procedure to implant the farspeak device that would allow Ravizu to control Lilith completely.

Turning to the other surgeons, Mishna said, "I've been asked, by my father, that only I perform the implantation. So, if you will, please excuse yourself until I call for you."

All the surgeons nodded, acknowledging his request. Once they left the room, leaving just the two of them, Mishna began to open the back of Ravizu's neck with a sharp knife.

Speaking under his breath, Mishna said, "Now...let's get a look at what is inside this so-called childhood scar of yours."

Pulling back the skin he continued to explore the site. "Hmm. It appears at one time you had a receiving farspeak. Now who would want to control a noble like they would a servant? Wait a moment, what's this?" asked Mishna as he began to examine what looked like foreign tissue fused to Ravizu's spinal column.

He continued to speak under his breath, "Well, well Ravizu. If I'm not mistaken, you are still under someone else's control, but I've never seen a biological device like this except in our labs, but I thought this was untested. Is this why Father asked me to do this alone? I will need to talk with him once I'm finished."

Mishna proceeded to implant the device above the other and then closed up the incision. It wasn't long before Ravizu was awake and able to leave with Lilith.

***

"Father, may I speak with you in your office please?" asked Mishna.

"Yes, I knew you would have a question once you finished," he replied while staring long at the younger version of himself.

Once they were alone, and the curtains drawn, Mishna continued, "I'm not sure where to begin. How long have the new implants been in use?"

Greyson looked at his shaky hands. "You know how long it's been since I've been able to perform my work?"

"Ah...no,"

"I needed someone else to do the work that I could not. In fact, I needed many others to do what I could do no longer physically. That is why I created you and all of my other children. All of you are me in almost every way. But the day I created you, you were more like a son to me. It was a joy to see you grow so quickly; which is why it pains me to do what I have to do. I hope you can forgive me."

"What do you mean, Father?"

"I wanted another to do the work, but he insisted on the best."

"Who insisted? You're not making any sense."

Soon, a knock came at the door. Bowing his head and looking away from Mishna, Greyson replied, "Please, come in My Lord."

King Zeul stepped into the room and took a seat next to

Greyson. Mishna was startled to see the Alemeleg in his presence. He tried to say something, but was interrupted by his father, who could no longer look him in the eye. He said, in a matter of fact tone, "You see my son. I needed you to do the work that I could not. Pure and simple. Now, that work is done."

"I don't understand Father, what are you referring to?" asked Mishna, with trepidation in his voice.

Greyson was about to speak when Zeul interjected, "What he's trying to say is, you've seen too much and your services are no longer required." Turning to Greyson, Zeul asked, "I presume the first implant is still in place?"

"Yes My Lord. My son did as I expected. He did a remarkable job if I must say."

"How would you know Father, you weren't there," said Mishna, growing angry and afraid of what he thought was to come next.

Greyson pointed to his head and said, "Oh yes, yes I was. I was always there my son."

Soon after, two MSS troopers came walking into the room.

"Mishna backed up against the corner of the room, knowing what was to come next. "What's going on?"

Zeul again interrupted, "Take him to the incinerator."

"Father NO!! What are you doing? I won't say a word. Why would I? Please!" screamed Mishna as he was being dragged from the corner of the room by the hideous beasts he helped to create.

"If I may Lord Zeul, please let me have a final word with my son before he goes?"

"Make it quick. I have other business to attend to," said Zeul dismissively.

As Greyson was walking towards Mishna, he quietly pulled out a small device from his coat pocket and placed it in his son's side pocket without Zeul or the MSS troopers seeing it.

"My son, this is nothing personal. It is…," he stammered while trying to clear his throat. "It is for the good of the kingdom that we do this. I will remember you always. Especially for all the work you did in creating the devices that controlled the MSS troops. It was a blessing to all of us," said Greyson as he motioned with his eyes to the device he just placed in Mishna's pocket.

Knowing he needed to keep up the ruse, Mishna spit in his face. Soon after, the MSS troopers escorted Mishna out of the room and down towards the incinerators, leaving the two of them alone.

Without even turning to Greyson, Zeul said matter of fact, "You did your duty and for that you will be rewarded."

"Thank you My Lord. If only I were able to do the procedure, then I would not have needed to eliminate him. But I understand the need for secrecy."

Zeul, now turning towards Greyson, put his hand on his knee and said in a softer tone, "For what is to come, we need your mind. You can always make plenty of servants like him to do the work."

"I understand My Lord. Even though I don't know what you have planned, I have complete faith in you. I am always at your service," replied Greyson.

"I know. You're an old friend, and I'm sorry we had to do it this way, but I know what it's like to give up something to accomplish your goals. It's hard the first time. But each one thereafter gets...easier," said Zeul as he paused several moments while staring off into oblivion.

After what seemed like an eternity, he continued, "Now, Ravizu's new companion. Have all the modifications been made as I requested?"

"Yes My Lord. No one knows but you and me. You can have complete control of her anytime you want. For Ravizu, you will still be able to see and hear everything. The new implant will be undetectable by him. He will only know of the one used for Lilith."

"Lilith?" asked Zeul.

"That is the name he gave her My Lord," replied Greyson.

"Hmm. A fitting name, isn't it," said Zeul with a chuckle.

"Yes My Lord. A fitting one indeed," said Greyson as he slowly turned his face away from Zeul to hide the tear that fell down his cheek.

Chapter 20

"Loha! I figured it out!" Pernel shouted triumphantly as he came rushing in to see Aaranon. Upon entry to their clandestine lab, he handed over the controller that Aaranon used to kill the MSS trooper at the pub.

Aaranon tumbled the device about in his hands. "What did you do?"

"Well...you mentioned earlier that the UAK possibly changed frequencies and codes on the MSS troops in order to prevent others from taking control."

"That's correct, but how did you figure it out?" asked Aaranon as he tried to fathom how a simple farmer was able to understand the intricate workings of a farspeak.

"This might sound odd, but I remembered one year we couldn't get a particular dolan to die that was eating all of our crops. They're pesky little bugs, but easy to destroy. In years past, we always used a dry cooking paste that we scattered on the leaves. Once it comes in contact with the dolan, its soft underside would dry out and crack open, killing it. But this one year, no matter how hard we tried we couldn't get rid of them."

"So...what did you do?"

"We realized that the dolan somehow adapted their shells to where the paste was no longer working."

"Adapted?" asked Aaranon while thinking about the various mingling experiments being performed by the UAK.

"Yeah...I mean...I think they adapted somehow. Something changed in them preventing us from easily killing them."

"Sorry, I interrupted. Go on," said Aaranon.

"Well...anyway...we used a type of dry soap that wouldn't harm the plant, but would eat through the shell of the dolan, thus killing it that way."

"Alright...so what does this have to do with figuring out the controller?"

"It made me think. The bug was the same except for a few changes. What if the UAK is still using the same set of codes and frequencies, but, they are changing them on a routine basis."

Aaranon was confused. "Go on."

"I took the same set of codes and frequencies and set them to change on a timed interval that I was able to derive from the frequency settings of the energy taps," replied Pernel.

"So you think the interval is set to the same frequency."

"That was just a guess."

"So what happened?" asked Aaranon looking perplexed at how Pernel figured it out.

"Well, see for yourself!" he replied, with a broad smile as he pointed toward the container. Inside the container was the farspeak device which was still encased in the flesh that Aaranon took from the MSS trooper at the pub. Keeping it inside the flesh prevented it from exploding and allowed them the opportunity to tinker with the device.

"Press the switch and see what happens," said Pernel.

Pausing for a moment before he engaged the switch, Aaranon looked at Pernel as if to say; *Are you sure?*

"Go on! Try it!" he said with even more enthusiasm.

"Uh...shouldn't we be back a bit further?" asked Aaranon.

"No, this will only create the electrical impulse that kills it. The explosion is on a different setting.

"Alright," Aaranon replied nonchalantly as he pointed the controller and pushed the button.

Immediately the piece of MSS flesh began to light up with sparks of electricity while it quivered and shook inside the container.

A proud grin worked its way across Pernel's face. "See...it works!"

Aaranon looked at Pernel, the controller, and then at the container, trying to figure out how Pernel solved the problem.

"What? You didn't think I could figure it out?" he asked in a slightly offended manner.

"No, it isn't that. It's just…I'm just glad you figured it out. Now we can program the others to do the same," he replied in a slightly apologetic tone as he continued to examine the device.

"I've already done that!" said Pernel, still smiling from ear to ear. "So…do you have anything else to say…O' mighty Loha?" he asked while bouncing his legs up and down in his chair like an energetic school boy.

"Oh yes. How rude of me. Please forgive me. Let's go find some dolans to thank for solving the problem."

Pernel wrinkled his face, turned away slightly and muttered, "Oh! Very amusing! Can't even give an udam a pat on the back, or a hardy thank you…"

Aaranon interrupted by putting his rugged hand on his friend's shoulder and, while looking into his eyes, said, "Hey… you did good Pernel…you did a superb job."

"Well…I was just teasing about that praise thing. We all do our part you know."

Aaranon replied, "So who do you think we should test this out on before we begin our first raid? I believe it should be someone who truly deserves a visit from us."

Aaranon and Pernel looked at one another intensely. They both knew who it should be without speaking a word.

Pernel said confidently, "Right! I know just where he is."

"Let's take Benohi with us. I'm sure he would like to see this," replied Aaranon as they both left the safety of their hidden lab.

Chapter 21

"I swear to you kind sir. I don't know of any forester named Loha in these parts."

"I am growing *so* tired of you lower-class scum holding out hope for some dacking redeemer. Just because he killed one MSS trooper, you all believe that he can now take on an entire company; as if he was the legendary heboram killer...whatever his name was.

"He was only lucky due to the ineptness of my predecessor. I can assure you that I will not make that same mistake. I can also assure you that the Alemeleg will not allow that to happen again. Therefore, it is in your best interest to let go of this silly little *myth,* and give me the location of your precious Loha," said Sayir. During his tirade, his MSS trooper continued to harass the local barkeep of a lower-class village near to Pernel's home.

"Please kind sir, I can assure you I know nothing of this..."

Growing tired of his constant pleading, Sayir gave the command through his implanted device to kill the barkeep. He then turned around to the crowd that was standing at attention; just as he had commanded them to do.

Lifting a mug of ale, high up in the air, he mockingly said, "Why don't you all raise your mugs to your former friend here. With bravery and dignity, he withheld the location of the one in whom you so naively place your hopes. Now, which one of you want to join him next?"

"I volunteer you," came a voice through the doorway which lead out into the muddy, rain covered street.

Dismissively throwing the mug to the side, letting it crash to the floor, Sayir slowly walked toward the entryway;

commanding his MSS trooper to follow. As his eyes pierced through the curtain of light that streamed into the pub, he could see a tall hooded figure brandishing two large blades.

Looking up at his MSS trooper, Sayir chuckled and said, "So…we have a volunteer." Looking back toward the hooded figure he continued, "And who might you be, my bold and fearless friend?"

Without removing his hood, leaving his face to hide in the darkness, Aaranon replied, "I'm not your friend."

"But I have lots of friends. Just look around," Sayir chuckled as he motioned toward the many lower-class villagers who were huddling nervously in the rain. "I can always use one more," he continued.

Pernel was hiding off to the side in the crowd, holding the control device that would kill the MSS trooper. Benohi was standing next to him, doing everything he could to contain his anger for the one who killed his beloved brother.

Aaranon slowly turned towards Pernel and nodded his head. Pernel acknowledged by pushing the button…but nothing happened. He pushed the button again and again, but the MSS trooper was still standing erect.

"Well…I don't have all day for this. I'm assuming you are the beloved Loha, and you've come to turn yourself in. Very admirable if I must say. As a show of benevolence, I will allow you to say a few parting words before my friend here has his evening meal."

Aaranon kept glancing at Pernel in a panicked state; wondering why it wasn't working.

"Alright…you had your chance," said Sayir. Turning toward the MSS trooper, he said, "Have some fun with him before you kill him. I want them to watch their precious Loha die…*very* badly."

The MSS trooper nodded, acknowledging his master's command and began walking toward Aaranon.

With his heart thundering against his chest, he muttered

under his breath, *DACK! DACK! DACK!*

Immediately, Aaranon took a defensive position as he realized he was going to have to face down an MSS trooper. As he removed his hood to see better, he looked up into the heavens and whispered; *remember me like you remembered Rohu.* Before he knew what happen, an intense pain emanated from his midsection. The MSS trooper, with one swift blow, knocked Aaranon off his feet and threw him back several *ama*, sliding head first into the muddy street.

"Splendid, superb! I think we all should give a round of applause for Loha," said Sayir as he motioned for the soggy crowd to clap. He continued, "Now, let's see what incredible feat of strength he will try next, shall we?"

Pernel and Benohi continued to fidget helplessly with the device, trying to do all they could to stop the monstrous beast that tossed their beloved friend around with ease. Aaranon slowly made his way to his feet, stumbling side to side, attempting to remove the mud from his eyes while looking for his blades. Quickly glancing around, he could not find them. He did however find a small iron plow to defend himself. As the MSS trooper came near to strike again, Aaranon, without a moment to spare, pulled the plow to his chest.

Once again, he was knocked back several *ama* into the muddy street. Not one of the villagers tried to help Aaranon, knowing it would be the death of them. But everyone tried to hold back their tears as they envisioned all of their hopes being destroyed with every blow.

"You're knocking him too far away, kick him back this way you scaly idiot," yelled Sayir. The MSS trooper looked back with a mild sneer and acknowledged his command.

As the mingled abomination slowly made its way towards Aaranon, it gave him some time to compose himself once more before the next merciless blow. Once again he grabbed hold of the plow to defend himself. At that moment however he heard a faint voice in his mind; *Turn the tip facing outwards.* Barely above a whisper and looking around, he said, "Rohu?"

Walking around to his backside, the MSS trooper grabbed hold of Aaranon's neck and began choking him as he held him high for all to see. The MSS trooper was about to throw him when all of a sudden, Aaranon swung his arms backward, digging the tip of the iron plow into the beast's cranium.

Releasing Aaranon, dropping him to the ground, the MSS trooper staggered backward and tried to pull at the plow. With a surge of adrenaline, Aaranon jumped up, yanked the plow out of its head and then repeatedly began swinging at the creature's skull. With every blow, hope was rekindled in the eyes of all who were watching, except for one.

Soon, the crowd started to gather around Sayir, preventing him from running away. They still kept their distance but made sure he couldn't escape or use his farspeak to call for reinforcements.

Pernel and Benohi pushed their way through the crowd that was watching Aaranon. They gazed at him as he continued to drive the iron plow deeper into the beast that terrorized the helpless villagers in the district. Memories of the first Loha flooded their minds. They remember the one who saved them from the giant heboram of long ago with just a simple plow.

With every strike, Aaranon vented the repressed rage and anger that permeated every fiber of his being. At that moment, he thought of no one but his father. He muttered under his breath repeatedly, "I hate you!"

After several attempts, Pernel was finally able to get Aaranon's attention. "Loha! Loha! It's dead! It's dead! You killed it."

Aaranon finally ceased beating the lifeless creature once he was covered, completely, in blood and filth. While still holding the simple iron plow, he struggled to get to his feet. Coming to his aid, Pernel and Benohi lifted him up. As he staggered back toward Sayir, the villagers began to bow at his feet.

Looking towards the crowd, Aaranon finally spoke with an

exhausted voice, "Please, stand up. Everyone, please stand up!" As the gathering of udamé slowly rose and stood firmly to their feet; Aaranon and Sayir locked eyes.

After several moments of watching the same terror sweep over Sayir that he inflicted onto others, he continued, "Never again will we bow to thugs like you. From this day forth, we will serve no king."

Looking at Benohi and then back to Sayir, Aaranon said through the gritting of his teeth, "He's all yours."

Without hesitation, Benohi pulled a knife from his side and ran headlong into Sayir, driving his blade deep into his heart, stabbing him repeatedly. As Sayir's life was slowly fading, Benohi whispered into his ear, "That was for Yaren, you bastard!"

Soon after, the villagers lifted Sayir's body up high and carried it away to burn it. They did not burn him on the traditional altar but placed him inside the temple and set the whole place ablaze.

Tired and exhausted, Aaranon watched Benohi and the other villagers carry Sayir's body away. Once they passed over the hill, he looked over at Pernel fidgeting with the controller.

"Loha, I think I figured out the problem," Pernel said.

"I don't think we can use it Pernel. It doesn't work," he said while holding his arms out to draw attention to his bruised and battered body.

"No, wait! I noticed that the board was wet. I just dried it off, so let me try it one...," said Pernel as he pushed the button. Immediately an enormous boom was heard behind them as the MSS trooper exploded into a multitude of pieces. Finishing his comment he said, "...more time."

Pernel, while holding up the controller, jumping up and down, screamed like a giddy little school girl, "YEEESSSS!! Ha Ha! IT WORKS!! "

With his face still covered in blood and nursing numerous pains, Aaranon said with an exasperated look, "Seriously?"

Chapter 22

Cadet Micah watched as Dihana walked nonchalantly through the halls of the Quayanin castle and towards him. "Your Highness, it's good to see you this morning,"

"Micah, correct?"

"That is correct," he replied, a half smile forming in the corner of his mouth as he watched her beautiful form walk past; leaving only the fragrance of her perfume in her wake.

Straightening her dress just a bit and clearing her throat, she said under her breath, *here we go.* Dihana stopped and slowly turned toward the young cadet. She didn't notice, in her former drunken stupor in front of her mother's quarters, how handsome and eloquent he looked as he stood at attention. "So how has your day been?"

"It's been wonderful. To stand in the palace of the Alemeleg is my greatest joy," he replied anxiously, as he did his best to continue standing at attention.

"Really? So you wouldn't prefer somewhere else? Perhaps outside where it's bright and beautiful?" she asked in a flirtatious manner as she gently glided back toward him.

"Oh no, Your Highness. My duties are clearly defined. I would not wish to break them," he said with the same half-smile.

Her tone was gently mocking as she cocked her head to the side. "So then…what are your *clearly defined* duties that you are so joyous to uphold?"

Fumbling every word he spoke, "It is my duty, given to me by my commander…Your Highness…to guard the members of this sacred home against the vile Apostates who wish to destroy this noble family and institution."

Stepping closer to her new, yet, growing infatuation she

quietly asked him, "Do you practice that dung-filled speech on a regular basis or does it flow naturally like those soft lips of yours?"

With his face growing red like the setting of Shemesh, and a mind running to places it shouldn't, he stammered, "Uh...oh... Princess I mean no disrespect. I honor my duties and..."

Dihana interrupted, "I tell you what. You can perform your duties by guarding me as I take a walk through the garden."

"I...uh...I...don't...uh...I don't think that would be a good idea Your Highness; my commander was explicit in his commands that I must stand guard in this location."

"But your duty isn't to guard a hallway, is it? But the occupants in the hallway, correct?"

"Uh...well...I believe that would be correct Your Highness."

She lowered her chin to reveal her long and beautiful fluttering eyelashes. "Well, of course, it's correct. So...are you not here to protect my weak little rear end from those dastardly Apostates?"

"Oh, Your Highness I would love to do more than guard your sweet little a...I mean, it's my duty to guard all those who are within these walls," Micah said, growing hot under the collar and feeling an increasing restriction in his breeches.

"So...you think my backside is little and sweet don't you?" Dihana asked as she gently ran her hand along his chest.

Fear started to coat his every word. "Oh dear! Uh...uh... Princess...I don't want to do anything that would offend you or your family,"

Before Dihana could say anything else, Micah's commanding officer was moving swiftly to where they were standing.

"Your Highness, is this cadet bothering you?" he asked without a smidge of compassion in his voice.

"No! But there is something bothering me," replied Dihana in a stern voice.

"I will most certainly take care of this matter and...,"

Dihana interrupted him and started poking him in the chest, standing on her tiptoes as the commander was much taller than she. "What is bothering me, commander, is that you will not release this young cadet to do his duty and guard me as I walk through the garden. Don't you realize how delicate my little... don't you know how delicate I am?"

Turning to Micah, the commander said in a very brash tone, "Why haven't you taken orders from the Princess, cadet?"

"Yeah! Why haven't you taken my orders cadet Soft Lips?" She may have sounded stern, but she had a tiny grin; threatening to break into a full smile. She looked back at the commander, "I think I can handle it from here commander. I will make sure to deal with him myself."

Immediately, she grabbed Micah's collar and yanked him down the hallway. After getting far enough away from the bewildered commander, Dihana let go of his collar, allowing Micah to straighten up and walk beside her.

"Your Highness, I didn't mean to offend you in any way. If I did, I would give my life to apologize..."

"Oh stop...you didn't offend me. And stop calling me Your Highness, or Princess, or any of that other nonsense," she said as she waved her hand dismissively in the air.

"If I cannot address you by your official title, then how may I address you Your High...uh...," he queried while tapering off his words.

"Just call me Dihana."

"But...what if...uh..."

"What if someone hears you? Alright, when others are around you can call me Your Highness, but when no one is near, just call me Dihana. I grow so tired of the pomp. It just disgusts me to no end."

Micah continued to walk alongside her, wanting to express his fear and concern over speaking with her, but also so desperately wanting to follow her lead and speak as if they were close friends. Looking over at him, she could tell he was finding it difficult to speak freely.

Dihana grabbed hold of Micah's arm, stopping him in his tracks. She continued, "I can tell, you're not used to speaking to a noble this way."

"Exactly!" he said with a great deal of relief.

"So why don't you just do what comes natural and comfortable to you and I'll do what comes natural and comfortable to me," she stated as she looked up into his dark blue eyes.

"Thank you Your Highness," he said as his body began to relax.

"Rather than worrying about me, I want to know more about you," she said while she continued to not only hold his arm, but caress his hand as well.

Mesmerized by her beauty, he found it difficult to speak.

She continued, "How about this, there is a garden here where you can speak freely. Why don't we go and visit it?"

"Alright…Your Highness…I will follow wherever you lead. It is my duty as you know," he said with a smile, as they both walked out of the castle into the beautiful light of Shemesh.

Chapter 23

"Do we really have to do this Darham?" Dihana demanded as she walked into his quarters without shutting the door.

Moving quickly to close themselves in, Darham whispered, "I told you not to say anything until I close these doors. I was only able to secure this room. We need to be careful."

"Yeah...I know. Anyway, why do we have to use him?" she asked in a slightly whiny tone.

"Dihana, I told you before, we cannot leave the kingdom without a military escort. We need Micah by our side when we escape."

Dihana walked over to Darham's bed and flung herself down while giving off an agitated grunt. "It's just that he's so nice. I don't want him to get hurt because he's helping us; even if he isn't aware that he's helping us."

He flopped himself down next to her. "Alright, let's go over this one more time."

"Darham, I understand the plan. I just don't like putting someone else in jeopardy."

"He's the best one for this. He doesn't have family, except for his father, who can get in harm's way and he...," Darham said before being interrupted.

Leaning up quickly and looking towards her half-brother she said, "Oh yeah, some father he is. He's just another chip off our dear ol' love-bucket of a father!"

"Yes, I know. That's why I picked him."

"If it weren't for that twisted piece of flesh...that...that... seed donor, Micah wouldn't even be in the military. Just because he was a highly decorated lower commander doesn't mean he should be able to ruin his son's life."

"Dihana I know all this. You insisted that I do all I could to minimize the number of people impacted by...," he said as he was interrupted once again by his enthusiastic Betwudam.

"Get this. His father was a drunk. And not your kind of drunk. But the kind that beats up his wife and rapes his own daughter. No wonder his mother died of a broken heart and his sister committed suicide."

"Well...for one, you know I still have to drink to keep up the appearance..."

"I know! And I have to keep up with my anger and rage moments as well."

"At least it comes natural to you," he chuckled.

"Oooo!! If you don't want me to use your sack as a chew toy for the celabs then you take that back," she said, her fist poised over his privies ready to strike.

"Alright! I take it back," Darham exclaimed as he immediately covered himself.

"Well, anyway, he doesn't deserve that wretch of a father. You should have heard what he had to endure growing up," she said as she once again flung herself back down on the soft mattress.

"Yes, I know. I did the background check on him. He's the perfect candidate. My guess is that he will not report us to the UAK when we leave. Wait a moment, how much did you tell him about yourself. Because you know we can't..."

"Don't worry. I didn't give away anything important. I only said enough to influence him like you asked. My wonderful brother is "dead", my mother was poisoned, our dear brother Ravizu used me like a sock hung on a windmill," she said while twirling her finger in the air.

"Sock on a windmill?"

"Look, he abused me alright? Micah got the picture, and now he wants to do everything he can to protect me. You got what you wanted, alright!?"

Exasperated with having to explain his logic to her continually, he said, "Dihana, it isn't what I want, it's what *we* need. He needs to want you more than his personal freedom if this is going to work."

"Yeah, yeah. It's done. He wants me; that much is clear," she blurted out while thinking, *and I want him too.*

"Good! Because you…I mean we…can't mess this up. If you let out too soon…"

"I know, I know! You don't have to keep telling me. I'm not that stupid."

"Dihana, I'm not calling you stupid. I just need for you to be careful with what you say."

"Alright! Now let me finish. I have more to tell you," she said while shaking off her anger to once again think about her new love. "You should hear him talk about his sister. You know what he called her?"

"Surprise me."

"His little rose," she said as she clasped her hands together, remembering Aaranon's name for her. Darham looked over and just shrugged his shoulders.

"HIS LITTLE ROSE!!" she growled. "Aaranon called me his little flower. GET IT!!"

"Oh no," said Darham as he realized her growing fondness of Micah.

"What?!" she barked as she looked over at him.

"You're in love with him aren't you?"

"Don't be silly! We need him to escape. I just don't want to see anyone get hurt," she replied as she ran her finger ever so gently across the covers, trying to hide her affections for her new love.

"Dihana we need to be careful. If someone thinks that you're in love with this cadet, it…,"

"This cadet has a naaaammme. His name is Micah," she said through a calm yet firm voice and clinched teeth.

"Alright, alright. Don't get upset. I'm just telling you to be careful," Darham said as he laid there with a smug look.

"What?" she asked.

"What do you mean...what? I'm just laying here."

"You're thinking something, what is it?"

"I just think it's cute that you have a fondness for this young lad. I know Aaranon would be happy for you."

"Really?" she asked in a more subdued and somber tone. She continued, with tears beginning to fall down her delicate face that has seen more pain than most, "Do you think we will ever see him again, Darham?"

"We will," he replied with a renewed confidence in his voice.

"What makes you so sure?" she asked.

Putting his hands behind his head and looking up towards the ceiling he said, "I just have this overwhelming peace about it. I can't explain it, but I know we'll find him."

Dihana didn't say anything, but she too felt the same peace and confidence.

While patting his half-sister on her leg, Darham sat up and said, "We need to get ready."

"Oh yeah. That stupid announcement. Why is he doing this anyway? I think this is the first time in the history of all this pageantry that a noble announces a Prince taking a Betwudam. I can understand a wedding announcement, but not this."

"The *official* reason given by our beloved father is that he wants the whole world to know we refuse to be bullied into fear by the Apostates. That we will continue to live our lives without concern; or some such thing like that."

"So...what is the unofficial reason again?" she asked.

"My guess is that he wants Aaranon to see the announcement and know that we are still alive."

"So...our sack-wad of a father is using us as bait?"

"Yeah, remember? We talked about this before."

"I know, I know. Well then...," she said as she headed toward the door.

"Where are you going?" he asked.

"If we are going to be bait, then I want to make sure I send a clear message."

"Uh…what do mean, Dihana? You know we need to be…"

"Oh, I know. I just want Aaranon to see that I know he's still alive. Trust me, I know what I'm doing," she replied as she playfully glided out of the room.

Chapter 24

"Loha, what are you looking for, maybe I can help?" asked Pernel as he watched Aaranon throw around the supplies looking for something.

"I left it right here! I know I did!" Aaranon growled.

"You left what?"

"Here it is," he said with short-lived satisfaction as he found his satchel.

"Alright...uh...is there anything else you need help with? Benohi and I can get it for you."

"Uh...yes. Be sure to scan everyone for any possible implants or trackers," said Aaranon to Pernel.

Pernel was frustrated. "Loha, we've scanned them several times now and they are all clean. I can assure you of that."

"Well then scan them again!" Aaranon walked out of their secret location and sheathed his blades in preparation for their first raid on one of the temples.

Waiting for Aaranon to exit the room before he spoke, he said in a slightly defeated manner, "Fine! I'll take care of it."

"Why is Loha so hot under the collar?" asked Benohi.

"I think he's just concerned about the mission."

"Well...yeah...but aren't we all? I mean, we've all lost someone."

"He knows. But...he's the one we're all looking to for hope and guidance. Can you imagine shouldering that burden? I don't think I could."

"Well...yeah...I never thought of it that way."

"So...let's go scan everyone again before we go," Pernel said, pausing to look at the scanner he just picked up.

"What is it?" Benohi asked as his friend since childhood stood there silently, looking at the ground.

"Thirty," he said in a matter of fact tone.

"Thirty what?"

"Only thirty of us. How in the world is this going to work?"

"It's a bit too late to ask that don't you think?" Benohi said with a snicker.

"Maybe."

"Pernel I think you know, as well as I do, that someone needs to stay behind to watch after our families. If too many of us were to leave the village, it could become evident where the group came from."

He looked downcast. "I know. I just hoped that others would come and join our cause. I thought when Loha killed the MSS in the village that more than just a handful of people would yoke themselves to our mission."

"Never underestimate the power of the kingdom over its subjects," replied Benohi.

"I know," he said as he continued to stare at the ground.

"Is there something else?"

As his eyes started to water, he said in a softer tone, "After you lost Yaren I feel I shouldn't be so selfish, but I can't stop thinking about her; I just want my wife back. I thought that others would feel the same about their loved ones who were still being held captive by this dacking…I just thought there would be others. I thought they cared about their families."

"They do Pernel. All of us do. But only a few will do something about it. But don't worry, you will see her soon."

"I hope you're right. I can't stand the thought of coming back here…and…" Pernel paused a moment to fight back the tears, "…and have my children see that she isn't with me."

"We will get her back. You saw what he did to that oversized leather-head. Even though we are few, word has spread that Loha has returned. Besides, you figured out the controllers."

"Yeah, but we almost lost him."

"But Pernel, that's the thing. We didn't. Listen, I was angry with him when my brother died. But when he destroyed that beast like the Loha of old, and with a small iron plow of all things, that meant something to me." Enthusiasm was building in Benohi's voice.

"Yeah?"

"Yeah! Look, you know me, I'm not much for believing in the ancient god or gods, or whatever, but what if we aren't alone? What if they've been here the whole time? You know, looking down on us. And now it's our time. This time, we get to decide who lives and who dies. We get to tell them what to do!" he said as he pointed in the direction of the capital city, Heock.

"Yeah, you might be right. Maybe it is our time. I'm sincerely sorry about Yaren. He won't get his time."

"That wasn't your fault Pernel. I took care of that problem already, remember?" said Benohi in a more sober tone as his longtime friend nodded in agreement. He continued, "So don't worry. How about this. We do this for him. We do it for Yaren."

"Yeah, for Yaren; and everyone else who was cut short of their day," Pernel said as they both clasped each other's' forearm and gave one another a firm embrace.

"Well...I better go scan the thirty of us, *just in case*. We don't want to find a traitor in our midst," Pernel said with a slight chuckle.

"Do you want me to scan you?"

"Uhh, no...I'll let Loha do that."

"Sure thing. Well then...scan away," he said as he lifted up his arms and spread apart his feet for Pernel to, once again, check for any tracking devices.

***

"May I have a word with you young Loha?" asked Isma as Aaranon was walking past the elder's humble abode.

"Sure," he said hesitantly, not knowing what unwanted advice he was about to receive.

"Please, have a seat."

"I honestly need to get moving. It's going to take several days to get to the destination and...," Aaranon looked away from Isma and pointed toward the north.

"You have time Aaranon. Please...have a seat."

Looking around to make sure no one heard him mention his real name, Aaranon cautiously decided to appease the aging elder and have a seat next to him.

"So I hear that you've found the location of Pernel's wife."

"We have. She is in the temple in Tuval."

"Well then, you do have quite a journey ahead of you."

"Ah...yeah...so if you don't mind I need to get moving...," Aaranon said before he was interrupted.

"That creature you killed. It was quite impressive I heard," said Isma as he looked up towards the heavens.

"Ah...I suppose. Not to be disrespectful, but can you get to the point?" he asked.

"I heard that you were muttering something under your breath as you buried that plow into him."

Aaranon ground his teeth. "I think you're mistaken."

"Maybe I am. Maybe you were not thinking of your father as you were releasing your aggression. If I may, just one more time, remind you..."

Growing agitated and impatient with Isma's comments, Aaranon retorted, "I know what Rohu taught me, Isma! I know it very well. I'm not seeking revenge. I only want to rescue my family. That's all. Then I'll take care of what Rohu asked... alright!?"

Isma gently said, "Your family?"

"You know what I mean. I certainly can't help mine if I don't help theirs now can I?"

"Well then...it seems you have it all under control," he said without looking towards Aaranon. He continued, "I will pray that the ancient one will watch over you and lead you home."

In a slightly calmer voice, Aaranon replied, "It's going to be a while before we come back. We can't return immediately for the sake of…"

"I'm not talking about your return to here, Aaranon," Isma said as he looked directly at him.

"What?"

Isma stood up from his worn out rocking chair and started towards the door. Before gently closing the door, he turned and spoke softly, "Be safe young Aaranon. Be safe."

Chapter 25

"Amana, would you mind handing me that hammer over there before you go?"

"Sure thing," she replied as she walked over to the daughter-in-law of Nahim. "Here you go."

"Thank you. So...are you all set for your journey?"

Setting down her fully laden satchel from her back, Amana replied, "I believe so. I know I said this numerous times at the feast last night, but I want to thank you and your family for everything that you've done for me."

"It was our pleasure. I just wish there were more like you."

"There's a world filled with people like me."

"Well...there's a world filled with those who have suffered just as you have, but very few who will listen to us so-called *Apostates*," she chuckled.

Amana shook her head. "If only they knew the real truth. Then they wouldn't call us that."

"That may be true but it comes as no surprise to us," she said as she continued to hammer away at the hot iron rivet. Looking over, she asked, "Is there something on your mind?"

Amana took a deep breath and lifted her head towards the heavens. "I know I keep asking this, and since this might be my last chance; do you honestly think it's coming? I know what your answer will be...I just want to hear it once more."

"I honestly do," she said, pausing from her work on the massive structure to look up as well.

While gently touching her friend's arm, Amana said, "Thank you. I've always appreciated your friendship, but I especially appreciate your faithfulness. I just wish I had your confidence."

She turned and gazed at the colossal structure that was three hundred *ama* in length and chuckled. "I'm glad you see it as confidence, because, for most of the people who pass by here, they look at that and think it's craziness."

Amana continued to stand next to her friend; wanting to ask another question that has long been burning in her mind, but finding it difficult to do so.

"Is there something else Amana? I know you have a long journey ahead of you and I'm sure you want to get started."

After a few moments of shuffling her feet, she finally said, "Can I ask you something personal?"

"Sure."

After several moments of trying to find the right words, Amana finally asked, "Is it possible for someone to love another person who has been...well, you know? I mean truly love that person? Because, I keep asking myself; who would want someone like...that?"

"You're thinking about Aaranon, right?"

Amana paused for a moment as a radiant smile moved across her face melting away the frown she so often carried. She continued, "We're from two *completely* different worlds."

"As far as I can tell, you're both from the same world. You both came from the same ancestor and you both have flaws like the rest of us. So, what difference are you referring to?"

"Look...I know what your father-in-law said and what I'm called to do but, Aaranon...he's...he's a noble," replied Amana, looking downtrodden and hopeless.

"Let me correct you on that. He *was* a noble. He is *now* an outcast like the rest of us."

Amana climbed up on a stack of boards and began to swing her legs back and forth as they continued their discussion. "When Rohu brought me here, the night after almost dying in the arena, he told me something that I can't get out of my head. For one, I was surprised to hear him speak. But also, he said that our paths were...linked."

"That is true."

Amana started to cry and looked away from her friend who took her in and loved her like a sister. "I know it's *true*, but I can't help but think that Aaranon and I could never be together. How could he ever want someone like me?"

"Amana, look at me." After waiting for a few moments for Amana to compose herself, she continued, "You know all of us love you, right?"

"Yes," she said as she wiped her tears.

"Now, if we can love you; this band of misfits," she said while waving her hand towards Nahim's other family members who were working on the structure. "Then don't you think that someone like a supposedly dead, but still alive, living in the trees, eating all kinds of who-knows-what, ex-noble can love you?"

As a smile, followed by laughter, quickly spread across her face, Amana said, "Well if you put it that way, I'm not sure if I want him now."

"I tell you what, you just keep reading the scrolls. They will put everything into perspective and then you'll know who is truly worthy."

"I can do that. I will do that," Amana vowed.

"Now remember, when you leave here, you're not alone. A multitude has been sent to watch over you. Aaranon has a greater purpose, and you're a part of that. You will find him. I know this to be true."

"Greater purpose? It doesn't seem so great when I think about what your family is called to do," Amana replied as she lifted up the satchel onto her back.

"It doesn't matter what we are called to do. What matters is our faithfulness in that call."

Amana gave her friend and newly found sister one last embrace. "Well then, I hope to see you soon."

Chapter 26

Aaranon motioned for his small band of mercenaries to gather around before they made their first raid on the temple in Tuval. "We've only got one shot at this. I know we've practiced this many times before, but let's go over it one more time. It's crucial we get it right."

He continued, "First of all, be sure to put on your masks before we exit the forest. We don't want any of the recorders to catch our faces. Now, as soon as the three energy taps that power this area are disabled, the UAK will be alerted. They won't know what happened, but they will send out a repair team to investigate."

Pointing to a layout on the ground he continued, "Pernel, once your team disables the taps; the outer wall will de-energize. Benohi will then lead his team and their ohemas to knock down the outer and inner perimeter. Ballac, lead your team immediately behind Benohi's. Rush toward the temple front gate and kill the guards. Their EBs will have manual rounds so you will need to keep a tight formation behind the shields. Eliminate all the guards, both outside and inside the temple. Kill the priests as well. They shouldn't put up much of a fight."

"What about the other entrances? Will they be guarded" asked one of the udam.

"Like I said before, ever since the attacks on the four hundred temples, they've tightened security on all city temples by sealing off all entrances but one. We'll enter in through the front."

"Why don't we use the ohemas to knock down one of the gates since it's unsecured?" asked Pernel.

Growing frustrated at their questions Aaranon said, "Doesn't anyone listen to me?" He continued, "Like I said before, it will take too long to break through because those walls are double lined. The perimeter walls are not as thick and rely mostly on the energy from the taps to keep anyone or any creature at bay."

"May I continue now?" Aaranon asked sarcastically. Pernel motioned toward the ground as he nodded sheepishly. "Good! As I was saying, we will enter in through the front. Benohi will position the ohemas in front of the gate to prevent anyone from coming in. Ballac, when the temple is clear, move back to the front. Each member of your team join with one member of Pernel's to be ready for anything that could come our way. Since the power will be out, the trigger devices will only have enough charge for one try. We will be well on our way before any forces show up. But if they do, do not use them until they are within range. Let's go ahead and distribute the triggers."

As Pernel distributed the devices, it was noticed they weren't powering on to receive a charge.

Growing frustrated, Aaranon yelled, "What the dack! Why aren't these working Pernel?"

Pulling at his hair, Pernel said, "They were working when we left! I don't know what's wrong. I still have the original one around my neck...," he said while pulling it out. He continued, "...see, this one is still working."

The others looked concerned while one spoke up, "Well that's it. We need to abort."

Pernel replied in a panic, "My wife is in there! We can't abort! We have one working trigger, and this might be our only chance! Please!"

Another crew member said, "I don't think we have a choice. We can't go in there with only one trigger. That would be crazy."

"Just shut up for a moment and let me think," Aaranon muttered as he walked around rubbing his head. He continued, "Alright, it's too late to change the plan now. Pernel's right, we still have one working trigger. Hopefully, if all goes well, we will be long gone before the MSS troops even show up."

Pointing to another member of the crew Aaranon said, "Hena's team will open all the chambers releasing the prisoners. Once released, we need to keep them in a tight formation around the cloaking device as we exit the temple and back through the breached wall. *That's* still working, right?" Aaranon asked as he looked at Pernel.

Pernel checked the cloaking device. "Yes, it's working."

"Good, if the prisoners get too far away from it, they will be tracked. Once we get them to the rendezvous point we can remove the tracking devices, but not until then," Aaranon said.

"But what happens if one gets loose? Not all of these prisoners will go with us willingly, so how do we handle that?" asked Ballac.

Aaranon's countenance was stern and his tone harsh. "We already talked about this! Didn't any of you pay attention these past four odes? You know what happens to them."

"Now wait a dacking moment! I didn't sign up for killing our own people. There has to be a better answer than that," one udam said.

"I told all of you what was at risk. It's either we get out alive or we all die. I don't like the choices we have to make today. But we didn't want this. They did this to us. So are you in, or you out," Aaranon demanded as he gazed upon the twenty-nine others.

After a few moments, all acknowledged they were committed to the cause. He continued, "Alright then. Everyone to your places."

***

"How much longer before we get to leave our post," whined Phillin, a cadet, fresh out of the Academy, assigned to be a temple guard.

"Not much longer young one," said Stralo, the older, more experienced guard.

"Hey, don't you find it strange that they only have two of us here, and no one inside?"

"Yeah, I do but that new duty commander thinks we can do more with less."

"Well, I don't like that. These longer work days are wearing on me. I just want to get home."

"I know how you feel. I need to get home as soon as possible myself. My son is getting back from his deployment, and I can't wait to see him," Stralo said.

"How long has it been?"

"Four years."

"Dack! Not only are the work days getting longer, but these deployments are getting longer and longer too."

"I know, with all this stuff going on, his mother worries about him."

"About what?"

Waving his hand in the air dismissively, he said, "Dacking Apostates."

"Ahh. I don't think she needs to worry about that. I believe the new Alemeleg has taken care of the last of them. I don't like all these new security measures though. It certainly makes life more restrictive, but if it keeps us all safer then, I guess I'm fine with it."

"I know, I know. I try to tell her, but...hey! What happened to the power?"

As a rumbling noise began to grow, Phillin asked, "What's that sound? Is it another ground quake?"

Pointing off in the distance Stralo shouted, "Look over there, those trees, what in tarsis is that?!"

Immediately, Benohi and his team rushed the perimeter while riding on the necks of the ohemas. It didn't take much effort for them to knock down both walls. Soon after, Ballac's team charged ahead.

"Holy DACK! They're knocking down the perimeter! Call central!" said Phillin.

"We can't! The power is out! Switch to manual rounds!"

"Here they come! Fire!"

Immediately, several arrows came rushing toward the guards from behind, what looked like, a moving fortified wall, killing Phillin instantly, but only wounding Stralo in the leg.

Screaming and writhing in pain, Stralo soon realized that his EB was empty of manual rounds. Crawling behind a small embankment, he hid himself as he watched the mysterious band of masked marauders storm the temple. Unable to reach Phillin's weapon he pulled out a small knife from his side to try and protect himself if he became discovered.

As Aaranon was running up the temple steps, giving direction to each of the teams, he stopped near Stralo's hiding place, unaware of his presence. As his team flooded the temple to release the maidens, his eye caught a glimpse of something. He turned to see, off in the distance, a large banner hanging on the side of the city's sporting arena. The image displayed the announcement of Darham taking Dihana as his Betwudam. Below it was the caption, *We Wish for Nothing but Your Peace and Safety.*

For just a moment, the world stopped for Aaranon. For the first time in almost two years, he could feast his eyes on his beloved sister. No one could see it because of the mask, but a smile started to emerge. He said to himself; *she must know.*

Stralo quietly moved behind Aaranon, knife in hand, hoping to kill the one he perceived to be the leader of the group. Stralo, with his wounded leg, lunged as best he could for Aaranon, who was still mesmerized as he gazed at his sister's image. With Stralo's knife poised to strike the small of Aaranon's back, Ballac suddenly grabbed Stralo from behind and wrestled him to the ground, knocking the knife out of his hand.

Lying there helpless and alone, Stralo begged for mercy as Aaranon looked down on him. "Please, I have a son! A family! Please don't kill me! Just let me go. I don't know who you are!"

Aaranon paused for a moment as he looked at Stralo

weeping for his family. Before he could respond, Ballac thrust his blade into Stralo's chest, putting to rest his desire to be with his family.

Aaranon and Ballac locked eyes for just a moment and Ballac said in a muffled tone, "For our families." Trying to put aside the image of an udam like himself crying out for his family, Aaranon just slowly nodded in agreement.

Wiping the blood from his blade onto his sleeve, Ballac looked over at the banner to see what captured Aaranon's attention.

"For a noble, she sure is beautiful. I can see why you were distracted."

"Yes...I guess so," Aaranon said, trying to hide his love for her.

"They sure do dress weird though huh? Looks like she's wearing a sea of little flowers."

"Yeah, she sure is," he replied, with a small grin that no one could see.

***

"Let's go! Move it! Move it! Move it!" yelled Aaranon as all thirty of them, along with the temple maidens, rushed out the front and through the breached wall, leaving the ohemas to stand guard in front of the temple.

Pernel ran among the maidens looking for his wife, screaming, "I don't see her! Where is she, I don't see her!"

From above they could see several Dargons moving in and releasing their MSS troops. As they ran past the temple and towards the forest, Aaranon looked over and saw scrawled on the temple wall; *We Serve No King - Loha Has Returned.*

Running alongside Aaranon, Pernel said to him, "Loha, I don't see my wife."

"There are many maidens Pernel; we'll look for her once we get out of here."

Looking upward, Pernel then pointed to the Dargons; "How can they fly? We took the power out!"

"Dack Pernel, I don't know! Just keep running!" Looking back, Aaranon could see the MSS troops drawing near at a rapid pace. He said, "Hold off until they get close. We need to make sure they're within range."

Nodding in agreement, Pernel pulled the device out from underneath his clothing. Just as he was about to press the button, a group of MSS troops emerged from the forest; arresting their forward progress. They were now completely surrounded without anywhere to go.

Pernel was about to push the button when Aaranon whispered to Pernel, "Wait! We need for those behind us to come closer. If we push it now, it will only kill the ones in front of us."

"But why have they stopped? What are they waiting for?"

"Their commander wants to take us in," Aaranon replied.

"They will torture us for sure. We can't let that happen," said Benohi with panic rising in his voice.

Aaranon directed everyone to form a tight perimeter and huddle behind the shields. Many of the maidens were crying and begging to return to the temple, not realizing that the UAK would kill them after being questioned. Their only hope rested in Aaranon and his crew.

As they huddled together, the MSS troops slowly moved within fifty *ama* of Aaranon's crew as they were directed and then stopped, awaiting further command. They were, however, still not close enough for the device to work.

"You are completely surrounded! You have nowhere to go!" yelled out the UAK High Commander. "If you give yourself up, I can assure you, your deaths will be swift once we have the information we need. But if you resist, we will still extract from you what we want. However, the MSS troops will take their time, prolonging the inevitable!"

"Now Loha? Now?" asked Pernel in a panic.

"Not yet, they need to be closer."

"But the power is back on, if it doesn't work the first time I can just wait for them to get closer, right?"

"No, it isn't, look at the device. It only has enough capacitance for one shot. Don't touch it until I say so."

"Then how can they fly?"

"Tarsis Pernel, I don't know!" growled Aaranon as he was trying to figure out how they got there so quickly. There wasn't enough time to setup a mobile tap unless...unless they knew. Unless they were waiting for them.

"But Loha, if they get too close we could be killed when they explode."

"Dack it, give me the trigger!" growled Aaranon as he reached over to yank the device from his trembling hands.

Pulling the device away, Pernel said, "Loha please, I don't want to lose my wife all over again!"

"Pernel! Give me the device!" yelled Aaranon as he once again reached for the trigger. In their struggle, Pernel inadvertently pushed the button.

Nothing happened.

"I see that you wish to take the prolonged approach to death. So be it!" yelled out the High Commander as he and his crew stood behind the MSS troops so they could watch them slowly move in to devour their prey.

"I'm so sorry Loha! I'm so sorry! I didn't mean it. I only wanted to save my wife," cried Pernel as he and all the others could feel their very souls slipping away into the great beyond.

Looking toward the banner on the arena wall, Aaranon fell to his knees. Tears flowed down his cheeks and into his now overgrown beard. The beard that she once embraced when they were together.

He whispered, with a lifetime of remorse filling every word, *I'm so sorry Dihana, I'm so sorry.* He could feel it all slip away. Rohu's forty years of service to him wasted because he couldn't listen to someone wiser than himself. She looked so happy standing there next to Darham. Why didn't he just listen?

As the MSS troops continued to move closer, the ground began to shake violently. The ohemas that were once standing still in front of the temple turned and ran back through the way they came. As they moved, they trampled several Dargons that were in their path, prompting the UAK forces to run for cover. The MSS troops, however, continued to move forward with a great deal of difficulty because of the quake. Nothing was going to stop them from their mission.

Looking down at the device that was in Aaranon's hand Ballac screamed, "Look Loha! Look!"

Aaranon looked down and noticed the device was indicating it had power and was fully charged. Without a moment to spare, Aaranon yelled to his crew and the maidens, "GET DOWN!"

He then pressed the button.

Chapter 27

BOOM! Zeul smashed down the gavel, breaking it into several pieces.

He shouted at the other members of the UAC. "Order! I will not begin until we have order in these sacred chambers!"

"Sacred? How can you call these halls sacred when those rebellious bottom-feeders dare to challenge our authority?" screamed one highly indignant magistrate.

"If you would all just calm down I can explain...," Zeul yelled before he was again interrupted by shouts and jeers against his sovereignty over the council.

"We gave you sole power over this council, and this is how you repay us," yelled King Lachish, of the house and kingdom of Tuval. "Why should we listen to what you have to say? We made a grave mistake when we put you in charge!"

Growing tired of the constant barrage of insults hurled at his ability to lead, he gently nodded his head towards one of the guards standing across from him. Acknowledging his prearranged order, the guard pulled a farspeak to his lips and muttered a few commands. Soon after, a large company of MSS troops came thundering into the council chambers and filled the aisles; causing the numerous UAC members to gasp in horror.

"What is this?" shouted one of the kings.

Zeul looked down on the assembly of kings before him and spoke in a calmer tone, "I suggest that all of you take a seat." Once they quieted down and found their seats; he then lifted up a trigger device similar to the one Aaranon had used.

"This, my fellow kings, is what it took to bring down the whole company of MSS troops," Zeul said as he continued to hold the trigger up high for all to see.

King Lachish still had more frustrations to air regarding the situation at hand. "It very well may have been that device that took down these dumb beasts, but it was your over-reaching policies that caused these peasants to riot against us in the first place! What did you think would happen?! You cannot expect the lower-class to sit back and do nothing as you continue to rob them of what little freedom they do have.

"They riot against us because you poison their crops with your experiments; you post MSS troops everywhere, and then you allow these law enforcement agents to operate with impunity. It is abundantly clear to me that you have brought this upon all of us. I was against your election from the beginning. Never before did we elect an Alemeleg from the lower-house!"

"Is that right?" asked Zeul while looking down his nose at Lachish.

"That's exactly right! I also wish to motion that we elect a new Alemeleg...*the proper way*," he said while looking around the room to see who would second it.

"Well then...," Zeul said as he motioned to the MSS trooper that was standing behind Lachish. As the creature lifted its claw, one of its talons extended forward and injected Lachish with a lethal dose of venom. The MSS troops have a few poisons in their arsenal from which they can choose. In this case, the MSS trooper could either inject a small amount of toxin, which would have killed Lachish after several days or a deadly dose which would kill him immediately. In this instance, the latter was chosen, and King Lachish collapsed to the floor. The other kings gasped in horror. Zeul, unfazed by the entire situation, continued, "...is there a second? Do I hear a second on that motion? Hmm...it appears we don't have a full motion for a new election. Therefore, with that nasty business taken care of, I will continue with my demonstration."

As Lachish lay lifeless on the floor, silence replaced the

confident shouts of the other kings. Zeul once again lifted up the device and continued, "As I was saying, before my former council member so rudely interrupted, this was all they needed to bring down our defenses. But now...," he said as he pushed the button, "...that will no longer be a problem."

Several of the kings ducked for cover; thinking the MSS troops were going to explode. Once it was evident that nothing was going to happen, King Vidas spoke up, "If I may, fellow council members, speak on behalf of our esteemed Alemeleg. As you can see, the MSS troops have had their explosive implants removed. No longer will these rebels be able to stop them in this manner."

Zeul then took over for Vidas. "Thank you King Vidas. Let me first assure you that none of you need to be in fear." Nodding towards one of the guards, Zeul indicated that the MSS troops should leave. Once they all left the room he continued, "I apologize that all of you had to witness this unfortunate event. But it was necessary for me to demonstrate to you what happens to traitors who lurk in our midst."

Several of the kings began to speak in hushed tones; wondering how one of their own could betray them.

Holding up his hand for silence, Zeul continued, "It came to my attention that a small band of rebels were forming a coalition to attack one of the smaller temples on the outskirts of Tuval. I wanted to be sure before we moved. Unfortunately, we were a few moments too late in our arrival. We were also not fully aware of their capabilities."

One extremely nervous king gathered enough courage to question Zeul. "If I may ask the esteemed Potentate, how was King Lachish involved?"

"As you know, the city of Tuval lies within the former King Lachish's kingdom. As it turns out, the temple was under-guarded with only two soldiers at the front gate."

Gasps came from the members. One king asked, "Excuse me My King, but were these not Apostates?"

"We believe they are a different group altogether, but we have not completely ruled that out. They are not targeting the temples for destruction but appear to only want to take our property."

"But what did Lachish have to do with this?" asked another. Realizing they were no longer in jeopardy of being assassinated, the council members began to calm down.

"As many of you know, Lachish has fought us on every front. He gave us resistance in every policy we have put into place. Let me say, I have no qualms with opposition, as long as it is brought to the council for debate. Even though, at present, I do hold complete and total authority, I still wish to operate within your wise council. However, it appears that Lachish wanted to undermine our efforts by creating a so-called rebellion that had no chance of forming on its own. It was his hope that I would appear inept and removed from office."

Zeul motioned for several mingled servants to enter the chambers and pass out sealed folders that contained all the information on his office's investigation into King Lachish. Once the servants left the room, he continued, "You may now open your folders. In them, you will find all the intelligence gathered on Lachish and his operation. Unfortunately, since he used multiple tiers of underlings to carry out his plan, we've been unable to discover the group that made the assault on the temple. We do, however, have numerous concealed agents in place who are providing us with inside knowledge."

"Why are we just hearing about this now?" asked another king.

"We didn't know the depth of compromise in the kingdoms until now. Releasing this information too early would not have been wise," Zeul said.

"Can you speak of their whereabouts? Since they escaped, have we been able to track them down?" asked King Vullkal.

"We think King Lachish supplied the rebels with equipment that made it possible for them to remove any and all tracking devices on the maidens. Since this temple was within his kingdom, we don't have any records of the maidens who were removed, therefore making it impossible for us to discover which villages or districts from which they came. It appears Lachish covered his tracks well, and we believe the operation he started has many more targets."

"Since you have discovered Lachish's plans, shouldn't this so-called rebellion now fall apart?" asked another king.

"Unfortunately, no. Numerous upper-class law enforcement agents across Araz have reported that many appear to be mobilizing to join this fledgling rebellion."

One angry and disgusted king went over to Lachish's lifeless body and spat on it. He then requested, "Give his kingdom to me, and I will take care of this rebellion."

"For now, in order to maintain the peace and safety of Araz, it will fall under the administration of my office. We need to know everyone involved within Lachish's kingdom before we can appoint a rightful heir to his throne."

"Why would you do such a thing? Neither he nor his family deserves to rule with us. They've forfeited that privilege," said one king, while many others shouted in agreement.

"I understand your displeasure over Lachish's actions. I, too, share your sentiments, but for the sake of stability, we cannot make any sudden changes that would awaken the masses to this incident. As you will read in your files, the official statement will be that King Lachish had fallen ill and passed away. Publicly, he will be honored for his service to the UAK. We reported the incident at the temple as a power glitch in the taps due to a recent quake; allowing several ohemas to wonder into a civilized area."

"So just like that!? We forget his treason? No one will know of the despicable acts he did?!" yelled another disgusted king.

"It will not be forgotten by this council or me! However, it will be hidden from public view. Even though it appears the resistance is growing slowly, can you imagine what the useless masses would do if they thought, for even just a moment, that a successful rebellion was on the rise?"

"They would riot in the streets!" shouted one council member.

"Precisely! I do not wish to take this route, but we have no choice. It's being forced upon us. Until we can root out Lachish's entire network and crush this rebellion, it is the path upon which we must walk. It's the only option at this time."

King Vullkal asked, "Are you saying it's now too late to contain it quickly?"

"Unfortunately, my dear friends, I believe that Lachish has unleashed a force that is far more sinister than the Apostates."

"What do you mean?" asked King Burnkal.

"Scrawled on the side of the temple in Tuval were the words, *Loha Has Returned.*"

"Loha?! He's nothing but a myth. A false story told to cadets to get them fired up."

"Don't be so quick to call it a myth young king. There are plenty of you here who knew the real Loha, and the legends surrounding him. In fact, we have a report from one of our agents in the field who heard from a reliable source that an udam standing over eight *ama* in height killed an MSS trooper. That he accomplished this seemingly impossible feat with nothing but an ordinary head of a plow," Zeul said as he looked down at the report in front of him. He continued, "I'm not one given over to ancient prophecies, but if this is true, then I'm concerned and you should be as well."

At the end of Zeul's statement, many of the older kings who knew the truth of Loha became white as a sheet. While others slowly sat down trying to catch their breath, one discouraged king could be heard saying, "No, no, no...not..."

Chapter 28

"Loha! I need to speak with you please. There is something I need to tell you before...," said Pernel as he tried to catch up to Aaranon as he walked briskly through the village.

"Not right now Pernel," he said dismissively.

"It's been almost two odes since the raid and you have been avoiding me this whole time. Now that we've returned I think it's time you and I speak."

"Now?! You want to talk now?"

"Yes, please."

"Fine! Let's talk. Follow me." Aaranon yanked Pernel into one of the hideouts near the village so no one could hear them speak.

"You don't have to be so rough. Why have you been avoiding me?" he asked, looking perplexed.

Without warning, Aaranon belted Pernel across the jaw, knocking him to the ground. He then grabbed him by the collar and pulled him close as he spoke through a clenched jaw, "Your wife was removed the day before our arrival. Care to tell me how that coincidence happened?"

After wiping the blood from his mouth, he said with a confused look, "I don't know! Don't you think I've been asking myself that same question? That's one of the reasons why I wanted to talk to you, but you've been doing everything you can to avoid me."

"You don't know! Well...how convenient. Those troops moved in like they were waiting for us! Like they knew we would be there!"

"If you're insinuating that I...," replied Pernel before being interrupted.

"And what about the trigger devices?"

"I told you they were working when we left. How is it...?"

"And why the DACK did you do nothing but fight me on every decision I made for that operation? You don't have the knowledge it takes to run a mission like that."

"You're right Loha; I don't! But how is it that you do?"

"Excuse me?! All of you asked me for help and then you question how I give it?"

"I'm not questioning the help you provide; I just want to know how it is that you know so much about energy taps, UAK policies, and temple operations. If I'm not mistaken, I think I should be the one asking you all the questions."

Aaranon let go of Pernel and picked up a scanner. "Stop trying to change the subject! You're hiding something. When I asked you to scan the others for tracking devices I don't recall you being scanned."

"Me?! What about you? The only thing that makes you *legitimate* around here is some shriveled up old geezer who stared at you for a moment and then gave you his so-called blessing."

"Come here," Aaranon growled as he tried to scan Pernel.

"No! Why don't you give me that scanner and I'll check you out," replied Pernel as they fought over the scanner.

Aaranon tried to wrestle the device out of Pernel's hands. "Tell me again how you got this equipment."

"I told you! Ballac and I got it off that no good agent Sayir. You can ask Ballac yourself, you dacking idiot!"

Aaranon now had Pernel's arms locked behind his back. "Agents don't have cloaking devices as standard issue. So, again, where did you get it?"

"Forester my ass. How is it that a simple forester like you can come to know so much about government operations?" Pernel said as he tried to free himself from Aaranon's grip.

Aaranon, after an intense struggle, was finally able to scan the back of Pernel's neck as well his hands. "Well, how is it that a simple farmer can figure out the code and sequence pattern required to kill an MSS with a complex trigger?"

"Satisfied, O' mighty Loha? So-called savior of us poor defenseless bottom-feeders."

After confirming that Pernel didn't have any tracking devices on him, Aaranon immediately jumped up and said, "Get up!"

Rolling over on his back, Pernel looked up at Aaranon and said in a more somber tone, "Why? Why should I get up? I'm getting this sinking feeling that I have nothing to get up for. My wife is gone. Do you get that? GONE! My children feel they've lost all hope of ever seeing their mother again. We all have a target on our backs. And now you are growing paranoid; you, our only dacking hope. So tell me O' great one...why should I get up?"

Aaranon just stood there for a moment looking at Pernel. He thought to himself, *He's right, what do any of us have left to look forward to? We are all dead.*

After several moments of just staring at one another, Aaranon finally reached out his hand to help him up. "Come on, get up."

Once he was up, Aaranon handed him the scanner. He then turned around and revealed the back of his neck which still bore the scar. "Go ahead, scan away."

Pernel could see the scar, but nothing showed up on the scanner. Aaranon then turned around and presented his hands, pointing to the scar on the back of his left hand. Pernel scanned again, but nothing was there.

"I was in the UAK forces for several years. I learned all I could before I left," Aaranon said as he held out his hand requesting the scanner from Pernel.

Handing the scanner back, Pernel said, "My great-grandfather...he was a servant to an upper-class UAK soldier in a time before they populated the whole dacking world with those mingled creatures. His master taught him many things.

He did so, because he believed that every udam should be free. So...in turn, he taught me when he was allowed to come visit. My father wanted nothing to do with it, and forbade my great-grandfather from teaching me. He was afraid, just like most of us. But I wanted to know, and my great-grandfather thought the knowledge might be useful someday."

"What happened to him?" Aaranon asked.

"His master was unwilling to sacrifice him for a mingled servant. He held off as long as possible. They gave him some leeway because he was a soldier, but one day they came for him. They sacrificed him like an old celab," he said.

"So why didn't you just say that before?"

"I could ask you the same Loha. Why didn't you mention your background?"

"Really? You think a bunch of farmers would help someone like me? An udam who worked for a government known for killing...peasants?"

"Peasants? I think it's fair to say that now you are lower than a peasant by our benevolent government standards."

Aaranon gently placed the scanner back on the shelf. "Well...yeah...but now we're all peasants together, huh? So I guess we have no one else but each other."

"So...if I may ask, without getting punched again, why did you avoid me all this time?"

Aaranon tried to think of an answer that would satisfy his question. Should he tell him of his concern that someone within the group, or the village, might have reported them to the UAK? Naturally after that brief altercation, Pernel now realized that Aaranon suspects someone of being a traitor. Or should he say how he feels? That he failed them, and if it weren't for the ground quake and the mysteries re-charging of the device; they would not have made it. Clearly, however, he cannot mention that his father is looking for him.

"Loha, did you hear me?"

"Yes, I heard you. Obviously...," he said while pointing at

Pernel's bleeding lip, "...I had my suspicions. I didn't want to say anything until we had returned all the maidens and got back to your village."

"Yeah, but we all had our suspicions. It did seem odd that only two guards were on duty for the entire temple, the devices not working; along with my wife not being there..."

"That's the other thing."

"Yes, I know. You think this has something to do with me, but I assure you....," replied Pernel as he looked away from Aaranon.

"No, it isn't that. I just...I feel like I let everyone down... especially you. No offense, but none of you were ready. I was impatient. I didn't prepare you like I should have. Plus, I underestimated their response." Looking down and away, he then said, "I always seem to underestimate him."

"Him? Who's him?"

Realizing his slip, he recovered by saying, "Sorry...I meant... them, the UAK. I think it's safe to say that we can no longer use the trigger devices."

"Why do you say that?"

"Because that is what they taught us in the military. Once your opponent knows your weakness, you either change your strategy or you discard the weakness."

"What do you think they will do?" asked Pernel.

"If I were them, I would remove the explosive devices from the MSS troops and look for another method of control."

"But doesn't that put them at greater risk? If the MSS troops know they aren't in immediate danger, isn't it possible they could rebel? Because, are they not part udamé?"

Aaranon rubbed his shaved head, trying to think of a solution. "I honestly don't know. I do know that we will have to come up with another way to stop them if they get close. Because if we don't, there isn't much we can do to defend ourselves."

"That's the other thing I wanted to talk to you about. I tried to talk to you earlier, but since you kept avoiding me, I decided to move ahead and..."

A sense of dread came over Aaranon. "What do you mean move ahead?" he asked with a stern voice.

As Pernel was about to explain, Ballac knocked on the door with a great deal of enthusiasm. "Both of you, get out here, you've got to see this!"

"Well dack, I guess you'll have to see for yourself," Pernel said as he gingerly walked by Aaranon and then out the door.

Chapter 29

After walking far outside the village, Aaranon was flabbergasted as his eyes landed on the forest floor; covered with udamé as far as the eye could see.

Aaranon looked out from behind a tree and addressed Pernel sharply, "Pernel, who are all these people and why are they here?"

"They're here to see you. They heard about what you did."

"What I did? I almost got us all killed," he said as he continued to look at the sea of people from all across the region.

"Loha, you led a small group of farmers and hunters up against the mighty kingdom and won!" Ballac said enthusiastically.

"Won? If that's what you call winning, I hate to see what losing looks like to you. No, this is too much. We can't have this many people here; it draws too much attention. Besides, I don't know these people. How can we be sure none of them are spies?" he said while pointing to the crowd and gritting his teeth to try and compose himself.

"Loha, we know them. Our families go back hundreds of years. We invited them here. It was Pernel's idea. Pernel, didn't you tell him?" Ballac asked, looking confused.

Aaranon looked at Pernel as if he was going to knock his jaw off.

"Ah...that's the other thing I wanted to tell you," he said while scratching his head.

Aaranon didn't reply but only gazed at Pernel with his eyebrows climbing his forehead and sporting a disingenuous smile.

"Well, you see...after the word got out that the not so

mythical Loha had returned...many began asking questions."

"Oh yeah! Who the dack put that on the side of the temple?" asked Aaranon as he looked back and forth between the two.

"I guess that would be me again," Pernel said as he slightly raised his hand. "I had a moment of..."

"Stupidity!" thundered Aaranon.

"I was going for enlightenment, but sure, that works. Anyway...since they're here now, we can't just ask them to leave."

"Yes you can." Aaranon sat down and put his hands on his head. He was feeling overwhelmed, frustrated, perplexed, and tired all at the same time.

"Loha, I don't think you realize," said Ballac.

"Realize what?"

"The revolution! It has begun, and we can't stop it."

"Revolution!? What revolution? I only committed myself to helping you rescue your families so you could in turn help me. In the beginning, I said we cannot go up against the UAK. Don't either of you remember that? Our best hope is to hide in the shadows and not get caught."

"Loha, this began when you killed that MSS trooper in the pub. You are the heboram killer like the Loha of old. What did you think people would say?" Pernel asked.

Aaranon's mind began to race as he tried to think through his predicament.

What the dack did I just do? I only wanted to rescue Dihana and Darham. I should have kept walking that day I saw Pernel. Better yet, I should have just kept going south to Nahim.

Why did I lie to these people? Am I becoming like my father? Is this how it starts? The end justifies the means? If I try to back out now, then what? If I leave, then I may never get to see her again.

It isn't any different than when I was a noble. I can't run around it. I can't avoid it. So now I have to go through with it?

"Loha? Are you in there?" asked Ballac while snapping his fingers. "We can't keep them waiting."

"No...we wouldn't want to do that," Aaranon said sardonically.

"That's the spirit! Now let's go give these people some hope!" said Ballac.

"Are any of your friends good at building sarcophagi? 'Cause we're going to need them...lots of them."

Looking over at Ballac, Pernel said, "Maybe the hope will come later."

"Much later," replied Aaranon.

"Oh...and one more thing. They think you are the original Loha. Alright then! Let's not keep them waiting, shall we," Pernel said as he moved out in front, leaving Ballac behind and Aaranon way behind, dragging his feet.

***

Staring at his massive frame, Aaranon slowly reached out his hand, "And who might you be?"

In a deep gravelly voice he said, "Sdra'de, Elder of the Criz tribe." He then leaned over, picked up Aaranon, and gave him a hug that left him breathless.

With a voice barely above a whisper, he squeaked out, "And what do you do?"

Setting him back down on the ground, Sdra'de cupped his hands to his mouth and made a call like that of the ananin. Soon after, the den of a thousand wings, beating against the wind, drew near to them. As the skies grew dark, Aaranon could see a multitude of ananin descending from the trees. As they drew near, he could see udamé riding gracefully upon their backs.

"Amazing," Aaranon said absently as he stood in awe and

admired their aerial acrobatics.

"We have waited a long time for your return. We are at your service," Sdra'de replied as he and the other members of his tribe bowed their heads.

Recalling Rohu's heralding adventure when he rescued Yohan, Aaranon said, "Well then…it is an honor to meet you."

"The honor is all mine, Loha."

Pernel then directed Aaranon over to another who was fully laden with multiple EB weapons. "Loha, this is our good friend Aveed bamé Denn. As you can see, he knows his weapons."

Aveed reached forward, grabbing Aaranon's forearm and then smacked his back a few times before he began his fast-paced diatribe against the nobles. "It is a fine dacking pleasure to meet the one and only heboram killer. Aveed the Great - as many call me - has been waiting for this dacking day all my life. The day of reckoning is upon the nobles, and I will finally get to play my part in this fabulous dark comedy we are about to enact.

"It is curtain time for those dacking uppity uppers. The day of our redemption is at hand! The end is near for those dacking wastes of skin, those unprofitable, gangly, ostentatious, blathering buffoons. Whatever you need in your arsenal of killage, I'm your udam. I have first, second, and third generation EBs, class I, II, and IV cannons - shoulder mounted, side mounted, and ground mounted. You want a put a manual round up the hind end of one of those tight-cheeked bloated fat bottomed magistrates? I have the weapon and the arsenal for that. If you want to separate that crown from one of them fat headed pus buckets, I can calibrate any and all EBs to do that faster than you can say…Aveed the Great."

"Well…that's quite impressive. How did you come by these weapons?" Aaranon asked apprehensively.

"Well now…Aveed doesn't give away all his secrets! But let me say this…,"he said while drawing nearer to Aaranon, "… from one legend to another, I have contacts on the inside that want this revolution more than you, I, or anyone here, can imagine. There is so much dissension in the ranks that the whole UAK is like a stack of leaves. All it's going to take is a strong wind to blow through there. And as I stand here looking at you, I can see a storm of enormous proportions about to blow. You pickin' up what I'm laying down?"

Aaranon just nodded at Aveed; as he could feel the enormity of what he and his inexperienced band of rebels had just unleashed. The anger he felt towards his father was nothing compared to the years of oppression experienced by everyone who were subject to the nobles. What started out as a simple rescue mission was only a catalyst that triggered a rage that had been brewing for eons.

Pernel then moved onto a somewhat rotund fellow, wearing large makeshift glasses that he continually pushed back onto his protuberant nose. "Loha, this is Drahcir bamé Kram. Uh… he…uh…well…I think it'd be easier if I just let him explain what he does."

Looking up at Aaranon, Drahcir began, "I would estimate that you are approximately five *ama* in height. Not that that is pertinent in any way shape or form, but I was under the distinct impression that you were closer to eight *ama* in height. Legends, of course, are always an embellishment of the truth, similar to my esteemed colleague here who likes to refer to himself in the third person."

"Hey! Shut up you bloated ohema dropping! I can blow your rotund pair of boulders, that you call a hind end, across this forest in the time it takes Aveed to field dress four EB class III cannons," he said as he lifted his chin to look down his nose at Drahcir.

Drahcir commented to Aaranon, "Makes you wonder if he's overcompensating for something, doesn't it?"

"Overcompensating?! If you don't shut up, Aveed is gonna pull out his *overcompensation* and knock your chubby rear end all the way to Heock. Overcompensation? The only way you can find your privies is with a bright light and some spelunking equipment," Aveed said as he walked away.

"Anyway...as I was saying before the walking mouth interrupted. I'm not given over to legend or myth. What I am given over to, however, are facts. The skill I wish to bring to your merry band of marauders is my knowledge of, shall we say, peering into the UAK's crystalline mind. From what I've been able to gather, they are very aware of your presence and are highly concerned about the movement you have spawned."

Growing slightly concerned over Drahcir's ability to gather data from the MCR, which holds information about Aaranon's past, he asked, "What do you mean?"

"It appears that the legends of you, or the one they call Loha, have spread among the UAC. They've been loading their breeches at the sound of your name. Your return, whether actual or contrived, has caused a great deal of concern; and for that, I am truly grateful. Therefore, I care not if you are the true Loha. It only matters that they believe it to be so."

Trying to take it all in, Aaranon's concerns began to mount with every conversation. Not only was he becoming a symbol of hope for them, but he was also moving headlong into the very thing he was warned against. Maintaining his composure, he just shook Drahcir's hand and thanked him for joining their group.

***

While directing Aaranon from one tribal leader to another, Pernel spoke briefly about where all this could lead. "Can you imagine Loha, what if the whole world joined our cause?"

"I'm still trying to understand what *our* cause is."

"I understand that we started out to only rescue our families. And I swear that I will do all in my power to help rescue yours. But look at what you've started...," he said as he motioned to the large gathering. "I know this isn't possible, but imagine if you were of noble birth. You could overthrow this tyranny and set up a new government that's ruled by the people."

Aaranon gave him a cautious look; questioning within himself Pernel's motives. He replied in a muffled tone so that only Pernel could hear him, "Pernel, I'm not...of noble birth. I'm no one. In spite of what you've told these people, I'm not the original Loha. I was only trained by him. You're turning me into a symbol of hope for them. I only agreed to help rescue families! Families in *your* village. That's all I offered. But this... this goes way beyond that."

"I understand that Loha, but things have changed. We can't abandon these people. Yes, I did embellish a little..."

"A little?"

"Alright...I'll admit I went overboard. But, I think you need to hear their stories. What my village has experienced is nothing compared to what others have faced because of this tyranny. For example, look over here. Come and meet Mara. Maybe she can change your mind."

They both walked over to a beautiful young wudam, with hair black as night, and eyes as green as the forest. She was standing in the midst of a pack of areyas that obeyed her every command.

"Loha, this is Mara, she is the last of her tribe."

Aaranon reached forward to shake her hand when, all of a sudden, a large male standing quietly next to her batted Aaranon's hand away with its massive paw, growled like thunder, and revealed two oversized teeth.

"Umba no!" she said as she stroked his beautiful golden mane. "Forgive him please. He is quite protective."

"I can see that," replied Aaranon.

"It is an honor to finally meet you," she said while bowing to him.

"Please, that isn't necessary. I'm not worthy for others to bow to me."

"I bow not in submission, but in gratitude. You see, for as

long as I could remember, at night my people would gather around the fire in the evening while the elders spoke of you."

Wanting to hear more about his beloved friend Rohu, he couldn't help but ask, "And what did they say; if I may ask?"

"They spoke of a day when you would bring freedom to our people. Day and night they sought for nothing but justice. Their desires live within me. I long for the day when the nobles are dragged through the streets and hung from the trees. I want to see them pay for what they did to my family."

A sinking feeling came over Aaranon and he wanted to restrain himself from asking, but he couldn't help himself. "What did they do to your family?"

"One of the noble families wanted to mine the land that our tribe inhabited for centuries. My people bled and died for that land; we were not going to move just because they wanted it. So they sent in their troops. Like cowards, they came at night; killing everyone and everything in their path. Babies were ripped from their mothers' wombs. Daughters were raped in front of their fathers before they were slaughtered. Sons were beheaded in the streets. I only escaped by hiding under my younger sister's body. I waited there for days for them to leave."

Knowing the dreadful answer, he asked anyway, "Which noble family?"

Looking up at him through a lock of hair that draped across her expressionless face, she said, "Quayanin."

Aaranon could no longer contain the hatred and disgust for the name his father longed to protect. Looking deep into her eyes he said, "They will pay for what they have done to you."

"I know. That is why I'm here to serve your cause."

"And what cause might that be?"

"Vengeance."

Chapter 30

"Dihana please; we need to go now! Besides you don't need all that stuff."

"Don't you think I know that Darham! If you want this to look...," she paused, realizing her words might be heard by others. In a more composed tone she said, "If you want me to look fabulous as your new Betwudam, then I need all these things for our trip to Heock."

Realizing she almost slipped he backed off a bit. "Fine, but can you move just a little bit quicker?"

"Since you sent the servants away...My Lord...why don't *you* come over here and help me pack," she retorted, growing frustrated with every word.

"I haven't a clue what you need for our *excursion*," said Darham as he sat on her bed, watching her throw various items into her luggage.

"You're right; you don't know what I need, so sit down and wait until I'm finished and ready to go."

"Alright! Just keep it moving."

While Dihana walked across her room to gather more items, Darham noticed a cylinder underneath some of the clothes. Reaching over, he pulled it out and inquired, "What's this?"

As he started to loosen the top of the cylinder Dihana immediately dropped the clothing in her hands and ran towards Darham. Before he could get it open she tackled him on the bed; sending both of them tumbling to the floor.

"What the dack is your problem Dihana?"

Whispering into his ear, she said, "Don't open that, just play along." Climbing off of him she said out loud, "Those are just some pictures I had of Aaranon that I'd like to take with me.

They remind me of him and I just prefer that no one touch them."

Looking confused and concerned, Darham looked up at Dihana and said in a calm voice, "Alright, I'll be sure to not touch them."

"Thank you. They are very…precious to me," she said as she hid them deep inside her luggage.

She continued, "I have just a few more things to pack, and then we can go."

Before Darham could speak, a knock came at the door. Walking over, he opened the door to see an older cadet standing at attention.

Looking very concerned, Darham asked, "Uh…where is cadet Micah?"

"He's been stationed to patrol the halls. I've been assigned to you for your trip My Lord. My name is cadet Leo," he said as he saluted Darham.

"Oh, look Dihana, Micah has been replaced by Leo. What do you think of that?"

Looking perturbed and exhausted, she dropped the clothes she was carrying onto the bed, swiftly walked over to the cadet, and then kicked him in his privies with the sharp end of her shoe.

Looking over at Darham, she said, "It's just an awful thing that Leo is experiencing stomach problems. I guess you'll have to call the commander and demand cadet Micah." Turning to look at Leo writhing in pain on the floor, she continued, "Isn't that right Leo?"

"Yes Your Highness," he said in a high-pitched squeal.

Dihana stomped back towards her bed. "Alright then…I'll go back to packing, since I have to take care of everything."

***

"I'm so sorry to hear about cadet Leo falling ill. He's an excellent soldier, and he would have been more than adequate to watch over you, Your Highness," said Micah to Dihana as he piloted Darham's sky runner away from Quayanin castle.

"Oh…I'm sure he would have been wonderful. But hey, how fortunate that we get more opportunity to talk. Oh, and remember, you can call me, Dihana."

"I'm so sorry Your High…I mean…Dihana. I forgot."

"In fact, from now on, I don't want you to call me Princess, or Your Highness, or anything like that. Just call me by my first name. Also, I spoke with Darham, and he wants you only to call him by his name as well. So…no titles."

"No titles? Not even among other nobles?" he asked, looking confused.

"Exactly! You see, Darham and I, we want to…oh how can I say this…we want to experience life as…uh…non-nobles," she explained with a flurry of hand motions.

"Non-nobles? Is that a game you play, Your High…Dihana?"

"Yes! Yes, it's a game we nobles play from time to time. It helps us better understand those who serve us. It helps us to better lead."

"Well…it's the first I've ever heard of it."

"Oh yes, we do this all the time. We dress up like the lower-class and pretend that we're one of them. It's very rewarding for us."

"Alright…if you say so," he said looking a bit confused.

"And you're going to do this with us. You need to remove that uniform off your gentle yet rugged exterior," she said as she paused while looking him over.

"Dihana?"

"Yes my dear," she whispered with a glazed look in her eyes.

"So…you want me to dress as a peasant?"

"A peasant? OH! Yes! A peasant," she yelped, bringing herself back to the moment. "All three of us will dress as peasants, and we must play the part. Darham can explain it to you more," she said while leaning against the flight console to get a better look at him.

She continued, "So, since you know what we do for fun, what is it that you do to relax? You know, when you're not protecting us defenseless nobles from those terrible Apostates."

"Fun? Well...I'm on duty all the time, so I don't have much time for leisure."

"They don't let you get away, or take a day off every once in a while?"

"They used to, but ever since they increased security, we've been required to serve every day. Besides, my father always said that rest was for the dead," he said as a deep sadness washed across his face at the mention of his father.

"But didn't you have the opportunity to do anything fun? Even as a child?"

A smile came across his face. "My mother, when Father was away, would read to us stories about our ancestors. She always told us to hide them in our hearts and to never let anyone know about them."

"Can you tell me?"

"I suppose I could. My mother has since passed, and I have no desire to see my father, as you know."

"Yes...that is something we both share," she said while she gently placed her soft hands upon his shoulder.

Growing flushed at her touch, he looked into her eyes for just a moment. He then looked back at the flight console and began, "Before she told us a story, she would have my sister and I go into my room. Once she closed the door, she would pull out these old looking scrolls from behind the wall. I guess she thought they were safe in my room."

"Scrolls?" Dihana inquired, wondering if they were the same as hers.

"Yes, she said they came from her ancestors. She was very careful with them. They were old and ragged, and you could tell pieces were missing, but she was always very careful when she opened them."

As she was about to ask Micah a question, Darham yelled from the forward cabin, "DIHANA!"

"WHAT!?" she yelled back, hating to be disturbed.

"I need to see you, please!"

Looking at Micah, she straightened herself up and said, "Well…at least he said please."

Micah just smiled as she moved out the door. Just before she completely turned the corner, she looked back to see Micah staring at her beautiful frame. As she smiled back, Micah quickly faced forward; trying to hide his embarrassment.

Slamming the door behind her, she said to Darham as his back was turned to her, "What is so urgent that you absolutely had to see me right now?"

Turning around with the scrolls in his hand, he asked, "What are these; because these sure don't look like portraits of Aaranon."

Chapter 31

Once the servants left his office, Zeul walked over to a large bookcase that was against the wall. After pulling on two different books in a particular sequence, a section of the wall moved back and to the side; revealing a small passageway. As Zeul crossed the threshold, he lit a candle to brighten the hall and then pulled a lever; closing the door behind him.

It didn't take long before he came to a small room with an old hand carved wooden chair in the center of the enclosed space. He gently placed the lit candle on a table reminiscent of those found in most lower-class homes.

As his eyes adjusted, he could see his coveted carvings on the wall; images that reminded him of better days. There was a word engraved on the corner of one of the carvings and Zeul gently rubbed his finger over the well-worn grooves created by the hand of a young child.

After pulling the carving down from the wall, he sat down on the chair and gently rubbed the arm rests just as he had done, centuries ago. In a time before there were kings and kingdoms, he rested in that chair after a long, hard day in the fields. He then blew out the candle, sat back, and waited for the tears to fall, just as they had so many times before.

***

It wasn't long after he exited the secret room that Ravizu arrived as requested.

Ravizu, with Lilith in tow, strolled into Zeul's office. "Hello Father, you wish to see me?"

Zeul motioned for Ravizu to enter. "Yes, please, have a seat.

Your servant, however, will wait outside."

Turning to Lilith, Ravizu said while caressing her hair, "Wait outside for me my love. I won't be long."

"Yes My Lord," she said, bowing her head slightly.

Once she had left the room, Zeul continued, "I have a task for you. I need for you to find Darham and Dihana."

"Find? What do you mean...find?" he asked.

"They left over seven days ago and have not been heard of since. They were to arrive here at Heock with a military escort five days ago, but they never did."

"I'm guessing you've tried their farspeak?" Ravizu retorted sarcastically.

Looking slightly disgusted, Zeul continued. "It appears their tracking devices and that of the cadet's are no longer functional. I'm beginning to worry."

"Father, if I may, this sounds like one of your...*plans*. Are you sure you don't have them secreted away somewhere, and this is all just a ruse to further solidify your power? Because if it is, I would be perfectly fine with it. You know me, I always love a good plan."

"I hate to disappoint you Ravizu, but no, this isn't my doing."

"Well then...what are your thoughts? Does this have anything to do with Dihana and those scrolls?"

"It's possible. But to be sure, I need someone I can trust to handle this. If it has to do with the Apostates, then I believe they are headed south, towards Tarshish. Take some of your hired mercenaries to track them down. I don't want anyone from the UAK involved. Understood?"

Grinning sinisterly, Ravizu asked for further clarification; hoping to be rewarded with a bit fun at Dihana's expense. "Understood. What shall I do with them, once I find them?"

"Aside from what you want to *do* with Dihana, I want you to bring both of them here to me; unharmed, and untouched."

"That leads me to believe that I may use whatever force is necessary to bring them back," he stated while raising his eyebrows and growing excited over the possibility of creating some havoc.

"Within reason Ravizu. I don't want to draw attention," Zeul said as he sipped on his glass of wine.

"Do you want me to keep you up to date on my progress?"

"Do not use any farspeak. I don't want anyone listening to our communications. Just find them and bring them back."

"Well then...I will delay no further," he said as he walked out of the office.

***

Lilith soon joined him as he walked down the hall. "We're going to have some fun with both of them before we return aren't we?" she asked, a smile beaming across her radiant face.

"Of course! Father wishes otherwise, so we'll just be careful not to leave any lasting marks."

"Excellent!"

"It's like...you know exactly what I'm thinking," he said while they both laughed maniacally.

As they walked down the hall, they passed by a small, older udam who stood in the shadows, unbeknownst to anyone.

***

When Zeul stood up from his desk and started walking towards the center of the room, the sound of crackling ice could be heard. As the lights dimmed and the room grew colder, a bright light emerged. Zeul bowed down and said, "My Lord, how may I serve you?"

"I see that Dihana and Darham have taken it upon themselves to leave. What a shame. However, I've been informed that they're moving to the south; to the forests of Tarshish," Halail said.

"That's my estimation as well, My Lord. I have sent Ravizu to find them. Have I done wrong?" Zeul asked as he trembled before Halail.

"What you have done is good. You need them to return if you wish to draw Aaranon in, and complete what you've started."

"I commanded Ravizu to bring them to me, and to use whatever force is necessary without drawing attention."

"Splendid. I believe Dihana and Darham are seeking an old enemy of ours. An enemy whose time for elimination is at hand."

"Who is this enemy My Lord?"

"You know about whom I speak."

"But…but I thought we could not touch…," Zeul remarked before being interrupted.

"Have your desires changed, Zeul?"

"No, My Lord. I have been loyal to you since that day."

"Good, excellent. Then you will need to find a way to eliminate our enemy," Halail said.

"Forgive me My Lord, but, in the past, I have tried to eliminate him and his grandfather, but to no avail. Our greatest enemy protects them."

"Well, it seems that you're at an impasse aren't you. You desire to ascend, but you're constantly unwilling to do what is necessary. Have you forgotten what I have offered you? Have you forgotten why you were chosen to be the ruler of the whole world?"

"No My Lord. I have not forgotten."

"Hmm…I thought you to be a worthy apprentice. I have allowed you to ascend to your present status without having completed the proper requirements. I am only allowing this because of your father. Perhaps I have misjudged. Maybe you are not able to do what is necessary to ascend," Halail said.

"No, My Lord! You have not misjudged. I will do whatever is necessary!"

"Good! Then it is settled. You will eliminate that so-called comforter - that giver of false rest - and bring Dihana and

Darham back. But what will you do when Aaranon returns for them? Will your love for him cause you to seek the alternative; the lesser of what I desire? To do so would only anger those brothers who have already made their sacrifice. But as the head of the Brotherhood, you can choose what you wish. However, it will only demonstrate your weakness."

"I promise you My Lord, I will do what is necessary," replied Zeul as he lowered his face even further to hide a tear that fell from his cheek and onto the frozen stone floor.

"Well then it's...WHAT!!" Halail growled before he disappeared abruptly.

Soon after, the doors to Zeul's office swung open. He clamored to his feet and said, while looking shocked and perplexed, "How did you get in here?"

"Come now old friend. You know how," Elder Isma said as he slowly walked into Zeul's office, carrying a small leather bound book.

Chapter 32

"Dihana, are you sure Darham knows what he's doing?"

"You know, I've been asking myself that same question for years," she sarcastically replied.

From the vantage of their secluded table, Micah looked around the lower-class pub while Darham spoke to an elderly wudam in the corner. "I understand we need to play these roles and don't get me wrong, the first ode was interesting...fun even...but after three odes I have to say, this has me greatly concerned."

She placed her hands on his and addressed him in a more serious tone. "Micah."

"Yes," he replied as he interlocked his fingers with hers, caressing them ever so gently.

"I think it's time I made a confession."

"A confession? Wha...wha...what kind of confession?" he stuttered, hoping she would say those words.

"Alright...here it goes. Darham wants to keep up the ruse, but I feel you deserve to know the truth," she said while growing nervous over how he would react.

He pulled back and let go of her hands. "Ruse? What do you mean?"

To hide her words she pulled in close and whispered into his ear, "We aren't playing a game, we needed to get away."

"Get away? Get away from what?"

"Our lives were in jeopardy. If we stayed much longer at the castle, we would have been killed," she said while looking around the room to make sure no one heard them speak.

"You're not talking about the Apostates are you?" he said as he realized there was more to their ruse.

"No."

He began to panic as he realized the only other ones they might be running from. He tried to keep his voice at a whisper, even though he felt like the more appropriate tone would be a shriek. "Wait a moment, are you running from the kingdom? If so...then I'm putting us all in jeopardy. They can track my whereabouts!"

"Actually, they can't."

"What do you mean they can't? I had a tracker put in me when I joined the military."

"I know, but Darham removed it."

"He did? When? Wait...*how*?"

"Remember that night when we played the drinking game? Well...I should have told you that Darham and I have had more practice than you when it comes to drinking; especially Darham."

Micah felt the back of his neck and asked, "What? What have you done?"

"Micah, I need for you to remain calm right now, please," she said as she now regretted telling him.

"Remain calm? Remain calm!?" he said through the grit of his teeth.

"Yes, please. I need for you to remain calm, or you will draw attention to us."

"Don't you know what you've done? I can't go home anymore! My career is over. My life is over. Oh no! They will think that I abducted you. They will kill me when they find me!"

"Micah please; I need for you to stay quiet. We can't...," she said before being interrupted.

"We can't what Dihana!? You dacking nobles are all the same. You will ruin whatever lives you please."

"That's not it Micah; we needed someone we could trust. Darham did a background check on you and..."

"He did what? So you profiled me? Made sure that I would be a useful idiot for your escape?"

Darham looked over to see Dihana and Micah arguing.

"Please Micah, it started out that way, but I wanted to tell you because..."

Micah stood up to look down on her. "Because why? You wanted to hurt me more? Why did you play this game with my life and then tell me now, when it's too late for me to return?"

"I wanted to tell you because...because...I...," she said through a multitude of tears before Darham interrupted.

"What the dack are you two arguing about? I'm trying to finish up a deal over here and you both are ruining it for us."

"Oh...you mean like how you both ruined my life," Micah said as he got into Darham's face.

"Listen here soldier, you need to calm it down right now or..."

"Or what Darham? You're just a prince on the run from your father."

Looking to Dihana, Darham asked, "What did you tell him?"

"He needed to know the truth," she said softly as she continued to wipe her eyes with the old garments they wore to hide their identities.

"Tarsis Dihana, why did you tell him?" whispered Darham.

"Because I love him, alright! I love him, and I can't lie to him anymore," she said while she turned away.

"You what?" Micah said in a softer tone as he walked over to her and bent down on his knee to then hold her in his arms.

She held him tightly. "I'm so sorry Micah. I never wanted to hurt you. I don't want to lie to you anymore. I don't blame you if you want to turn us in. I'll tell them it was all my fault. I don't deserve you."

"Dihana?" Micah asked, trying to get her to look at him.

"What?"

"Dihana, please, look at me."

As he looked up at her, he placed his hands on her cheeks; removing the tears with his thumbs and brushing the hair out of her eyes. He said, "I wanted to hear those words for so long."

"You mean the ones about lying to you."

"All of them. Especially those same words that I wanted to say to you."

"Well, go on, say them to her finally," Darham said as he looked at both of them with a smile.

"Yeah, do what he says. Say it," she said as she grabbed his cheeks.

"I love you. From that first day I met you outside your mother's room, I knew you were different."

"You like drunk wudamé who want to rip off your sack and use it for a purse? You're a little twisted Micah," she said with a mild grin.

"Well, I do love that. But it was your humility. You had every right and reason to look down on me, but you didn't."

"Why would I? You and I are equal in the eyes of the Creator. How could I ever look down on you? I love you."

"I love you too," Micah said before they passionately embraced one another.

Feeling uncomfortable standing next to the two of them while they kissed, Darham said nonchalantly, "Alright...it's time we get a move on. We need to be out of here before nightfall. I have our next destination. I got it right here. In my hand. Yes... right here, in my hand...ummm...I'll be waiting outside."

Chapter 33

Lilith continued to pound the dead mercenary's head into the side of the ship as Ravizu sipped his wine and ate some fruit.

"Alright, that's enough. I think he and the rest of our confused crew understand the point I was trying to make," Ravizu said as he slowly stood up from his seat on his sky liner. Looking over at Lilith, he instructed her, by thought, to throw the body over the side; letting it fall to the forest floor, a few thousand *ama* below.

He then continued to address his group of exhausted mercenaries, "Now, what have we learned in the last three odes? Can anyone take a guess?"

"Lord Ravizu, we have looked...," one disheveled udam said before Lilith silenced him with her EB.

"Apparently, he didn't understand my rhetorical question. It's a simple answer really. Let me see if I can put this succinctly. We don't know where...THE...DACK...THEY...ARE!" he screamed while throwing his chair over the side of the ship.

"You," Ravizu said while pointing to an udam, "Go after my chair."

The udam just sat there, looking confused. Looking over at Lilith, Ravizu commanded her to throw him overboard.

As he screamed all the way down, Ravizu continued while looking at Lilith, "I loved that chair; it was a gift from King Persiel. I sure hope our friend finds it for me."

Turning back to look at his wearied crew, he continued, "Apparently, the clandestine approach to finding them isn't working. I think it's time we employ other methods in our search, don't you?"

Pacing back and forth while rubbing his chin, Ravizu

pondered how to find them.

"Ravizu?"

"What?" he asked as he looked at one of the frightened udam.

"Ravizu, can you hear me?"

"Who said that?" Ravizu demanded as he looked back and forth at his crew.

"Who said what My Lord?" Lilith asked.

"You didn't hear...," he said, before pausing to leave the room. Once he was by himself; he continued, "Who is this?"

"This is Mishna. You don't need to speak out loud."

"How the dack are you doing this?" he thought.

"There is something you should know about your father."

"There is something you need to know about me, you sniveling piece of lint! I'm going to hunt you down and kill you slowly!"

"Your father had you implanted with a newer undetectable farspeak. I saw it when I performed your surgery."

"He did, did he? Well then...go on," Ravizu thought in a slightly calmer tone.

"As I suspected, he also put a farspeak in Lilith. I've gone ahead and reprogrammed both yours and hers. He can no longer hear your every thought. I've also reprogrammed them both with false tracking information."

"What do you want?" he asked.

"I want to return to my father. Zeul order him to have me exterminated because I knew too much. My father would never do such a thing unless he had been ordered to do so. I don't know what Zeul is planning, but he apparently wanted to keep track of you and Lilith at all times."

"What makes you think I won't go to my father and tell him what you've done?"

"Because...I've been watching and listening to your thoughts for the past several odes. I know what you want, and I can help you get it."

"Hmm...go on," Ravizu thought as excitement began to build.

***

"Where are we going My Lord?" Lilith asked as they entered the elevator that would take them down to the tunnels.

"I want to see if what my new friend says is true. If it isn't, then I should not be able to enter the sacred library. There would be guards there waiting for our arrival."

"Library, My Lord?"

"There has been a nagging question on my mind for a very long time now; why does my father want Dihana and Darham kept alive? They serve no purpose. It would be far more prudent to extinguish them immediately. But, for some reason, he wants them protected."

"He must want them for something," she said.

"Correct, but what is it?"

"This library, what information are you looking for?"

"To become a full member of the Brotherhood, you must pass a series of tests. I've heard that one of those tests requires a sacrifice of some sort."

"Like those in the temple?"

"Similar, but apparently it must be something, or maybe someone who is very important to you; but I'm not certain. I've only been sealed. I'm not yet privileged to know all their secrets."

"Do you think we will be able to enter?"

"Since this library holds their most coveted knowledge, if Mishna is truly working for me, and my father is unaware of our location, then we should be able to enter unimpeded. Then maybe I can find something to help me understand why he wants to keep them alive."

"But what of your master, Halail? Will he allow you to enter?" she asked.

"Good point! Hmm...I guess we shall learn quite a bit on this little excursion," he replied while pulling her closer.

***

As the doors opened, prompting them to cease from their passionate embrace, they looked out and observed that there was no one there to stop them.

"Hmm...I'm guessing this is a good sign. Let's continue and see what may come," he said.

Exiting the elevator, they moved down the dimly lit hewn tunnels until they came to the massive doors that secured the library.

"How do we enter?" she asked.

"I'm not sure; there are no handles to speak of, I...," he said before the doors opened of their own accord.

Looking at Ravizu with a sinister grin, Lilith said, "What do you make of that?"

"I don't know if that is good or bad. But let's find out," he said as they entered the long room that stretched for several hundred *ama*.

Looking down the long corridors that rose high up into the darkness, they could see ancient books and scrolls of all ages, piled one on top of the other.

"Where do you begin My Lord? It could take years to find what you are looking for."

"Well, I suppose we just...," was all he could say before a large, leather bound book slid off the shelf, gently settled to the floor, and then opened up before them.

He picked it up from the ground and set it on a small table near them. "Ah...I'm going to say we take a look at this one."

"What does this mean My Lord? Is your master helping you?"

"It might be a bit too early to say, but I think that's a reasonable assumption."

Once the book was open and they were able to examine its contents, Lilith asked, "What is this writing?"

"I don't recognize it. I wonder if there is a way to translate the text," he said while looking around.

"My Lord, look!" she yelped.

The words on the page began to change in front of them. At the top, it read; *Offering Of The First Born*.

As Ravizu began to read, another book fell from the shelf behind them.

"Grab that," he said.

After she had brought it to the table, he could see that it was the genealogical record of his family. As he perused the pages, he made an interesting discovery.

"Would you look at that! The Brotherhood...really is a brotherhood. It's an actual family," he said.

"Who is this person?" she asked, pointing to the only name at the top of the page.

"According to his chart, he is my grandfather. But wait! I thought he was only a myth...a legend." he said looking baffled.

"A myth? Who is he?"

"I'll explain that later. But notice this...Zeul was the son of a concubine when his father was of an old age. That might explain why we don't have any family records," he mused.

"What do you mean?"

"Children of a concubine are seen as less."

"I can understand that," she said.

"Uh...yes...I'm sure you can," he said dismissively.

"Your grandfather's name. It's similar to Quayanin," she noticed.

"Well...being the son of a concubine might explain why Father took a different name. Or maybe he wanted to hide his heritage. I'm not entirely sure."

Confused, she asked, "If he was considered less, then how could he rise to be the Alemeleg?"

"Order of selection is based on bloodline purity. If there were no pure bloods by a wife, then the son of a concubine would be next."

Pointing to a section of the chart that appeared crudely removed, she asked, "What's this here? It looks like your father had another family before yours, but the information is no longer there."

"Interesting," Ravizu said as he moved his fingers over the removed section.

"I see this is a surprise to you. So what *do* you know of your heritage, My Lord?"

"Virtually nothing. There are only a few sarcophagi in the family mausoleum; most of them are the ones I put there. Especially that detestable Aaranon and his constant seeking of the truth. The other three were easy to kill, but Aaranon was much harder to...wait a moment?"

"What?"

Moving down the page of the first book he found what he was looking for, "Look what it says here of the first born."

For the sealed to ascend, he must pass his first through the fire. If the first however be greatly beloved, then the sealed must redeem the first by three; two who are beloved by the first, and another that is next.

"Redeem by three? What does that mean, My Lord?"

"My father said that I was the one he waited for all his life. *The one to rule by his side*, he said to me. But what if I'm not the one he wants?" he asked while thinking to himself, *This is what I get for believing a master betrayer.*

"I don't understand the two, but the next, isn't that you, My Lord?"

Ravizu turned around to look at the bookshelves and then back again at the two books; pondering the significance of why they were given to him.

"What is it My Lord?" she asked.

After pausing a moment to collect his thoughts, he closed the books and put them back in their place.

"Let's go," he said.

"Where to, My Lord?"

"To the location where Aaranon supposedly died."

***

The two servants of Halail closed the massive library doors behind Ravizu and Lilith. Turning around and seeing nothing but the doors closing of their own accord, they quickly made their way back to the elevator.

"Don't you find this most peculiar?" asked one of the servants.

"I do not always understand Halail's requests, but I do know to question him would be unwise."

"But doesn't this seem contradictory?"

"How do you mean?"

"Are not Ravizu and his father working towards the same end? Why pit them against one another?"

"Maybe Halail knows that their goals are not the same. Maybe one of them is changing their allegiance. Besides...what do we care? Our only goal in all of this is to break the line forever. These pathetic imbeciles are nothing but stepping stones for our use."

"Changing allegiance? Ahh...that would make sense."

"Yes it would. Let us go. Halail will want to know of their progress."

Chapter 34

"Are Pernel's forces in place?" Aaranon asked as he nervously paced back and forth.

"Let me confirm," Drahcir answered as he manipulated his mobile CR console once again. "Yes. His teams of three have arrived at their respective energy taps and are awaiting your signal," he said while rolling his eyes.

"What about our eyes in the sky?"

"Sdra'de and his team report that the heavens are clear. No Battlecruisers, Armadas, or Dargons in sight except for a few patrol ships."

"I find that a bit unnerving, don't you?" asked Aaranon as he continued to bite at his nails.

"It would if it contradicted the information I gathered from the MCR. They shifted most of the patrols in this area for combat training. That's why we picked this sporting arena, remember? I believe your band of marauders have prompted the kingdom to double down on its preparedness."

"Let's hope that's the case," Aaranon said openly as he then thought to himself, *I can't help but think he knows I'm coming.*

"Give me the status again on Ballac."

"One moment," Drahcir said while letting out a short huff. "As reported earlier, Ballac and his team have made it to the prisoners' quarters. They are ready to push up through the floor…on your signal."

"And what of Aveed and his team?" Aaranon asked.

"He's about to fill his breeches with excitement, but again, they are waiting for you."

"He knows that I only want military targets hit, right?"

"I believe he is fully aware of your wishes. Whether or not he and his band of crazies can refrain from shooting everything that moves and breathes is yet to be seen."

"And what of Mara, is she prepared?" Aaranon asked as he continued to pace.

"According to her previous check in, she and her golden posse are fully awaiting your orders," Drahcir said once more, growing slightly agitated over Aaranon's apprehension.

"What about Pernel? Did he remember to tell his team to disengage the new locks entirely? If he doesn't do that, the taps will immediately reset, and they won't be able to get back in."

"Loha, may I speak freely?" Drahcir asked while pushing up his prodigious spectacles to look up at Aaranon.

"Sure," he said dismissively as he looked out over the sporting arena from his distant vantage point in the forest trees that came near to the city.

"For almost six odes we've been preparing for this. We've been over this about three times now since the teams have been in place. I can assure you, everyone, or should I say, almost everyone is ready to go. I believe the question you are not asking is; are you?"

Aaranon looked down at Drahcir and then back toward the arena. He crossed his arms and thought to himself; *am I?*

"Not to push you, sir, but our window of opportunity is closing."

"I know, I know," Aaranon said in a matter of fact tone. He grabbed hold of the farspeak and raised it to his lips, "Teams ready?"

"Ready," came their unanimous response.

"On my count. Three, Two, One, Go."

***

"RUN! Back to the forest!" yelled Pernel as he tried to carry Benohi, the only member of his crew that was barely alive.

"Did you see that!? Those dacking ships came out of that

black hole in the sky! What are they?" screamed Ballac in a panic while hobbling along next to Pernel with only a few of his team members left.

"I don't know! Just shut up and run!"

"Oh no, LOOK OUT!" yelled Ballac as several Dargons began firing upon them from above.

An EB burst struck next to Pernel, knocking him to the ground leaving Benohi cut in half by the blast.

"Help me, we can't leave him," he yelled out as he tried desperately to put his friend back together.

"Look at him he's dead. We can't take him; we have to go." Ballac cried as he tried to pull Pernel off of his beloved friend's body.

"I just can't leave him like this!"

"We have no choice Pernel. We have to go! Let's go, NOW!"

Soon, Mara came rushing up next to them while riding on the back of an areya. She yelled to Pernel and the others, "Jump on; they can move faster than you!"

Each of the few remaining udamé jumped onto one of her areyas to be swiftly taken out of the city and into the forest. Looking back, Pernel could see several Dargons setting down next to the sporting arena. The forces quickly surrounded the prisoners, preventing them from escaping.

Ballac and his team were able to release the prisoners by leading them out through a tunnel system that lay underneath the arena, but they were unable to lead them to safety. As Ballac watched, they methodically killed each of the prisoners.

Looking up, Pernel could see Sdra'de and his tribe forcing the Dargons to chase after them; allowing the few who were left to escape back into the forest. Unfortunately, there were far too many ships in flight.

"Here they come again!" yelled Ballac as he pointed to several Dargons moving in their direction. Within moments, the Dargons began firing at their position. With every passing moment, the bursts came closer and closer.

"What's that?" yelled Pernel, pointing to a large ohema running in their direction.

"The ohema?"

"No, the thing on its back!" he asked.

Within moments, large manual rounds from an old cannon were being fired from a turret mounted on the stampeding creature's back.

"You want some of this?! Here ya' go, you stupid mother dackers! Make sure you send the Alemeleg all my love! Tell him to kiss this you blowhard butt smacking buffoons!" screamed Aveed as he fired his cannon up toward the Dargons that were chasing his friends. One by one he was able to knock out most of the ships that were attempting to remove the battered and torn remnants of Aaranon's crew.

It wasn't long, however, before one of the Dargons was able to fire a damaging burst into the ohema, knocking it to the ground. Aveed was soon airborne and about to meet an untimely demise with the side of a kyder tree. All of a sudden, Sdra'de swooped in, letting his ananin grab hold of him with its two claws; treating him as gently as a new born.

As the remnant of the failed mission was nearing the edge of the forest, they could see Aaranon running to meet them. Waving him back as she rode towards him, Mara tried to get him to stop, but he just kept coming.

Pernel reached out his arm to grab hold of Aaranon; prompting him to jump onto the large golden beast with him. With both of them now seated firmly on its back, they raced further into the forest. From above, they could see MSS troops being dropped over the sides of the mysterious ships that were completely sealed and had no outer decks.

The MSS troops jumped from tree to tree at breakneck speeds, moving like a swarm of harbes, drawing nearer to their position. It was becoming readily apparent that they were not going to make it, but they had no other option than to run.

Some of Sdra'de's tribe was able to fly through the trees, but they were soon met by MSS troops leaping from the massive branches; striking them with their deadly claws which killed them swiftly.

Aaranon waved Sdra'de and his crew away, trying to tell them to get to safety, but Sdra'de continued to do all he could to save the battered remnant who ran for their lives.

From out of the corner of his eye, Aaranon could see a small white wind runner moving rapidly through the trees. He couldn't focus on it long because of the innumerable amount of MSS troops coming at him and his crew. They blanketed the forest floor and covered the trees at every level; halting their forward progress.

Because of the density of the woods, the Dargons were unable to move below the forest canopy. Sdra'de and his remaining tribe members landed next to the remnant, unwilling to seek refuge above or try to save their lives.

As Aaranon stood in the middle, surrounded by his crew, he turned in a complete circle and saw every square *ama* of the forest covered in MSS troops.

Aveed moved next to Aaranon and said, with the most serious tone he could muster, "I have enough explosives strapped to me to take out half of these bastards and most of the surrounding forest. Just give me the word."

Sdra'de and the others looked at Aaranon and nodded in agreement. They were all willing to fight to the end.

Soon after, the MSS troops started to edge closer; moving at a slower pace. It appeared, this time, the UAK was not willing to negotiate. When they were just over two hundred *ama* away, they quickened their pace, running as fast as they could towards the rebels. Their monstrous growls and the beating of their clawed feet against the ground drowned out every noise of the forest.

Aveed turned to Aaranon and somberly said, "Just tell me when."

Aaranon held up his hand for him to wait until they were

closer. Aveed maintained his steady hand on the trigger, waiting for the signal.

All of sudden, however, the white wind runner flew in and came to a rest over the top of the rebels. Immediately, the MSS troops ceased their forward progress and then stood at attention. The silence was now far more frightening than the din that had preceded it.

The tall figure on the wind runner, his face hidden by an all-white helmet, gently stood up and pointed towards the city. The MSS troops immediately took off in the direction the mysterious udam pointed leaving Aaranon's crew standing there dazed and befuddled.

Soon after, they heard the screams of the UAK forces as the MSS troops began to devour them one by one. Any soldier left on the ground found a swift death.

The rebels continued to watch in astonishment as the MSS troops then boarded the Dargons and flew towards the Armadas and Battlecruisers. Some boarded the ships to annihilate the crew; while others fired upon the fleet, destroying both ship and crew.

As the astonished rebels looked at one another with complete confusion, the mysterious udam slowly landed the wind runner and walked toward Aaranon.

He then took off his helmet, reached out his hand and said; "Forgive me for my late arrival. I believe you are the one they call Loha."

Having learned, the hard way, to not trust so easily Aaranon refused to extend his hand. "And you are?"

Pulling his hand back, the stranger said, "My name is Mishna."

Chapter 35

"Princess Whihany. There is a young wudam in the foyer who is here to see you," the mingled servant said.

"I'm not expecting anyone; so who is it?" Whihany replied, in a frustrated manner.

"She only said that she had a message for you from Lord Ravizu."

Finally! Maybe now this waiting game can end, she thought. "Send her in immediately."

"Right away Your Highness," the servant said, bowing before leaving the room.

***

"So, has Ravizu finally decided to uphold his end of the bargain? My father will be greatly pleased to see me in my beautiful wedding…," Whihany said before being interrupted.

"Let us forget the small talk, shall we? I'm here because he has another mission for you."

"Another mission!? But I did everything he asked and now it's time for him…"

"Aaranon is still alive," Lilith said as she slithered around the room after closing the doors behind her.

Upon hearing those words, Whihany dropped the glass of wine she was holding and began to shake. Trying to compose herself, she continued, "That is just…preposterous! I was there at his funeral. Why would he think that…that…that Aaranon is still alive?"

"He wants you to use your…magic as you did before."

In spite of knowing the answer, Whihany still asked, "Magic?

What do you mean magic?"

"My Lord is now fully aware of what your father has taught you; seeing that he has not a single son to pass on the knowledge of the Brotherhood."

"Don't be silly. A wudam isn't allowed to know such things," Whihany said as she now feared for her family as well as herself.

"Tsk, tsk, my beauty. The proper response should have been, *what Brotherhood?*"

Realizing her revealing response, she only grew more impatient with Ravizu's pet. "So what? So what if my father tells me a little here and there? That means nothing."

"A little here, a little there? Come now. We both know your knowledge is far more than a little here and there. However, if the brother kings knew of it, then it would be…shall we say… most unpleasant for you and your family," Lilith said as she continued to glide around the room.

"So what does he want me to do now? Lure Aaranon into false love like before? What purpose will that serve?"

"He has his reasons," Lilith said as she examined several items on a small table in the room.

"Well…I care nothing for…Aaranon. I was glad to see him… die," Whihany said as she turned her face away to hide her true feelings.

"Then you will gladly see him die again. You realize this isn't a request, correct? Or have you forgotten what My Lord holds over you?"

"Holds over me! Has he forgotten that I willfully gave myself to him with the knowledge that we would be together!" she yelled, recalling the night Ravizu repeatedly destroyed her chastity.

"Willfully you say? Not if he was swayed by a sorcerer as powerful as you, correct?"

"What? He wants to threaten me and my family? Well then…you tell *My* Lord that there is no need whatsoever to browbeat me or my family, for I know where my loyalties lie."

"Good then. So you understand?"

Whihany moved out onto the balcony of her room to get further away from Lilith. She tried to prevent her from seeing a tear that was welling up in her eye.

"Yes. Yes, I understand. I will do anything for my...love. He knows that," Whihany said in a dismissive manner.

"Are you sure?"

"Sure? Sure of what!? I don't appreciate this constant barrage of accusations and threats from his pet."

Lilith growled at that insult. "Are you sure that you are loyal to Ravizu?"

"I just told you my loyalties are with him," Whihany said as she turned slightly to look back at Lilith.

"So, I can assure My Lord that you were never in love with Aaranon?" Lilith asked as she slowly moved closer to Whihany; causing her to back up against the railing that prevented her from plummeting over the edge.

Looking backward to glance at the great distance to the ground below, Whihany turned to look Lilith in the eye and said through the grit of her teeth, "Never."

While gently brushing Whihany's hair, Lilith said, "Good. My Lord would be so upset to know if his future wife's loyalty was... in question."

With her hands grasped firmly on the stone railing, Whihany replied, "Here's what you can tell *My* Lord Ravizu."

Leaning forward, Whihany passionately embraced Lilith for several moments.

After taking a bit of time to compose herself, Lilith wiped away the smudged lipstick and said, "Well then. I will be absolutely sure to give him that message."

Whihany sneered. "You do that."

"One more thing," Lilith said before exiting the room.

"What?"

"Just to be clear, you say nothing of this to anyone, not even your father, understood?"

"I can assure you; My Lord has nothing to worry about," Whihany said with a look of confidence.

***

"Servant! Get in here and clean up this mess before I sacrifice your worthless life!" Whihany yelled as she poured a strong drink to calm her nerves once Lilith had completely exited the castle.

"Yes Your Highness," replied the frightened mingled servant.

Looking at her servant with disgust, Whihany began to take out her frustrations on it.

"You dacking creatures are so fortunate, aren't you? You don't have to deal with such things as love or compassion...or regret, do you? I see you move about these halls, without a care or concern for a mate. Someone who can love you unconditionally. Someone to speak to you like you were a real person and not a toy to be played with, or a celab to kick around. Someone who can truly see you..."

"I'm sorry Your Highness, but...,"

She shrieked, "Did I say you could talk?"

As the mingled servant cowered, Whihany unleashed her pent up rage.

"You can only talk when I say you can! You don't move unless I say move! And you can't love ANYTHING that you care about unless I say...," she said before she began to cry uncontrollably.

She continued in a softened tone, barely above a whisper, "Just get out. Leave it, and get out."

Walking over to the soft couch next to the fireplace, Whihany laid herself down and cried until she fell into a deep sleep.

***

"What is this my daughter; why are you so sad?" asked King Davison as he caressed his daughter's hair while she slowly woke up.

"Oh...Father...I didn't know you were here. I'm sorry. Give me a moment while I clean myself up," Whihany replied.

"There is no need for that. Of all my daughters, you are the most beautiful. What is troubling you?" he asked.

"It's nothing. I just wasn't feeling well, and I needed to lie down."

"I may be old, but I'm not blind. What is wrong? You can tell me. Are you growing with anticipation? Waiting for your marriage to Prince Ravizu? I can speak with the Alemeleg if you wish."

"No, it isn't that. It's just...uh...,"

"Go on my dear."

She whispered, "I know I'm not supposed to speak of the Brotherhood when we're here."

While King Davison slightly shook his head to indicate she should cease speaking, Whihany continued, "I need to tell you something."

"If anything needs said, we will say it once we go below."

Leaning close to his ear, she whispered, "Zeul lied to us. Aaranon is still alive."

"What?!"

"It's true. My beloved, Lord Ravizu, sent a messenger to inform me. I believe he only wishes the best for us, Father."

"Say nothing else. I will take care of this," King Davison said sternly, and then walked out of her room.

Turning to look outside, Whihany gazed into the forest and thought to herself, *Wherever you are sweet prince, please...run. Don't ever come back.*

Chapter 36

"Loha! Where are you going?" Pernel shouted as he ran to catch up with Aaranon.

"I need to take care of something Pernel. Just go back."

"Let me go with you. I can help."

"Tarsis Pernel! I don't want your help. I need to handle this myself."

"Well...based on what you're carrying, it looks like you don't plan on returning."

"Dack Pernel, I don't have to run everything past you before I do it."

"Will you please stop so I can talk to you face to face instead of like this?"

Aaranon stopped but didn't look back. Letting out a sigh, he said, "I'm going back to get my family."

"Now!?"

"I can't keep doing this."

"Doing what?"

Aaranon stared at Pernel for a moment. "You just don't let go do you?"

"No. So what is it you can't keep doing?"

"Putting you and everyone else in jeopardy! I might as well go at this alone. At least then I know that I'm the only one in harm's way."

"You can't just leave us. Not now! We've come so far," Pernel said, panic rising in his voice.

"Come so far!? What are you seeing that I'm not? I'd sincerely like to know because all I see is bloodshed. Do you know how many we lost in that last raid?" Aaranon demanded, looking tired and remorseful from head to toe.

"Loha, that isn't your fault!"

"Stop saying that! I'm tired of hearing that! It *is* my fault! I should never have asked any of you to help me. This isn't going to work. I only offered to help rescue your families. I didn't sign up for taking down the whole dacking government."

"How could we have known about those ships coming out of those...holes in the sky?"

"That's my point! They have better knowledge, training, and weaponry than we could ever have, or even hope to have. It should now be abundantly clear to you, and everyone else, that this isn't going to work. And who knows what they will do now after what Mishna did...or whatever his name is," Aaranon replied as he threw his bag down and took a seat on a large fallen limb.

"Listen, I just heard from Drahcir that the UAC is recalling all of their MSS troops. That one incident was enough to scare them into taking drastic measures."

"Yeah, I know. But they will then come up with something else that will make it impossible for Mishna or Drahcir or me or you or anyone else to penetrate their defenses. And all of THAT...means more of US...die! Don't you get it? Do you want that on your conscience? Because I can tell you, with no uncertainty that I don't!"

"Alright, well...here's something for *you* to get. They're killing us anyway. You've seen the temples, and the sporting arenas, and the hired thugs who wander the forests, fishing for souls to sell. So do you get it!? Our people are dying anyway! So why can't their deaths mean something? Why can't they die for something meaningful? Why do they have to die for the pleasure of those dacking nobles and upper-class?

"Let me tell you something Loha, their deaths brings hope. And not just for me, but everyone who has committed themselves to this cause. It means something to everyone out there who are still trapped and unable to be set free. So, I can't sit back and watch you walk away because you don't want to get any more blood on your hands! Their blood is on mine as well, and we will remember them!"

"I never said I would forget them," Aaranon said as he continued to look down at the ground.

"Then don't abandon them! We need you. We need what you stand for."

"What I stand for?" Aaranon chuckled. "What I stand for? Apparently, all I seem to stand for is running. You're the one they should look to, not me."

"Loha. You can't leave us. Please...not now," Pernel pleaded.

"Why? Give me one good reason as to why I should stay and continue to lead you to death's door."

"Well...because...you seem to be the only one who knows where that door is," he replied with a sarcastic grin.

"Dack you," Aaranon chuckled as he punched Pernel in the arm.

"Alright, joking aside...we need you Loha. We need you because you're the first, in a very long time, who was willing to run up against the kingdom gates; and not just run against them, but move them ever so slightly. I know we've all lost a lot, but so much more has been gained. And there is much more yet to be gained. But it will all be for nothing if you leave."

"Yeah."

"Yeah...what? Yeah...you're coming back, yeah...there has been much gained, yeah...Pernel you're always right, and I should just listen to everything you say," he said, trying to lighten the mood.

"I always seem to find myself caught between doing what's right, and doing what is convenient. But this time, I don't know what's right."

"You speak of right as if there are absolutes. But there are no absolutes in this world, Loha. We have to look at what is before us and determine what is the right thing to do *now*. I say, the right thing to do now is to come back and lead us."

"No absolutes?"

"Nope, well…that's my opinion at least," said Pernel.

Aaranon couldn't resist some mild teasing at Pernel's expense. "Are you absolutely sure?"

"Absolutely!" he replied, realizing the absurdity of his statement.

"There is another reason," Aaranon said, recalling Rohu's warning.

"And what's that?"

"The real Loha - the one who is better than me - he warned me."

"Warned you? About what?"

"Vengeance," Aaranon said.

Pernel started to grow slightly agitated. "What about it? Because…isn't that what this is about? Getting back our families and making sure that these dacking rulers get a taste of what they've forced down our throats for hundreds of years?"

"He said that vengeance, once it has run its course, would turn on you and destroy you."

"Well, let me tell you what I think. It's my love for my wife and sister that drives me to find them. But vengeance? Vengeance is what gives me the strength to do it. Without it, I would be like the rest of these dacking mooks who sit back and wait for their turn to die. Not me Loha. If I need vengeance to find my family; then that's the tool I'll use to do so and I'll just deal with the consequences later."

"That's what I'm afraid of; the consequences. What comes after this? I've seen what vengeance can bring."

"Oh yeah? And I've seen what doing nothing can bring. At least I know I've tried. I tell you what Loha, leave the vengeance to me and the others, while you come up with some other reason to justify our taking down this dacking kingdom."

"You know that many of those who serve the kingdom are just like us."

"What the dack do you mean? They are nothing like us!"

"That guard at the temple who almost killed me; he begged

to see his wife and children."

"So."

"So? He wanted the same thing we want; to be with his family."

"Don't tell me you have sympathy for those uppity uppers. You know what they do to our udamé and wudamé in those temples, right?"

"Yes, I know!"

Frustrated, Pernel asked, "So what are you saying?"

"I'm just saying it doesn't matter if you're a noble, an upper-class, a lower-class, or the lowest person on this planet; everyone's been hurt in some way. To think that our cause is greater than another, or that our vengeance against them is different than their vengeance against us; it's...well...absurd."

"You're making no dacking sense whatsoever; do you know that? How could you have sympathy for a dacking noble?! They do *not* deserve to live!"

"Then who does Pernel?! Who deserves to live?"

"We do, Loha!"

"Why? Why do we deserve to live, and they deserve to die? What gives us the right to say that? Because, from where I stand, we have done *nothing* different than what they have done to us."

"There you go again, talking as if there are absolutes. When we kill them, it's righteous indignation. They deserve to die for what they have done."

"Yes, they do deserve punishment, but don't we also deserve punishment for our crimes? How is it that two sins can equate to righteousness?"

Pernel started laughing and shaking his head. "Wow...how much have you been talking to Isma?"

"What?!" Aaranon asked as he watched Pernel double over in laughter.

"You're starting to sound like a dacking Apostate."

"I'm not joking. I'm serious."

"Alright, you're serious. Just give me a moment," Pernel bowed before Aaranon, "I didn't realize I was in the presence of The Holy One."

"Shut up, you idiot. I didn't say I was holy; I just wanted to explain."

Once Pernel stopped laughing, he continued, "I get it."

"Do you?"

"Yes, I get it. You don't want to commit the same crime against them that they've committed against us, right?"

"Right!"

"So why don't we commit different crimes? Then that will even it out. There! Problem solved," Pernel said as he continued his laughter.

"I hate you," Aaranon said with a melancholy smile.

"No you don't."

"Yes I do. I'm trying to explain what's going on in my head, and you keep turning it into a joke. I'm serious; this is serious. It bothers me enough to want to turn around and keep walking out of here."

"Look, we will do all we can to abstain from *iniquity*, alright? But you know, as well as I do, that things might go bad."

"Yeah, I know."

"So...are you coming back?"

He paused for several moments as he looked back and forth trying to decide what to do. Turning to Pernel he finally said, "Every time you talk me into something, things seem to go wrong."

Pernel reached for Aaranon's arm to pull him off the limb. "There he is! I tell you what, when we take down the UAK, and you declare yourself the new and improved Alemeleg, or whatever name you want to give yourself, then you can hate me all you want."

"Fine! As long as I get to hate you."

"Don't worry, I'm sure there will be plenty of opportunities for you to hate me in the future," Pernel said in a more serious tone. One that went unnoticed as he pulled Aaranon in to give him a hug.

***

As they were walking back, they could see a lonely udam walking through the forest. Ducking behind a tree, they watched and observed; wondering if he was possibly a scout looking for them.

"Who do you think he is?"

"He doesn't look like one of us," Aaranon said.

"Do you want me to take him out? Just to be sure," he said while pulling out his bow.

"No…wait. Stay here,"

"Loha…what are you doing?"

"Just stay here," Aaranon said as he moved from out behind the tree and made his way toward the stranger.

***

With Pernel far enough away, Aaranon was able to speak with the stranger without being overheard.

"Aaranon? Is that you? Is that really you?"

"Shhh…yes, it's me. It's good to see you Yosef."

"Oh my goodness! I did not expect to see you here. You look so…different," he said while hugging Aaranon for a few moments.

"Yes, things have changed, haven't they?" he chuckled.

"In more ways than one."

Looking back at Pernel to make sure he couldn't be heard, Aaranon turned to Yosef and said, "I'll explain everything later, but for now, do not call me Aaranon. Call me Loha."

"Well...that explains a whole lot," Yosef said as he continued to be amazed to see him alive.

"Can you tell me how Sohan and Alyya are doing? I feared for them and you after I learned the truth of my father."

"That's why I'm on the run. The three of us left the city when we heard of your death. We figured if they could get to you, then they could easily get to us."

"What happened to them?"

"We were able to get out of the city but, soon after, we were caught. They took us to this underground tunnel system. I've never seen anything like it. When we got down there, they put us in this prison with many other people. One by one they took people away and then I didn't see them after that."

"So how are you here? How did you make it out?"

"As you know, I worked for the Mosan family. When I was down there, I could tell they built most of those structures in the tunnels. I'm guessing your family carved the tunnels while the Mosans did the rest."

Aaranon thought about that for a moment. "Sounds about right."

"Well...to make a long story short, my knowledge of how they constructed those rooms made it possible for me to navigate through the substructure underneath. I tried to get to Sohan and Alyya to get them out, but it was too late; they were gone."

"Do you know where they are?"

"I have no idea. Once I made it out and to the surface, I ran as fast as I could."

"So how did you end up here in the forest?"

"You haven't heard?" asked Yosef.

"Heard what?"

"You, or should I say, Loha, has turned the whole world upside down. Everyone is talking about you, and I mean everyone - the nobles, the upper-class, the lower-class, and everyone in between. I, for one, wanted to come and join the fight. So, here I am. How can I help?"

Before Aaranon could speak further, Pernel came up from behind and said, "I figured that all was well, so I decided to join you."

"Uh…oh…Pernel…uh…this is Yosef. He's a friend of mine from…"

"From?" Pernel asked with a skeptical look.

Yosef extended his hand to Pernel and said, "Loha and I, we go way back."

"Way back? So how do you know each other?" Pernel asked.

"Uh…well…Yosef's son and I served in the military together. We were part of the same unit. Yosef came out to join us."

"Oh! That's good. Well, it's a pleasure to meet you Yosef. My name is Pernel."

"Pernel? You know, you look very familiar to me," Yosef said as he examined Pernel's facial features carefully.

"Uh…no…I don't think so. I must have one of those faces I guess," Pernel replied as he, too, examined Yosef carefully; knowing he knew him from somewhere but unable to place his face.

"Loha, one of the reasons I came to get you was because Drahcir heard the Alemeleg was going to make an announcement about the new security measures. He was able to pull up a visual of the announcement, and he suggested we take a look at it," Pernel said.

"Well then, let's all head back and see what we have to fight against next." Aaranon led the way as the three of them returned to the hideout.

Chapter 37

They were only three odes away from the annual festival celebration to the Ayim, and there was a looming threat of an open war against the kingdom from the growing resistance. The UAC decided it was the perfect time to introduce the next generation of MSS troops, as well as the increased security measures. The UAC determined that a public demonstration was necessary to adequately emphasize the futility of a rebellion. The council chose the central sporting arena in Heock as the venue through which they would make their point abundantly clear.

As Zeul moved to the podium in the center of the arena, a place upon which an Alemeleg never before stood, the crowd grew deathly silent, awaiting for his mysterious announcement. He gently removed the crown from his head and set it directly on the ground; a profound and significant statement of humility.

He began once the multitudes' fervent applause subsided. "My fellow citizens of Araz, almost four years ago, our beloved King Darvan spoke during a time of great despair. The kingdoms have never been more united than they were at that time. Unfortunately, it took a great affliction to forge our hearts together into one. I must say, with the utmost humility, that tragedy has, once again, found its way back into this beautiful land we call home."

Gasps and whispers were heard coming from every corner of the arena.

Zeul continued, "This time, however, it is no longer the Apostates; for we have removed them from the face of Araz. No longer shall they return."

The crowd immediately leapt to their feet to applaud the defeat of their enemy; an enemy they believed to be the source of all their problems. As Zeul held his hand up, the ebullient crowd became silent once more.

"Behind every victory, however, there is always a new battle and a new enemy. It has come to our attention that a small band of rebels has decided that they no longer wish to participate as peaceful citizens of Araz."

Hissings and curses echoed against the stone walls of the arena for several moments before Zeul was able to continue.

"The Apostates fought for an antiquated way of life. These rebels, however, are nothing but ordinary robbers and thieves. They take what belongs to you - the faithful citizens of Araz - and use it for their greedy, personal gain. They have disrupted our tranquility for their own selfish ambitions."

Zeul paused once more, allowing their anger and resentment to build into a fever pitch.

"You have all been through so much, and many of you have shown concern over the new security measures. I, too, share your concerns, but I can assure you that we have no desire to limit your freedom nor your privacy. However, in order for us to keep you safe and maintain peace, we needed to take drastic measures. Measures we hope…no…that isn't correct…we *will* remove these measures in the very near future, once we eliminate this pointless threat."

Many of the audience members and those watching through the visuals at home or on the public displays, began to applaud once more; believing their Alemeleg had their best interests at heart.

Watching from Drahcir's console many of Aaranon's crew began to chide and sneer at Zeul's colorful lies.

"I can't wait to shove a hot iron rod up his rear end and watch it burn the bottom of his throat," Aveed said.

"Security and Freedom? This blowhard might as well exchange the words security and freedom for war and slavery.

They are the robbers and thieves, not us! He cares nothing for the people. We are the ones who actually care," Hena said with many responding in agreement.

"Why do these idiots believe this drivel?" asked Ballac.

"They don't honestly believe. They only do what they're instructed to do out of fear," Sdra'de said.

Once the applause subsided, Zeul continued, "As it was with the Apostates, so it is with these new rebels. We did not invite this tyranny. It was forced upon us. Therefore, it will be made abundantly clear that we will not stand for their acts of cruelty against this benevolent institution. An institution that has stood for several hundred years."

Aveed pointed an EB at the console. "What a mother dacking load of smack this wrinkled ohema privy is shoveling out of that lie hole of his!"

"If you would, please, holster your weapon before you do anything you would regret," requested Drahcir without looking at Aveed.

Aveed continued waving his weapon at the console. "Just put me within a few hundred *ama* of that piece of dung and I'll easily put a few hundred rounds through that condescending face of his!"

"Everybody, please keep it down, I want to know what he's planning," Mishna said while Aaranon remained silent as he watched his father increase his grip on the world.

"As your Alemeleg I have decided, along with the unanimous wisdom of the council, and by the gracious leading of the Ayim, that it is time for us to introduce to you the third generation of MSS troops that will continue to maintain peace and safety throughout all of Araz."

Once Zeul finished speaking he lifted his hands toward the heavens. Soon after, the skies filled with numerous portals opening, allowing Battlecruisers, Armadas, and Dargons to pass through. As the crowds watched in amazement, seeing the portals for the first time, creatures of all kinds leaped over the sides of the ships. Some had wings like that of an ananin and flew throughout the sky; while others leapt to the floor of the arena. Other portals opened in the midst of the arena, allowing numerous MSS troopers, and other kinds of mingled creatures outfitted with mechanized weapons, to come running through.

Pernel looked panicked. "Mother Dack! Did you see that!?"

Ballac turned to Aaranon, "They came out of thin air, just like they did before."

Aaranon watched calmly as he realized that some of these third generation MSS troops were the same ones that came through the portal at the monument to the first udam. He also noticed that the energy taps were not interrupted; indicating another source of power was being used to open the doorway.

"How did they do that?" demanded Sdra'de.

"Dack that! Look at those weapons! I've got to get me one of them. It's like the whole uniform is a weapon. That is a dacking thing of beauty," gushed Aveed with growing excitement over the advanced weaponry.

"If you wouldn't mind, I need to hear this," Mishna said with a mildly smug attitude.

"Well, well…looks like pretty boy here is a bit scared at what he sees. Are you telling me, that when you were a prisoner in their labs, you never saw one of those things?" asked Aveed with his all too frequent short temper.

"What!? Don't you believe me? I told you; they held me captive against my will. They wanted me for my mind and not my brawn you halfwit," he said while looking down his nose at Aveed.

"Halfwit? Halfwit?" came Aveed with his hand ready to pull his weapon.

"Yes…halfwit! Are you deaf as well?"

Breaking his silence Aaranon yelled, "SHUT UP! I need to hear this!"

Zeul continued once the crowd settled, "As you can see, there is no place safe for them to hide. And neither will they see us coming. As an added measure for your safety, every citizen of Araz will be offered a small implantation that will identify you as a faithful citizen in good standing. This implant will insure that none of these new protectors of the kingdom will ever come near you or harm your precious loved ones."

"Come on people, stand up! Your lovely leader has just put you into further bondage; you sack-licking suck ups!" yelled Aveed as he watched the once joyous crowd give a lackluster applause for what they just heard.

"Quiet!" Aaranon commanded with his eyes glued to the screen.

"As a demonstration to ease your minds, we will now bring forward a group of rebels; caught in the act. Some of them have the implant while the others do not. Let's see if you can tell the difference because none of them know who has the implant and who does not," Zeul said as he motioned for the guards to release the prisoners.

"Oh dack, look! They didn't die in that raid," Pernel said as he looked at Aaranon with deep concern.

"What if they talk? Dack, what if they've already talked?" asked Ballac.

Aaranon looked around the room as, one by one, they became silent. Before Zeul motioned for the Supreme High Commander to give the order for the MSS troopers to attack; he gave the rebels the opportunity to confess their crimes and give up their comrades. One of the rebels moved forward and gazed up toward the silent masses. He then looked back at his friends who all nodded towards him, indicating solidarity. He then shouted; "We serve no one! For Loha has returned!"

Many of those who were younger and not familiar with the stories of Loha began to throw down curses at the rebels. But for those who were well stricken in years, it was all they could do to hide their shock and bewilderment.

Looking upward, Zeul gave the command. Immediately, all MSS troops in the arena and those flying above, rushed towards the prisoners placed at the center. The rebels tried to huddle together but were, instead, ruthlessly separated into two groups. For those with the implant, their lives were spared for the moment. For the others, however, death didn't come fast enough.

"Turn it off. I've seen enough," Aaranon said to Drahcir.

Each member of Aaranon's crew tried to hide their sadness for the loss of their friends. Instead, they channeled their energies into sheer hatred for the UAK.

After a few moments, Aaranon turned to Mishna and asked, "What do you know about those things?"

"Quite a bit actually," he said.

Others gathered around to listen. "Care to elaborate?"

Enjoying the audience that was around him, Mishna continued, "I was the one who created the new interface and control mechanism for those *things*, as you called them."

Aveed angrily expressed what the others were thinking. "Those dacking *things* just ate half of our friends, and I'm sure they will eat the other half later. So stop acting like you're so dacking high and mighty, or I'll string your lovely little hind end up a tree and watch those *things* eat you! Got it?!"

Aaranon put his hand on Aveed's shoulder to calm him down and then calmly asked Mishna, "Can they be stopped?"

"Yes, but not as easily as the previous generation."

"What do you mean?" Pernel asked.

"For the second generation, they employed a standard farspeak interface, which is a point to point connection. That's why I was able to control the others directly. The third generation however is no longer using point to point. They utilize a central command hub to verify all commands."

"Can someone like you or Drahcir get around that?" asked Ballac.

"We can't get around it, but we can pass commands through the hub as long as we use a verified controller," Mishna said.

"What do you mean verified?" asked Aaranon.

"There are three levels of verification and each one is harder than the last. At the first level, you need an authorized implant. They insert them through the nasal cavity into the base of the brain instead of in the back of the head along the spine. Fortunately, I installed one into me before I escaped."

"And the second?" Drahcir asked.

"At the second level you need an authorized console that is synced to the implant. At present, one department in the Ministry of War holds the implants while another department in the Ministry of Knowledge holds the authorized consoles. The two are separate until they join them together; which, of course, requires authorization from the UAC."

"And the third?" asked Aaranon.

"To activate the console, a drop of fresh male noble blood from an active member of the UAC is required."

"Huh?" asked Aveed.

"Every male of noble birth has had their blood analyzed and registered with the UAK. It's how they can know precisely who is and who isn't of noble birth. The console is programmed to begin operation once it detects the correct marker. After that, the console is operational."

"So is that it?" asked Sdra'de.

"No. You still need to pass commands through the central hub. Each command gets weighed against a set of operations. If the command appears to be rogue or false, it isn't passed; which, of course, makes you vulnerable to being caught."

"So every mission that an MSS trooper goes out on, it needs an operational objective," Aaranon asked.

"Exactly."

"So these things will never attack a UAK soldier or its commander?" asked Drahcir.

"In theory, that is correct."

"Well is that all? I thought this was going to be hard," said Aveed with a hefty dose of cynicism and sarcasm.

"I have the implant, and I might be able to create the

console, while Drahcir might be able to hack into the operations MCR to discover their operational objectives…," Mishna said before being interrupted.

"But where will you get a drop of male noble blood," Pernel said while turning to look at Aaranon.

"I think we're not looking at the obvious," Aaranon said.

"And what's that," asked Mishna.

"If we could do all of that, and be able to submit commands to the MSS troops, the best we can hope for is to stop them from attacking us."

"Isn't that better than being attacked?" asked Mishna.

"Yes, but then what? We still have to get past these new ships and weapons. Not to mention their ability to appear at will with those portals," he said.

Mara raised her hand and said, "May I ask a question?"

"Go ahead," said Aaranon.

"These things; they are part udam and part beast, correct?"

"Yes; and part foliage as well," replied Mishna.

"What motivates them? I mean, why do they follow orders?"

"They know that if they don't, they will be eradicated immediately by an internal kill box that stops their hearts. Visions of bliss and happiness, along with images of fear and despair also motivate them. Whatever it takes to make them follow commands is given to them. To reduce variability, all of them were created from one udam and one set of beasts."

"So…what motivates one will motivate another?" she asked.

"Hmm…yes, I suppose so. I never thought of that," he replied as his mind conceived of an alternative.

"Thought of what?" she asked.

"Virtually every beast of the forest is motivated by scent in one way or another; whether it is with respect to mating rituals, dominance among the pack or marking its territory. The right kind of scent can be used to evoke a particular response. If we can't motivate them by direct command, then maybe they can be motivated by scent; which just so happens to have a direct link to memory."

Aaranon interjected, "Alright then. It looks like we have some direction. Drahcir?"

"Yes, Loha?"

"Work with Mishna on that console, and see if you can access the MCR for those objectives."

"I'll get right on it."

Aaranon turned. "Mara and Sdra'de, the two of you might have a better chance of getting close enough to extract what we need from a beast than any of us. Can you work with Mishna on extracting whatever is needed to create these...*motivational scents?*"

"Will do," they both said.

"Aveed, Pernel?"

"Right here, Loha," Aveed said, stepping forward.

"See what you can find out about these portals. Since you two have the most experience with electrical sources, see if you can come up with a way of detecting their presence before they even appear."

"We're on it," said Aveed.

"Yosef?"

"Yeah A...ah...yeah, Loha."

Smiling ever so briefly to acknowledge his slip, Aaranon said, "Why don't you and I see if we can find some noble blood? Everybody else, back to what you were doing. We have a lot of work ahead of us."

Chapter 38

So how much further to our next stop, Darham?" she whined as she looked around the pack animal to see her brother's face.

"It isn't much further, Dihana. I purchased a small house and I had it fully stocked. We can stay there for several days before we set out again," he replied.

"Good, I can use the rest."

Micah, trying to lighten the mood, teased the object of his affection. "Not used to walking on these types of roads are you, my dear?"

"Of course not. My delicate feet know only of the soft fluffy pillows fit for a princess," she said while looking up at him with a pompous yet sarcastic look.

Micah chuckled a little while Darham rolled his eyes at their constant flirting. Micah then said to his new love, "Have I told you how beautiful you look today?"

"No...yes...but you can say it again if you want to," she said while playfully smacking his arm.

"Well then...you are the most beautiful former princess turned peasant I've ever had the privilege of gazing upon."

"And you, my former soldier turned hostage turned peasant, are the most handsome udam in all the world."

"I'm going to puke," Darham said.

Dihana turned a piercing glare towards her brother. "Well then, puke over there somewhere so we can continue fawning over one another without you interrupting."

"Sorry Darham; I just can't help myself," Micah said.

"Don't apologize to him. He's just jealous. Aren't you Darham?"

"No...I'm just growing tired of this infantile petting between you two."

"Petting!? Well, if it wasn't for you keeping us apart every night, then maybe we could do more than just *pet* one another," She turned and wiggled her eyebrows at Micah, "if you know what I mean."

"The trees know what you mean, Dihana," Darham replied.

"Why wouldn't they...they are made out of wood you know," she said with a cheesy grin.

"Funny...can you stop with the innuendos? That is even worse than the flirting."

"How about the eyebrows?" she asked while wiggling them again. "Do you want me to stop them too?"

"He's right Dihana. Let's try to be more serious."

"Thank you," said Darham.

"Kiss ass," Dihana said to Micah.

"Is that a command Your Highness?" Micah asked while he, too, wiggled his eyebrows.

"Alright you two...please...stop!"

"But why dear brother?"

"For one...it isn't good to hear my sister talk that way...,"

"Reminds you of the temples...huh?" she asked.

"No...it's just...we need to be careful what we say. We don't want to draw attention."

She waved her hands around, gesturing towards the empty woods. "Attention? What attention? There's no one here, Darham."

"I'm sure Micah would agree with me, but these woods are crawling with bandits."

"I would agree with that. I'm sorry. I'll be more careful," Micah said.

"Oh! Now you two need to relax. Don't we have these weapons to take care of anything that comes our way? I know how to handle these things. Aaranon taught me you know," she said while reaching for her concealed EB.

"Yes, but I don't want to use them unless we absolutely need to. If we use them, it will just draw further attention to us since *peasants* are not allowed to possess weapons," Darham said while motioning for his sister to return hers to its concealed holster.

"Fine, but I'm only doing this for Micah," she said while caressing his arm.

"Whatever...just try and act like disheveled peasants and not like nobles."

Dihana moved next to Darham so she could speak softly and asked, "So...what do you think our noble father is up to? Do you think he's sent the whole kingdom to look for us?"

"I don't think he'll do that."

"Why not?"

"I don't think the council knows that Aaranon is alive. In order for Father to become the head of this Brotherhood, or whatever it is, I believe he needed to sacrifice him. Now, since that didn't happen, if he were to use the UAK forces to come looking for us, it might bring up too many questions that he doesn't want to answer."

"I don't think he would just let us go though, so who would he send if neither the government or this Brotherhood couldn't know? Does he trust anyone?" she asked.

"At this point, I think he only has one person he can trust, if you want to call it trust."

"Ravizu?"

"Yes...and probably his hired band of thugs. But that's a guess. In fact, my plan is based on him not using the UAK or the council to track us down. Because if he did, I don't think we would have made it this far."

"So you don't think he would put up posters everywhere asking, *have you seen this prince and princess anywhere?*"

"No...it's too risky. He needs to be quiet about this," Darham said.

Dihana was about to speak when, all of a sudden, five udamé carrying bows and blades surrounded them. They emerged from concealed pits that had been dug out of the ground; covered in limbs and leaves.

One of them yelled, "Stop right there, or I'll kill you where you stand!"

Darham immediately put up his hands while Micah put Dihana between himself and Darham. As Micah was about to reach for his weapon, he felt a sharp arrow poke him in his back.

"Don't grab that weapon lover boy, or I'll just put this through your heart," another udam said while reaching for his weapon to remove it.

Another one of the filthy thugs came closer and removed Darham and Dihana's weapons and began searching them for any knives or blades.

"Take whatever you want. We don't want any trouble," Darham said, trembling from head to toe.

One bandit, looked Dihana up and down and liked what he saw. The tone in his voice made it very clear as to what he wanted to take. "Oh I will."

Another asked, "So, how is it that poor folk like you came into possession of weapons like these?"

"We found them...along the road," Micah said calmly.

"Really? Just lying there...out in the open?"

"Yes," Dihana said, looking disgusted.

"I don't believe you," another bandit said.

"I don't care what you believe," she barked.

"You need to keep a leash on this one," one bandit said while looking at Micah.

After looking at Darham and Dihana intensely, the leader of the bandits, Valmor, said, "Wait a moment. These two? They look familiar."

He turned to his fellow bandits; "They look familiar to you?"

The three of them tried to remain calm, but their fears were becoming evident.

"Yeah! You, I don't know...," he dismissed Micah, then turned his attention to Darham and Dihana, "...but you two...I think I know who you are."

"You don't know anything," Micah said while pulling Dihana further behind him.

"Yeah, you look like those two on the side of the arena in the city," he said while he continued to intensely examine their facial features.

Darham and Dihana looked back and forth at one another; realizing he was referring to the large banners their father had installed.

"Ah, ha, ha! You know what we've got here, you mooks? Gold! Pure gold! I bet someone would pay a whole lot for the two of you," Valmor said with excited laughter.

"What are you talking about," another bandit asked.

"These two are nobles. I *knew* I heard her say she was a princess. Oh Dack! We are going to be rich!"

"Listen, I can give you anything you want. I have a house fully stocked not far from here, you can have it all if you just let us go," Darham said as he continued to hold up his hands.

"So you *are* nobles. Sounds like you two don't want to get caught. Which can mean only one thing. I tell you what, Your Highness," the bandit said as he slightly bowed, "You can keep your house, and we'll then turn you in for a reward."

"Listen to me please," Darham said, "They will not give you a reward. Once you turn us over, they will turn on you and kill you. Do you understand?"

"Well then...maybe we'll just give up only one...and hold the other until we have our money. Thanks for the advice, Your Highness," he said.

"I'm telling you, you're making a big mistake. They will not give you anything, I can give you more than you could ever imagine if you just let us go," begged Darham.

"No...I don't think so. Earlier, when you were on the road, I could hear you whispering. It's one of the gifts from having lived in the forest; unlike you two. I think we will contact this...

Ravizu fella...and have a talk with him. I'm sure he's a reasonable udam."

"Trust me when I say this," Dihana said looking the bandit in his eyes, "He will show you no mercy when he finds you. All of you will die! Do you understand?"

"Oh I understand, Your Highness. I can see that none of you want to get caught. That's what I understand. I tell you what; we'll just make our way to this house of yours, see if we can contact Ravizu and get our reward."

"You're making a big mistake," said Micah.

"I'll be the judge of that," Valmor said as he motioned for one of his crew to go and get the enclosed cart to put them in for transport.

"Please, I beg of you, don't do this," cried Darham.

"Can you believe this!? A high and mighty noble, groveling at my feet! My my, how the world has changed. Now...if you would ever so kindly...get the dack in there and shut up," he said as he pushed the three of them into the cart and locked the door.

***

As the bandits moved down the dirt covered road, Amana stepped out from behind one of the trees. She thought to herself, *What are they doing here? This can't be a coincidence. I need to follow them.*

Chapter 39

They arrived at the location where Aaranon and Rohu's cargo carrier went down. Ravizu motioned for one of his mercenaries, who fired the missiles, to come near.

He nervously said, "Yes, Lord Ravizu?"

"Where was it again that you said you thought you saw something fall out of the carrier?"

"It was over the top of the lake we just flew over, My Lord."

Through his thoughts, Ravizu instructed Lilith to turn the sky liner around to hover over the top of the lake.

"Where exactly do you think it was?" Ravizu asked while drawing near to the frightened mercenary.

Swallowing deeply, he said while pointing to the southern end of the lake, "Right there, My Lord."

"Right here?"

"Yes."

From behind, Lilith shot the mercenary, leaving a gaping hole in his chest. She then pushed him over the balcony and into the lake below the sky liner.

Looking over the edge, Ravizu yelled, "Was it like that? Did he jump into the lake like that, or was he pushed? Hmm...I guess he can't hear me. Lilith my love?"

"Yes, My Lord?"

"Why don't you set us down next to the lake."

"Very well," she said as she moved back to the cabin to set the sky liner down.

"Gather around my merry band of misfits," Ravizu said to the crew. "I want you to turn this area of the forest upside down, and inside out. I am of the conviction that my dear brother knew, somehow, that your former friend and his companion were coming to kill him. Therefore, I believe that somewhere in this area we might find a clue as to his whereabouts."

"Yes, My Lord," they said in unison.

"Let me make myself perfectly clear, you better find something this time, or none of you will be leaving this forest. Now go!"

Quickly, the mercenaries shuffled off the sky liner and into the forest to look for any trace of evidence that would indicate Aaranon survived.

***

After waiting on the sky liner half the day without any results, Ravizu turned to Lilith and asked, "What do you think my love? Should we just kill them all when they return?"

"If I know you, which I do; then I know you are not asking me."

"Look at you! You know me so well. Come here beautiful while I violate every part of your lovely flesh," he said as he began to remove his clothing, prompting her to do the same.

With both of them standing there naked, one of the mercenaries came running up the plank yelling, "Lord Ravizu! Lord Ravizu! We found something!"

Both of them turned to face the stunned mercenary who couldn't take his eyes off of their exquisite forms. Ravizu then asked, "Well...what is it?"

Holding up the container that held the scrolls that Aaranon left behind he said, "I found this long tube."

"Well, would you look at that; a long tube. What do think of that Lilith?"

Looking down at Ravizu's midsection and then back at the tube she said, "It isn't that long."

Immediately, they both laughed, leaving the stunned mercenary to let out a little chuckle. Ravizu then walked over to take possession of the container and opened it. As he pulled out the scrolls, the letter written by Rohu fell to the floor.

The dazed mercenary continued to stare at Ravizu as he read the note. He finally said, "There were more items in the cave where we found this. Did we do well, My Lord?"

"Yes. Yes...you did well. You and the others get to eat another day. Now get the dack out of here until I call for you," Ravizu said as he turned and walked towards Lilith. Once the mercenary was gone he said, "Well, well. If I'm not mistaken, which I never am, I believe I know who the leader of the rebels is."

"Your brother!?" Lilith chuckled.

While nodding his head, he added, "...and I can't help but think Father has something to do with it."

"What do you mean?"

"The Apostates...they were a farce. They were only there as a false opposition to the kingdom."

"You mean they never existed?"

"Oh...they existed, and probably still do. But they never committed any crime against the kingdom except to believe some crazy doctrine, which I now seem to have in my hands."

"So what does this have to do with the rebels?"

"My guess is that the Apostates have run their course; based on my father's announcement in the arena. Therefore, he and the Brotherhood need a new opposition to solidify their power even further. And this type of opposition seems to be anywhere and everywhere."

"Meaning...it could be anyone?"

"Exactly. With that type of enemy, you can easily convince the masses that they need to give up everything to the kingdom; even their very soul if they think it will keep them alive."

"Do you think your father and Aaranon are working together?"

"Knowing them both, I would have to say that my brother is an unwilling and unknowing stooge in my father's plans. More than likely he's manipulating him like he does everyone else."

"Everyone else? So...what about you, My Lord?"

"What about me?" Ravizu asked.

"Is he manipulating you as well?"

"Of course he is. I would expect nothing less."

"So what should we do?"

"Well...if Whihany does what I think she'll do, then my plans are already in motion."

"What do you mean, My Lord?"

"Oh...sometimes I forget that you don't know everything I'm doing. Regardless...the reason I had you deliver that message to her was not for her to lure Aaranon in."

"I don't understand...I thought that is what you wanted her to do. Did I do something wrong in delivering that message?"

"Oh no, my dear. You did exactly as I asked. As you know, I saw the whole thing. Even down to that passionate embrace, which I must say...I truly want to repeat, but with the three of us next time. Anyway...as you know, secretly she and I had agreed to be married. Her father was desperate to make an alliance with my family. I however wanted to use her to poison Aaranon with one of her concoctions. I knew she was a powerful sorcerer, but I wasn't fully aware of how that came to be."

"So what happened?" Lilith asked.

"That crazy witch fell in love with him; that's what happened! After that, I knew she could not be counted upon... until now."

"Why until now?"

"Not only is she a boiling cauldron when you cross her, but she's also a wudam in every sense of the word. Her anger over the news of Aaranon being alive will need to find a place to land."

"So what do you think she will do?"

"Let me put it this way; it's time to betray the so-called master betrayer," he said.

"But what will happen to you if the Brotherhood discovers

that your father betrayed them?"

"Well...I believe Davison will spread rumors among the brothers. He is well known for not being able to keep a secret for long. Zeul will do whatever he can to squelch the truth. Once he traces those rumors back to Davison, he will then realize that I know. Hopefully, by that time we will have found Aaranon."

"Will you eliminate him?"

"This is where it gets tricky. I need Aaranon alive, but under our control, in order to sway my father from the throne."

"So...once you become the head of the Brotherhood and the new Alemeleg, then you will destroy Aaranon?"

"Precisely. I will then remove Davison and that witch daughter of his. That way, our family honor is still intact with the Brotherhood, but my father will be out of my way," he said while pulling her closer to continue where they left off.

However, before he could continue his romp with Lilith the farspeak signaled an incoming call.

"Well, that certainly isn't my father. Excuse me love while I see who this is. Hmm...it's my office." Waving his hand over the console he said, "This better be urgent."

"Lord Ravizu, we received a call from someone named Valmor that claims he has a package you might be looking for."

"A package? What kind of package?"

"Two packages to be exact. Apparently something of immense value that you might have lost."

"I see. Well then, send me his location and let this Valmor know we shall see him very soon."

"Yes My Lord."

Ravizu ended the call and turned to his beautiful servant, "Lilith my dear, this day is getting better and better."

Chapter 40

"Darham, I am so sorry," Dihana whispered through her tears.

"I am too. I knew better," Micah replied as the three of them sat in the small cage, waiting for the inevitable.

"Well I'm not," shouted Valmor as he walked out of the house to give them some detestable concoction to eat. "You might want to eat up. I don't want this Ravizu to think I've been starving you when he arrives."

"He's coming?" asked Darham with dread filling every fiber of his being.

"Of course he is. Why wouldn't he?"

"I'm asking you once more, please let us go. When he finds us, none of your udamé or you will live to tell about it."

"Don't you worry about me and my udamé. They can handle their own if anything happens. We caught you didn't we? And now, since we have you to thank for those nice EBs you were carrying to protect you, we'll be able to handle this Ravizu character if he decides to not play so nice. Oh! That reminds me, once my udamé return with the other cage, I'm going to separate one of you for safe keeping. The question is, which one should I give to him first?"

"Take me," replied Micah.

"What do you take me for you idiot? You mean nothing to him. It's these two he wants. I'm sure he'll kill you immediately. Better yet, maybe I should take care of you myself," Valmor said while pulling the EB from his side and aiming it at Micah.

"No!!" screamed Dihana as she jumped in front of him.

Darham tried to grab his sister and put her behind him. "Dihana, no!"

"Leave me alone Darham I'm not going to let this walking

dung heap have his way with us," she said while spitting on Valmor.

Valmor then pointed the weapon at Dihana's head and said, "You dacking nobles need to learn your place in this forest. I'm in charge here; not you! If you know what's best, you'll do what I say, when I say. When my udamé return tomorrow, we are going to separate you and then see what kind of bargain we can... uh...uh..."

A blank stare came over Valmor for a few moments and then his eyes rolled back in his head. As his body fell to the ground, they could see an arrow sticking out the right side of his back. Off in the distance they caught a glimpse of a hooded figure running towards them.

"Oh no! I'm so sorry Dihana. I thought I could save us," Darham said as he could feel the blood coursing through his veins. As he continued to stare at the dark figure moving towards them he leaned forward, narrowed his gaze and said with a smile, "Amana?"

"Shh, we don't have much time. I saw them leave, but I'm sure they will be back soon."

"Amana? You're Amana? I've heard so much about you!" Dihana said, a smile forming across her face.

As she searched Valmor for the keys, she said, "We can do the introductions later, but for now, we need to get as far away as possible."

"But what are you doing here?" asked Darham.

"I'm looking for Aaranon."

"So are we! We're going to Emet to get help," Dihana said with a great deal of enthusiasm.

"Aaranon was instructed by Rohu to go there as well but he never did. In fact, he's now the leader of the rebels and goes by the name of Loha."

"Huh?" Darham asked.

"What?! How do you know that?" Dihana asked.

"Because Nahim and his family told me after Rohu took me

there."

"Rohu did what?" Darham asked.

"Look...I can explain it all later, but right now we need to get all of you out of there and leave."

Micah pointed towards Valmor and said, "Roll him over, I think I saw the keys in his front pocket."

As she rolled him over, Valmor reached up and grabbed Amana by the throat. With blood spewing from his mouth he muttered, "You dacking whore."

Dihana screamed, "Hit that piece of ohema smack in the privy. Hit him! Hit him!"

As Amana pulled at his hand, Valmor once again passed out and let go of her.

"Hit him! Hit him! Kill that son of a wench! Dack you, you dacking piece of dung!"

"Dihana. Dihana!" said Micah as he tried to get her attention.

"What!"

"It's alright, he's unconscious."

Dihana paused for a moment to collect herself but then collapsed into his arms; trembling and crying profusely. Micah did his best to console her by holding her tightly while she continued to pour out her pent up frustration and anger she kept hidden.

"I can't take this anymore, Micah. I just can't take it. I'm tired of these filthy udamé doing what they want. I'm tired of running. I'm done fighting. I can't handle this!"

Amana soon found the keys and opened the cage. Dihana immediately dashed out of the cage and proceeded to punch and kick Valmor with all her might.

"I want you dead. I hate you! I hate you! I hate you! I want you dead Ravizu, Why won't you just die you dacking ignoramus, filthy cretin, arrogant prick!"

Micah leapt from the cage and grabbed Dihana. Darham cautiously emerged from their temporary prison and looked at Amana with gratitude and bewilderment.

"We need to move now. Grab what few supplies you can find and let's go," Amana said before running into the house to search for food and weapons.

"You're alright Dihana. I'm here. You're alright," Micah said.

"You take care of her, I'll help Amana," replied Darham as he ran into the house.

"Why?! Why is this happening to us?" she asked while she clung to Micah.

"We'll figure it out together, Dihana. It will be alright," Micah said as he continued to hold her fragile body.

"And on top of all of this, I'm now going through the dacking change," she said as she continued to hold onto Micah.

"Change?" he asked.

"Yeah…change. You know," she said with her face buried in his chest.

"Uh…I need some help. I'm not sure what you mean."

"Change! Change! You know…the time when a wudam gets her…"

"Oh! Change. Right. I know what you mean."

"You do?" she asked with a look of relief.

"Not really. I'm sorry. I don't want to upset you and I don't want to make you mad."

"You know…the change from a child to a full grown wudam. My mother told me it would happen someday. Along with the bleeding and the wretched smell, comes wild fluctuations in my emotions. Aaranon called it the *days of rage*."

A look of understanding crossed his face. "Oh…ooohhh… now I know what you mean."

Valmor began to stir slightly prompting Dihana to pick up a limb and beat him multiple times before Micah could pull her off of him.

After she finally calmed down, Micah said in a gentle tone, "Days of rage…huh?"

"Yeah…days of rage," she replied in a softer tone and then said, "You still love me?"

"Always. Nothing could change that."

"Good…because you're going to need to keep that attitude when I'm pregnant with our first child," she said while smiling up at him.

"Huh? But I thought Ravizu…"

"Poisoned me! Yeah, that was a lie like everything else that comes out of his mouth. Apparently it was only temporary. Long story on how I found that out."

"Oh…," Micah replied, looking a bit nervous.

"Sorry my love. I forgot to mention that part. As it turns out, I'm as fertile as a newly plowed field. Hey, you alright? You look a little pale."

Amana and Darham soon emerged with several packs filled with supplies and the few EBs they could find. Darham looked over at a pleasant looking Dihana, but a confused Micah. He then turned to Amana and asked, "So where to?"

"North of here. I have an idea as to where Aaranon is," she replied.

"Alright then, lead the way," he said as he handed the other packs and weapons to Micah and Dihana.

***

After he spent a night and part of a day on the ground, Valmor's udamé finally returned with the second cage,

As Valmor continued to writhe in agony, one asked, "Boss! Boss! Are you alright?"

"You dacking idiot, do I look alright to you," he muttered just above a whisper.

"Who did this to you, was it that Ravizu?"

"No you fool. Get this arrow out of me," he demanded.

"We got the cage, but where are the prisoners?"

"You really are stupid aren't you? Isn't it obvious? They escaped," replied Valmor as he continued to groan in pain.

"How did they escape?"

"They had help. Now shut up and get this dacking arrow out of me before I kill you with it."

"Right boss, I'm on it."

As Valmor's udamé were working on him, Ravizu's ship maneuvered over top the house. Several mercenaries repelled over the side and secured the area before Ravizu and Lilith came down on one of the wind runners.

After making a sweep of the area, one mercenary approached Ravizu, "My Lord, they don't appear to be here. This peasant Valmor said that several udamé raided the place and took them, but from the looks of it...I would say that's a lie."

"Well then, let's see what we can extract from them before we give them a full helping of death, shall we? Lilith my dear, I believe we will be using your art of persuasion once again."

"It would be a pleasure, My Lord."

Chapter 41

Aaranon looked out across the growing group of rebels that were, under his tutelage, becoming a well-organized machine. Aaranon realized, after the previously botched rescue attempt in which many died, they needed more training; the few who had narrowly escaped had Mishna to thank. Aaranon decided to train for a few more odes before carrying out their next mission as many new recruits came to join the fight. Since they were still yet unable to perfect the console needed to control the MSS troops, Aaranon decided to use the untested concentration of foul smelling scents - extracted from the hormonal glands of various beasts - as their last line of defense against the vicious beasts.

After pausing for a few moments for the group to quiet down from their idle conversations, Aaranon began, "I understand many of you have concerns as to what I think we are actually doing here. You've asked me, *Are we only rescuing families and friends, or are we taking down this dacking kingdom?*"

Immediately, the rebels began grunting and beating their chests, indicating their desire to destroy the UAK.

Aaranon held up his hand to quiet the crowd and let the noise of their enthusiasm absorb into the massive forest surrounding them. He continued, "It took the wise counsel of a good friend to help me see through my confusion." Aaranon paused for a moment to look over at Pernel, who was standing by his side.

After exchanging glances, he continued, "I am now of the opinion that they are not two distinct objectives, but one in the same. How can we rescue the ones we love, if we do not, at the same time, destroy their captors?"

The rebels erupted into an enthusiastic roar that shook the forest floor ever so slightly. Holding his hand up once more to quiet the crowd, he continued, "But let me make myself clear as to who our real enemy is. It isn't the line worker in the factory who molds and shapes the iron used to build weapons of war. It isn't the stone cutter who builds the monuments to the Ayim that others are forced to worship out of fear. It isn't the farmer who is made to work from the rising of Shemesh until its setting to feed those who never even touch the ground. It isn't even the creatures that have no choice, but to carry out its master's every whim.

"Our true enemy barely moves a muscle as it commands these to do its bidding. Our true enemy will not stop until every soul is enslaved or sent to the great beyond. Our actual enemy sits in a lofty tower, barking orders to those who have no voice to shout back. Therefore, let me say this; they now have a voice!"

Unable to contain their zeal, Aaranon just stood back and allowed them to express their eagerness to enact vengeance by hurling shouts and jeers against the kingdom.

After a few moments, as the roar of the crowd diminished slightly, Mara climbed atop a fallen tree and from that platform, she began to sing an old hymn. It was one rarely sung, if ever, but it wasn't foreign to its listeners, and it wasn't long before they all grew silent. They stood quietly and listened to her haunting melody as it moved throughout the tall kyder trees.

It was a song sung to them by their grandmothers and great-grandfathers. It spoke of the promise of a new land that knew nothing of pain or sorrow. It promised rest to the weary soul and healing to the broken hearted. The young recruits didn't understand much of its original meaning, but it was fitting for the moment.

As Aaranon stood there listening, he vividly recalled a memory of his mother and father singing the same old hymn to him as he lay in his crib. What he saw next shook him to his core.

He could see Sari and Zeul embrace one another with a kiss; Sari then exited the room, leaving Zeul behind. His father reached down and picked up Aaranon to hold him in his arms.

Making sure that his beautiful wife could not hear him, Zeul gently spoke to his new born son, "Hello my son. When I look upon your beautiful countenance, I realize the curse that plagued my father did not pass to me. I was such a fool to think it so. The Great One has blessed me once again with a family; giving back to me what I had lost. Ever since that day, I thought of nothing but vengeance. How silly of me to think of such a thing; who am I to tell Him how to rule the world? I now know it wasn't me, nor my father, but this fallen world that took them away. Thank you for making that clear to me. I hope such rage never blinds me again. Please forgive me if I do."

To knock him out of his daze, Pernel tugged on Aaranon's sleeve, "Loha. Loha!"

"Yeah..."

"We're ready for your orders."

"What?"

"Your orders...for the mission."

"Ah...right. Yes, the orders," Aaranon said as he tried to compose himself quickly. "Sorry, I was just caught up in that song. Thank you Mara. I needed...we all needed to hear that."

"You're welcome Loha," she said as she jumped down from the limb, letting her four-footed companions follow her into the crowd.

After composing himself further, he began, "As many of you know, we have countermeasures we're still working on to deal with the new threat. We have a few solutions, but until then we need to continue our fight. Each of your commanding officers has their orders. Please confirm your mission with them.

"Please remember, we are only looking for the smaller drill that can bore a hole about four ama in diameter. Any of the other drills will be too cumbersome to carry out so don't try to remove them. The specifications are on its side; so you'll know it once you see it. Once any of you find it, alert me or your commander.

"The mine we are going to should only have a few workers on sight. Drahcir confirmed the information, so we shouldn't see too much opposition. However, let me stress this clearly; we only use deadly force if required. These workers are no different than us. We are no longer a band of misfit peasants; as they like to call us." Aaranon paused as he looked over at Yosef. "We are, in every sense of the word, true Arazians."

As the rebels cheered and embraced one another; unbeknownst to them, the servants of Halail were watching the whole event from high above.

"Look at them cheer and encourage one another as if their hearts were pure."

"Idiots! They fight for something that will come to naught. These pitiful beings are good for nothing but the fire."

"Well, if all goes as planned, then that will be their end."

"Oh yes and what a glorious day that will be."

"Glorious indeed."

"And that fool doesn't even see the path he is treading. *Oh... let's not destroy the precious souls that are like us. Oh...let's not kill our fellow Arazians.* How pathetic can they be? Their words will come back to haunt them in that day of reckoning. Not a single one of them knows honor or truth. They do nothing but lie to themselves continuously."

"I knew Aaranon would not be able to resist the path of vengeance. No matter how he tries to explain it away, his carnality will always win. He is just like his father."

"Don't be so sure."

"What do you mean?"

"Halail will not speak of it, but I can see his concerns. Zeul seems to be wavering in his loyalties. After that old shriveled piece of meat visited him and gave him that book, he no longer is as he once was. It appears that his cold heart has received some new found warmth."

"What is in that book?"

"We don't know. We cannot get near it. But whatever it contains, it isn't good for us."

"And what of our plans with Dihana and Darham? We allowed them to escape to the forests of Tarshish in the hopes that it would compel Zeul to go after them."

"He sent Ravizu, didn't he?"

"Yes, but now Amana has gotten them turned around."

"But Zeul doesn't know that yet."

"Yes, but he will."

"You seem to forget that Halail isn't the one who see all things. He must put multiple plans in place since he is unable to foresee their outcome. I believe that is why we were instructed to assist Ravizu."

"Hmmm...just one more thing to concern ourselves with."

"You sound as if you are wavering again."

"I'm not wavering! I just have concerns they'll thwart our plans."

"Sounds like wavering to me. You've been around these mortals for far too long. You're starting to sound like them."

"Whatever. Let us return to Halail and give our report. I'm sure he will want to know more of this new mission to the mine."

Chapter 42

"Are these all the workers?" Aaranon asked while removing his mask.

"They're the only ones we could find," replied Pernel.

"Only eight?

"Yeah."

"I knew the staff would be small, but not this small."

"Looks like good fortune for us."

Aaranon didn't want to express his concern, but he knew that was too small of a staff for one of his family's mines. He knew something was amiss, but what?

"Yeah, that is good fortune," Aaranon said. Pulling a secure farspeak out of his pocket, he signaled Drahcir. "Be sure to notify me the moment you see any troop movement. We have the countermeasures in place, but hopefully, we won't need them."

"As of right now, you are free and clear," replied Drahcir from his secluded hiding spot on the outskirts of the forest, located near the mine.

He then contacted Sdra'de on the farspeak, "Those portal detectors may or may not work, so be sure to keep your eyes open as you're moving around up there."

"That won't be a problem. Our ananins will also alert us if they see anything out of the ordinary."

"Excellent," replied Aaranon as he put the farspeak back in his pocket.

Soon after, Mishna approached and asked, "Loha, if I may, I would like to keep watch over the workers."

Aveed interjected with his standard sardonic tone, "What's a matter feather toes? You afraid of the dark?"

"Of course not. I lived exclusively underground for most of my life. I only wish to be of service the best way I know how."

"By being an infant watcher?"

Aaranon jumped in quickly before they continued their normal bantering, "That's fine Mishna, but only use your EB if necessary."

"Are you sure you know how to use it? Let me show you. Just point that end with the hole at your ugly bulbous head and then pull that trigger," replied Aveed.

"Aveed!"

"Yes, Loha?"

"Why don't you walk point just in case we come under attack," Aaranon suggested.

Turning to look at Mishna, Aveed smugly said, "You see that sack licker? Loha needs his best out in front."

"Or more like cannon fodder to protect...," replied Mishna before being interrupted.

"Enough! Just do your jobs, alright?"

As Aveed and Mishna turned to walk away, Yosef came running up to Aaranon. "Loha, you've got to see this."

"What is it?"

"Food! Supplies! Everything you can imagine! And it's just sitting there, waiting to be taken."

"Aveed, grab your crew. Let's check this out," Aaranon said as they all walked down the dark tunnel, toward the vaults leaving Mishna behind to guard the workers.

Looking around to make sure he was alone, Mishna closed the door to the office where the captured workers were being held and began to speak quietly to them. "Listen to me very carefully. I'm with the UAK, and I need your help. Now, which one of you is in charge here?"

Micum raised his hand as best he could since they were all bound and gagged.

Still holding his weapon, Mishna waved Micum over to him so he could remove the bindings. Once removed he continued,

"What's your name?"

"Micum."

"Micum, do you know Prince Ravizu of the house and kingdom of Quayanin?"

"Yes sir, I do. This mine belongs to his family."

"Wonderful! I need for you to get a message to him. He is my...ah...liaison to the government. Only he knows of my activities. Let him know that I can no longer use the farspeak for it's too dangerous. The rebels' capabilities have increased, and it's far too dangerous to use. Therefore, I need for you to give this coded message to him. Let him know that Lilith will be able to decode it."

Mishna handed him a slip of paper and continued. "Do you know of another way out of here? The main shaft is being guarded so you won't be able to exit that way and it's absolutely vital you make it out of here safely. I'm depending on you; you're my only link to Prince Ravizu at this point."

"Yes, I know all the exits out of here."

"Good. Now go, before they return. I'll let them know you got past me while I had my back turned."

"What about my co-workers? What will happen to them?"

"I'll take care of them, don't you worry. Now go!" Mishna said as he watched Micum move quickly out the door and down a side tunnel that was unoccupied.

Looking over at an enormous machine just outside the office that was shut off, Mishna walked over and turned it on; creating a deafening noise. He then walked back into the room where the workers were being held. He closed the door and then mercilessly killed all seven of them. Pulling a knife from his side he then cut open the backs of their necks to remove the new implants given to every citizen of Araz.

***

"Can you believe this, Loha," said Pernel as he moved his hands across the glass-like stone door that was used to seal the massive vault.

Yosef said, "It looks like it could be air and water tight to me Loha. This vault is better than any construction I've seen, and I should know."

In awe, Aveed walked among the reams of sacks, filled with all kinds of grain, piled up to the ceiling. "You know how many people we could feed with this dacking food?"

"What do you think it's for?" Pernel asked.

"Obviously they're hoarding supplies, but to what end?" Aaranon wondered as he recalled his terrifying dreams.

Looking down the tunnel, Pernel said, "This just seems to go on forever. They must have been doing this for a very long time. And if you look, you can see the ones in that direction are all sealed. This one and a few more the other way are all that are left to fill. Whatever they're preparing for, it looks like they're almost ready."

Just then, Mara came up to Aaranon and said, "I believe we've found the drills you wanted."

"Thank you Mara," he said and then turned to everyone who was standing in and near the vault. "Grab what food you can. We need to get out of here."

"I hear that," replied Aveed as he shouldered his weapon and grabbed several sacks of grain.

"Loha...can you hear me," came Sdra'de over the farspeak.

"Yes...I can hear you."

"I think something is happening. The meter on this device is showing strange fluctuations. I don't see anything yet, but you might want to find what you're looking for and get out."

"Thanks Sdra'de, we've got it and we are leaving now." Turning to the others, he said, "Let's go!"

Fully laden with food and a few drills, they headed back

towards the exit; with Aaranon bringing up the rear to make sure there were no stragglers. As he was about to pass by the office, he put on his mask. He was going to let them know that someone would come to free them, but when he opened the door, he found them all dead with the backs of their necks cut open. Looking around for Mishna, but unable to find him, he decided to head for the exit and question him later.

"Loha, you need to get out of there now. The portals are opening, and I don't think you have much time left," came Sdra'de over the farspeak.

"Get your tribe out of there and tell the others to abandon their guard at the entrance. We'll leave out the secondary shaft like we talked about," he replied.

"Understood!"

Aaranon shouted to the others, "We can't go out the main entrance; the UAK forces are heading this way! We need to take the secondary route!"

Still looking around for Mishna, Aaranon asked Mara, "Have you seen Mishna?"

"I believe he's up towards the front," she said.

"Thanks. I need to talk with him."

"If it's about the countermeasure, I believe it will work. It took Sdra'de and me awhile to extract what he needed, but you can tell he knows what he's doing."

"Ah…good…that's good to know."

Running past the others, Aaranon finally found Mishna. "Can you please tell me what happened back there?"

"What? Oh, you startled me. I was running up ahead to find you. Yes, there was a problem."

"Mind explaining?"

"Well…at first they were quiet and didn't do anything. I assured them that no harm would come to them and that they'd be free once we'd left. I think that was a mistake to let them know that."

"So what happened?"

"All of a sudden, one of them lunged for me. He must have gotten the restraints off somehow. He then pushed past me, knocked the weapon out of my hand, and then ran off. Once I picked it back up, the others were starting to remove their restraints as well. I just…I just panicked. I fired that infernal weapon to scare them, but…,"

"But…what?"

"I didn't mean to kill them all."

"Really?"

"What…you don't believe me?" replied Mishna.

"Loha," came Sdra'de over the farspeak again.

Aaranon leveled a steady gaze at Mishna. "We'll talk about this later." He then turned his attention to more pressing matters. "Go ahead Sdra'de."

"The MSS troopers are headed down the main entrance. It's only a small unit of about twenty, with several UAK soldiers behind them."

"Alright, we are almost near the exit. Hopefully, the countermeasures will work to give us some time."

"I'll see you when you make it out," replied Sdra'de.

"Loha…I think I can hear them coming. This version moves faster than the previous one," Pernel said.

Looking over at Mishna, Aaranon said, "I hope this works."

"Of course it will work…I made it."

The last of Aaranon's udamé exited the tunnel, jumped on their pack animals, and rode back to their hideout. Once they were clear, Aaranon set up a recorder at the exit of the mine so they could see what would happen, from a safe distance.

***

Putting his arm around Mishna, Aveed jovially queried, "Do we have any more ale we can give to my new friend here? I want to get as drunk as I can with this mook and watch this thing over and over again."

"Oh…it was nothing," replied Mishna, enjoying the spotlight.

"Nothing?! That was the funniest dacking thing I have ever seen. Come on, let's watch this again. Hey Loha! You want to watch this again," yelled Aveed.

"Once was enough for me. You enjoy yourself," he replied as he walked back to his room to rest for the evening.

"Hey...I dacking will. Now play that again you fat pimple," Aveed said while poking Drahcir.

"If you call me that one more time, I'll castrate you and feed your privies to Mara's friends."

"Hey now! Don't be so mean. You don't want to choke her furry pets. Only an ohema can digest these," Aveed slurred while grabbing himself suggestively.

"If you would please, Drahcir, play it once more for my friend," replied Mishna while holding a rather large mug of ale.

"Fine, but this is the last time," Drahcir said begrudgingly.

As several of the rebels gathered around once again, they could see on the recording the MSS troopers rushing toward the exit and then abruptly stop.

"Again, what was it you used," Aveed asked while wiping his mouth.

"Urine, for the tenth time," said Drahcir.

"I wasn't asking you Sir Fatty; I was talking to my friend here," he replied sloshing ale all over himself and Mishna.

Trying not to laugh, but having difficulty doing so, Mishna said, "Well, to be precise, it's a highly concentrated form of what we in the knowledge community like to call...piss."

Barely able to sit up, both Aveed and Mishna were falling over each other as they laughed.

"Piss! You get it! You dacking...," Aveed said while punching Drahcir in the arm.

"That's it! I've had enough of your juvenile antics, you... you...you idiot," Drahcir replied

Aveed placed his hand over Drahcir's mouth. "Shh...shut up. Here comes the funny!"

On the screen, the MSS troopers began to back away from the exit area coated in a concentrated form of ohema urine. Once the UAK soldiers caught up from behind, the lead commander could be seen giving orders to the beasts to move forward, but none of them would obey. Soon after, a small explosive went off next to the UAK soldiers; showering them in a putrid concoction of concentrated female scent that aroused the MSS troopers.

The stocky beasts then raised their noses in the air and performed a mating ritual similar to a male ananin attempting to attract a female. As they danced in circles, flapping their arms, the UAK soldiers tried to compel them to cease their activity and go after the rebels. Soon after, one of the MSS troopers grabbed hold of a UAK soldier and attempted to mate with him.

"Here they go! Here they go!" yelled Pernel.

Yosef stared in disbelief and asked, "Why are they doing that when they don't have any privies?"

"Well…like I said earlier, even though they don't have the parts they need, the scent of a female in a concentrated form will still trigger their natural instinct to want to mate," he replied.

As they watched each of the MSS trooper grab hold of a UAK soldier, they laughed uncontrollably as the soldiers tried to break free from the hideous beasts. Some of the soldiers were ripped to shreds while others died from the poisonous claws that dug into their tender flesh. Eventually, one of the commanders enabled the trigger that stopped the hearts of the creatures, but not before a large portion of the udamé suffered mutilation.

As Mishna stumbled to his feet, he walked over and turned off the console. He then faced the crowd of drunken rebels and said with much labor, "Let me say this to all you dacking peasants, who are now my most coveted companions. When I avenge my father and bring down this maniacal regime, I will be sure that all of you receive rewards for your efforts. Therefore, raise your mugs!"

About half of the inebriated rebels raised their mugs while the other half were well on their way to a long night's rest.

"Come on…raise them high. I swear that I…Mishna son of

Greyson will stand..."

They soon heard a loud thump as Mishna passed out onto the floor. As the others sloshed their mugs in agreement, no one picked up on what Mishna said, except for Drahcir, who was hiding just around the corner.

Speaking softly to himself, Drahcir said, "That explains a great deal. I'm sure Loha would like to know this."

Chapter 43

"How do I look, My Lord?" Lilith asked as she spun around to show off her peasant clothing.

"You look stunning my dear. It doesn't matter what you wear, I still want to rip it off and enjoy every square *ama* of your delightful flesh," Ravizu said as he gently caressed his servant.

"Are you sure you don't want me to harm that quivering brother of yours?"

"Oh...you do share my passion, don't you? Eventually, we will, but for now, we need to use him for our purposes. Do you have the console Mishna asked for?"

"Yes, I have it here in my beautiful peasant satchel, underneath my resplendent peasant cloak."

"Good! That Mishna is brilliant don't you think? I wonder what else he's done to you that I'm not aware of," Ravizu asked, backing away slightly and looking skeptically at her.

Trying to hide her concern she asked, "What do you mean My Lord?"

"Well...I wasn't aware of your ability to decode complex cyphers, so I can't help but wonder if he's done something else to you that I'm not aware of."

Pulling him close, she said, "I swear to you, My Lord. I would rather die than do anything to harm you."

"I know my dear. I know," he said as he kissed her forehead and then pulled her closer. As he continued to caress her hair, he gently reached for one of her weapons she kept stored on her backside in anticipation of the unexpected. Soon after, one of the mercenaries boarded the sky liner and knocked on the cabin door to his private quarters.

"What?" yelled Ravizu.

"Forgive me, My Lord, but the cargo ship is ready."

"Good. Lilith will be down in a moment. Now leave us." Waiting for the mercenary to leave, he continued, "Be sure that one of the mercenaries delivers the console to Mishna. I don't want him getting near to you."

"I understand, My Lord," she replied.

"Did you install the tracking device in the console like I asked?"

"Of course, My Lord. I concealed it like you asked. Is everything alright?"

"Ah...yes," he said hesitantly.

"You don't seem alright. Are you concerned about this meeting with the Brotherhood?"

"Well, I'm certainly not looking forward to it. As good as I may be at hiding the truth, Father is even better at discovering it."

"You're concerned he will learn that you know of Aaranon?"

"Of course, along with all the other plans I'm putting in place. The less I'm around him, the better."

"If I may say, My Lord; you deserve to be the King of Kings."

He immediately put his hands to her lips and whispered in her ear, "True, but let's keep that to ourselves; shall we?"

She nodded in agreement and said, "I'm sorry, My Lord."

"No worries my love. Now...after you deliver the console, dispose of the two mercenaries that will be traveling with you. We don't want any loose ends. Then meet me back at the castle in a few days. And be sure that you don't use your farspeak at all."

"Yes, My Lord," replied Lilith as she turned to walk away.

"What? No kiss?" he asked.

"Oh...forgive me, My Lord," she said as she returned cautiously to embrace him once more before she left.

***

"Did you wish to see us, My Lord?"

"Please come in. I wanted to speak with you both before we begin with the other brothers," Zeul said as he motioned for King Vidas and King Mathal to come into his private quarters deep within the tunnels.

"If you would, please, shut and seal the door," Zeul said as he sat down at his desk instead of sitting around the informal seating area. Without giving them a chance to speak Zeul continued, "I wanted to talk about Lachish and make sure we are all…in agreement on what has transpired."

"What do mean My Lord? No one but the three of us know of your using him to create the new uprising," replied Mathal, looking a bit confused.

"Yes, but I've heard rumors circulating that some believe Loha to be my deceased son, Aaranon."

Vidas quickly chimed in, "That's preposterous! We all saw the body, and it was clearly him. His implants made that abundantly clear."

"Yes they did, but there are some who wish to undermine my authority by claiming that I have not offered up my first born like the rest."

"I will find this scoundrel and crush him myself!" Mathal thundered as he slammed his fist atop the desk.

Zeul tried not to look at them directly. "I appreciate your loyalty, but we must determine the source of this lie before it spreads too far. We are so close to our goal and with the razing upon us; we cannot have a pathetic rumor such as this circling among the brethren."

"We will most certainly find the malefactor and report him to you, My Lord," came King Vidas.

"Since we're discussing the rebels; any word as to who this Loha truly is? I'm not given to prophetic buffoonery but, from all the reports I'm getting, this Loha appears to be guarded by the one whose name we do not wish to speak," said Mathal.

"Like what for instance?" asked Zeul.

"I cannot say for certain…," Mathal paused as he attempted to feel with his spirit as to whether or not they were being watched. Leaning closer in to whisper, Mathal said, "…but I have sensed that our master and his servants are fearful that this Loha has a greater purpose. One that could destroy everything we are working towards."

Vidas then leaned in as well. "So…for the network of spies that you put together from the bottom feeders - the ones who were captured and then implanted here in the tunnels - has anything of value come from them? Anything that we can use to our favor?"

"We know that the rebels' capabilities are limited, but growing every day," Zeul replied.

"But can they overrun us?" Mathal asked.

"Don't be silly old friend. Everything they have achieved has been done to give them confidence. They need to feel as if they are winning; which gives us recourse to increase our control. We can crush them at any time," Zeul said as he pulled up an image of the forest on his console showing the exact location of the rebel encampment.

"Superb! I knew you had this under control. And trust me when I say this old friend; we will discover who is the source of this terrible lie you spoke of," Vidas said.

"Good. Take no action, but bring it to me. We need to handle this delicately. He is our brother and not an outsider like King Lachish," Zeul replied.

"Of course My Lord. We will bring it straight to you."

"Good. I have a few things to attend to before the gathering. You may see your way out and, please, close the door behind you," Zeul said as he got up from his desk and walked into another room.

***

Closing the door behind them and walking a considerable distance down the tunnel, Vidas turned to Mathal and motioned for him to turn into a side room. He drew near and whispered, "What do you think?"

"What do I think? Did you see him when he spoke of Aaranon?"

"Yes. He couldn't even look at us."

"I fear the rumors could be true," replied Mathal.

"What do we do then?"

"What can we do? Zeul has all the power in his possession."

"If they are right, then why does our master continue to allow him to reign?"

"Maybe he has given Zeul a chance to offer him up once more."

"But he knows the location of the rebels, you saw it. If Aaranon is this Loha, then he could capture him at any time," Vidas said.

"How should I know," understanding dawned in his eyes, "Unless!"

"Unless what?"

"Unless he wants to offer up the lesser sacrifice."

"The lesser! If that is true, then he's protecting Aaranon."

"That begs the question then; where are Dihana and Darham? He will need them to offer the lesser."

"But how could he? Doesn't he know that it will put his rule into question with the Brotherhood?"

Mathal stuck his head out the door to make sure no one was coming and then said, "I say we move forward; behave as if none of this is authentic. We find the source of the rumor and confirm it. Once confirmed, then we bring it to Zeul. We cannot risk him questioning our loyalties."

Vidas replied, "I agree."

"So where do we start?"

"We look at those for whom Zeul or his family has slighted."

Mathal chuckled, "Maybe a better question is; who hasn't

been slighted?"

"I mean…in a personal way. They would be the ones who would spread such a rumor."

"Ah…King Davison! His daughter was betrothed to Ravizu secretly, but they have not yet married."

"Wasn't she the one who fell in love with Aaranon?"

"Yes! She grieved deeply when he passed. And if she knows he's alive…"

"Then she may want vengeance upon Zeul. Davison and his family seem to cause the most problems for us and that daughter of his. She never knows her place. Nothing but trouble she is."

"Well then…let's begin with Davison."

"I agree. Now let's go. They will be starting soon."

As they both walked down the dimly lit tunnel, a small mingled servant stepped out of the darkness and scurried back toward Zeul's office.

Chapter 44

With the massive stone doors shut, the Brotherhood once again gathered far below, in secret, to discuss their plans for the coming razing. Zeul sat upon an opulent throne, reminiscent of the one at the UAC headquarters. Once the others settled down from their idle chatter, Zeul rapped his scepter, indicating the start of their meeting.

"King Vidas," Zeul said, "Please give us an update on the preparations at Mu'udim."

"Yes My Lord," Vidas said as he stood up from a large round table that took up a tremendous portion of the room. "The colony is now fully stocked with all provisions needed for a stay of up to five Arazian years. It includes enough for all of our families and the mingled servants. The atmospheric generators are also fully functional throughout the tunnels on Mu'udim. We certainly won't have the amenities we have on Araz, but we will have all we need to survive the coming cataclysm."

"What about the portals between here and there? How are we progressing in that area?" Zeul asked.

"We have successfully moved a small recon ship through the portal, but, unfortunately, the occupants inside didn't make it. We are continuing to look into the problem."

"Well, that is most unfortunate. If we cannot move one simple ship and its occupants through a portal to Mu'udim, then I fail to see how we will accomplish moving against the ancient one," Zeul said in a calm demeanor.

"I understand My Lord. Let me assure you, our desire is stronger than ever. I know that, soon, we will be able to break through the heavens like that of the Ayim and remove the mark placed upon our father," replied Vidas.

"Agreed!" shouted many of the brother kings in unison, as they knocked their fists against the stone table.

"What about the old prophet and his aging grandfather? I hear they're building some primitive structure in an attempt to survive," Zeul asked, once more with little emotion in his voice.

All of the brother kings began to laugh; knowing what Nahim and his family were attempting to build.

"Well, for one, it's abundantly clear that this so-called *structure* will save no one. I'm surprised they've been able to get this far without it falling on top of them. However, if Your Majesty so wishes, I can have it removed with one thermal-collapser," Vidas replied as he and the others laughed through his whole statement. All of them knew, however, the futility of trying to remove the structure for no one could stop their progress; not even their own master. The laughter only reinforced the lies they continually told themselves.

Zeul replied in a dismissive manner, "That won't be necessary. I will personally see to it that it no longer remains."

"Is our King looking for some target practice," one of the brothers joked as the others laughed and knocked their fists on the table once more.

Zeul gave a slight grin before he continued, "King Mathal, what of the preparations in the mines here on Araz?"

As the laughter died down, Mathal stood up and said, "Out of the eight hundred storage facilities scattered throughout the tunnels, seven hundred and ninety of them are filled to capacity and sealed. Vidas may have only five years' worth of supplies, but I have over twenty years of supplies for all of us."

"Well, if I only had to move the supplies a few *ama* then I, too, would have as much as you," replied Vidas in a playful yet competitive voice.

As the others laughed, Davison remained silent as he slowly raised his hand, requesting to speak.

Zeul motioned for him to speak. "Yes, King Davison. Go ahead."

Waiting for the others to complete their laughter, Davison eventually stood up and said, "Thank you, King Vidas and King Mathal, for your updates. It is wonderful to know that much has been done to maintain the continuity of our existence. I do, however, wish to speak of the growing threat that this rebellion is causing to our plans. I've heard that one of our supply mines was recently raided and, as I understand, it was one of your mines dear King Zeul. Therefore, may we have an update on what is being done to end this nuisance?"

"Yes, it is true. The rebels did happen upon one of my family's mines. They stole a few supplies and got away. However, they took nothing of significance. I believe the new security measures we've put into place will eventually crush this group. It's only a matter of time," replied Zeul.

"Agreed!" shouted many.

"Forgive me for belaboring the point, but early on it was reported that this rebel leader could very well be the return of Loha. However, as you speak, I detect that you now know differently. Is that correct, My Lord?"

Zeul shifted slightly in his chair as he lowered his gaze to look at Davison. "Even if this is the prophesied return, I am confident that we will crush this feeble attempt of an uprising before it goes any further."

Davison, unfazed, continued to sow discord against Zeul, "Forgive me, once more, as I continue to address this issue. How is it that they just happened upon the one mine that was not adequately guarded? As I understand it, there were only eight workers. Seven were found dead in the mine, and the other has not been heard of since."

"I very much appreciate your concerns, dear King. But why don't we cut to the quick; what are you getting at?" asked Zeul, cocking his head slightly to the side while the other kings shifted in their seats.

"Oh, please don't misunderstand me My King. I believe the brothers would agree with me that all of us are united in our cause, and not just in our cause, but in our faith in you to lead us to our destiny."

"Agreed!" shouted the others as they banged their fists even harder against the table.

"When we discovered, long ago, that you were the son of Qayin in his old age, we knew it did not matter that your mother was a concubine. Your blood was of a greater purity than the rest of us. We were just mere descendants of our great father, while you were his direct offspring. It was our joy to help you build your kingdom from nothing."

The brother kings began to stir once more and look inquisitively at one another. To mention they helped to build his kingdom was a mild insult, to say the least, but to mention that his mother was a concubine was clearly a backhanded slap.

Davison continued, "You have set the example for all of us by offering up your own son, so that we may ascend to the heavens through our master Halail and enact justified vengeance for what the ancient one did to our beloved father."

"Agreed! Agreed!!" they all shouted.

"If you wouldn't mind dear brother, get to the point," Zeul said.

"How is it that this so-called Loha is always so fortunate? From what I hear, he cannot be killed, and no one can stop him. It's as if...someone is helping him," Davison said while looking around the room. He made it a point to look at each king for a moment and then finally, with his last word, his gaze came to rest on Zeul.

Silence filled the cavernous room. All eyes were locked on Zeul, waiting for him to dispel their growing concern.

Zeul's eyes penetrated King Davison and, in a calm, steely voice, asked, "Who do you think it is...brother?"

It was soon quite clear, to all in attendance, that Davison did not expect a turn of the tables. He had miscalculated, hoping Zeul would cower upon his throne, rather than put him on the spot. Davison finally muttered out as best he could, "It must be...uh...the ancient one?"

All eyes, in unison, shifted back to Zeul, waiting for his response. Only Vidas and Mathal took a moment to shoot a quick glance at one another.

Without the light of Shemesh to indicate the passing of the day, one might have thought that eons had elapsed before Zeul answered. Lifting his hand slowly and then making a fist, Zeul slammed his hand down onto the arm of his throne, cracking it ever so slightly. He then spoke in an eerily gentle voice, "Agreed."

With a voice barely above a whisper, Davison said, "Agreed... My King."

No one vocalized their thoughts, but it was clear that Davison had successfully sown the seeds of doubt; he did so, however, at a hefty price.

Before anyone could say another word, Halail materialized in the same fashion as before, prompting all to bow down before him.

"Rejoice Brothers! Your time of redemption is close at hand," thundered Halail.

"Praise almighty Halail," they all shouted.

"I see that all of you are making great strides. I could not be ever prouder. Only you, the sons of Qayin, are worthy to ascend and sit by my side, to rule with me. It's only a matter of time before we remove those abominations from their throne and establish our rule over the heavens."

"Agreed!"

"And now, I ask that you all leave me to converse with your worthy brother and king," Halail said, through the blinding white light.

Once the others had left the room, closing the doors behind them, Halail for the first time manifested himself apart from the light.

"Zeul, you may look upon me now."

Zeul slowly lifted his eyes to gaze at the most beautiful

creature he had ever seen. With hair white as wool, feet like that of bronze burning in a fire, and a long white robe that was whiter than any fuller on Araz could clean; needless to say, he was beyond impressive.

"Zeul, please, have a seat with me," Halail said while motioning towards the round stone table.

Noticing his labored movements, Halail reached out his hand and helped Zeul to his feet.

"It's alright. You don't need to be frightened of me. Please, have a seat."

Once they both made it to the table and sat down, Halail said to his servants, who had just manifested, "Please, get us both a glass of wine. I believe Zeul needs to calm his nerves."

"What...why...uh...," Zeul stammered, trying to understand why he was now seeing Halail in this form.

As the servants set the glasses of wine down, Zeul stared at them as well, bewildered by their appearance.

"Zeul, I know what you are going through. You remind me of myself, so long ago."

"I do?"

"Yes. I sense within you a wavering that does concern me, but isn't unknown to me. You see I, too, wavered once. As well as all my brothers," Halail said while motioning to his two servants standing off to the side. Within a few moments, however, the whole room was filled with a multitude of servants.

Halail waited for a few moments, allowing Zeul to take in the scene before he spoke. "But in time we knew what we did was right. We could no longer be told what to do and where to go, or what to obey. We wanted to create our own destiny, rather than let another decide for us. And you want that as well; I know that. Wouldn't you agree?"

Having difficulty taking it all in, Zeul finally spoke, "Yes...I want to decide what happens to me."

"Exactly! You see, we want the same thing. We all want the same thing," he said while motioning toward his servants. "To be the captain of our own destiny; the master of our own fate. But to do that, we had to make a sacrifice. You understand?"

"I understand."

"Besides, there is no returning for us, and there is no returning for you. Once you have crossed over, you cannot return. So what will you do?" Halail asked as he took a sip of wine.

Looking around the room and up toward the ceiling once more to take in the majesty of it all, Zeul finally looked upon Halail and said, "I'll do the right thing. I will bring Aaranon to me and finish what I started."

"Magnificent, my brother. Superb! Soon, you will join with us and lead your brothers to a state of being you've never experienced before. Then, we will put an end to the plans of the wretched one and break his line for all eternity."

Chapter 45

"This looks good. In fact, it looks fabulous! It's cooled down enough for us to move through here. It brings back memories," Aaranon said as he ran his hand along the smooth stone they recently cut.

"Memories?" asked Pernel as he set down one of the drills.

"Uh...yeah...I use to drill stone before I went into the military," he said, recovering his slip.

"So how much further to the temple?" Ballac asked.

"According to my calculations, we should be just under it right now," replied Drahcir.

"What about the alternative shafts? Are they complete?" Aaranon asked Pernel.

"Yes. They'll need to cool before we can enter though. Some of the rock didn't flow very well into the crevices, so we had to pull that debris out. We will need to rig each shaft just in case they chase after us."

"Good. Hopefully with these smaller shafts it will be difficult for those MSS to maneuver around down here; especially those mingled creatures with mechanized weapons," replied Aaranon.

"Well, if I'm any indication, then I would say yes, they will have difficulty moving," replied Drahcir as he tried to turn his rotund body around so he could exit the shaft.

"You know, we could use Drahcir to plug the hole to keep them from coming after us."

"Aveed, enough," Aaranon said.

"I'm just saying. Plus they could gnaw on his hind end for a long time. That would give us plenty of time to get away," replied Aveed with the same sarcastic grin.

"Loha," said Mishna.

"Yes."

"I might have a lead on that console we needed."

"A lead?"

"Yes, even though they locked me away, I still happened to make a few friends in the government."

"Who's your contact?"

"Uh...I don't know his name, but he was able to acquire one console."

"How do you know he isn't working for the government?"

"Oh...I can assure you Loha; he despises this Alemeleg with all his heart. He is more than happy to assist our cause."

"So...how are you planning to get it?"

"We're still working that out, but I will let you know as soon as I know."

"I would like Aveed and his group to go with you when you pick it up," replied Aaranon.

"Wonderful! I would be happy to have Aveed and his group by my side," Mishna said, patting Aveed on the back.

Drahcir turned back to look at Mishna; wondering when he would get a chance to speak with Aaranon about what he'd learned of their resident genius.

"What?" asked Mishna, looking at Drahcir.

"Just keep moving grease trap," shouted Aveed.

"Both of you...," said Aaranon pointing at them.

"I got it. I'll try to stop making fun of fatty pants over there...I mean Drahcir," replied Aveed. Looking towards Drahcir, he said, "Nothing but love for you bulbous...I mean... brother. Tarsis, I can't stop, can I?"

Looking slightly disgusted, Aaranon said, "Anyway...let's get out of here and let all these shafts cool. Then we'll come back later and rig all of them."

***

"Don't move or I'll blow that ugly skirt right up through that privy hole of yours and out your throat," shouted Aveed to one of the temple priests as he exited the shaft inside the temple.

Within a few moments, several of Aaranon's udamé came pouring through the opening and began releasing the temple maidens and setting the bombs to destroy the temple.

"Rachael! Rachael is that you?" yelled Hena as he looked at his wife for the first time in over two years.

"Hena? Is it truly you," she said while trembling with fear and excitement.

"Oh love, it's me. I'm here. I'm here."

"Sorry priest, but you just heard way too much," said Aveed as he proceeded to kill him and a few others who heard the exchange between Hena and his wife.

"Let's move everyone! We don't have time," yelled Aaranon as he looked over at the dead priests and then up at Aveed.

"Couldn't help it Loha. They heard too much," said Aveed.

"I know," Aaranon said. He then turned to the others and shouted, "Keep moving! We don't have much time!"

"Loha," came Sdra'de over the farspeak.

"Go ahead."

"They're coming."

"Everyone, let's go! Down the shaft! Pernel, do you have the explosives set to bring this thing down?"

"Yeah, they're all set. Why don't you go. Mishna, Aveed and I will take up the rear. You get the rest out," replied Pernel.

"Why? That's not what we talked about."

"Loha, you're more important than us. Besides Mishna has a new deterrent he wants to try."

"New deterrent?"

"Yes. I believe this will help us tremendously," replied Mishna.

Due to the urgency of the situation, Aaranon decided not to argue over the change in plans. He headed down the shaft, leaving Mishna, Aveed, Pernel, and four others to bring up the rear.

Looking down the hole to make sure they were far enough away, Aveed said, "They're gone." Rubbing the back of his neck he said, "I sure hope this dacking thing works. I'm counting on you being right."

"Have I failed you yet?" Mishna asked. "Now hurry up and cover that hole, but let the other one stay exposed." He instructed Pernel to cover up the hole through which the others escaped, but to leave another shaft exposed that was empty, yet rigged with explosives.

"Hide your weapons," Aveed said to the others.

"Alright, here they come. Get ready," said Pernel as he watched the temple become flooded with MSS troopers.

In a deep gravelly voice, one of them ran up to Mishna and said, "Where did they go?"

"They ran down that shaft over there. Hurry, I'm sure you can catch them."

Immediately, every last MSS trooper dove down into the hole that was rigged with multiple explosives. Soon after, several UAK soldiers came running into the temple. By this time, Pernel was removing the cover from the other shaft. Everyone but Mishna made it into the hole before the soldiers were near to him.

"Stop, Thar bamé Luden! What are you doing," asked one of the soldiers while reading off the name from his console.

"Oh...so sorry. I'm not Thar. That must be the name of the one I killed. Let me show you something," Mishna held up a trigger device and pushed it. A massive boom shook the temple, sending a mountain of dust up from the shaft the MSS troopers dove down into, and knocked many of the soldiers off their feet.

"That was for my father. And this...," he said as he dropped down further into the shaft before he pushed another trigger which destroyed the whole temple; killing everyone who was left inside, "…is for me."

"Holy Dack, they worked," yelped Aveed.

"Of course they worked," replied Mishna patting the back of his neck.

A voice spoke from the shadows of the tunnel. "What worked?"

"Dack Aaranon! Don't scare us like that, I could have shot you," replied Aveed.

"Mishna was able to create seven of those citizen implants they've been giving out. They worked! They didn't attack us," Pernel said with great enthusiasm.

Aaranon recalled the seven dead workers at the mine and then shot an angry look at Mishna.

"Oh! Don't play coy with me Loha! You know what happened, and you know it was necessary," Mishna barked.

"You and I need to talk once we get out of here," he said looking frustrated and angry.

"What did I miss?" asked Aveed.

"Nothing. Mishna and I just need to work something out. Let's go!" Aaranon said as he moved ahead of the others; leaving the three to lag behind and talk amongst themselves.

"What's wrong with him?" whispered Pernel to Mishna.

"I don't know. I thought he would be excited. Maybe he's upset that we killed those soldiers."

"Yeah, he didn't look too happy that I killed those priests either," replied Aveed.

"Let's just get out of here and talk it over later. I'm sure he has a good reason for being upset," Pernel said.

Hoping to sow discord into their minds about their leader, Mishna whispered, "Pernel, you don't have to keep defending him. I know everyone believes that he will lead us to this great victory. Even though he gave us that stirring speech, I still think he is wavering as to what our actual purpose is."

Turning to Pernel, Aveed said, "Don't get me wrong Pernel, I love Loha. I wouldn't want anyone else by my side fighting, but I think Mishna is right. He wavers too much on what our real goal is."

"Like I said...let's get out of here, and we can talk later," he said, gently pushing the others to move forward.

Chapter 46

"Has anyone seen Loha? I need to speak with him," Pernel asked several of the rebels as he walked through the camp.

From high up above in the trees, Aaranon placed his finger to his lips, requesting Yosef to remain silent.

"Why don't you want him to know we're up here?" asked Yosef.

"I just need a break. We've been going for so long, I feel like I haven't had time to sit and just think," Aaranon replied.

"Well, you do have your hands full that's for sure. I don't know what you're going through, but I can tell it's wearing on you."

"It is Yosef. I'm glad you're here. At least with you I can be more open. Could you imagine what Pernel and the others would do if they knew the truth about me? They would think I was a spy, or a tool being used by the government to create a rebellion."

"What do you mean?"

"The government was only using the Apostates to create a false opposition. It allowed them to solidify their power."

"So you think they're using us for that purpose; because they've really clamped down on everything. You can't take a dump in the city without their permission."

Aaranon stroked his beard and looked up. "You know that makes me wonder."

"Wonder? About what?"

"What if our fortunes, accomplishments, narrow escapes; what if they're not due to our abilities, but due to the UAC permitting us to create havoc?"

"I don't see how that's possible. I haven't been on every raid, but from what I've seen, those soldiers and MSS troops are unrelenting. They're doing all they can to stop us. I mean look at all the security they've put in place."

"I don't know why this just now hit me, but this sounds like something my father would do. If the Apostates were no longer useful, he would need to find another enemy with which to further solidify his power over the kingdoms. Apparently, we are that new opposition."

"Hmm. I never thought of that."

"Yeah...why did I miss that," Aaranon replied, recalling the ineptness he had toward his father the first time.

"That's seriously evil Aaranon. How could anyone think like that? That's just so deceptive."

Aaranon didn't vocalize it, but he believed everyone was capable of that level of deception. Even he was using the same tactics, like that of his father, to get others to fight for him.

"You in there Aaranon?" asked Yosef.

"Oh...yeah. Sorry. I get caught up in my thoughts."

"So what do you want to do?"

"Do?"

"Yeah. If they're using you as you think they are, then what should we do?"

"If they're using us as controlled opposition, then that means someone in the group, or several someones are here on their behalf. I suspected this before, but I thought the UAC would send spies in to take us down, not to prop us up."

Looking out over the limb, Yosef could see Pernel walking further into the woods by himself.

"Now where do you think he's going?" asked Yosef.

"Who?"

"Pernel. He's walking away from the camp, and he keeps looking back; like he's checking to make sure he isn't being followed."

"Well, I thought he was looking for me," replied Aaranon.

"You think maybe we should follow him to see what he's up

to?"

"Good idea, let's go."

**

After following Pernel for several hundred *ama* outside the camp, he finally stopped at the edge of a cliff and sat down. Aaranon and Yosef continued to hide up in the trees, waiting to see what he would do.

"Looks like he's doing what you were doing."

"Yeah...getting away to think. We all need to do that don't we," Aaranon said with a mild grin.

"We sure...wait! Look over there. Looks like an old cargo carrier coming this way."

"Those are common around here."

"They sure are, but that one looks like it's heading straight for Pernel. And he isn't looking to run and hide."

As they watched, Pernel boarded the small cargo carrier and then flew away.

"Now what do you think that's all about?" asked Yosef.

"I don't know. But I need to find out."

"Aaranon, what if he's the insider like we talked about? If I were you, I would keep an eye on him."

Aaranon didn't want to believe it, but he needed to be honest with himself and admit that not only could Pernel be working for the UAK, but anyone else as well; even Yosef.

"What in tarsis is going on!? Look over there Aaranon," he said, pointing in the other direction.

"That looks like Mishna. I wonder if this is his contact for the console."

"It might be, but where are Aveed and his crew? I thought they were all going together."

"Hmm, that's what I thought too," Aaranon said as they both watched two udamé and one wudam step off their wind runners. As the two udamé came near to Mishna, the wudam pulled her

EB and killed them both. She then holstered her weapon and handed Mishna the console.

"What the dack is going on?" asked Aaranon.

"I have no idea, but you need to keep an eye on both of them. Look! She's leaving now. And she just boarded that cargo vessel hidden behind that cliff."

"Yeah, and Mishna is going the other way; and he's just leaving those two bodies there. Let's go and check them out."

***

Once Mishna was far out of sight. Aaranon and Yosef climbed down the tree and rushed over to the bodies.

"Mercenaries! You can tell by their tattoos," said Yosef.

"Yeah, and not just any mercenaries. These belong to my brother, Ravizu."

"Are you serious? Dack! This just keeps getting worse. Do you think your brother knows that you're Loha?"

Aaranon scratched his head. All he could say was, "I have no idea."

Chapter 47

"Two ales please," asked Darham as they sat around the far corner table of the old pub, hoping to speak in private. Looking at Amana, he asked, "So how much further?"

"I only know that we're near, but I'm not exactly sure how close we are. I heard this was the pub where he killed an agent and his MSS trooper. That large indentation on the floor is supposedly where the beast fell," she said motioning toward the cracked stone floor near to the opening.

"That's true, I saw it happen right there," said one of the patrons who couldn't help but overhear their conversation as he sat, without being noticed, nestled in the dark corner. "It was a day I will remember for the rest of my life. He didn't even move a muscle to kill that thing. Clearly he has returned from the gods."

"Hogwash!" shouted an older patron sitting nearby, "He's nothing but a menace! He needs to stop all that before more innocent people get killed."

"Oh no. Here they go again. Why don't you two just drop it before that dacking agent gets here," said another patron sitting on the opposite side.

"Dack you, you old coot. You've lived your life; I have many more years to go, and I would like to live it in freedom."

"You can kiss what freedom you have goodbye if that so-called savior of yours keeps it up. Your best bet is to shut up and live your life; you cripple."

"Oh...blow it out your rear," he said. Moving next to Darham, he whispered, "Don't worry about them. They're too old to care. Biltner is my name."

Reaching out to shake his hand, Darham answered, "Pleased

to meet you."

Looking at the others, he said, "I can tell you ain't spies. I have an eye for that, you know." Pointing to Amana, he said, "You. I can tell you've spent time in the temples."

Slightly bewildered but curious, she asked, "Really? How can you tell?"

Raising his dirt filled hand to his eye, he said, "It's in the eyes. My sister looked the same. I was only able to visit her once. I'll never forget it."

"What happened to her," Dihana asked.

Averting his eyes as he recalled the dreadful memory, "She didn't make it out. I tried to earn enough to buy her back, but it wasn't enough."

"I'm sorry," replied Micah while Dihana reached over to grab his hand.

Pushing aside the memory, he looked back up with a smile and said, "You three, however, don't look like peasants."

Darham started to grow uneasy until Biltner said, "You look like upper-class that have come to join the fight. Plenty of them are joining up."

"Yes! Exactly," Amana said, "In fact, it was his brother who freed me. We've heard that he joined up with the group, and I want to pay him back for all he did for me."

"Sounds about right. That Loha said our true enemy isn't folks like yourselves, but the ones who rule this world. I would join the cause myself if I had a good pair of legs to stand on," he said while pointing to his legs that were missing from the knee down. "Lost them to one of those dacking beasts. The former agent who wondered these parts had his slave bite my legs off because I looked at him funny."

"You didn't look at him funny; you insulted him to his face," the old patron yelled.

Biltner replied, "Well I looked at him funny when I said it!"

"Do you know where we can find Loha?" Darham whispered.

"Nobody really knows where he is. They seem to move about

quite often to avoid detection. Don't want to get caught, you know. But there is a village not far from here that can help you. When you leave here, head west until you come to an old road that leads south. That will take you to the village. Ask for Elder Isma. He can help you. A little crazy, but very helpful when he wants to be."

"Thank you," Amana said.

"No trouble at all," he said as he scooted out the door using his hands to move himself.

Drawing nearer to one another to whisper, Amana said, "I know that name, Isma. Rohu mentioned him to me."

"We must be headed in the proper direction, right?" whispered Dihana, hoping she would soon meet up with her brother.

Before they could speak further, the old patron who was arguing with Biltner came over. He pulled up a chair with its back to the table, sloshed down his drink, crossed his arms over the back of the chair and began his story.

"My name is Vultnor, if you have a care to know. And I'm not a shill for the government like that cripple tells everyone. I've lived for over eight hundred years, and I've seen the ups and downs of this life. None of you look to be over fifty, so listen up because this is the best advice you'll ever get."

While he paused for a moment to take a drink, Darham tried to interrupt but was unsuccessful. "There was a day when we udamé...huh...funny how even words have fallen like the rest of this world. Anyway, there was a day, so long ago, when the world wasn't as small as it is today. You could knock yourself out a nice bit of land. Farm it. Live on it. Breathe on it. It was wonderful. The Ayim had already arrived, but we still had freedom.

"I seen them once. From a distance. Beautiful. Couldn't take my eyes off 'em. But I knew, on that day, that things would change. Then came the heboram. Massive and fierce. Ugly looking things if you ask me. That's when Loha began his quest.

I was excited then. I honestly was. I was also young and idealistic." Vultnor paused as he looked at the deep wrinkles reflected in his mug of ale.

"And then he did something that changed my mind about him. He began killing whole villages - fathers, mothers, brothers, sisters, children, and even infants. Anyone that he thought was helping the heboram, he slaughtered them. Burned their villages," pausing to look up. "He even burned mine."

The four looked back and forth at one another in confusion. Amana asked in disbelief, "The first Loha? He killed your family?"

"Hard to believe after hearing all the wonderful stories, isn't it? Since many in my village worshipped those disgusting Ayim, he thought we helped their monstrous offspring. Others may have, but for me and my family, we didn't. But that didn't matter to him. He was out for vengeance, and nothing was going to get in his way. Not even the truth."

"But that doesn't sound like the Loha I heard of," replied Dihana while trying to contain her feelings.

"People only remember the parts they want to, the sins just get forgotten. There were stories told that he grieved over what he had done. Ran away they said. Never to be seen again. Legend says he was taken to the gods. I don't know about any of that. I only know he took my family. And now they say he has returned."

Each of the three who knew Rohu the best, couldn't fathom what they had just heard. They only knew him as a kind and gentle udam who wouldn't hurt anyone. To think of him any other way was incongruous.

Vultnor continued his slow droning, "They praise him all across this village. I tried to warn them, but no one listens. They praise him for fighting against the kingdom, but I hear about those who died while he was seeking his revenge. Many of the young say, 'It's better to die on your feet, than to serve on your knees.' But for me; I would much rather hold my children on my knees than to stand on their graves."

Vultnor stammered to his feet and sloshed his ale as he went. He paused for a moment. Without turning to face the four, he left them these sobering words, "If you find this Loha, and it's really him, tell him...tell him I forgive him. A few hundred years of anger is long enough for me."

Watching him waddle his way back to the bar, Amana turned to the others and said, "I knew Rohu had deep regret for something, I just didn't know the full extent."

Dihana, looking bewildered and confused, said, "It broke my heart to hear that. We've got to find Aaranon now and put a stop to this before it goes any further. I can't imagine he could..."

Dihana turned into Micah and held onto him as she tried to hide her tears.

Grabbing her shoulder, Darham said, "Don't worry. We'll get to him."

Reaching out to touch her chin, Amana said, "Dihana, look at me dear. Aaranon has a greater purpose. Rohu told me what that was."

"What do you mean?" she asked.

"Move in closer, she's about to reveal the secret," said one of Halail's servants.

"Shut up, we need to hear...LOOK OUT!" cried the other servant, moving quickly out of the way as the multitude that surrounded Amana moved closer in to protect her.

As Amana continued to speak, not realizing the protection she and her traveling companions received, one of the servants of Halail said to the other, "Dack! Why didn't you tell me they were there?"

"How could I know they were there? You didn't see them either."

"We speak none of this to Halail. Agreed?"

"Agreed!"

While the patrons of the bar stammered in and out of the pub, Amana revealed all that she knew of Aaranon's destiny.

"Oh my!" Dihana said while she tried to slow her heart rate and catch her breath after she heard all Amana had to say.

Holding his head, Darham asked, "Are you sure Amana? I don't understand."

"I know. I don't understand it either. Besides, that isn't just laid before him, but before us as well."

Wanting to focus on the task at hand, Micah said, "Sounds like we need to go then."

Holding his hand and looking up at him in concern, Dihana said to Micah, "Are you sure you want to do this?"

"Being by your side is my purpose. So wherever you go, I go."

"Well then. Here we go," Darham said while standing up, prompting the others to do the same.

Chapter 48

"Loha! There you are. I've been looking all over for you," Pernel said as he walked into the room of the newly created hideout.

With his back to the door, Aaranon quickly tucked away his necklace, shrugged off his emotions and said, "Really?! You were looking for me?"

"Well...yes," he answered, trying to see what Aaranon was doing.

Looking Pernel up and down, Aaranon retorted sarcastically, "That's interesting because Yosef and I...we went looking for you as well. You know...out in the forest."

"Why are you looking at me that way?"

"What way?" he said, shrugging his shoulders.

"This way!" he replied, quickly looking Aaranon up and down in a mocking manner.

"You look different. I'm not sure what it is, just...different. The hair maybe?"

"Have you been drinking?"

"No. Your hair has that windblown look. Kind of like Sdra'de looks after he comes back from riding the ananin. Have you been riding one of the ananin?"

"Uh...right. Anyway...uh..."

Not giving Pernel a chance to speak, Aaranon reached for the back of Pernel's neck and said, "I see that new deterrent Mishna created worked quite well."

"What are you doing, Loha? You're acting weird."

"I am? Because I find it odd that seven of you stayed behind at the temple to *test* a new deterrent and that just happens to be the same number of mineworkers that Mishna *accidently* killed."

"What are you talking about? Mishna said you released them when you left."

"No. As I was leaving, that was my plan, but Mishna said they tried to escape, so he shot them all. Accidently of course. Apparently he isn't too good with those infernal weapons, as he put it."

"What?"

"However, it does appear he's reasonably good with a knife. He put a stolen device in you, not a created one like he said."

"Wait a moment! He said he created them."

"Yeah, right. He lied."

"Loha, I didn't know he did that."

"That seems to be the norm around here now, doesn't it? People going off and doing things that others don't know about. What did you want to tell me that was so urgent, Pernel?"

Pernel took a moment to rub the back of his neck. "Loha, I'm sorry. He said he created them. I honestly thought..."

"Well...you thought wrong, Pernel."

Pernel began to rub his head once more as if a tremendous pain was washing over him again. Aaranon didn't notice, however, as he continued his thought, "I'll deal with Mishna later, but let's deal with what you need to tell me."

"Uh...I...uh..."

"Spit it out, Pernel."

"Well...you're not going to like this."

"Oh dack. What is it?"

"Since you gave us a few days to recover before the next raid, some wanted to blow off some steam. So a few days ago, Mishna, Aveed, Ballac and the others with the implants took the drills and went to one of the nearby kingdoms."

"What?! I didn't authorize that. What are they doing?" Aaranon grabbed his blades, a few EBs, and some supplies while Pernel hesitantly spoke.

"Since the deterrent worked, Mishna and I decided..."

"You two decided?!"

Frustrated, yet confident, Pernel said, "Yes! We decided!"

"And what did you decide?" Aaranon demanded while getting up in his face.

"Before I go any further, let me remind you of the speech you gave not too long ago."

"Go ahead, *remind me.*"

"You said our true enemy isn't the peasants, nor the lower or upper-class, but the nobles, right? The ones who do nothing but push us around while they just sit on their hind ends. Do you remember that?" Pernel retorted, getting even closer to Aaranon.

"Yeah, and what about it?"

"We followed your lead and decided to take the *fight* to them."

"Is that right?"

"Yes it is, *Loha!*"

"And what family are you taking this to, may I ask?"

"King Davison!"

Aaranon's heart skipped a beat. Whihany!

Backing away slightly, trying to hide his angst, Aaranon asked, "What did you tell them to do?"

"Uh...well..."

"What did you tell them to do, Pernel!?" shouted Aaranon.

"I wanted them to kill only the King. You know, to use his blood for that console. But Mishna wanted to make it clear that none of them are safe!"

"What is he going to do, Pernel!?"

"I tried to tell him different, but he was emphatic."

"For crying out loud Pernel, say it!"

"They're going to kill everyone and burn the place to the ground."

Without hesitation, Aaranon yelled, "We need to go...NOW!"

"But...isn't this what you wanted?"

"You fool! What have you done?!" he said as he ran out the door.

Without moving a muscle, Pernel shouted to Aaranon as he ran out of the room, "There were no guards near the castle. It was the easiest of targets! I thought you would be proud of us!"

**

Climbing up through the hole that led into the grand foyer of Davison's castle, Aaranon could hear screams coming from the second floor. With the fire already spreading throughout the first floor, he could barely make his way up the stairs. With his mask on to hide his identity, he ran from room to room looking for Whihany.

As he entered the room where the screams emanated, he could see Aveed on top of a wudam while two others held her down. Pulling Aveed off, he could see that it wasn't her.

"What the dack! Hey, glad to see you could make it!" Aveed said with a smile beaming from ear to ear.

"What are you doing?" Aaranon asked, trying to conceal his concern for Whihany.

"Now...I don't think Aveed needs to explain to a robust udam like yourself on the finer things in life, but if you need a demonstration..."

"You know what I mean. Why are you raping these wudamé?"

"Uh...why not? She's gonna die no matter what. Mishna said it might be the only time we'll ever get some royal lovin'...so... *have at it*, he said."

"Are there any more wudamé here?"

"Now you're talking! Yeah...there is one left that I know of; she's in a locked room on the highest floor. But be careful with her though. She has some tricks up her sleeve. Just about cast a wicked spell on me."

Hiding his disgust, Aaranon said, "Before I have my fun with her, do you know where Mishna is?"

"Not sure. He said he was going to get some blood for that

console of his. Did you know that idiot went and got it without me? He's getting bolder the longer he hangs with me."

Aaranon quickly headed out the door, leaving Aveed and the others to destroy the young princess. Coming to another room, he found King Davison bleeding profusely from the chest, just barely alive. Aaranon pulled his mask off and said, "Is my father using me like he did the Apostates? Is this another game he's playing?"

With blood spewing out of his mouth he said, "It's you. I knew you were alive."

"What is my father planning? Tell me!" he shouted while pulling on his once beautiful robe.

"Please, I beg of you. Save my daughter. Save Whihany...," he said before he collapsed into his arms. Aaranon attempted to revive him and ask more questions, but it was too late. Putting his mask back on, he began running again from room to room to find her. As the flames climbed every floor, he feared the worst.

Running up the stairs and down the hall to the room on the end, he finally found her. With the doors locked, he repeatedly kicked until they opened. Once inside, he saw her from across the room, standing on the railing of the balcony, ready to leap to her death.

"Stay away from me!" she shouted.

Aaranon quickly closed the door behind him, took off his mask and spoke softly to her, "Don't jump, it's me."

"Aaranon? What's going on?"

"I need to get you out of here."

"Why are you doing this? Why?!"

"I didn't authorize this. I didn't command them to do this. You have to believe me; this isn't my doing."

"Is it because of Ravizu?"

"What?"

"He knows you're alive. He wanted me to...I'm so sorry I lied to you. He made me do it. I didn't want to, but he made me," she said, tears running down her cheeks.

"Look, I don't know what you're talking about, but let's worry about that later. You need to get out of here right now. I can get you to safety."

"There's nowhere safe Aaranon. There's nowhere safe."

"Yes there is Whihany, just step down and I can get you out of here."

Looking back at the cliff that dropped several hundred *ama* below the castle, she slowly moved closer to the edge.

"I shouldn't have told my father," she said. "I don't know how, but I know Zeul sent you."

"What?"

"Don't be like them Aaranon. Oh please, don't be like them. You're too good for this. Don't be like them," she said while staring deep into his eyes. She whispered, "Don't be like me."

Flames could be seen breaking through every window below them. Off in the distance, UAK Dargons were racing towards their location, but it was too late.

Moving closer to try and grab her, he said, "Whihany you're not making any sense. Just step down and let me save you."

With tears falling onto her gown like a gentle summer rain, she gazed into his beautiful blue eyes and said, "You can't save me. No one can. Please...know this. I loved you from the moment I met you. When I was near you, my spirit soared like never before. You are too good to let them destroy you. Don't let them destroy you like they did my family...like they did me."

He continued to plead. "Whihany, please. Just step away. I can take care of you. I can fix this. I just need..."

"Goodbye my love."

"NO!" Aaranon flung himself against the railing, but it was too late. He watched as she fell, her beautiful gown flowing majestically around her as she floated down and into the cold mist below.

Turning himself around to sit with his back against the railing, he watched as the flames engulfed the once alluring room that Whihany called home. It grabbed at every tapestry, furnishing, and painting it could find; consuming every memory of her with the greatest of ease. The inferno was unrelenting in its quest to devour anything and everything in its path. It knew nothing of mercy or grace. It was devoid of any type of love.

Feeling the heat of the blaze as he sat there, his chest began to bounce ever so slightly. At first he thought it was someone else's voice he heard, but he soon realized it was his own. The chuckling morphed slowly into laughter; and not just a simple cackling, but a hysterical laugh that bordered on insanity. It didn't take long, however, before the unrestrained laughter turned into a wailing that drowned out the roar of an approaching cargo vessel. With all his might, Aaranon yelled into the fire, "YOU WIN!! Can you hear me you dacking bastard? You win!"

Pernel opened the side door of the cargo vessel as it neared the edge of the balcony and screamed, "Loha! Get in, they're coming. We need to get out of here!"

In a voice barely above a whisper, he replied, "I don't care. Just leave me."

"Loha. LOHA!" he screamed to get Aaranon's attention. He didn't speak but only turned to look at Pernel.

"We know where we can find the Alemeleg!"

Aaranon finally stood up. With the flames licking at his back, he looked at the cargo vessel; realizing it was the same one that picked up Pernel in the forest.

Acknowledging his inquisitive looks, Pernel replied, "I know, I know...I should have told you." Turning to the pilot, Pernel said, "This is our new friend. He came to join the fight. His name is..."

"Sohan," Aaranon said in a matter of fact tone. Looking at one another, Sohan was expressionless, except for his eyes. They sought to warn Aaranon, but the son of Zeul already knew.

"Yeah...how did you know?

Chapter 49

"The two of you can leave," Zeul said to the two high commanders, allowing the four MSS troopers that surrounded the captured rebel to remain.

"But Your Highness, this wretched piece of filth obliterated the Davison family. Don't you think...?"

Raising his hand to quiet them, "Clearly, he is bound and chained. He's going nowhere. I will have the MSS take care of him when I'm finished here. Now leave us."

"Yes, Your Highness," they replied, leaving them alone in Zeul's office at the UAC headquarters.

Setting his glass of wine down next to the old leather bound book given to him by Isma, Zeul motioned for the prisoner to sit across from him.

"Dack you," he said while spitting on the ornate sofa.

With a mild shrug, Zeul said, "Suit yourself. You will deliver something to Loha for me."

"Yeah right. I'm not going to stroll back into camp after being here. For all I know, you're going to pack a bomb up my hind end or implant a tracking device. No...dack that! You can just get it over with and feed me to these bloated buffoons," he retorted while kicking the leg of the MSS trooper next to him.

Zeul turned a console around that was resting on the gold encrusted table for the prisoner to see. "Is this the camp you're referring to?"

In disbelief, he stared at the visuals that displayed their current location.

"Or how about this one where you store your supplies? Or this one where you train new recruits? Or this small village where it all began?" Zeul asked rhetorically. Turning the console back around, he then stood up and looked toward the center of the room. The sound of cracking ice signaled the opening of the portal. Zeul only glanced at the MSS troopers. He commanded them, by thought, to pass through. Once the portal was closed he then sat down and sipped his wine while motioning for the prisoner to sit.

After several moments of trying to understand the predicament he was in, the prisoner finally shuffled his chained feet over to the sofa to sit down. Wiping up the spit with his sleeve he gingerly asked, "So…if you know…then…"

"Why haven't I stopped Loha? Well…*that*…is the question, isn't it? The natural place for me to begin would be at that cliff, so long ago. But I think I need to go back much further if I wish to be convincing."

"Huh?"

"I had a home in a beautiful valley, just a few days journey from here. I was away when it happened."

"What is he saying!?" one of the servants of Halail screamed at the other as they hovered outside; looking in through the window.

"Again, you ask such infantile questions. Can you not see the book? If I could get closer, I assure you, I would know precisely what they are saying. Therefore, stop asking!"

"Well then, maybe you can answer me this...why is this rebel here in the first place?"

"Don't you think I've been asking myself that same question?"

"What purpose does he serve? Do you think Zeul is so bold as to try and deceive us?"

"Him? Deceive us?"

"Yes, I guess you're right. That is impossible. No one can deceive us."

"Clearly!"

"But yet, there he sits."

"Will you be quiet and let me think!"

"Always with the thinking. Why do you need to think? We are only here to gather information and report back. You act as if you're the one in charge."

"You still don't get it, do you? We may be his servants, but he expects us to anticipate their moves and advise him of it."

"Well, you're not doing such a fine job of it, now are you? You once thought Zeul was wholly given over to Halail, but now you think otherwise. What makes you think you can discern what will happen next?"

"Getting bold aren't we?"

"I'm not bold, just observant. Instead of trying to figure it out from here, I think I'll just move in and listen for myself."

"I guess I'll let you do the thinking then. Go right ahead. Let's see how that works."

"Fine!" the servant said as he moved through the window and came near to the two. "I don't know what the problem is. I don't see anyone approaching. That fool *thinks* he knows it all."

As Zeul continued to tell his life story to the prisoner, unbeknownst to them, the heavens ripped open, exposing a multitude of warriors, similar to the one who visited Aaranon in his dream.

The one servant still standing outside the window, said to himself, "He will never learn."

Like a flash of lighting, one of the warriors, beaming from head to toe in a blanket of white light, came down and stood between Zeul and the servant.

"You know this one belongs to us! Why are you protecting him?" Halail's servant yelled.

"Leave." the warrior said calmly.

"Or what?"

Several more warriors, brandishing shields of pure gold and blades of crystal, flashed down in an instant, filling the entire room. The warrior, with eyes like flames of fire and hair white as wool, pointed towards the window where the other servant was standing.

"Fine! But you all know that Halail will bring an end to your Lord and Master. Then you will find yourselves on the wrong side."

In a flash, Halail's servant moved back to his companion.

"So, did you get to hear anything...genius?"

"Shut up. At least I tried; which is more than I can say for you."

As the prisoner held the chalice and looked at his reflection in the wine, he asked Zeul, "And that will convince him?"

"I don't know if it will convince him of my plans, but I know it will convince him that we spoke."

"Clearly, I'm not a religious man; and, like you, I've done things I'm ashamed of, but...don't you think there's redemption for udamé like us? I mean, you can't think of any other way to do this?"

"The ancients spoke of something they called, *The Returning*. For those who had fallen from the true path, they believed that one could return," Zeul said while averting his eyes to hide his regret.

"But you don't think that's possible?"

"For you? Maybe. For me? No. I'm too far gone."

"So why..."

"Because...if I cannot return; then maybe I can help others who can. Maybe, I can help him before it's too late."

When Zeul finished, he walked over to remove the bindings from the prisoner. Soon after, the portal opened, revealing the backside of the rebel hideout.

With the chains removed, the prisoner walked to the edge of the portal, turned around and asked, "So when should I tell him?"

"I believe you will know when the time is right," Zeul said.

"You're right. Like you said before, things just seem to happen at the right time when you're around him. Thank you, Your Highness."

"You're welcome, Aveed."

Chapter 50

King Vidas quickly stepped out of a small cargo vessel as it set down near King Mathal's castle.

Mathal was there, waiting to greet him. "I'm so glad you could make it, did anyone follow you?"

"No, I made sure to retrace my path a few times to be certain. Are the other brother kings here?" Vidas inquired as they moved hastily towards the castle.

"Yes. They're here," Mathal said as he scanned the skies for any UAK forces.

"Do they share our suspicions?"

"I believe so. At the very least, they're all concerned after what happened to Davison."

"They do know about the removal of troops from their posts at his castle before the rebels arrived, correct?"

"Yes, of course. This event clearly has Zeul's signature all over it. Since he broke the code and killed a brother king, none of us feel safe," Mathal replied.

"We need to move quickly before Zeul moves against us. Otherwise, we too, shall find our kingdoms burned to the ground."

"Agreed!"

As they entered the castle, unbeknownst to them, several hooded figures, camouflaged by a mist of evaporating ice, stood at the edge of the forest, watching.

***

After spending half the day deliberating over a solution, they still could not come to a consensus as to how to best unseat Zeul from the throne.

"Brothers! Brothers!" Mathal screamed as he banged his fist on the table to get their attention. "We need to make a decision on a course of action now! If we deliberate too long, he *will* move against us."

"We've been over this a thousand times!" shouted King Darvan. "He has sole control over all UAK forces. We cannot attempt a coup. Besides, to do so now would arouse the non-brother kings' awareness to the Brotherhood. We cannot allow them to be even remotely aware of our existence."

"What about an assassination?" asked another king.

"Again, who would we get to do that? All of the kingdoms' assassins are under Zeul's control," yelled Mathal.

"Clearly we cannot use direct means, therefore, let us cease from this course of discussion and think of another way," said King Parvalle.

"The manufactured plot that was used against me; can we not do something similar?" asked King Darvan.

"That is preposterous! We cannot do such a thing without him immediately attacking us," Parvalle replied.

"Obviously, we can't bring up a vote of no confidence, you imbecile. We would influence several of the non-brother kings to do so," replied Darvan.

Parvalle sneered, "Imbecile?! Watch your tongue brother."

"I have sacrificed more for this family than all of you, so don't speak to me that way, you insolent piece of filth," Darvan said while looking down his nose at Parvalle.

"Insolent? Insolent!? I'll have you know I have sacrificed all to stand with the brothers to avenge our father, and I will not be spoken to like that from a puppet Alemeleg. You were good for nothing but a stepping stone."

Vidas shouted, "Both of you, stop! Fighting amongst ourselves isn't helping! Darvan is correct; we need to bring into question his leadership through the other kings, and it can't be linked to us. Now, what can be done to make that happen?"

One king spoke up, "Right now the other kings have no reason to call his leadership into question; or at least not enough to go against him. They need to feel the pressure from the serfs in their kingdoms before they'll make a move."

"Agreed!" yelped another. "The other kings will not put pressure on Zeul to step down unless they feel the pressure themselves as well."

"But how? How do we accomplish that without any forces being at our command?"

Mathal looked over at Vidas and said, "The agents."

"Yes! The agents," replied Vidas.

"What about the agents?" asked Parvalle.

"The agents are under my jurisdiction," replied Vidas. "Each agent has an MSS trooper assigned directly to them. We don't have access to UAK forces, but we do have access to each upper-class law enforcement agent."

"That's right! We can't remove them from their district, but we *can* send a direct message to each of them to step up their harassment and arrests of the lower-class," said Mathal.

"Not only that," said Darvan. "We can also have them imprison the upper-class in their districts on charges of aiding and abetting the enemy. We'll use the law in our favor."

"Precisely!" Parvalle said, excitement growing in his voice. "We could easily plant evidence against the upper-class."

"We're only six days away from the festival to the Ayim. The people need to feel the pain. Zeul has served for three years now, with sole power for most of that time. We cannot allow him to serve another. If we do, I believe none of us will see the light of day."

"However, before we proceed we need to know for certain. Is Aaranon still alive? If he isn't, then we're the ones making a mistake," asked Darvan.

"Yes! He is!" Ravizu shouted as he, Lilith, and his broad band of mercenaries entered the room. Holding up his hands, as if to embrace them, he said, "Brothers, fear not! For I am here to help you with your predicament."

Trembling from head to toe, Vidas ask, "How?"

"Let's just say, Halail has heard your cry and he has sent me to assure you that all is well."

Chapter 51

Anger and dissension against Zeul swept across Araz as agents escalated their efforts against everyone who wasn't a noble. Evidence implicating the innocent as supporters of the rebellion were in abundance, as the legal courts for the upper-class filled to capacity. The sporting arenas were soon turned into mass prisons to accommodate those who were being forcibly removed from their homes and places of work.

The lower-class, however, bore the greatest brunt of the Brotherhood's conniving ways. Because of their status, they were not given the privilege of legal recourse like that of the upper-class. The agents ruled as judge and executioner. For most, they were pulled out into the streets and the village squares to be killed mercilessly in front of their loved ones without even a shred of evidence. Needless to say, the Brotherhood's plan was producing the desired effect; not only against Zeul, but against the rebels as well.

Deep within the forest, reports of their atrocities buffeted Aaranon, like the MSS trooper who attacked him over a year ago. Unlike his previous victory, however, this was a fight he could not win. A few cried out for his help, but most blamed him and the others for all the death and mayhem that was now befalling them.

Lying down on his bed alone, or so he thought, Aaranon took an account of all that lay before him. After spending half the day attempting to find a way through, he could only come to one conclusion; choosing to speak openly to those whom he'd lost, he poured out his heart.

"Rohu, if you could only hear me, I would beg you for your forgiveness. I should have listened to you. You never spoke except that last day, but your silence could have filled all the books in the world. What a fool I was not to heed them.

"I sacrificed those words for a quest; one in which I am no closer to than when I first began. And then, in exchange for looking for Dihana and Darham, I've allowed others to lead me astray and for what; freedom, glory, vengeance? I turned the whole world upside down for nothing. Am I worse than a naive fool?

"You sacrificed your life for me. You demonstrated to me how a real udam should be; kind, compassionate, showing love to others more than yourself, and countless other examples. How does one come to such a place? How did you become such an udam? All I see in this life are wretched, miserable souls who think of nothing but themselves. I lied to myself, saying I wasn't one of them. However, I was wrong. I am chief among them.

"I know you felt regret for killing the heboram, but did those monsters not deserve what they received? Then again, am I not a monster as well? Don't I deserve the same? To know you never stepped across that line, as I have, brings me comfort; but will it be enough to carry me for an eternity? I wish I could cross back over. But I feel it's too late for me. There is far too much blood on my hands. There is no returning for one such as me. I have become like my father.

"I believe he not only knows where I am, but he has been using me, somehow, to foment a rebellion. For what reason? I can only assume it was used to solidify his power. But then again, how can I proclaim to be innocent of the same? I used him as well.

"Ever since that day I heard your voice, I thought, somehow, you were helping me. But why would you be a part of this?

"Other than Dihana and Darham, you were the only one I could trust. I know this camp is full of enemies. I know they're here, but I don't know who they are. It's clear that if I do have any friends, the number is miniscule.

"Enemies. Who is this Mishna? How is he connected to

Ravizu? Whihany said that Ravizu knew I was alive. Does Mishna know who I am? Drahcir says he has information about him that might be useful, but every time he tries to tell me, that dacking Mishna shows up. And now Whihany is dead. She said I was too good for this. If only she could see into my heart. But it's too late for that.

"And then there's Sohan. What the dack did they do to him in those tunnels? I tried to ask, but it's no use. He claims he doesn't remember.

"Even now, at this moment, I seek justification! What a miserable wretch I am. It doesn't matter. Soon it will end. If you can hear me, please know, I'm grateful for all you did. Please forgive me."

Aaranon paused for a moment as he glanced down at the weapon resting next to him on the floor, underneath his satchel.

"Mother, if you can hear me, I'm sorry. I had the opportunity to do what was right. I should have read those scrolls. I think you need to know why I didn't read them.

"For as much as I act like I want to know the truth, I now realize, I want to know the truth about everything else...except myself. I was afraid those scrolls would peer into my soul like that voice I heard in the dream. If the voice I heard wrote those scrolls, then I didn't want to see the real me. But, as time has shown, to ignore your sins is like trying to cheat death. One day, sin and death will find you. Ironic how the two will meet on the same day. I, too, hope you can forgive me."

After pausing for a few moments to wipe away his tears, he then continued, "Yohan! Oh Yohan. I am so sorry. I didn't see what Zeul and Ravizu were doing to you. I was too wrapped up in myself. I was excited that you and I reconnected. I know we could have been the best of friends. But now, that too, is too late."

As he paused once more to wipe his tears, Dihana, Darham and Amana listened from around the corner as Yosef and Micah stood guarding the door. They so desperately wanted to interrupt, but Amana felt he needed to pour out his heart if they were going to have any hope of convincing him to leave.

"Dihana. Darham. I know you can't hear me. But if you could, I want to tell you I'm sorry." They both covered their mouths to keep themselves from wailing.

He continued, "I thought I knew what I was doing. I thought I knew best, but I was wrong. Rohu believed in the ancient one. I believe now that he knew we would be protected if I went to Nahim. Who knows, you both might be there right now waiting for me."

Reaching over to pick up the weapon, he set it gently on his chest. Barely able to speak with tears streaming down his face, he said while lifting the weapon to his head, "It's too late for me, Dihana. I love you so much. Remember me as I once was. Remember our long trips down the river; but not like this. I hope you can forgive me for what I'm about to do."

-Click-

Chapter 52

"NO! STOP!" Dihana screamed as she and Darham jumped onto Aaranon and knocked the weapon away before it could fully discharge.

"DIHANA?! DARHAM?! How?!" he yelped as they all embraced one another, holding on tightly.

"What are you doing, Aaranon? Why were you about to do that?" Dihana cried out; her voice muffled as she wrapped herself around him further, not willing to let go.

Crying even more, Aaranon, barely able to speak, said, "I'm so sorry. I thought I lost you. I'm so sorry. Please forgive me. I'm so sorry."

"It's alright brother, we're here now," Darham said while they all continued to hold onto one another on the dirt floor.

Yosef and Micah stood outside the door to keep watch while Amana stood just inside, crying as she watched them embrace one another.

After what seemed like an eternity, Aaranon, exhausted and overwhelmed, whispered, "How long were you standing there?"

"Long enough," Dihana said.

"How did you find me?"

Darham pointed up to Amana and gently said, "An old friend."

With tears still falling down his handsome face, he grabbed hold of his chest to feel the necklace underneath. He could only say, "Amana." Motioning for her to come near he reached out and held her tightly.

Not knowing how he would receive her, she hesitated. However, it didn't take long before it was abundantly clear that he longed to see her once again.

"How?" was all that Aaranon could say.

Through her tears, she whispered, "Rohu."

Needless to say, everyone continued to hold onto one another, unwilling to let the other out of their sight.

After several moments, Yosef came inside, leaving Micah to continue his vigilant watch. "Please forgive me Aaranon, I don't want to end your reunion, but I think you all need to leave as soon as possible."

Dihana was finally able to back up just a smidge to look at his bald head. She ran her hands over his darkened skin, examining the tattoos. With tears still flowing, she said, "I can't imagine what you went through."

"I'm alright, Dihana."

"Apparently not, you almost ended it all. I would hit you right now, but I don't want to add to your pain."

"Please don't cry anymore, I can't stand to see you cry. I truly am alright now. You're here. Darham is here," looking up at Amana from the edge of his bed, he continued, "Amana is here."

"I knew we would find you. I never doubted it," Darham said, firmly grasping his brother's shoulder.

Unable to hold back his emotions, Aaranon cried and said, "I can't lie to you anymore. I'm not alright. I've done things. Terrible things! I don't want you to know what I've become. If you know, then...then...you won't love me anymore."

Grabbing hold of his beard, Dihana lifted his head up and said gently, "Look at me."

Shuffling his hands on the bed, unwilling to look her in the eye, she said once again in an even softer tone, "Please, Aaranon, look at me." Finally, he lifted his blood-shot eyes to look at his beautiful sister.

"I want you to listen to me right now because you need to know this. First of all...you smell...terrible...quite atrocious actually. I hate what you've done to your hair and beard. And those tattoos look like a small child drew all over your head. And on top of all that, I have to deal with several days of uncontrollable rage and erratic emotions because my body is ready to produce small, time-consuming annoyances. But in spite of all those changes, no matter what you've done, you cannot make me stop loving you. Do you understand me?"

Unable to speak, Aaranon, grabbed hold of his little flower, unwilling to let go.

Straining to speak, Dihana said, "Seriously, you smell like the hind end of an ohema. And don't get me started on your breath."

"It's you. It's truly you," was all Aaranon could say.

"Of course it is. Oh, one more thing."

"What?"

"I want you to meet my future husband."

Aaranon immediately pulled back and shot a look that said, *Not if I have anything to do with it.*

"Really! You know we're not nobles anymore, right?"

"Where is he?"

"Uh...hold on now. He's a good udam. He loves me, and I know you will love him too."

Just then Micah cautiously stepped in the room.

Dihana stood up and grabbed his hand, pulling him closer. Putting her arm around him, with Micah reciprocating she said with a smile, "Aaranon, I want you to meet Micah."

Jumping up quickly and standing next to him with a terrible frown forming, Aaranon inspected Micah by circling him.

"What are you doing," Dihana demanded to know.

Holding up one finger, Aaranon indicated he wanted her to be quiet.

"Aaranon?" Dihana huffed.

Finally, Aaranon wrapped his arms around Micah and gave him a hug. As everyone smiled at their embrace, Aaranon said while he was still holding Micah, "If you touch her before you're married, I'll wrench off your privy."

Without losing a beat, Micah said, "You don't have to worry about that. Dihana already has it somewhere for safe keeping."

With everyone laughing uncontrollably, Aaranon said to Micah, "You are indeed the one for my sister. I think you will do just fine."

"Aaranon," Yosef said.

"I know. We need to leave," he replied.

"If it wasn't for Mishna and a few others, I think you would be safe."

"What do you mean?" asked Aaranon.

"Drahcir told me that Mishna was the son of Greyson, from the Grenaldi clan."

"Huh! Well...that explains a lot. That might explain his connection with Ravizu," Aaranon replied.

"What?!" asked Dihana and Darham.

"I'll explain later. Why didn't Drahcir come tell me?"

"At first, it was because he was having trouble getting near to you without Mishna around."

"And now?"

"I think he's switching sides."

"Sides. What do you mean?" Amana asked.

"Mishna is taking control of the group by spreading rumors that you no longer want to go up against the kingdom."

Dihana, Darham and the others looked at him, fearing he wanted to continue on this dangerous path.

As he smiled at each member of his current, and future family, he replied, "Well then...I guess the rumors are true."

Pulling each other closer, they all embraced; grateful he no longer wanted to travel down the same dark path that Rohu once took.

"If that's the case, then we all need to get out of here," Yosef replied.

"You said a few others. Who are the others, other than Mishna, that are causing problems?" asked Darham.

"Like I mentioned about Drahcir switching sides; he's now helping Mishna to perfect that console to control the MSS troops. For as much as he once admired you, he now wants to annihilate the kingdom altogether, and he believes that Mishna will be the one to do it."

"I can see that. Who else?" asked Aaranon.

"Remember when I first meet Pernel, I said I knew him from somewhere, but I couldn't place him?"

"Yeah."

"Well...when I saw Sohan, I remembered where I saw him."

***

As Halail's servants observed their every move, Aaranon and his family, along with Amana, Yosef, and a soon to be brother-in-law, scurried out the back of the camp without being noticed.

"Alright...now what?"

"It appears they're traveling towards Isma. I assume, if they make it, they will then make their way to the old prophets in Tarshish."

"Hmm...maybe this will work in our favor. Won't Zeul be forced to go after them?"

"You assume too much. We need to inform Halail. He will decide what to do with this information."

"But wouldn't it make sense to let them go all that way? Isn't that what we wanted long ago when we allowed Dihana and Darham to escape?"

"Plans change you fool! Why do I always need to explain this to you?"

"You need to explain nothing. I understand it all."

"Clearly not! If Zeul is truly *returning*, as these pathetic marionettes say, then he is no longer reliable."

"But what of Ravizu? Isn't he being prepped to take his father's place?"

"It appears as such, but I don't know. Do I look like Halail to you?"

"Well...you clearly want to be."

Raising his hand, while bearing his six clawed fingers, the servant took a swipe at his naive partner.

"What was that for?"

"Next time...watch your tongue, or I will remove it. Now let's go. He will need to know this immediately."

Chapter 53

With only three days until the festival to the Ayim, the dissenting members of the Brotherhood decided to, once again, meet at Mathal's castle to further strategize. As each of the members poured in, including Ravizu, they could not contain their excitement over the immediate impact their plan was producing. Once they'd all arrived, the meeting began.

"Everyone, please, come to order, we need to begin," shouted Vidas.

"Brilliant! Just brilliant, dear King Vidas. This plan of yours is working wonderfully," shouted Darvan.

"Let's be very careful to not count our victory before the time. Zeul is clearly feeling the pressure from this surge of arrests, but that's no guarantee that he'll move to crush the rebels along with his own first born."

"What reports are coming out of Zeul's office?" King Parvalle asked.

Mathal responded with pure glee, "As most of you know, there will be an emergency UAC meeting this evening, which several non-Brotherhood members called for. As we suspected, their bottom-feeding constituents have applied the appropriate pressure."

Laughter immediately erupted from all the kings, including Ravizu.

Mathal continued, "With the courts and prisons filled to capacity, the citizens are on the verge of rioting. They're calling for either the head of the rebellion or the head of Zeul."

"Has Zeul contacted any of you," King Darvan asked.

Vidas answered, "Yes. As we suspected, he immediately contacted my offices. We were able, thanks to King Parvalle, to produce all the evidence needed to validate the agents' actions. He may suspect a move from us against him, but he cannot take any legal recourse. If he were to claim that all of the UAC was treasonous, he would appear to be a lunatic; which, of course, would further guarantee a call for a vote of no confidence. Therefore, he has no choice but to act."

"Wonderful! Wonderful!" screamed one of the kings.

"Let us be clear, however, that at tonight's emergency meeting we need to side with Zeul, or it will appear that we are the conspirators," yelled out one king.

"Exactly," said Mathal, "We cannot appear to side with those who are calling for his resignation. According to our last count, there are enough dissenting kings on the council who can call for a vote of no confidence if Zeul refuses to take action."

"So it's clear then. He must move on this group of rebels that he, with the help of King Lachish, created. Created without any of our knowledge or permission," Vidas said as he paused, ever so slightly, to look over at Mathal, hiding his deception from the others. He continued, "Since he started this, then it's his responsibility to clean it up. Once this rebellion is taken care of, then, as promised, he can relinquish his sole power over the council, thus returning a portion of the UAK forces back under our command," replied Vidas.

"But are we ready for that? I mean, are we adequately prepared for the razing? The whole reason we struggled for years to give Zeul full power was for the purpose of preparing without the other kings' knowledge," asked another king.

"Unfortunately, Zeul has been keeping some of the details to himself, but for the most part, yes, we are ready," replied Mathal.

"Once we deal with Zeul, then we will once again have control, and then we can begin preparations for our departure to Mu'udim," King Vidas said.

As they were giddy over the success of their plans, the two servants of Halail appeared in their midst. Waiting for them to calm down, one of the servants spoke to Ravizu, "Ravizu, Dihana and Darham are with Aaranon. He and the others have left the camp and were walking towards a small village to the west. Send your mercenaries to capture Dihana and Darham and deliver them to Zeul but do not harm your brother, Aaranon."

"Uh...but, I thought Halail was preparing me to...," muttered Ravizu before being interrupted.

"You have your orders. Now go," the other servant said before they both disappeared.

While the kings began to talk amongst themselves, Ravizu was clearly agitated over this new information. Without speaking, he rushed out of the room and headed towards Aaranon's location - using the tracking device on the console to find the camp.

As the brother kings wrestled with Halail's request, fearing it would destroy everything they were attempting, the two servants continued to watch, unbeknownst to the others.

"Before you call me an idiot for asking this question, do you understand this request?"

"No, I don't fully understand, but I have a theory."

"By all means, please share."

"Pride."

"Ahh...yes. You believe Halail doesn't want to lose Zeul."

"Yes. Especially to the ancient one. Imagine how the other servants will look at him if he cannot retain someone like Zeul. To betray Halail like that would send shockwaves amongst the others."

"It would be devastating to his leadership."

"Exactly. We need to go. He'll want to know of our progress."

Chapter 54

"Order! Let us come to order please," Zeul said in a calm demeanor as he rapped the gavel.

One agitated king shouted, "What are you going to do about this? We are on the verge of an uprising and these measly peasants who serve us appear to care less and less about the consequences of their actions. They will not give into our threats like before. If you don't do something now, then we will be forced to move against you! I hope I don't have to remind you that the law allows us to remove you from your current position of sole authority with only a vote of three-quarters, and we clearly have that."

Many rapped against their tables and shouted 'Agreed!' leaving Zeul to wait a moment so his voice could be heard when he started speaking.

Once the ruckus subsided, he continued, "My fellow kings, I concur with your assessment. My only desire was to protect this institution that has lasted for centuries. It appears, however, that my efforts have been too far reaching. Therefore, here in my hand, I give to you, my resignation."

Gasps filled the UAC meeting hall at the shock of his announcement. Many of the Brotherhood were unable to hide their concern over this unforeseen move.

Zeul continued, "I will formally resign as Alemeleg the day following the festival to the Ayim. Therefore, for the next three days, I will do my utmost to remove this rebellion. I want you to know that we have finally discovered the rebel hideout."

Mathal turned to Vidas and whispered, "What do you think he's up to?"

"I don't know; I didn't expect this to happen," replied Vidas.

Zeul motioned for the mingled servants to pass out the security briefings to all the kings to review. Once they left, he continued.

"As you can see, they are quite large, but clearly they are no match for our forces. At this present moment, troops are preparing to move against their main base of operation. Although the evidence against the prisoners was unquestionable, I have chosen to pardon all of those arrested. This act is a gesture of goodwill to the upper-class," Zeul said as he looked directly at King Parvalle.

He continued, this time shifting his gaze to Vidas and Mathal. "I have also decided that reparations will be paid to the peasants to compensate for their loss; though I believe nothing will truly quell their anger against the kingdom for what has taken place."

Growing uneasy in their seats, the three anxious kings dared not glance at one another.

In a calmer demeanor, one king asked, "Why, then, are you choosing to step down? Our threat of removal was only for the sake of prompting you to act. It appears, however, that you've been doing so all along so there's no need to remove yourself from power."

All the kings sat in silence as Zeul paused for several moments to gather his thoughts.

As Zeul was looking upward to find the words, Mathal whispered to Darvan, "It appears he's making a move to protect his family. If he steps down of his own volition, then no one will question his loyalty to the kingdom. What does that mean for the next Alemeleg?"

"It took us years to position the Brotherhood in order to seize the throne. Since he has done this, we have no guarantee of being sovereign over the council."

"So in one move, he's protected his family and denied the Brotherhood of absolute rule."

"Precisely," replied Darvan.

"But this doesn't make sense. How does this fit into Halail commanding Ravizu to bring back Dihana and Darham; leaving Aaranon untouched? Does Zeul know that Aaranon and his family aren't with the rebels?"

"He must know. Why else would he then move against the rebels?"

"What if he plans to go to Mu'udim with only his family? What if Ravizu isn't telling the truth of his ambitions?" Mathal asked, panic rising in his voice.

"You need to calm down. We will figure this out, but now isn't the time."

Finally, Zeul gave an answer, "Why am I resigning as Alemeleg, you ask? It has taken me some time to discover this truth. After pondering this for a while, I've come to this conclusion; to reign over Araz is a privilege best suited for one greater than myself. It is an honor best reserved for one with wisdom greater than I possess." He once again paused to look out over the gathering of kings who looked back at him in bewilderment.

One king stood up from his seat and began to applaud, slowly at first. Then another joined, followed by another, and then another. The last to join in, however, to their own detriment, were the members of the Brotherhood. Soon, the applause was followed by shouts of praise and thanksgiving for Zeul's service to the council. Without speaking any further, Zeul removed the crown from his head, placed it on the throne behind him, and walked out of the room.

Having to shout because of the sheer volume of noise, Vidas said to Mathal, "This isn't good. This isn't good at all."

***

Mishna was in a panic. "Has anyone seen Loha!?"

"I thought I saw him leaving last night, but it was dark, so I'm not sure," Sdra'de said.

"I saw him the other day with Yosef. Why? What's wrong?" Ballac replied.

"Drahcir just learned that multiple troops are coming this way! They've discovered where we are!"

"What?! How?!" Mara shouted.

Just then, an enormous boom came from just outside the small bunker they were occupying; knocking them to the ground.

"What do we do without Loha?!" screamed Ballac.

"Listen to me!" yelled Mishna, "I can get us out of this, I have the console. Drahcir is working on changing their mission objective in the underground trench on the other side of the camp."

"Well let's not stand around here and talk about it. Let's move!" screamed Mara as she ran out the door.

As they all fled out the door and up to the surface, they could see the skies filled with multiple Battlecruisers, Armadas and Dargons descending on their location. Dodging missile fire, they all ran to the area of the console; hoping to gain control of the forces that were coming at them.

"Sdra'de! Can you and your tribe draw their fire while we try to get the console working?" asked Mishna as they all huddled inside the hidden trench.

"We'll do what we can but what good will it do if Loha isn't with us?"

"We don't need him. In fact, he isn't the true Loha, we've all been lied to," Mishna said while looking at Ballac.

"What?!" Mara yelled as the bombs continued to fall around them.

"Tell them Ballac! Tell them what you told me!" Mishna said.

Cringing with every blast that fell, Ballac finally said, "It's true, Pernel told you it was him so you and the others would join the fight."

"Then who is he?" Sdra'de shouted as he yanked Ballac near to him.

"An elder of our village said he walked with Loha, but it isn't him," he said, feeling ashamed for having misled the others.

Pushing himself onto Ballac and grabbing his throat, he screamed, "Are you dacking telling me I allowed over half of my tribe to die for a dacking lie!?"

Trying to speak, but barely able to because of Sdra'de's grip on his throat, he eked out, "We only wanted to get our families back. I'm sorry."

"You're sorry?! You're sorry?! It was all a lie! And now our backs are to the wall and, Loha, or whoever the dack he is, isn't here! How dacking convenient!" Sdra'de shouted, ignoring the troops that were now surrounding their hideout as he continued to strangle Ballac.

"Kill that dacking liar," shouted Mara, while one of her golden beasts stood atop Ballac.

"Stop!" shouted Mishna. "We cannot fight one another. We aren't the enemy! *They* are!"

Sdra'de and Mara pulled back, leaving Ballac gasping for air.

"Drahcir, are we ready to use the console?" asked Mishna.

"I'm close, but they've locked down the MCR. They've closed many of the back doors I was using."

"Well, hurry up! We don't have much longer before they destroy us all." Picking up Ballac from the floor, Mishna asked, "Where are Pernel and Aveed?"

Barely able to speak, he said, "They were in their quarters before the attack, but I don't know now. The enemy has surrounded the camp so they could be dead for all I know."

Pointing to the door that was shut, Mishna said, "All of you guard that door while Drahcir and I try to take control of these troops.

Soon after he finished speaking, a large force began beating against the door. With every thrust, the door opened slightly. Ballac, Sdra'de, and Mara did all they could to hold the door shut, but the strength of the MSS troopers pushing against it was too much. With one final blow, they knocked down the door; flinging the three against the far wall.

Mara's beast was no match for the MSS troopers and was destroyed right before her eyes. As they all huddled in the corner waiting for the inevitable, the MSS trooper began to shriek a blood-curdling sound they never heard before. Needless to say, they all turned away, fearing the worst. Soon after, they heard multiple, massive thuds, like large boulders hitting the floor. When they turned around they couldn't believe their eyes.

Sdra'de said to Mishna, "Did you do that?"

"No, they did," he replied, pointing to three large udamé who just killed the MSS troopers with their bare hands.

Unable to stand erect in the bunker, because of their massive frames, one of the udamé rumbled, "Where is the Guardian of the line?"

Chapter 55

While Aaranon and Amana climbed up into a tree to see the night sky, Dihana, Micah, Darham, and Yosef tried to get some sleep in their tents below.

Amana sat silently next to him, trying to find the words to say, but unable to speak. Aaranon, of course, was having the same problem. They never spent any significant time with one another, but their love for each other was overwhelming, to say the least.

Looking down at her hand, he slowly moved his over top hers. She flipped her hand around so she could interlock her fingers with his. While she caressed his hand she could feel the rough, calloused skin underneath. She pulled his hand up closer to examine the years of pain that left his body battered and scarred.

Aaranon then took her other hand to examine the scars inflicted upon her by many tormentors.

As she examined a scar on his wrist, he said, "That was from the first MSS trooper I killed."

"How were you able to do it?" she gently asked, still caressing the scar.

"I'm still asking myself that same question. I thought for sure it was over. But, as that thing lifted me up in the air, I heard Rohu's voice. He told me to turn the plow around. I then drove the tip of it into its head...I don't remember much after that."

"Did you black out?"

Giving out a sigh, he said, "I'm sorry. I lied to you. I remember what happened."

"What do you mean?"

"I didn't want you to know what I said, but, I can't keep lying.

As I was beating that beast with the plow, I was thinking of my father. I kept saying, I hate you; I hate you."

Amana pulled him in closer and put her arm around him. Leaning her head against his, she whispered, "We'll get through this. I know where your mind is right now."

Leaning into her bosom, he said, "I'm so glad you're here. I know we don't know each other that well, but I feel as if we were created for one another."

Amana tried to contain her tears, but she couldn't. They gently fell atop his head, prompting him to look up.

"What's wrong," he asked.

"You know just what to say, don't you?"

"I hope I do now. I'm so tired of lying. Ever since that night at the temple, I knew you and I would, somehow, come together. I just didn't know how."

"Rohu said...," Amana replied before he interrupted.

"You spoke to Rohu?"

"Yes, that night he took me away from the arena, while you stayed back. He told me...," she said before she paused.

He looked into her deep, beautiful green eyes and asked, "What? What did he tell you?"

"He said I was called to rescue you, like you did for me."

Drawing close to her, his lips almost touched hers. "Is that all he told you?"

"No," she sheepishly replied.

Wrapping his arms around her tighter, he asked, "So what else did he say?"

"He said..."

"Yeah..."

"He said...your breath stinks."

After laughing for several moments, Amana grabbed the back of his head and answered, "He said you and I were destined."

"That's all I needed to hear," he said before pulling her closer to caress her soft lips with his.

After several moments of getting to know one another like never before, Amana said through the kissing, "Just so you know, I want to be married first before we go any further."

"Oh...yes...absolutely...I agree. Isma can help us out with that."

"Oh...and...how far away is he," she asked while Aaranon nibbled on her ear.

"If we start running...right now...we can be there...by morning," he said while moving down her neck.

"Alright...but what about...your family?"

"Who?"

"Your brother and sister. What about them?"

"Oh...right...uh...give me a moment," he muttered as he moved back to her lips.

As they continued their passionate embrace, an enormous boom could be heard off in the distance. Ceasing from their activities, they both looked up to see numerous military ships hovering over the rebel camp.

"What's that Aaranon?"

"Oh no. It looks like they found the camp."

Fearing the worst, she asked, "Are you going back?"

"I...I can't. I just can't. Maybe it's for the best. Perhaps my father will think that I died in the attack and then he'll leave me alone."

Looking at him, she could see the conflict that was brewing in his mind.

"I know this must be hard for you, but I think it's for the best," she said.

"I wish I could have told them the truth, the truth about who I am. I feel like a coward for running off in the night."

"I know...but...," Amana replied, before being interrupted by shouts and cries for help coming from below.

"What?! Oh no! They've got Dihana and Darham!" he shouted. He looked down and saw Lilith and several mercenaries dragging his brother and sister into the woods to a small cargo vessel that was quietly resting on the forest floor. Micah and Yosef tried to fight them off but were left unconscious.

Even though they climbed down as fast as they could, they were unable to rescue the two. Running back to the tents, they found Yosef and Micah badly injured, but still alive.

"Micah! Yosef! Can you hear me? Are you alright?" he asked.

"Yeah...yeah...I'm sorry Aaranon. We tried to stop them, but there were too many of them," Yosef replied while Micah was crying uncontrollably on the forest floor.

Amana asked, "Can you both move?"

"Yeah," replied Yosef, with Micah only able to nod his head.

"What do we do now, Aaranon?" she asked.

"Those were Ravizu's mercenaries. They could have easily killed us all, but they didn't. I'm guessing they want me to go after them."

"Where did they take them? Do you know Aaranon?" Yosef asked.

"I'm not sure, but I know somebody who does."

Chapter 56

Bursting through the doors without even knocking, Ravizu and Lilith dragged Dihana and Darham bound in chains into Zeul's office.

"Well, it is a beautiful morning, is it not Father," Ravizu shouted, catching Zeul off guard.

"What's going on?" he asked.

"What's going on? Did you not commission me to find Dihana and Darham and bring them back to you? To bring them back to you unharmed? Well, here they are, *My Lord.*" he answered with sarcasm and fury dripping from every word.

"Ah yes. I haven't heard from you in such a long time, I was beginning to think you had forgotten," he said in a calm and dismissive manner, hiding his concerns over the two being brought to him at this point.

"Oooo! Did you not command me to refrain from communicating on the farspeak? As I recall, you didn't want me to use UAK forces for this. Which begs the question Father; why not? What are you planning? What are you hiding?" Ravizu shouted as he and Lilith threw their two prisoners down on the floor, along with the scrolls that Dihana found in her mother's bed.

"That will be all, you two can leave while I speak with my son and daughter," he said.

"NO! I am NOT leaving until you explain to me what the DACK is going on!"

"Ravizu, I will call for you when I'm ready to speak. You will go now."

"NO!" he said while pulling out two EBs and pointing them at their heads. "You either explain to me why Halail's servants had me bring these two in or I will kill them both."

Since Ravizu confirmed Zeul's concern as to why they were now being brought to him, in a calm fashion, Zeul stood up from his desk and walked near to them. He then glanced for just a moment at Lilith. She immediately and effortlessly removed Ravizu's weapons and pinned him to the floor.

"What is this? What are you doing, Lilith?"

"I don't know My Lord. I cannot control myself," she said while crying, yet still restraining him.

Zeul walked over and picked up all the weapons that were on both Lilith and Ravizu. He then handed them to two MSS troopers who were standing guard in a darkened corner. Soon after, Zeul released Lilith, allowing them to both stand up.

"You had her implanted!?" Ravizu shouted. "And you didn't tell me! And what about me?! Am I still your dacking *hand*?!"

Dihana and Darham continued to lay on the floor quietly; trying to comprehend what was happening.

"Ravizu, I will speak with you later. You may go now."

Lilith tried to grab Ravizu's hand, but he yanked it away and walked out of the room. Looking dazed and confused, Lilith just stood there for a moment, while she looked at each of their faces. All she could say was, "Why?"

Without speaking Zeul motioned toward the door, prompting her to leave quickly to find Ravizu.

Zeul then commanded the MSS troopers and the few mingled servants to wait outside the door. Once the doors closed, he walked over and helped his children off the floor and onto the soft white couches that surrounded the fireplace. He removed the shackles that bound their hands and feet, reached down and picked up the scrolls, and with a smile on his face, he gently set them down on the table.

After sitting across from them, he took a moment to gaze at the scrolls, as well as the book given to him by Isma. Looking out the window, wondering if he was being watched, he finally spoke.

"An old friend came to visit me and said something that was, needless to say, very profound."

Dihana and Darham looked at one another, wondering what would happen next.

Zeul continued, "For most of my life, I thought no one could fool me. He said, *If your master taught you to betray others, what makes you think that he has not betrayed you?* Such a simple idea really. It was one that never crossed my mind. He then left me that book."

All three looked at the worn leather book that sat on the table that separated them; bound by a leather string that had not yet been loosened.

"He suggested that I read it, and then give it to Aaranon. Unfortunately, I have not yet read it. Fearful, mostly, of what I will find."

Dihana, restraining her anger towards her father, finally asked, "Why are we here?"

"Why are you here? That's a fair question. It's one I asked myself as you walked in, but I have an idea as to why. So much has changed since I sent Ravizu to look for you both. I had my initial reasons, but..."

"Bait!?" she said, letting out some of her anger.

"At first, yes. I wanted to use both of you to lure in Aaranon."

"And now," asked Darham, in a calm voice, unlike his sister.

"And now? Now I believe you're being used as bait by someone else," Zeul replied.

Dihana and Darham looked at each other with confusion, not understanding anything he was saying.

"Would you mind being a little bit clearer...*Father,*" she said calmly while her body language screamed obscenities.

"I don't blame you for hating me, Dihana. I have destroyed this family."

"Destroyed?! It's more like ripped it to dacking...," she said before Darham interrupted.

"Dihana, please, I want to hear this."

"So do I Darham, but for him to sit there and now act apologetic, it makes me sick. You killed my mother and my brothers. You stood by and allowed, or who knows, even told that ohema dropping out there to rape me...*repeatedly*...while you plotted your rise to become Alemeleg."

"Dihana, let's listen to what...," Darham pleaded before Zeul interjected.

"It's alright Darham. Let her speak."

"And then...you tried to kill Aaranon. My brother! Your son! What the dack is wrong with you?! If I didn't fear for my life, I would climb over this table and do whatever I could to rip your dacking throat out," she screamed through her tears.

"You're right. I did more than destroy this family. I have broken it beyond repair. I won't be able to make you understand because, frankly, I don't understand. I just hope that in time - for what time we all have left - that you will find it in your heart to...no, I don't deserve that. That would be too selfish for me to ask. All I can do now is make sure the both of you and Aaranon are safe."

"What?" asked Darham.

"The Brotherhood will not stop their fight against me or my family. And Ravizu...well...he'll never relent either. It isn't in his character to give up on something he wants. Therefore, I must do something that I hope will keep you safe."

"This is just another lie! Why don't you get it over with once and for all? Just kill us, you sadistic piece of garbage," yelled Dihana.

"Wait!" hollered Darham, "You're a part of this group? I suspected you were, but I was never absolutely sure."

"Yes, I am. And since you two are here, I suppose my master does not want to let me go so easily."

"Your master?" asked Darham.

"He goes by many names, but we call him Halail; which is the name given to him by the ancient one."

"But aren't you afraid he's listening to you right now?" asked

Darham.

"He can't come near us," Zeul replied.

"Why?"

"Because of Dihana."

Confused she asked, "Me? What about me?"

"Because you believe this," Zeul said while picking up the scrolls. "I cannot return to that true path. It's too late for me. But for the both of you there is still hope."

"Wait a moment," Dihana said while opening up the scrolls to find the note from her mother.

"Mother wrote this," she said, handing him the note. "It said that I was to give this letter to Aaranon, which let me know he was alive, but I didn't understand the other part that had to do with you."

As Zeul read the note, tears began to pour down his face. He said, "How's this possible?"

"What does it mean? What does it mean when she talks about you...*returning*?" Dihana asked.

Putting the paper down and reaching for the book, Zeul untied the wraps and found the place where Isma told him to read. Unable to see through his tears, he asked Darham to read the passage. As he held the book in his hands, he read out loud.

"I never thought it to be true until today. After having destroyed so many lives, I never thought that one like I could return. I still cannot remove the images from my mind - villages burning, parents begging for mercy, children crying out through the flames. All of it done by my hands. For what? Vengeance! Vengeance because they took my family? The irony is so thick.

"I began this quest to annihilate the heboram for what they did to my precious loved ones. I determined it was justified retribution, but my anger didn't subside. I became a tool in the hands of the evil one, and I didn't even see it. It's true what the ancient scrolls say; sin begets more sin.

"I lost all hope. Believing the lie that I could not return, but I know now his hand is never too short. He can reach me, even in the darkest corner in the deepest sea."

When Darham finished reading, he turned to the front of the book. Noticing the ink was newer than the passage he'd just finished reading, he was shocked to read the following; "Aaranon, when vengeance has run its course, and all hope seems to be lost, let these words comfort you. Rohu."

Dihana looked at Darham, both of them recalling the story about Rohu told to them by the old udam at the pub. Looking back at Zeul, they watched as he put his hands on his head, unable to contain his emotions.

Unable to move, both Dihana and Darham just sat there, with their hands over their mouths, incapable of finding even a single word to say.

Chapter 57

As the secret door opened in Zeul's office, Zeul, Dihana, and Darham stepped out. Turning to her father, she said, "You need to tell him."

Hanging his head down, Zeul replied, "I'm afraid he won't understand."

"Maybe not at first, but give him time," Darham replied.

Zeul looked over at the center of the room where a portal had just opened. On the other side was a small stone cottage, covered in vines. Zeul motioned for the two of them to walk through. He said, "I will meet you once he arrives."

"Aren't you concerned about Halail?" Dihana asked.

"He won't show. He can't, not anymore," he said with a smile forming in the corner of his mouth.

Dihana leaned forward to give him a hug, but Zeul backed up and said, "I don't deserve that. Not after what I did to all of you."

"I must admit it really isn't for you. Mother would want me to," she said as she leaned in to hug her father. Zeul, however, found it difficult to embrace his daughter, knowing the damage he had done.

With renewed tears, he whispered, "Your mother was wonderful. She prayed at night for me. She didn't think I heard her, but I did."

"She still is wonderful. You will see her again," Dihana replied as she pulled away and wiped his tears.

Darham only placed his hand on Zeul's shoulder and said, "We will see you soon."

Picking up Rohu's journal and the scrolls, Zeul said, "Don't forget these. Aaranon will need them for the journey ahead."

Once Darham and Dihana passed through the portal and it closed, Zeul then used the farspeak to summon Ravizu back to his office.

***

Bursting through the doors, this time flanked by two MSS troopers, Ravizu entered and began spewing his anger.

Pushing the MSS troopers aside, he said, "I sent *your* pet to my sky liner to wait for me." Looking pointedly at the troopers, he said, "I see you don't trust me to be alone with you."

"I understand your anger son…"

"Understand me?! Dack you! You don't understand me. You don't know me; you don't care about me. It was always Aaranon, your precious Aleudam - the dacking heir to the throne. That's why he isn't dead right now! Because you want him over me."

"Son, if you would just calm down, I can explain…"

"You don't need to explain anything to me. When I sat here, almost two years ago, and you told me I was the one you wanted I thought that you finally saw me. ME!"

Wiping a tear from his eye, Ravizu continued, "For once, I was your favorite! I really thought you were proud of me that day I pushed him over that cliff. But now I know you were planning on killing me along with Dihana and Darham. To offer up what? The so-called *lesser sacrifice* so that you can keep your precious son."

"Son, things have changed since then, I need you to understand…"

"Dack you. It doesn't matter. Aaranon won't give up Dihana and Darham to stand by your side. And when that happens, you will be removed from the Brotherhood. Halail will not allow you to rule any longer."

"Son, I'm begging you to listen to what I have to say," Zeul pleaded, but to no avail.

"Begging?! Now you're begging me? Good! Get used to it

because if I have any say over it, I will rise to be Alemeleg and ruler over the Brotherhood. I will serve Halail faithfully, and not waiver like you. Then I'll take care of the dirty work you didn't want to do yourself. Just like old times, huh, Father? But this time, I'm both the mind and hand. I'll be the one giving the orders. Not you!"

"Ravizu, I was wrong. I was wrong for what I did to you and everyone else. I want to make this right. I need to make this right with you."

"Make it right? It was right! You gained the whole world, but you're throwing it away for what? Why can't you just pick me?! You and I are the same. We want the same thing."

"Not anymore. I don't want any of this!" Zeul shouted.

"Why? How can you give all this up? How!?"

"I started on this path long ago to seek vengeance against the ancient one. I thought a curse was on me because of the mark placed upon my father. When I lost my first family in that flood so long ago, I decided I would fight against him with all I had. That's when the Brotherhood found me. That's when they told me about Halail. They wanted me to rule over them; to lead them through the portals of heaven to storm the gates of that great city and remove him. But I was a fool!"

"Why would you follow someone who has cursed you because of your father?"

"That's just it! I will not be judged for the sins of my father, but for my own. Before that day at the cliff, I believed that the curse was gone. I thought the ancient one showed me mercy. But when you pushed Aaranon over, I gave up hope. I thought he was only playing a cruel game with me."

"Yes! And?"

"But every time we tried to eliminate Aaranon, he was spared. Even when everything was against him, he lived! I watched it all. He should have never lived, being my son, living under the curse, but he did!"

"So what! Who cares that the curse did not pass to you or

your family? Why let the world go?"

"Because it was never ours to possess, and neither does it belong to Halail. He's a liar. If he commands us to lie, don't you think that he is lying to us as well?" Zeul asked, hoping that Ravizu would see the truth.

"No. You're wrong. We have been lied to by the ancient one. He's the one who's played games with us and misled us."

"You're wrong, Ravizu. I was wrong."

"Even if you were right, there is no returning for us. We've made our decision. Well, at least I have. And I'm not changing it."

"Ravizu, no! Please don't. We can return!"

"Are we done here? Because I have some business to attend to."

"I'm begging you, please don't go down this path. I was so wrong. Please learn from my mistakes!"

Wiping the tears from his eyes, Ravizu said, "Oh, I have learned from your mistakes. I'll be sure, *not* to repeat them."

Turning around, Ravizu pushed aside the MSS troopers and walked out the door.

***

As Ravizu boarded the sky liner, he called for four of his largest mercenaries to follow him to his cabin. Moving down the hallway, Lilith could hear them coming. Checking herself out in the mirror, she tried to make herself look as beautiful as possible for her lord.

Only Ravizu however stepped through the doors as they opened.

Bowing to him, she said with trepidation in her voice, "My Lord, I didn't know he..."

Interrupting, Ravizu gently pulled her close and said, "It's alright. We'll fix this. I know you couldn't control yourself."

Trying to hold back her tears, she whispered, "I'm so sorry. I never wanted to harm you. I love you more than life itself."

While reaching for a blade hidden in his sleeve, he said, "And I love you. When I saw you that first day, I didn't realize I could love another as much as I loved you. Even Ballar could not compare to you."

"I tried to fight it, but…"

"Shh, shh, I know. I know. It's alright. It will never happen again…" he whispered as he quickly plunged the blade into her back and straight into her heart. Immediately, on cue, the mercenaries came in to restrain her arms, but she didn't resist.

"My Lord?"

While holding her head, and kissing her soft, beautiful lips, he whispered, "My father will pay for what he did to you." He continued to look into her eyes and said, "Can you see me Father? Do you see what you made me do? You have cursed me. I will love no one, ever again."

Holding her tightly he then shouted, "Leave us!"

Once the mercenaries left the room, he gently removed the blade from her back, being careful not to ruin the beautiful dress she was wearing any further. He rested her gently on the bed and then laid next to her while caressing her long, pitch black hair. He repeated himself in a whisper, "I will avenge you. I promise. I will avenge you."

Chapter 58

As Aaranon, Amana, and the others walked back into the rebel camp, they could see bodies strewn throughout the forest. Some of the bodies were MSS troopers, others were UAK soldiers and rebels, but some looked like a mix of MSS troopers and udamé. Looking over the landscape, one could see fires as they raged across the forest, spewing black smoke. The smoke covered most of the sky; leaving very little light to creep through the thick brush. Walking past a crashed Dargon, they could see that massive claws had ripped open the cargo doors and destroyed the occupants inside. The further they moved in, the worse it became.

Amana drew near to Aaranon and asked, "What are these creatures here? I've never seen anything like them."

"They almost look like MSS troopers, but they're more like an udam than a beast. I've never seen them before," he said.

"There are so many of them," Micah replied.

Yosef crouched down and examined the bodies carefully. "I'm a bit older than the three of you; they look like the first-generation mingled soldiers."

"First generation? But I thought they destroyed them," said Aaranon.

"They did eliminate most of them, but not all."

"Why did they do that?" Amana asked.

As he continued to examine the bodies, Yosef said, "Unlike the second and third, the first generation wasn't born. The first generation consisted of regular udamé who were altered. However, their will was too strong to manipulate and, when they couldn't control them, they killed them."

"So then, how is it possible for these to be here?" Aaranon

asked.

"Stories were told that some of them escaped to the farthest north, in the forests of Ashal, to get away from the general populace. Whether in the far north or the far south, like the forests of Tarshish, you can't set public energy taps because of the unstable energy fields. Smaller taps, like a temporary military tap, can be set for short durations, but not a permanent one. As long as they stayed up in the north, the military never went after them."

"So, why are they here?" asked Micah.

"Legend says that one of the soldiers began to worship the ancient one. He then led the others to believe as he did. It also says he was given a prophecy to protect the Guardian of the line."

"Guardian of the line?" Aaranon asked while recalling his dream.

"Yeah, but I don't know what it means."

As the four of them stood there, looking at the dead soldier, Aveed was walking near to them. Pulling his weapon up he shouted, "Who is that? You better start talking, or I'll...Loha! Where the dack have you been?"

Holstering his weapon, Aveed ran up to Aaranon and gave him an uncharacteristic hug. He then said, "I need to tell you something. You are not going to believe this."

Soon after, three large first-generation soldiers came walking up. Aaranon and the others were about to pull their weapons until Aveed instructed them otherwise.

Turning to the leader, while pointing at Aaranon, Aveed said, "Is he the one you're looking for?"

Walking up to Aaranon, standing at least two ama higher, he said, "Yes. He is the Guardian of the line." Extending his hand, he said, "My name is Salem. I was in the far north when I witnessed the prophecy come to pass. The stars have begun to shift, and the hosts of heaven are moving out of their course. The razing is upon us. What are you orders, My Prince?"

Yosef whispered to Aaranon, "What does he mean?"

Aaranon gazed up at Salem and then back at the others. He then said to Yosef, "I think I understand now. But first, I need to do something."

***

While Aaranon climbed atop a large fallen tree, the remaining surviving rebels gathered around to listen.

Pausing for several moments, he looked out across the sullen faces; covered in blood and soot. He wasn't nervous over what he had to say, just saddened for waiting so long to say it.

As he looked down at Amana and smiled, she said, "You can do it."

He looked back at the crowd, took a deep breath and began, "My real name...is Prince Aaranon bamé Zeul, of the house and kingdom of Quayanin."

Immediately, Mara sent her beasts to attack Aaranon. If it weren't for Salem and his soldiers to stop them, he would have been easily killed.

She then shouted out, "You dacking liar! Your family killed those I loved! How could you use us like that?"

Sdra'de shouted, "My tribe! My family! We bled and died for you! A DACKING NOBLE!"

Soon after, the remaining rebels began shouting and throwing rocks and limbs at Aaranon. The first-generation soldiers under Salem encircled Aaranon, Amana, Mishna, and Yosef to protect them.

"You don't have to believe me, and you don't have to listen to me but you do need to know the truth; my father sought to kill me."

Drahcir yelled out, "Well then, at least we now have something in common with a noble!"

As the calls for his death increased, Salem and his soldiers pulled out their weapons.

"No! No! Let them speak," Aaranon said as he motioned for Salem and his troops to lower their weapons. "You're right. I lied to you. I mislead all of you. I wanted your help to free my family. But even when I had them back, they were taken from me again. Maybe they were never mine to have."

"So where is the real Loha?" Sdra'de asked.

"He died a few years ago. He was my servant, and he taught me many things. But the one thing he taught me, that I cannot seem to follow is…never to seek vengeance."

"That's a lie!" shouted Mishna. "All the legends tell us that Loha sought vengeance and won. He never turned the other cheek."

"That is untrue!" shouted Isma as he slowly walked, with assistance from a family member, toward Aaranon. Several of the rebels parted as he came near. Once he reached the fallen tree he raised his arms, indicating his desire. Salem lifted him up and set him down next to Aaranon.

He continued, "The real Loha did, at one time, seek vengeance. However, he learned from the error of his ways. This path that you are set on will only lead to your destruction. All of you must repent and return to the true path."

"Dack you, you old udam!" shouted Drahcir. "We don't need your drivel!"

Mishna then climbed up on another fallen tree, opposite of Aaranon, and shouted, "Listen to me! Drahcir and I have figured out the console and have full access to the UAK's MCR. We can now take down the whole government! For those who wish to follow our pathetic leader - the noble in disguise - then stand on his side. For those who want to gain freedom from tyranny, then come to me."

Aveed, Pernel, and Sohan moved near to Aaranon while the remaining rebels moved over to Mishna.

Looking at Pernel, Ballac asked, "What are you doing?"

"Leave him alone, Ballac," Isma said. "He knows what he's doing. Don't you Pernel?"

Pernel only looked away, hiding his long-held secret.

Mishna looked at his remaining band of rebels and then back to Aaranon. "I will allow you and your pathetic followers to leave in peace. But if I see you again, I will not be so kind."

Aaranon turned to the others and said, "Let's go. I don't want to cause any more problems." Unable to look them in the face, Aaranon hung his head until they were far outside the rebel camp.

Walking next to him, Amana asked Aaranon, "What are you going to do now? We need to get Dihana and Darham back."

Aaranon stopped immediately and began to chuckle. The others gathered around to see what was so amusing.

Micah asked, "We are going after Dihana, right? We need to try and get them back. Please, Aaranon."

Aaranon continued to laugh even more until Isma put his hand on his arm.

Sohan asked, "Why are you laughing?"

Holding his hand up in exasperation, Aaranon replied, "I'm back at the beginning. This is how all of this started; me, using all my knowledge to go after my family. It's what brought down temples, killed families, and now, apparently, has disrupted the whole world. All because I wanted to save someone who I'm apparently not allowed to save."

Micah begged, "But we can't just let Ravizu have her! You know what he's going to do to her, don't you? Please, you can't just sit here laughing like you don't care."

"I don't care? Who are you to say that I don't care? I moved the world to get them, but it appears they are not mine to have. So, you tell me; what can I do? How about you Isma? What should I do? Because, frankly...I'm out of options."

"No, you're not. Is he Aveed?" Isma said as he turned to look at him.

"Huh?" Aaranon asked, looking at Aveed.

"Oh! Now's the time! One moment. I've been holding onto this so I would be ready," Aveed said as he set his satchel down on the ground to find what he was looking for. "Ah, ha! Here it is. Give me a moment. I have to do this right."

Aaranon tried to see what Aveed was doing, since he had his back to him. Before he could walk around to see the item in his satchel, Aveed immediately stood up and threw a glass of wine on Aaranon.

With Aaranon, standing before him, dripping from head to toe in wine, Aveed said, "Too much? I wasn't sure how much I was supposed to use, but your father said that you would know what this means."

As the others looked dazed and confused at Aaranon, Isma said, "Your father is ready to see you now."

"But...how?" Aaranon asked. "I don't understand. I don't even know where he is."

Looking over at Pernel and Sohan, Isma said, "Not to worry. Pernel will take you."

Chapter 59

As Sohan piloted the cargo vessel, Aaranon, Amana and the others sat in the back, wondering what was to come next.

Looking at Pernel, Aaranon realized something. He said, "The first time I saw you, you didn't assume I was one of the bandits, did you?"

Hanging his head down, Pernel replied, "Yeah. I thought you would figure that out sooner or later. When I saw you that day, I wasn't for sure if you were going to let me down. They made sure that we knew everything about you. From your eyes to your height, and even your voice. It was your voice that let me know it was you."

"So what did they do to you and the others?"

"They inserted an implant, not like the ones they put it in the back of the neck. They put it up through the nose. They didn't even bother to numb the pain," he said while rubbing his forehead.

Looking up at Aaranon, he continued, "When I finally figured out where I'd seen Yosef before, I thought he'd expose who I actually was; especially when you saw Sohan."

Leaning back against the cargo vessel, Aaranon said, "I had my suspicions from the beginning. But when I saw Sohan, I knew then you were connected to my father somehow."

"Then why didn't you do something?" Pernel asked.

Shrugging his shoulders, and shaking his head, he replied, "I just didn't care anymore. At Davison's castle...as I looked into that fire...all I could see was him, consuming everything I cared about. I just gave up. I decided that it needed to end." Grabbing Amana's hand, he continued, "If it weren't for her and my family, I wouldn't be here right now."

"Do you want to know why?" Pernel asked.

"Knowing my father; I'm sure he manipulated you, somehow, into doing it. Did he take your wife and sister?"

"Yes."

"Then I don't blame you. I would have done the same."

"When I was in those tunnels, I saw thousands of people. Your father wanted to bring you in from the forests. He knew he couldn't do it with UAK forces, so he took us. Whoever was the one that found you first would be the one to get their family back. But when he saw that a rebellion could be possible under your command he decided to see if it would work. He wanted to create a new enemy against the kingdom."

"That's why your wife wasn't there at the temple."

"Yeah. I was supposed to find her there and take her home. But he needed me to keep you going. So he took her away," he said while drying his tears.

Reaching forward to put his hand on Pernel's knee, Aaranon said, "I'm sorry for what he did. Unfortunately, I seem to possess his same skill for manipulating people. Whatever you did, I forgive you. I just hope you can forgive me some day."

Looking up, with eyes as red as the evening sky, Pernel said, "I don't deserve that."

"And neither do I, Pernel. But forgiveness has to start somewhere, doesn't it? It might as well begin with me."

"Thank you."

"So what changed? Obviously, with what Aveed did and what Isma has said, something must be different with him."

"I'm not quite sure. But every time you miraculously survived, I could sense something different in his commands to me. Whether it was with the MSS trooper you killed with the plow or the triggers not working or the ground quake; every time we should have died, a miracle happened. With every miracle, I could sense he was changing somehow. It was as if, on one hand he wanted the rebellion to succeed, and then on the other, he wanted to see if you would survive an impossible escape. It was so strange. I didn't understand it."

Sohan turned his head slightly, so the other's could hear, "It's true Aaranon. I couldn't say anything before, without jeopardizing my wife, but something is different with your father. In the beginning, those of us captured were charged to find you. Once we found you, he then directed us to help foment the rebellion across Araz. But then it all changed. That's why we can tell you this now. Before, we would have been killed immediately."

"I know we're headed to him. And I'm guessing he can see and hear all of this, but I don't care anymore. He can do with me what he likes. I just want it to end. I'm tired of compromising the truth. I'm tired of seeking vengeance. I'm tired of putting my wants and my needs before others. It's all vanity," Aaranon said, staring out through the glass portal on the ceiling.

Isma then turned to Aaranon, gently placed his hand on his shoulder and said, "Now, you are ready to listen. Now, you can begin the journey home; this is your returning."

"Is that where we're going; home?" Aaranon asked.

"What I speak of Young Prince is spiritual, not physical. But yes, we are going to your father's house."

Looking out the windows, Aaranon said, "This doesn't look like Hoshier. I'm not familiar with this place."

While patting Aaranon's knee, Isma said, "We are going back to where it all began."

Chapter 60

With only two days left until the festival and the fear of another retaliation from the kingdom, Mishna and the remaining rebels mobilized their forces to attack as soon as Aaranon and the others left. Having gained access to the MCR and full control of the MSS troops, Mishna and Drahcir commanded all troopers to imprison all UAK soldiers and their commanding officers. He couldn't command them, directly, to kill the soldiers, but he had another way to eliminate them.

With most of the military bases in disarray, the rebels moved quickly to take control of any ship they could find. With numerous upper-class rebels joining the fight, it wasn't difficult to find capable pilots. Mishna and Drahcir alone, with the aid of a few MSS troopers, commandeered the lead Battlecruiser. They began directing all ships to destroy every temple, sporting arena, and prison once the maidens and the prisoners were clear; leaving the soldiers behind to suffer their fate.

"Give me a status report," Mishna shouted while looking out the window from the ship's bridge.

"So far, all temples, prisons, and sporting arenas have been destroyed," Drahcir replied.

"How close are they to taking back control of the MSS troops?"

"They've broken through four of the locks I created. Once they break the sixth, then they will gain access and take back control."

"When they break the fifth, send the signal to the MSS troops. We cannot let them take control," he shouted with glee as he watched the mayhem unfold several hundred ama below. Under his breath, Mishna said to himself, "It won't be long now

Father. Soon, Zeul will fall from his throne, and I will return to you. We can build a whole new world from the ashes. You'll see. We will make it a better world."

"I'm sorry…but what did you say," asked Drahcir.

"Nothing! I was just going over my plans."

Looking back at his console, Drahcir shouted, "They broke the fifth lock."

"Now! Do it now!" he screamed.

Immediately Drahcir sent the command that activated the internal kill switch which stopped the heart of every MSS trooper across Araz. As they looked around the ship, the few MSS troopers that were on board fell over where they stood.

"Good! Good! Now, put this ship on a collision course with the UAC headquarters and let's get out of here," he said as he ran towards one of the Dargons on the flight deck.

With Drahcir running as fast as he could, while carrying his console, but having difficulty keeping up due to his size, Mishna quickly boarded the Dargon and fired up all resonator cores. Before Drahcir made it to the ship, however, Mishna began to pull away.

"Wait! Wait! What about me?"

Opening the side window, Mishna yelled out, "Your usefulness has run its course. But I do appreciate all that you have done." Pulling a weapon from his side, Mishna pointed it at Drahcir and fired, knocking him down onto the flight deck. He then yelled out, "Thank you, you fat pimple!"

With blood running out his mouth and out through his side, Drahcir pulled his makeshift console onto his chest so he could see it. Once he connected to the Dargon Mishna was flying, he took control of the ship, forcing it to fly back to him.

Fighting the controls, but unable to direct the Dargon, Mishna soon realized that Drahcir was bringing it back. Opening the window back up as it drew near, he tried to plead with Drahcir. "My father is the creator of all the mingled servants. He can fix you up if you just let me go."

Pulling the ship closer, Drahcir looked up and said, "Can your father trim away my fat?"

Looking confused, he said, "Why yes, he can remove anything you want."

"That's funny."

"Why is that funny?"

"Because I can too."

"What?"

Drahcir looked back at the console that was controlling the Dargon. He then set the resonator cores to overload. Soon after the bluish haze that surrounded the cores expanded.

"What are you doing?" shouted Mishna.

"I'm going to remove all your body parts."

"NO!"

As the Dargon exploded, it destroyed only a portion of the deck, killing both Mishna and Drahcir. It wasn't enough, however, to change the ship's course.

***

As Zeul was about to walk through the portal in his office at the UAC headquarters to meet up with Dihana and Darham, he could see, through his office window, the approaching lead Battlecruiser. As he looked at the flames that leapt from the ship, he quoted to himself a passage from the scrolls.

Since the beginning, I have sent foreseers among you, but you did not repent. Therefore, for thine iniquities, will I raze all things.

Chapter 61

All the servants of Halail gathered together at his immense fortress; set on one of the heavenly bodies that faithfully circled Shemesh. He appeared calm as he sat upon his throne, but a billowing anger was creeping out with every moment that passed. No one dared to speak, but only waited for their master to give them the assurance that they needed. With the loss of Zeul to the ancient one, he needed to invigorate his forces with hope that retribution was still within their grasp, but time was of the essence.

"Brothers, friends...and fellow rebels," he shouted with a mild sneer.

At the last word, the servants all cheered and roared a dreadful noise that would have quickly destroyed any udam that stood among them.

He continued, "I know I don't have to explain to you the urgency of the moment in which we find ourselves. As we look to the southern heavens, the obvious is becoming abundantly clear to all. Except, of course, for the useless souls that litter our kingdom!"

Once again, Halail waited for his servants to quiet down from their jubilation over their master's claiming Araz as their possession.

"Some of you may have concerns regarding Zeul's returning, but understand this. My plans never rested in Zeul. He was only a stepping stone for another," he said; every word dripping with deception. "As you can now see, there is one who I've been preparing since birth."

Shouts of praise and adulation reverberated against walls of the darkened fortress. They cheered, not out of belief, but out of fear. Their fates are set, unlike those on Araz. They had no choice but to serve the father of lies.

"Soon, I will exalt him to the throne. Soon, I will make him head of the Brotherhood. He will serve me with unwavering faith. He is the one who will break the line!"

Once again, the din was so great, that even the servants felt the pain from the sound.

"The time is at hand! Soon, the ancient prophecy will fail. With your own eyes, you will see his broken word. Then, I will ascend into heaven. I will exalt my throne above the stars. I will sit upon the mount of the congregation, in the sides of the north. I will ascend above the heights of the clouds. I will be like the most High!"

As Halail observed his servants shout praises to him, he could only dwell upon the destruction of Aaranon; for he was the Guardian of the line. So many other Guardians have come and gone; anointed from above to be the one who kept the ancient prophecy alive. But Aaranon was the second to the last; for all the others had been gathered to the fathers.

He continued, "The rebellion against the kingdom is going as I have planned. Millions of these creatures will die in the ensuing conflicts. As they are busy fighting amongst themselves, they will not hear the calls of repentance. They will not return to the truth path. They will be lost, for all eternity! Now...move about the world that belongs to us. Keep them from the ancient one. Then you will have your reward."

As Halail sat upon his throne, he watched the servants disappear in a flash of light, eventually leaving him alone, to watch from a distance.

Chapter 62

Setting down in a large valley, Aaranon and the others stepped out of the cargo vessel to see a quaint stone cottage covered in vines. It was a pleasant day, like that of the dreams Aaranon had experienced. As they stood there, looking around, the door to the small home opened and several people stepped out.

Once Pernel's gaze landed on his wife and sister, he could not contain his emotions. As he called out her name, she grabbed hold of her chest and started to weep. Behind her was Alyya, Sohan's wife. Sohan dropped to his knees and cried; ashamed of what he had done in order to see her once again.

Soon after, Dihana and Darham stepped out. Aaranon still couldn't believe he was looking at them once again. It felt like he was in a dream, but this time it was for real. As they all ran to one another, Zeul was seen standing in the doorway.

After several moments of embracing one another, Dihana said to Aaranon, "Will you talk with him? I know so much has happened, but you need to hear what he has to say."

"I don't know if I can," he replied. "I heard all the stories on the way over about his change, but…I just can't trust him."

Opening his hand to place the note from Sari in it, she said, "Then do it for Mother."

"What?"

"Just read it."

As he opened the note and read it, he looked back at Dihana, tears streaming down his well-worn face.

She understood his questioning look. "I saw her in that same wheat field as you did. She told me where to find it."

"You could hear her?"

"Yes…and Yohan…as well as Rohu."

Fighting his emotions as best he could, but failing to do so, he just hugged his beautiful little flower, thanking her for all she had done.

Darham wrapped his arms around Aaranon and said, "Just listen to him."

"I'll try."

As he walked towards the door, Salem, and the other two soldiers who escorted him in the cargo vessel started to follow him. It wasn't until he reached the doorway that he noticed they were following him. Aaranon turned and said, "I should be fine; you don't need to come in."

Zeul replied, "Salem, would you please come inside? I will need your help with something."

Looking confused, but allowing it, Aaranon stepped aside as Salem was the first to walk into the home. Once all three of them were in, Zeul shut the door.

***

"Please son, have a seat," Zeul said, gesturing towards a hand-carved wooden chair next to a table. Zeul sat across from him while Salem continued to stand in the dark corner.

After a few moments of awkward silence and fidgeting, Aaranon asked, "Where are we?"

"This…this was my home. The home of my first family," Zeul replied.

Looking over at the fireplace mantel, he could see, from the light shining in through the windows, there were several hand carved figurines. Pointing to them, Aaranon asked, "May I?"

Motioning towards them, Zeul replied, "Yes, please."

Aaranon stood up and looked at each carving. Without turning around, he asked Zeul, "Were these your children?"

"Yes," he said while standing up and walking to the mantel. "This one is Raccab; she was my oldest daughter. This one is Kiela. She was always curious; always wanting to know more.

Like you."

"And which one is this?" he asked pointing to the tallest carved figure that looked eerily similar to him.

Finding it hard to speak, he finally said, "Uh...hum...uh... that...that is Aaranon...my first born."

Looking into his eyes for the first time since that day he saw him through the visual in the cave, Aaranon could see years of pain and anguish, coupled with shame and regret. Before Aaranon could reach towards his father, Zeul backed away, hiding his face.

Setting the carved figure back on the mantel and turning around, Aaranon tried to ask but couldn't put together the words. "What...? Why...? Uh...I don't know where to begin."

Zeul chuckled softly. "Well...that makes two of us."

"I saw you through the visual Rohu gave me. From then until now...what happened? What changed?"

"You."

"Me? What do you mean?"

Looking up at the mantel, he continued, "When I lost my first family, I lost a part of me. I knew the stories about my father, but I didn't believe that a curse upon a father could fall to the son. But when I lost them, I thought it was true. But then you came into my life. Your mother..." Zeul paused as he again started to cry as he thought about what he did to Sari.

He continued, "Your mother was wonderful. She gave me hope again. The Brotherhood approached me to be a part of their quest to remove the mark of Qayin and restore their family name, but...I had you in my arms. Then, as you grew, and other children were born to me, I knew for sure that all was well. There was no curse.

"But then...it all changed. That day...it all turned. I thought the creator had played a cruel joke on me. He gave me another family only to watch them be ripped from my hands again. But this time, slowly, instead of all at once. That's the day I swore vengeance against him. When you went over that cliff, my heart, my compassion, my love for anything...died. My rage blinded me. It was Halail and the Brotherhood that allowed me to release my anger."

Doing everything he could to fight back his emotion, but unable to, he said through a river of tears, "But every time I tried to harm you, the Creator...he...he saved you. He continuously pulled you out of the fire. I was a fool, Aaranon. I believed that father of lies, instead of the father of truth and light. Oh...please...don't ever do what I did."

Aaranon wanted to move over next to his father and embrace him, but he still had difficulty trusting him.

Zeul continued, "I don't blame you for not believing me. I wouldn't believe me after all that I have done."

After several moments, Aaranon finally said, "So what do we do now? You and I have turned this world upside down. I don't think there's anywhere safe for us to go."

"For me...no. But for you, you have a mission ahead of you. And I'm going to make sure that you see it through. Isn't that right Salem?"

"That is correct," he said.

Aaranon chuckled and said, "I would ask how you knew, but I've learned that you have eyes and ears everywhere."

"Since I will step down from the throne the day after tomorrow, the council will not be able to go after our family legally. But I know they will not relent once they've seen what I will do."

"What are you going to do?"

"I cannot stop the Brotherhood, but I can slow them down. Just moments ago, the rebels destroyed nearly half of the military forces. The council will soon be able to confirm that I was the one who gave Drahcir and Mishna access to the MCR."

"Father, once they know that, they will not let some measly law stop them. They will come after you. They'll come after all of us."

"It's best that I don't tell you what I'm going to do. I don't want you involved, and I don't want you to try and stop me. Want I want you to do, is to follow what Rohu told you to do. Can you do that for me?"

"Are you sure? I can help…"

"No…you can help me by doing what you know is the right thing to do," Zeul said while standing up, indicating it was time to leave.

"But…will I see you again?"

With a confident smile, he said, "Yes…I know for certain, that you and I will be together again."

Finally able to hug his father, Aaranon embraced him for the last time on this side of the great beyond.

"Now…if you would, leave me alone for a moment with Salem. I need to ask of him a favor," Zeul said as he opened the door for Aaranon to exit.

Turning around to look at his father one more time before he left, Aaranon said, "I'm not going to see you again, am I?"

"You will…I promise."

***

Once the door was shut, Zeul turned to Salem and asked, "The poison in your claws, can you measure it out?"

"Yes. How many days?"

"Just until tomorrow night. I should be able to complete it by then."

Extending his claw, Salem injected the poison into Zeul's neck, giving him just enough time to help his son.

Chapter 63

At the same time Zeul was meeting with Aaranon, the Brotherhood had gathered, once again, to discuss their next move. Needless to say, not one of them knew what direction to take because none of them knew what Zeul was going to do next.

Shouting loudly to be heard, as they all gathered at Mathal's castle, Vidas said, "Does anyone have any information that would be useful to this discussion?"

Waiting for the others to calm down, King Darvan said, "My sources have informed me that they believe, very strongly, Zeul is the one who gave the rebels access to the MCR. They cannot completely confirm that since Zeul has full control until his resignation is complete, but they are highly confident that it was him."

"Did you see how he looked at us at the UAC emergency meeting?" asked King Parvalle. "He knew that it was us. I don't know about the others, but I say we move against him and his family, immediately!"

"We must be careful! Legally we cannot do anything...," Mathal said before being interrupted.

"I don't care about the dacking law! Zeul needs to die!" shouted Parvalle.

Soon after, the meeting hall erupted once again into a shouting match, each king presenting his view as to how to handle the situation. Eventually, Vidas was able to grab their attention.

"Brothers! Brothers, please! We must be united in this. We cannot split our decision."

One angry king shouted, "But what of our master? What

does he want us to do? We cannot do anything without his consent."

In a calmer fashion, many of the kings rapped against the table with their fist and said, "Agreed."

Another king said, "But why has he been silent on this? We haven't heard a thing since that day he appeared in the sanctuary and asked us to leave. Does anyone know what transpired between him and Zeul?"

Suddenly, in their midst, a great light appeared. Immediately, the kings bowed down. This time, however, Halail stepped out of the light with Ravizu standing next to him.

"Brothers!" he shouted. "Rejoice, for I have come to strengthen you."

No one dared to look up. After observing them for a moment, Halail said, "You may all look upon me for the first time."

Slowly, the brother kings looked up to see the most beautiful creature standing in their midst. Most of the kings, at first, didn't even see Ravizu standing next to him. As time passed, however, they could see Halail had his arm around Ravizu.

"I know all of you have been wondering what's taking place. Let me assure you that all is going according to plan. I have with me your new leader and the new heir to the Throne of Thrones."

King Darvan immediately cried out, "Praise Halail, and praise our new Alemeleg, King Ravizu, of the house and kingdom of Quayanin!" It didn't take long before the others cried out the same; doing so out of confusion and fear.

"I know you have many questions, but soon you will see the wisdom of what has just transpired. Soon, you will see all your dreams come to pass. But first, Ravizu will pass through the trial that all of you have completed and I can assure you; he will not hesitate."

Looking over at Ravizu, he said, "Now go, and do what's necessary. Then you will be the ruler of Araz."

"Yes, My Lord," he replied. Ravizu then turned around and walked back through the portal.

Chapter 64

Ravizu stepped off his sky liner with a young udam walking behind him. Together, they walked up to the small cottage that belonged to Zeul. While opening the door, he said to the young udam, "Wait outside for a moment." He then closed the door behind him.

Alone in the room, he walked over to the figurines on the mantel. As he gazed at each of them in turn, he began to cry. He examined each one by moving his fingers across their facial features. When he came to the one of Aaranon, he picked it up and walked over to the window.

As he looked down at it, he said, "All I wanted was for you to love me. But I wasn't good enough, was I? It was always about him. You want to know why I pushed him over that cliff? Because…you never saw me until that day. You never looked at me…the real me. Then you said…I was the one you wanted. The one for whom you were looking. I so longed to hear those words. But it was all a lie. You betrayed me. Now, I will destroy you and every memory of you."

He then grabbed hold of the head of the figurine and snapped it off. He then walked over to the door, opened it and said, "Son, you can come in now."

The young Aleudam asked, "Father, why are we here?"

Without his son seeing, Ravizu, while holding back his tears, pulled a blade from his sleeve and said, "I'm here to settle some family business."

***

As he exited the cottage, flames started to burn through the roof and out the windows. With the blood still dripping off the blade, Ravizu walked toward the two servants of Halail who were observing his sacrifice to Halail. Throwing the blade at their feet, Ravizu said, "Good enough?"

One of the servants quietly replied, "For now...yes."

Chapter 65

As Vultnor entered the pub, he could see Biltner on the floor, in the corner, drinking his ale. Walking up to the bar as he always did, he sat down and asked for the usual. Looking over at the visual he asked the barkeep, "Can you turn that dacking thing off?"

"Today is the festival to the Ayim. You know it's required to be on. Besides, the Alemeleg is going to make a special announcement."

"I'm sure they will try to assure us all is well after those dacking rebels destroyed everything, including the UAC headquarters."

"Why don't you just shut up you old coot. I want to hear how they're going to spin this one away," yelled Biltner.

As the visual came to life, Zeul could be seen sitting down on his throne at castle Hoshier.

"Wow! He looks terrible. What's wrong with him," one patron asked.

"Looks like the war against the kingdom is wearing on him," Biltner laughed.

The barkeep shouted at his patrons, "Shut up, I want to hear this!"

With a great deal of labor, Zeul finally spoke. "It is...with much sadness and regret...that I come to you this day. For hundreds of years...the Alemeleg would come before you...and pronounce the beginning of a...joyous occasion. However, I... cannot do that."

"That's right you dacking blowhard! The rebels are coming for you," shouted Biltner.

Vultnor turned around and threw his mug at him, "Shut up

you cripple!"

"Oh, now you want to listen," he replied.

Zeul continued, "As your Alemeleg, I want to ask, no...I beg...for your forgiveness."

"What?" asked Vultnor.

"I have lied to all of you. I am a member of a secret organization called the Kahe'Akaba. We are the descendants of that murderer, Qayin."

"Holy Dack!" shouted one patron.

"Every atrocity you have experienced was performed by our hands. From the razing of the four hundred temples that we blamed on the Apostates, to the raising up of the rebellion. This was all done to solidify our power. As of right now, I have disclosed all information to those kings who are not members of the Brotherhood."

"Yes! Yes!" screamed Biltner and several others.

"And, as my last act as Alemeleg, I have nullified all laws that have bound every citizen of Araz. I deactivated every implant, and sent every agent home. I've also put to death the remaining MSS troopers. I know that once I am gone, the tyranny will not stop but, in this my final act, I ask that you seek out the ancient one. Find the ancient scrolls that were once illegal, but are no more. Read them. Abide in them. Listen to that faithful word. For they are the way, the truth, and the life. There are no other means by which you will be spared."

At his last word, Zeul gave up the ghost and went to be joined with the fathers, and with his family.

Looking around the pub, Vultnor, with a smile on his face and a mug in his hand, said, "Now...it is a joyous occasion."

Chapter 66

"Can we stop at that crossroad for a moment? My feet are killing me," Dihana asked.

"We sure can, my beautiful wife," Micah said while leaning in to give his new bride a kiss.

"Yeah, let's all rest for a moment," Aaranon said to Salem and the other soldiers. Looking around, he realized where he was. "Uh…wait a moment. This is it. Yeah! This is it!"

"What's it?" Amana asked her new husband.

"The road where I was supposed to turn."

"What?" asked Micah.

"Oh…the road to Emet. Yeah," exclaimed Darham.

"This is the place where I sat down and decided to continue walking east, back to find you two. Wow…it's amazing to think back through what has happened since then. Let's sit for a moment before we head to Emet."

As they were sitting down, Amana said, "Did you know we should really pronounce it as, Emeth? It's an ancient word that means truth."

"Really? So **Rohu** told me to walk to Truth," he said.

"Yes," Amana said as she smiled and fed him a piece of fruit.

Darham searched his memory and said, "You know, I remember that old udam from the pub. He said something funny about the language even falling down like the rest of the world."

"Did you know we mispronounce udam and udamé as well?" Amana asked.

"Huh? What do you mean?" asked Dihana while she leaned against Micah.

"The proper way to say it is, adam. It comes from the word

for ground which is, adamah."

"How do you know all this?" Dihana asked.

"Well, when I was with Nahim, as you call him, he taught me."

"As you call him?" asked Aaranon. "Isn't that his name?"

"Not exactly. Nahim, or Nachim, as it is correctly pronounced, means *shall comfort.* It was a prophecy about him."

"Alright. So…what's his real name," asked Aaranon.

"His real name?" she smiled.

"Yeah. What's his real name?" they asked in unison.

"His real name…is Noah."

Epilogue

As he waited on the phone, he looked down at his watch, April 25, 2016 - 11:58am.

"Come on, come on! What's taking so long? I don't see why I had to call you from a stupid pay phone."

Finally, a voice came on the line, "He cannot be disturbed right now. Please call back later."

Frustrated, Aaron gritted his teeth and said quietly, "Look, you told me to call him from a payphone at a later time. Well, it's now a later time! If he doesn't want to talk to me, then you tell Rabbi Moshe this; Dr. Geoff Seegertun is dead, and it's probably the Rabbi's fault. So he better start talking to me right now, or I'm going to the police with the evidence I have against him. You got it?!"

After a long pause, she finally said, "One second."

"Yeah...now you're going to talk to me," Aaron said while tapping incessantly with his pencil on the wall next to the payphone in the college library.

The woman on the other end finally said, "Take down this address."

Once he wrote it down she continued, "He will meet you there in seven days from now. Leave your cell phone behind. Stay off any and all phones and computers."

"What is this run around you're giving me?"

"Look around you," the woman said.

"What?"

"Just look around! Do you see anyone in a black suit, white shirt, black tie, and black sunglasses?"

"Huh?"

"Just do it?"

Turning around, he saw no one at first. But then, off in the distance behind the psychology section, he spotted an extremely tall and burly man staring at him.

"Do you see him," she asked.

"Ah yeah...who the hell is he?"

"You need to get out of there now. If he comes near you, just say the following name..." The woman then uttered a name that Aaron had never before heard.

"And what will that do?" he asked.

"It will cause him to back away."

"Wait...you can't leave me hanging like this. What is this all about?"

"Fine! Read Matityahu twenty-four."

"What? Is that an archeology book?"

"It's the Bible you idiot. Matthew, chapter twenty-four."

"The Bible!? Listen lady...I'm an atheist and I don't believe in that fu..."

"Watch your language young man. Listen to me, and you may just get out of this alive. Now go!"

Coming soon

Part III - The Rising

Contact information

JADavis@IntoTheEast.org

www.IntoTheEast.org

www.TheRazing.com

www.facebook.com/IntoTheEastNovelSeries

CPSIA information can be obtained at www.ICGtesting.com
Printed in the USA
LVOW04s0554280115

424637LV00007B/27/P